CW01648240

The Island's Call

LK Wilde

ISBN 978-1-0685491-0-6

Cover Design by Jarmila Takač

PART ONE

Chapter 1

Spring, 1950

Annie's hand shook as she held the card in her hand. From the front it looked innocuous enough, a printed image of blue and white flowers, *Congratulations!* written in gold leaf above. It was what she'd read inside that made Annie's head spin.

Congratulations on your wedding day. You deserve all the joy in the world and we wish you a long and happy marriage. We promised to never mention the secret we share, and hope that by providing you with the enclosed gift, you don't feel we dishonour that promise. The gift needs no explanation, but will serve as a reminder of the sacrifice you made for our happiness. Every day, we thank God for you and the gift you gave us. Perhaps, one day, the truth will come out, but until that day we are bonded not just by secrets, but by the love we all share for the child at the heart of them.

"Annie?"

The card slipped from Annie's fingers and she dropped to the floor, grabbing the card and shoving it back in its faded blue envelope. She ran across the room and slipped it in the drawer beneath her mother's neatly folded underwear. Before she could close the drawer, her mother appeared in the doorway.

"What on earth are you doing in my bedroom?" Marnie's eyes were not on Annie, but the open drawer. In three strides, Marnie crossed the room and slammed the drawer closed.

"I'm sorry. I was looking for a pair of stockings."

"And did you find what you were looking for?" Marnie's eyes were narrowed, her face unusually pale.

"I'd only just opened the drawer when you walked in," lied Annie, somehow pulling her face into a smile.

"Good. Well, next time you want to borrow something of mine, please ask first."

"I will, I'm sorry, Mum."

"Ah, come here," said Marnie, letting out a long breath before scooping Annie up into a tight hug. She kissed the top of Annie's head, then released her, holding her at arm's length. "Your first dance. I can't believe it. Have you chosen which dress to wear yet?"

"Yes, I think so."

"Good. Why don't you get it, and I'll dig out a pair of stockings for you?"

"Alright."

When Annie entered her room, she closed the door behind her and leaned against it, taking slow deep breaths. What had she just stumbled upon? There was no address or postmark on the envelope, and no signature to indicate the sender of the letter.

"I've found you some stockings," called Marnie.

Annie shook her head free of the questions pinning her to the spot, pulled her dress from her wardrobe and carried it through to the bedroom Marnie shared with her husband, Frank.

"Oh, you've lit the fire," said Annie.

"Yes, I thought you could use this room to get ready in as it's the largest, but it was feeling chilly, so I got the fire going for you."

"Thank you," said Annie, taking the offered stockings.

"Ah, you've chosen that dress, have you? It's a good choice if you ask me. The green goes so well with your lovely blonde curls."

"Thank you."

"Feel free to borrow any of my jewellery, and you can pinch some of my makeup, too."

"Thank you." Annie couldn't help feeling Marnie was trying to make up for her earlier sharpness.

Marnie gazed at Annie, brushing her fingers against Annie's cheek. "I know things haven't been easy for you since you returned to Lowestoft after the war, but it makes me so happy to see you making friends and going out dancing. Are you beginning to feel more settled?"

Annie nodded, for what else could she do? Tell Marnie how much she still missed Padstow? Admit how her peers at school laughed at her West Country accent? Explain that despite loving her stepfather Frank dearly, he could never fill the hole left by her dad's death? But she could tell none of this to Marnie, for it would only set her off worrying again, and that wouldn't help anyone.

"I'll leave you to it, but shout when you're ready."

"Will do."

Marnie left the room, and Annie walked over to the fire to warm herself. As she looked down into the flames, she spotted a fleck of blue. Annie crouched beside the hearth, and taking the poker from its stand, prodded the coal. Before she could rescue it, the card she had been holding only minutes before melted into the flames, folding in on itself and turning to ash. Whatever secret the sender spoke of, one thing was clear: Marnie had no intention of anyone finding out what that secret was.

Chapter 2

December, 1952

Angry waves careered into the sea wall. Annie couldn't see them, but the noise filled the air around her as she walked towards the factory looming against a brooding black sky. She pulled her coat tighter around herself and hurried along the street. Today there were no kiddies out playing, no women leaning against open front doors, chatting with neighbours. The streets of The Grit were devoid of people and full of weather.

The no man's land that stretched between Christmas and New Year left Annie impatient. Everyone was tired and irritable after using up all their jollity on the Christmas celebrations. These days were the dregs of 1952, an uninspiring year of rebuilding and penny-pinching as folk tried to rebuild from the devastating war years.

Annie was counting down the days until they could see the back of 1952 and welcome in 1953. She had a calendar pinned to the door of her wardrobe, thick pencil marks crossing off each passing day. Annie knew there was no guarantee the next year would be any better than the last, but deep inside, she knew it would be a time of change. In four months' time, she would turn eighteen and become an adult. Quite what this meant for her life, she couldn't yet say, but she knew it meant *something*.

As she stuffed her fingers deeper into her coat pockets, they brushed against paper, and Annie smiled as she remembered the letter from Sam she had carried with her since it arrived. She missed her best friend, but he was doing well with his National Service and she felt an almost sisterly pride while reading his latest news. HMS St Vincent down in Hampshire felt a long way from Lowestoft, but knowing Sam was excelling in his training made the distance feel worth it. Annie considered pulling out the letter and reading it again, but the sound of heels tapping on the pavement grew louder and, without turning around, she knew it would be her friend Beryl.

"Good Christmas?" Beryl fell into step beside her, and Annie did a double take.

"What's happened to your hair?"

Beryl pulled down her headscarf to reveal new platinum locks. "Who do I remind you of?" she asked, twirling round in the street and posing as if on a magazine shoot.

"Doris Day?"

"Close. I was aiming for Marilyn Monroe. What do you think?"

"It's, um, different."

"You hate it."

"No, no, not at all," said Annie, linking arms with her friend. "It will just take a bit of getting used to, that's all. I'm used to brunette Beryl, not blonde bombshell Beryl."

"Yes, well, it's all right for you. You don't need to get either colour or curls from a bottle."

Annie's hand went to her headscarf, checking it was in place. "My curls are unruly, about as far from Marilyn or Doris as it's possible to get."

"Yeah, yeah, whatever you say. Goodness, what a foul day it is today. I could have done with another day off after all the sherry I've been drinking."

"I know, but the work at Birds Eye doesn't stop because you've got a hangover."

"Don't I know it," said Beryl. "Hear much from Sam over Christmas?"

"I had a letter and a card. He has leave around New Year although I'm not sure when or for how long."

"Miss him?"

"Of course, he's one of my best friends."

"Future husband, you mean."

"Let's not get ahead of ourselves," said Annie, laughing.

"Oh, don't give me that," said Beryl, nudging Annie. "If it weren't for his National Service, the pair of you would be stepping out by now. You're childhood sweethearts, after all."

"Beryl," said Annie, blushing, "we've never even kissed!"

"What about that time you were fourteen and playing sardines?"

"I wish I'd never told you about that," said Annie, pouting. "It was an accidental kiss."

"Pah! An accidental kiss? Pull the other one. Oh, look, we're early," said Beryl, checking the time on a new silver watch.

"Let me see that," said Annie, grabbing her friend's wrist. "Paul?" she asked, raising an eyebrow.

"Of course."

"He must be madly in love with you to have given you such an expensive gift."

Beryl grinned. "That isn't all he gave me." She pulled a leather glove off her left hand and wiggled her fingers.

Annie took hold of Beryl's hand and screamed. "Is that what I think it is?"

"Yes," said Beryl with a wide smile. "You'll come to the wedding, won't you?"

"Of course I will," said Annie, pulling her friend into an embrace. "Come on, we've got half an hour before our shift starts. I'm buying you a cup of tea to celebrate."

The two girls hurried along Whapload Road towards the harbour. They ducked into a small café, the lamplight from its windows warm and inviting.

"Make sure you close the door," called a woman behind the counter as they stepped inside. "There's a chill breeze coming in from the north and we don't want it stealing our heat."

Annie closed the door firmly behind her. They were the only two people in the café, and the woman behind the counter looked bored from lack of custom.

"I wasn't sure anywhere would be open today," said Annie, pulling off her headscarf and gloves.

"We're usually run off our feet with business from the new Birds Eye factory. You heard how much they spent on that new plant for the frozen peas? Seventy thousand pounds. That's right, seven zero zero zero zero, for peas, and frozen ones at that. I don't even know a soul who owns a freezer. Where are all these folks supposedly wanting frozen peas? To my mind, it's some mad idea stolen from the Yanks. Imagine what you or I could do with seventy thousand pounds. I certainly wouldn't be squandering it on peas." The woman laughed. "Anyway, that's enough talk of peas and I shouldn't complain, as Birds Eye has been good for my business. On a normal day, you'd be lucky to get a seat in here."

"I suppose a fair few people have taken time off over Christmas," said Beryl.

"Yes, and I'm wishing I was one of them. What can I get you, ladies?"

"Two cups of tea, please," said Annie. "Would you like a bun?"

"No," said Beryl, "I need to watch my figure if I'm going to squeeze into a wedding dress."

Annie paid for the tea, and they settled themselves at a table in the window.

"There's talk of more factories being built along here," said Beryl.

"Goodness, The Grit will be unrecognisable soon."

"Yes, but that's no bad thing. And think of all the jobs they'll bring to the town."

"That's true enough."

The café owner had clearly been listening in, for when she appeared with their cups of tea, she joined the conversation. "My Fred was here in 1913, the year they had that record catch. Over five hundred million herring they reckon was caught that year. Now there's no fish and everyone's turning their hand to peas."

"Not us," said Beryl, "we work trimming runner beans."

"And a darn sight easier that must be than the work of a herring girl."

"My aunt Clara worked briefly as a herring girl," said Annie. "It's hard to imagine it now."

"Half the women in this town worked as herring girls," said the woman. "And what a sight they were."

"I also know men who still fish," said Annie, thinking of Sam and his dad Bobby.

"Annie here is destined to become a fishwife," said Beryl, earning herself a kick under the table.

"Is that so? Well, good luck to you, I say. I'll leave you girls to it," said the woman.

When she was busy behind the counter, Beryl lowered her voice. "For all that woman's doom and gloom, I don't think the arrival of industry is a bad thing. Times change, and we must change with them. We've got an exciting year ahead, what with you turning eighteen and me getting married. I say we raise a toast to the year to come."

Annie lifted her teacup and clinked it against Beryl's. "To 1953," she said.

"To 1953."

Chapter 3

January, 1953

The pearl brush slipped through hair as fine as silk. With gentle hands, Annie curled her grandmother's white locks against the nape of her neck and secured it with pins. She picked up a string of pearls and fastened the clasp, letting them rest against Sally's translucent skin.

Sally reached up and squeezed Annie's hand. "Thank you, my darling girl."

"You look like royalty," said Annie, admiring Sally's reflection in the dresser mirror.

"I'll take your word for it," said Sally, her cloudy eyes searching for clarity among the blurred shapes in her vision.

"I think the only thing missing now is a shawl. Would you prefer teal or rose?"

"Whichever you think is best."

Annie held each shawl up against Sally's dress. "I think the teal works best with your dress. Here you are." Annie covered Sally's shoulders with the shawl, careful not to catch the pearls.

Sally's hand groped for the pearls around her neck. "Your granddad gave these to me on our wedding day. He'd be pleased I'm still wearing them."

"He always was an old romantic," said Annie, her voice catching as she glanced across to the bed where Roy had slipped away peacefully several months earlier. She still couldn't get used to not having him around, and could only imagine how much worse it was for Sally. "Right, madam, I think you're ready to see in the New Year."

"Then I'd better make the most of it, as it will probably be my last," said Sally, her voice matter-of-fact.

"Don't talk like that, Nan. I want you around for a long time yet."

"Ah, you think that now, but believe me, you're ready to spread your wings. You don't need an old fogey like me holding you back."

Annie surprised Sally by wrapping her arms tightly around her. "Please don't go anywhere, Nan. You're my favourite person. I'd be lost without you." With Sally one of the few fixed points in Annie's young life, the thought of losing her felt like a ship slipping its anchor.

"Don't let your mother hear you talking like that," said Sally with a chuckle.

"I love Mum too. Of course I do. But she has Frank. I have you."

"Now, now, enough of this silliness. Don't we have a party to go to? In fact, I'm sure I just heard a knock at the door. My eyes may not be as sharp as they once were, but there's nothing wrong with my hearing. Come on, we don't want to be late for our guests."

Annie released Sally from her embrace and the two women linked arms. From the top of the stairs they watched as Marnie opened the front door to her best friend Kitty, Kitty's husband Bobby, their son Stevie, and Stevie's wife Carol.

"I'm afraid the rest of my boys had other plans tonight," said Kitty.

"That's alright," said Marnie. "We'll make do with Stevie. Oh, and I see you've brought Missy the dog with you as well."

"I hope that's alright," said Stevie. "She doesn't enjoy being left alone in the house."

"Tell me about it," said Sally, navigating the stairs with Annie's help. At the sound of Sally's voice, Missy bounded up the stairs, almost knocking Sally off her feet. "Ah, you're a good girl. Come on, I'm sure I can find you some treats in the kitchen," said Sally.

"Don't let that mutt get too close, Sally," said Frank, "or you'll be sneezing all night."

"She's worth it," said Sally, pulling a handkerchief from her sleeve, waving it at Frank, then bending down to pet Missy again.

"You're looking lovely, Sally," Bobby called up the stairs.

"And you're an old charmer, Bobby Thorn," said Sally with a smile.

Annie helped her grandmother down the remaining stairs, making painful progress as Sally's joints left her so unsteady.

"There you are," said Kitty, leaning forward and kissing Annie's cheeks. "I wondered if you'd have been out with your pals tonight."

"No, I'd rather be here with the family," lied Annie. In truth, she was missing a dance she longed to go to, but knowing how frail Sally was had convinced her to stay in.

"That's just as well, as we brought a surprise with us."

"A surprise?"

Kitty stepped away from the door, and Annie experienced a flush of simultaneous warmth and surprise as Kitty's youngest son, Sam, walked through the door.

"Sam, lovely to see you," said Annie, stepping forward and letting her oldest friend kiss her on each cheek. "I didn't know you were back."

"I've only got a few days' leave."

"How are you enjoying the navy?" asked Frank as the group made their way into the living room. "I expect you're wiping the floor with all the other chaps given you've spent so much time at sea with your dad."

"I'm not sure enjoying would be the right word," said Sam, "but it's an experience and I'm learning so much."

"You must be one of the youngest there."

"Yes, there's only one other lad who volunteered. Like me, he has a family boat to get back to, so wants to get his National Service out of the way as soon as he can."

"Don't wish the time away," said Frank. "My years with the navy were some of the happiest of my life. You'll have plenty of years to enjoy being skipper of the *Sally Ann*."

"Who said anything about skipper?" asked Bobby, a look of mock horror on his face. "There are plenty of years left in this old sea dog before I need to hand over to the next generation."

"My apologies," said Frank, grinning and slapping Bobby on the back.

"I've got a lot to thank the navy for," said Kitty. "They've taught him how to make a bed and clean up after himself. He'll make a good husband one day, thanks to the navy."

Annie felt her cheeks grow hot and looked at the floor. She knew both families expected her and Sam to wed, and sooner rather than later if they had anything to do with it, but she and Sam had yet to discuss the matter. "I'll get the drinks," said Annie, rushing through to the kitchen to avoid any further scrutiny.

In the kitchen, Annie placed a glass against her cheek, feeling the heat of moments ago receding. She loved Sam, and always had, but with her eighteenth birthday approaching, and unable to shake the feeling she was an impostor in someone else's life, marriage seemed an impossible dream.

"Annie."

Annie spun around to see Sam leaning on the kitchen door. "Hello, Sam."

An awkward silence stretched between them.

"So..." they both said.

"It's good to see you," said Annie, meaning it. Sam might dredge up a host of confusing feelings, but at the root of them all was pleasure in seeing her oldest, best friend again. He had seen her through the difficult post-war years as she struggled to adjust to her new, old life, and had, at times, been her only friend in the world. Since leaving school, things had been more settled, with new friends like Beryl arriving on the scene, but Sam knew Annie better than anyone, and it had been so strange without him since he began his National Service.

"It's good to see you, too," said Sam. He smiled at Annie in a way that caused butterflies to dance in her stomach and allayed some of her fears. "It won't be easy to catch up this evening with so many people around. I wondered if you fancied a trip to the pictures one evening? Just the two of us. I'm not due back at base until the end of the week. Of course, I understand if you've already got plans."

"No, I don't have any plans, and a trip to the pictures would be lovely."

Sam grinned like the cat who got the cream and Annie's skin tingled as they locked eyes.

The evening passed in a pleasant mix of games, chatter, and the occasional song. When the clock struck midnight, cheers rang out, the singing of 'Auld Lang Syne' a tradition none would forgo. Whilst the others were mid song, Sam pulled Annie towards him, his lips brushing hers with such lightness she wondered afterwards if she had imagined it. She turned, smiled and pushed down any confusion she felt over their burgeoning relationship. They had officially entered 1953, a year Annie hoped would bring a sense of belonging, peace, and the possibility of romance.

Chapter 4

January, 1953

Annie paused her brushing as she heard a knock on the door.

"Annie, Sam's here."

"Coming."

Annie tilted her head and checked her appearance in the mirror. She pinched her cheeks and blotted her lips on a handkerchief. After tugging a comb through her hair, she stood, smoothed out her full skirt, and went to meet Sam.

Sam was looking very at home in an armchair beside the fire. Opposite him, Frank was puffing on his pipe, a newspaper spread across his legs. The pair were discussing politics while Marnie sat working on a fishing net.

There was a lot less call for the work Marnie used to do, and beatsters no longer filled the area by the Denes, but there were still fishermen needing nets, and they knew Marnie to be a trusted pair of hands. She supplemented her income with shifts in the Steam Laundry, and Annie was convinced the steam kept her mother's skin looking so youthful. Frank had tried to persuade Marnie there was no need for her to work, but she insisted on keeping her financial independence, and Frank knew better than to argue.

"Where are you off to tonight?" asked Marnie, looking up as Annie walked into the sitting room.

"I'm taking Annie to the Odeon to watch the new *The Gambler and the Lady* film."

"How wonderful," said Marnie, trying to smile.

Annie leaned over and gave Marnie's shoulder a reassuring squeeze. She knew the cinema's history and the feelings it dredged up for her mother. Marnie hadn't been able to cross the threshold of the Odeon since the night of the Waller's raid eleven years earlier. Even walking past the grand façade seemed to bring back memories of a temporary mortuary and the fear which filled the air. The Waller's raid was one of many experiences Marnie seemed to keep locked deep within her, and Annie longed for the day when her mother would trust her enough to hand over the key to her secrets and memories.

"It's an intriguing title for a film," said Marnie, breaking into Annie's thoughts. "I hope it won't be too violent, or fill your heads with ideas of illegal gambling."

Sam laughed. "Oh no, I think we'll be quite safe, and I'll bring Annie home before she's tempted to fill out any betting slips."

Marnie smiled. "And how's your mum?"

"Fine, she said you should call in for a cuppa one day this week."

"So she's all settled in to the new place, then? I haven't wanted to intrude before she had time to unpack, but I'm dying to see your new home. It's so strange being at opposite ends of town after living so close for so long."

"She says the same. And yes, her and dad have mostly unpacked. There are a few boxes left, but they'll probably get shoved into the attic and forgotten about."

It was strange to think of Kitty living anywhere but The Grit. It left Annie feeling uneasy, as though she was standing on shifting sand, and living through a time of change when what she craved was stability and an elusive feeling of belonging.

"What's the new house like?" asked Annie.

"New," said Sam with a smile. Annie sighed, and Sam laughed. "It smells new, new carpets, fresh paint. It's warm, and we still can't get used to the luxury of an indoor bathroom."

"So Kitty's not missing The Grit?"

"I think she is, but there's a few other Gritsters living up on the new estate, so that helps."

"Come on, you two," said Marnie, "you don't want to miss the film."

Sam and Annie left the house. As they walked up Mariner's Score towards town, Sam took Annie's hand in his, and a strange awkwardness crept through her. There had been no official request to step out, no first date. It was as though their lifelong friendship had morphed into something more without her noticing. It wasn't until Sam volunteered that Annie had thought anything of it, but he'd been gone for months, and in that time some of their easy familiarity had been lost, on her part at least.

"Fancy some chips before the cinema?" Sam asked.

"Maybe after. Have you heard there's a new fish shop opening next to the Kumfy Café?"

"No, I wonder if Dad knows. If he gets in quick, he might be able to supply them."

"Have you been out on the boat since you got back?"

"I've not had a chance with the house move going on. I'd like to though. Dad is counting the days until my National Service is over and I can join him full time. Do you think Tom would have approved of me eventually becoming skipper of the *Sally Ann* one day?"

Annie thought it was likely her dad would have approved. He'd have been proud of how Bobby guided the *Sally Ann* through challenging times, and the thought of the boat passing to Bobby's son would have pleased him. "Yes, I think so."

"There would be something quite poetic about it, don't you think?"

"Poetic?"

"Yes, if we... I mean... if our families were joined in some way... it would be like the boat returning to where it started."

Uncertainty rose from the pit of Annie's stomach. Was Sam referring to marriage? Surely he couldn't mean anything else. She knew she loved him, but it was far too soon to be thinking about settling down. They weren't even adults yet. "It's raining, we'd best hurry." Annie dropped Sam's hand and held her bag above her head.

The foyer was humming with young couples, all seeking a warm dry place beyond the watchful gaze of their parents on a miserable January evening. Painted panels depicting cartoon characters in sporting events filled the upper walls and added to the jovial atmosphere.

"Wait here," said Sam, making his way to the island box office to purchase their tickets. When he returned, Sam not only had their tickets but two tubs of ice cream.

"Thank you," said Annie, digging in a small wooden spoon and taking a bite. "Delicious."

"We'd better find our seats," said Sam. "It looks like a popular showing."

Annie laughed. "You know this cinema can seat about one and a half thousand? I don't think we're in any danger of not finding a seat."

Sam smiled, and they walked up a sweeping staircase into an impressive Art Deco auditorium. The back few rows were already full of couples slyly holding hands, waiting for the lights to go out.

“Let’s find a seat near the front,” said Annie, before Sam could suggest an alternative. They made their way down an aisle between the stalls.

Once settled, Annie noticed Sam reach his arm across the back of her seat. She knew he was too much of a gentleman to try anything on once the lights went out, but couldn’t decide if that left her relieved or disappointed. Shaking her head, Annie decided now was not the time to untangle the complicated feelings she held for her friend. The film was about to start, and she intended to enjoy it.

Chapter 5

January, 1953

Dear Grace,

Happy New Year! I can't believe we're already in 1953, and that means it's now almost ten years since I last saw you. How is school? How are Aunt Helen and Uncle Richard?

I can't believe in a few months' time I shall turn eighteen. Of course I'm excited, but I don't mind admitting I'm also a little scared. Eighteen means I'll officially become an adult, and I'm not sure I'm ready for that. I think Mum and Frank expect me to live with them until I marry, but I'm feeling the need to spread my wings and find my place in the world. I don't know whether it's because I was evacuated down to Cornwall, but Lowestoft and The Grit have never really felt like home. Truth be told, things are a little depressing around here these days. There are so many empty houses and people are hankering after the new council houses in town which have hot and cold running water. I suppose I should be grateful for an indoor bathroom, as most of the houses around here don't even have that luxury.

I miss Aunt Helen's cottage with its views over Padstow harbour. The sea is so close to this house, but there's a massive great gas works blocking any views we might have had. There has also been a new Birds Eye processing plant built at the end of our road, although I shouldn't complain about that as I've got myself a job there. It's not the most exciting work, but I have a good friend called Beryl, who works on the same line as me, and I'd rather be in the factory than working with Mum mending nets or ironing laundry.

Anyway, on to more interesting topics, I saw Sam on New Year's Eve and again this week when he took me to the cinema. On New Year's Eve we shared a kiss at midnight, but it was rather chaste and not all that exciting with all the parents watching! I wondered if he'd try to kiss me again when we went to the cinema, but he was the perfect gentleman.

To be honest with you, Grace, I'm not sure what I think about me and Sam. I've always loved him, but he's so certain about his future, while I'm still fumbling in the dark. Since he started his National Service, we've both changed, and are not as close as we once were. I suppose that's inevitable when you spend months apart, but it leaves me feeling confused. To commit to Sam means committing to Lowestoft, and I'm not ready to do that just yet.

You'll probably be too young to understand what I'm talking about, although at almost twelve, you must have started noticing some of the local boys. Is there anyone special you've had your eye on?

Mum's calling me so I'd better go. Send my love to Aunt Helen and Uncle Richard. I'm going to ask Mum if I can visit you in the spring. It's been far too long since I saw you. Write soon, lots of love, Annie.

"Annie? What are you doing? We need to head out to the shops."

Annie sighed, slipped her letter in the envelope, licked the seal and addressed the front.

"What's that you've got there?" asked Marnie as Annie ran down the stairs.

"A letter for Grace."

"I see."

Annie frowned at her mother, wondering, not for the first time, why she showed so little interest in Annie's friend and pen-pal. Marnie had still been living in Padstow when Grace arrived, so Annie would have expected her to take more of an interest in her development. Perhaps she received enough news in her regular correspondence with Helen not to need information from Annie.

"Is Frank at work?"

"Aye, he won't be back till six. Is Sally alright up there?"

"Yes, she's having a doze. I checked on her ten minutes ago and she was out like a light, so shouldn't be needing us for a while."

"I hope you know how much we all appreciate your help with her."

"It's not exactly a chore," said Annie, rolling her eyes.

"I know, but most seventeen-year-olds would rather be out on the town than looking after an ageing relative."

"I know," said Annie, "it's hard being surrounded by so many old people, but I've learned to cope."

"Oi," said Marnie, batting Annie on the arm. "I'm not that old."

"Mum, fifty-three is ancient. It's about time you accepted it." Annie grinned at her mother, who was still beautiful despite her hair turning white and the thickening of her waist. Their relationship wasn't always an easy one, so Annie relished any moment of closeness. The lost years when they'd lived apart during the war had taken their toll, but Annie knew Marnie worked as hard as she did to bridge the gaps between their lives and experiences.

"Enough of your cheek, lass. Come on, let's get to those shops before Sally wakes up and needs us."

Mother and daughter left the house and walked the length of East Street, turning up Nelson Road towards Christchurch.

"That's where me and your dad married," said Marnie, pointing at the church. Annie already knew this, but never tired of hearing memories of her dad. "Here we are," said Marnie, stopping first at the grocers where Mr Grieve greeted them with his usual wide smile and good humour. "He's making a good go of that shop," said Marnie with a smile as they left. "It's changed hands a fair few times over the years, but that shop's been here longer than I have."

"It doesn't look like these houses will be here for much longer," said Annie, as they walked past a row of empty cottages, their windows boarded up, the glass which had once been there long since gone. "Have you ever thought about moving up to town like Kitty has?"

"I'd never make Sally leave her home. It's the final tie she has to Roy and her boys. I couldn't do it to her."

"But when Nan's gone, what then?"

"Then I'd consider all our options, but I'm hoping that day won't be for a while yet."

Annie hoped so too, but of all the family she spent the most time with Sally, and was best placed to spot the rapid decline in her grandmother's health. She kept quiet, not wanting to upset her mother, who had lost too many loved ones already.

When the moment they were all dreading arrived, Annie knew there would be hard choices to be made. While their home was well located for her job at the Birds Eye factory, Frank worked up in the town, and The Grit, or Beach Village below the cliff, was in what Annie feared was a terminal decline. If it was up to her, she'd move them all up into town before things got any worse.

Chapter 6

January, 1953

"I wonder what my dad would think if he could see me now," said Annie, pulling off her hairnet and gloves. "He used to joke I'd go into the fishing business. Instead of fish, here I am trimming runner beans in a factory."

"We're lucky to have these jobs," said Beryl.

"Oh, I know, I'm not complaining, just commenting on how much has changed since my dad's day."

"And thank God too. Can you imagine us out in all weathers as herring girls? No, thank you. Give me a factory any day."

"From what Kitty and Clara say, being a herring girl wasn't all bad. Of course, it was gruelling work, but they had their fair share of fun, too. Girls got to travel, earn their own money."

"Marry locals, like my grandmother, who came down from the Highlands."

"Exactly. How are your own wedding plans coming along?"

"Good," said Beryl, "and just in the nick of time." She smoothed down her skirt to reveal a tiny bump.

"You're not?"

"I am, but I'm keeping it hush-hush until after the wedding. I know it's the 1950s, but attitudes haven't changed that much."

"How far along are you?"

"Only a couple of months. How about you? How are things going with the handsome Sam?"

Annie rolled her eyes. "Fine. It's fine, Sam's fine."

"Wow, what a ringing endorsement," laughed Beryl.

"Sorry, Sam's lovely. I miss him, that's all. Since he's been away on National Service, it doesn't feel as though we're as close as we once were. There's also this pressure from our parents. They decided when we were babies, we'd get married one day. I don't like the feeling of someone else deciding what my life will look like or where I should end up."

"It's not exactly an arranged marriage, though, is it? I mean, you've been keen on Sam for ages. Are you honestly telling me you like him just to please the parents?"

"Of course not. We've always been so close. Developing romantic feelings was probably inevitable. Besides, you've seen him, I'd have been mad not to be a little keen on him."

"He's a looker alright. If you don't want him, they'll be queuing round the block when they hear he's available."

"I never said I didn't want him. What I'm saying is I don't want to decide the course of my entire life before I've even turned eighteen. There are things I want to do before I settle down."

"Such as?"

"I want to go back to Padstow, where I lived during the war."

"Where's Padstow?"

"Cornwall."

"Why do you want to go all the way down there?"

"I don't know, I can't explain it. I just have this feeling it's an important place. Like something happened there that is lurking at the corners of my memory." Annie considered telling Beryl about the card she had found several years earlier but thought better of it. Instead, she turned to her friend and smiled. "Do I sound mad?"

"Yes, you daft old bat. Come on, let's get some grub or our break will be over."

The two friends walked to the canteen, greeting friends and colleagues as they went.

"So apart from Padstow, what else do you need to get out of your system before you settle down?"

"I want to go back to the island my mum's from."

"Why? No, don't tell me, you have a *feeling* about the place?"

Annie knew Beryl was teasing and knew she couldn't explain the connection she felt to the island. But she had felt it all those years ago at Marnie and Frank's wedding. It was as if she knew the place already, despite never having been before. And like Marnie said, Annie had island blood in her veins, whether or not she'd lived there. Perhaps in either Padstow or Holy Island, Annie would find the belonging she craved, and answers to the questions which hovered just out of reach.

"Don't you ever feel a connection to the Highlands? What with your grandma coming from up north?"

"Nah, Gran made Lowestoft her home the second she met Granddad."

"And you've never been curious to see where she's from?"

"Up in Scotland? Not likely. From what Gran's told me, it's bloody cold and there's not much to do. She's from some small village right up in the Highlands. She never got on with her family, which is why she jumped at the chance to be a herring girl, and then to stay put when she came down here and met my granddad."

"But what about when you were evacuated? Didn't that leave you feeling unsettled?"

"No, if anything, it made me appreciate Lowestoft even more. Don't forget, I was housed with an evil old bag who resented every second me and my sister were with her. There was no seaside idyll for me."

Annie sighed, wondering if there was anyone who understood the restlessness she was feeling. "I suppose you're right, and we should be grateful for what we have here."

"Yes, mind you, if you're that desperate to go to Padstow and your mum's island, it would be better to do it now than when you're saddled with a bunch of kiddies and a husband. I can't see Sam putting up with your gallivanting once he's got a ring on your finger."

Before Annie could discuss her plans further, the bell rang, signalling it was time to get back to work. With all the noise of the factory, there wasn't much time to talk, but plenty of time to think. As she got back into the rhythm of her work, a plan for the coming year formed in Annie's mind. She would go to Padstow, and to the island. If a marriage with Sam was meant to be, their relationship could survive distance. It would be a good test, a chance to clear her head.

The only fly in the ointment Annie could see was work. She'd not been at the factory all that long, certainly not long enough to be taking lots of time away. Padstow was manageable, but if she wanted to go to the island, it would be a bigger commitment. She'd need to leave her job and find work up there. Perhaps a summer season would work? Annie's heart fluttered at the thought. 1953 was shaping up to be an exciting year.

Chapter 7

January, 1953

Annie gripped tight to Marnie's arm as they forced their way along Whapload Road. The wind howled around them, tearing at windows, trying to pull them from their hinges. A large piece of cardboard hurtled towards them and Annie yanked Marnie out of its path in the nick of time.

"I've never known it so fierce," yelled Marnie, her white curls dancing around her head, her eyes half closed against the sand and dirt swirling around them.

"We have to get back," said Annie. "Nan will be terrified with all this going on outside."

"She'll be alright, she's a tough old bird."

"Come on."

They bent their heads, forcing their way through nature's ferocious barrier as it tried to pull them off their feet. When they turned the corner into their street, the rows of terraces provided a little protection, and Annie swept the tears from her eyes.

"Are you alright?" asked Marnie.

"Oh yes, it's just the wind getting in my eyes."

Once at the house, they forced open the door, slamming it behind them and leaning against it to catch their breath.

"It's such a relief to be out of that wild weather," said Marnie, tugging her scarf from around her neck and hanging it on the bannister. She moved to the bottom of the stairs and called, "Are you alright, Sally?"

"I'm fine, love, but what about you? It's blowing a hoolie out there."

Annie walked into the sitting room where the wind squealed up and down the chimney breast. She shivered and closed the curtains, despite it not yet being evening.

"I'll make us a pot of tea," said Marnie.

"Good idea. I'll go up and check on Nan."

Annie climbed the stairs and found Sally sitting up in bed, a radio spitting static into the room.

"There's something wrong with the signal," said Sally, waving a hand in the radio's direction. "It must be the wind. I couldn't see to turn the damn thing off."

"I'll do it," said Annie. The sound of a branch banging against the window and the wind's ghostly howl replaced the radio's static. "Mum's making us tea. Would you like me to read to you for a while? It must have been very dull up here with no radio to listen to."

"It was more irritating than dull," said Sally. "And yes, I would love for you to read to me, but only if you have time."

"Nan, it's my day off, and with the weather as it is, there's nothing else I'd be doing." Annie picked up a well-worn book, its pages yellow and thin as tissue paper. "Is *Emma* alright for you?"

Sally smiled. "There's never a bad time to listen to a bit of Austen. Her humour always cheers me up."

"Me too. Right, where were we..." Annie found the page they were on and began to read. By the time Marnie appeared with a tray of tea and scones, Annie had read two chapters.

"Oh, I love that book," said Marnie, noticing the cover as Annie placed it on the bedside table. "The moment I could read Austen, I knew Jimmy's hard work had paid off. It makes me shudder to think of all I'd have missed out on had he not taught me to read."

"How is that lovely brother of yours?" asked Sally.

"Very well, by the sounds of things. When I last spoke to him, he had just arrived back from a meeting about a new causeway across to the island. There is some opposition to it from local taxi drivers who make a living by being in the minority of those who can navigate the sand in a vehicle. Others, particularly businesses which rely on visitors, are all for the idea. A causeway would certainly do wonders for Clara's business."

"Goodness, building a road across all that sand with the tide coming in and out will be quite the job. I don't envy the poor chaps having to take on that challenge. Send Jimmy and Clara my love, next time you speak to them, and tell them a visit is long overdue."

"I will do," said Marnie. She poured out three cups of tea and settled in a chair beside Sally while Annie perched on the bed.

"I hope the spring tide doesn't bring us any trouble," said Sally. "If Roy was here, I know he'd be fretting over it. He always kept a close eye on the weather and tides. Oh, I miss him."

"So do we," said Marnie, reaching over and squeezing Sally's hand.

The front door slammed and Annie jumped, spilling some of her tea onto Sally's blankets. "Surely Frank's not back from work already?"

"Only me," called Frank. The women heard his treads on the stairs, and his smiling face appeared round the door. "They let us off half an hour early thanks to the storm. There's already a bit of water bubbling up through the drains. I don't expect it will get too bad, but I'll move a few things upstairs just in case."

"See," said Sally, "it's always a good idea to keep an eye on those tides."

"Don't worry, Nan. The storm will blow itself out in no time. If this house survived the war, it can survive anything."

"True," said Sally, taking a sip of her tea. "Although I wouldn't mind one of those new council houses they're building. Did you hear they've got gas heating?"

Marnie's eyebrows raised at Sally's revelation. "I'll start making supper," she said. "We'll eat early tonight, then we can all be tucked up at a reasonable time and sleep through the storm."

"That sounds like a good idea," said Frank. "While you cook, I'll begin moving a few things from downstairs. Better to be safe than sorry." He gave Marnie a quick kiss as she left the room, then followed her downstairs.

"Would you like me to read some more?" Annie asked Sally.

"May as well," said Sally. "There's not much else we can do."

Chapter 8

January, 1953

The strange weather had an unsettling effect on the household and they were later getting to bed than usual.

"I'm heading up the wooden hill," said Marnie, pushing herself up from her armchair and kissing Frank on the cheek. "Don't stay up too late."

"I'll finish this article," said Frank, lifting the newspaper in his lap, "then I'll be right behind you."

Marnie kissed Frank again and climbed the stairs to their bedroom. "We're off to bed, and you should be too," said Marnie as she met Annie on the landing.

"I tried to get to sleep, but that howling wind kept waking me," said Annie. "I thought I'd make myself a cup of tea, then try again. Would you like one?"

Marnie yawned and covered her mouth with her hand. "Not for me, but Frank might. He's downstairs finishing his paper."

"Alright," said Annie. "Goodnight."

Downstairs, Frank had finished reading, and was folding his paper when a hammering sounded on the door. He leaped out of his chair and ran to open it. From the top of the stairs, Annie looked on in horror as water rushed across the threshold.

"What on earth?" said Frank, looking from the man at the door down to his feet, now ankle-deep in water.

"I came to warn you about the flood," said the landlord of the local pub, "but you can see for yourself." He was breathless from running, his face only just visible through his waterproofs. "It's bad. Really bad."

"This is worse than anything I've seen before. Surely, this isn't all coming from the drains?"

"No, the waves have breached the sea wall. There's a storm surge and a wall of water coming down Whapload Road. You need to move to safety."

"Where should we go?"

"Oh, no, there's no chance of leaving the house," said the man, "but get yourselves upstairs and be quick about it."

"What on earth is going on?" asked Marnie. She pushed past Annie and ran down the stairs to Frank. From her position on the landing, Annie heard the splash of footsteps as Marnie made her way along the hall. "Where's all this water coming from?"

"There's a storm surge," said Frank, grabbing hold of Marnie's arm and forcing her toward the staircase. "Get back upstairs, quick."

"What about you?"

"I'm assuming I can be put to good use?" Frank asked the man.

"If you're game, it's a case of the more hands, the better. There are plenty of folk asleep who don't know what's happening. We need to alert all we can or things could turn ugly."

"Give me a moment," said Frank. He sloshed along the hallway, grabbing his wellington boots and raincoat from the under-stairs cupboard.

"I'm not sure how much use those boots will be," said the man at the door, glancing behind him to where the water level on the street was steadily rising. "Let's get going."

"Be careful," called Marnie, as Frank let himself out of the house.

Annie grabbed her dressing gown from the back of her bedroom door and met Marnie on the landing. "I'm not sure he should go out in that."

Marnie walked into Annie's bedroom and sighed. "You know what Frank's like. He's never been so happy as his days in the navy. His job in the office keeps him busy, but I know deep down he hankers after something more exciting."

"I'm not sure risking life and limb can be called exciting. And he's not as young as he was." Annie frowned, concern over her stepfather overriding anxiety about the flood.

"Frank will be fine," said Marnie, taking hold of Annie's hand. "I know it's a worry, him being out in this weather, but there's no time to dwell on it. Can you help me move as much upstairs as we can? Frank has brought all the photographs and ornaments up already, but neither of us expected things to be so bad."

"Of course," said Annie.

"Oh good God," said Marnie, pausing at the top of the stairs.

Annie looked over her shoulder to where the water had risen as high as the fourth step. "Where's it coming from?"

"Wherever it can get in. Quick."

Mother and daughter ran down the stairs, their feet meeting icy salt water as they descended the last few steps. The water was brown, churning with some invisible power that pulled on their limbs and made staying upright a task in itself.

"Keep hold of anything fixed down, door frame, windowsill, anything. The last thing we need is to be pulled off our feet."

Annie and Marnie waded into the living room, the water already above their knees. Vinyl records floated around them, eased from their stand in the corner of the room. When they waded towards the kitchen, a saucer floated towards them. "Mum, this is a fool's errand. Look at how quickly the water is rising. Nothing down here can be saved, but our own lives could be at risk if we stay down here too long."

"You're right," said Marnie, taking hold of Annie's hand and turning back. Their nightdresses were weighed down with brown, stinking water, their dressing gowns suffering the same fate.

"Have you seen floods like this before?" asked Annie.

"No," said Marnie, grabbing hold of the bannister and pulling herself and Annie to higher ground. "It reminds me of the island, when the tide would cover the sand in a matter of minutes. I learned then never to underestimate the sea or nature's power."

Their stockinged feet squelched as they climbed the stairs. When they reached the landing, Marnie paused, caught in a moment of indecision.

"Mum? What should we do now?" Annie tried and failed to keep the shake from her voice. All her bravado at approaching adulthood was gone, replaced by childish feelings of fear, and a desire for her mother to take control.

Focus returned to Marnie's eyes. "Change out of your damp clothes. Put on as many warm layers as you can find, then we need to do the same for Sally. I don't like how quickly this water is rising. We may need to move higher."

"Higher? Higher where? It's not like we can perch on the roof with Nan."

“No, but we could climb up into the attic if needed.”

“Surely it won’t come to that?”

Marnie glanced back to the stairs, and Annie let out a whimper of fear at the sight of brown water licking the fifth step.

“The water has risen at least a foot since we were down there. We need to be prepared, just in case. Now be quick, get yourself changed. The last thing we need is you getting pneumonia.”

Annie ran into her room, peeled off her sodden clothes and threw on as many layers as she could find. She grabbed an armful of blankets, a coat, and two pillows, then went to find her mother and grandmother.

“Annie!” Sally’s hand reached out in the darkness.

“I’m here, Nan, don’t worry, we’re all here.”

“Annie, you sit with your grandmother while I light some candles. Sitting in the dark won’t help anything.”

“You’re shaking,” said Sally, clasping Annie’s hand between her own.

“I’m scared,” Annie whispered.

“Everything will be alright. Think of all we’ve endured. If this storm thinks it will get the better of us, it’s picked a fight with the wrong women.”

Annie laughed and reached over to kiss Sally’s cheek. Around them the wind howled, the sound of lapping water all too close. Annie hoped Sally’s optimism would prove wise, but either way, she knew they were in for a long night.

Chapter 9

January, 1953

Annie sat cross-legged on the landing, a candle flickering beside her. Her eyes were transfixed on the water, which had reached the seventh step. A few inches higher and the first floor would be breached, and they'd somehow need to get Sally up into the attic.

"Don't you dare," whispered Annie, her candlelight glinting against black water. "You leave us alone, you hear me?" *What the heck am I doing talking to floodwater?* wondered Annie, the thought almost making her laugh. Almost, but not quite. Their situation was too serious for any joking around.

It had come as a relief when both Marnie and Sally had finally drifted off to sleep. At least here, beside the water, Annie felt a sense of purpose. She could do nothing to hold the water back, but she could monitor it, raise the alarm if needed.

Where was Frank? Was he safe? Annie couldn't bear the thought of her stepfather out amidst the floodwater. There would be no walking back through the door in the manner he had left, the water was too deep for that now. Had someone found him a boat? Annie experienced a rush of anger. Why did he have to play the hero? Didn't he know she needed him, that Marnie needed him? Annie had allowed him to fill some of the hole in her heart left by her father's death, and this was how he repaid it? Guilt swiftly followed the anger. Of course Frank would have gone to help with the rescue effort. That was the sort of man he was. It was why they all loved him.

Annie stood up and stretched. Her limbs felt heavy and despite all her layers, she couldn't shake off the cold. It was as though the floodwater had spread its dampness beneath her skin, chilling her to the bone. And as for the smell, if Annie wasn't so frightened, she might have given in to the nausea it inflicted.

Settling back down into her position on the floor, Annie rested her head against the wall beside her and allowed her eyes to close for a moment. She must have drifted off, for when she opened her eyes, the water had receded as far as the sixth step. She rubbed her eyes, and held her candle closer to the water, checking she wasn't imagining it. No, there was a definite brown stain on the walls left from the floodwater's height. Satisfied that they would remain safe as long as they stayed upstairs, Annie climbed to her feet and went to find her mother and grandmother.

When Annie walked into Sally's room, Marnie lifted her head and frowned. "Where have you been?"

"Keeping an eye on the water level," whispered Annie.

"And?"

"And it seems to be receding."

"How high did it get?"

"Too high."

"Any word from Frank?"

Annie shook her head. "Why don't you go to bed for a while? I can sit here with Nan."

"We should stick together."

"You'll only be in the next room. Besides, there's nothing anyone can do. It will be hours before the water's gone down far enough for us to get out of here. You may as well get some rest."

"It should be you resting. I've already dozed off for a while."

"I'm not arguing about this," said Annie. "Go to bed."

"It should be me mothering you, not the other way round," said Marnie, managing a small smile.

"Go."

"Yes, ma'am." On her way past, Marnie kissed Annie, gave her a tight squeeze, then wearily walked towards her bedroom.

With Marnie gone, Annie sat down beside Sally and took her grandmother's hand. It was icy cold, and Annie tucked it beneath the blankets, and secured the many layers covering Sally tight around her. It wouldn't do her any good to get too cold. Her health was precarious enough as it was.

Annie picked up a book but found she was too tired to read. Instead she stood, walked to the window and tried to peer out into the gloom. Deciding it couldn't get any colder in the room, she opened the window and leaned out. Above the whine of the wind and roar of waves in the distance, the sound of shouting reached her; men's voices, engaged in a common purpose. She heard a scream, and somewhere nearby a baby was crying.

Annie closed the window. "I'll be back in a moment, Nan," she whispered, leaving Sally's room for her own at the front of the house. The inky black of night was seeping into a lighter grey, and as Annie peered through the glass, she saw their street was submerged, the wind whipping small crests on the surface of a dark river that swirled between houses, trying to find a way in. Objects flowed along the street; a broken chair leg, a doll, a cushion, a joint of beef, what remained of a dresser.

"Are you alright in there? How's Sal?"

Annie looked up and saw Mrs Blythe from across the road, leaning out of her own bedroom window.

"We're alright," called Annie. Mrs Blythe cupped a hand to her ear and Annie opened the window and leaned out. "We're alright. How about you?"

"We're alive, and I suppose that's all that matters, but I dread to think what we've lost. We went to bed early, see, so the flood caught us by surprise."

"Let's hope the water level goes down quickly."

"Yes, but then we'll have the clean-up to face, and from experience, I'm telling you that's the worst part. If I were you, I'd be thinking of somewhere you can stay for a while. It will be a job getting these houses dry."

"Oh dear," said Annie, "I'd not thought beyond tonight."

"Don't worry, love, and I'm sorry if I've alarmed you. We'll get through this like we always do. Folk will turn out to help, you'll see."

"Let's hope so," said Annie. "I'd best close this window now. I don't want Nan getting too cold."

"Quite right," said Mrs Blythe. "I'll call round as soon as the water's gone and see if you need any help with Sal."

"Thank you, Mrs Blythe."

"No problem, love."

As Annie closed the window, she considered that despite the dreadful circumstances they found themselves in, some things never changed. The strength and spirit of Gritsters was hard to beat and although they faced hard times, the community would face them together.

Chapter 10

February, 1953

Annie blinked. Had she been sleeping? She rubbed the back of her neck and stretched. She was still sitting on a wooden chair, but had fallen forward, her face planted on Sally's bed. Annie rolled her shoulders, trying to tease out the stiffness. Sally's eyes fluttered, the muscles in her face tightening, before relaxing again with a gentle snore.

Annie rubbed her eyes and let out a loud yawn. It had been a long night, and it was a relief to see weak wintry light seeping through the threadbare curtains. She climbed to her feet and stretched her arms above her head, yawning again. As she crossed the room and drew the curtains, her hand flew to her mouth when she rubbed the windowpane free of condensation and looked at the yard below.

Instead of the neatly positioned flowerpots and ornaments Annie was used to seeing, there was a pool. From the way its water lapped against the back gate, Annie guessed it must be several feet deep. The shed door had been pulled from its hinges, debris from Roy's days spent tinkering had been ripped from the shelves and now floated on the surface of murky brown water. She opened the window to get a better look, and an awful combination of mud, seaweed, and sewage filled her nostrils. Annie slammed the window shut, coughing and taking a sip of water to rid the smell's aftertaste.

"Annie?" Marnie poked her head around the door, peering into the gloomy room. "Sorry, I must have fallen into a deep sleep."

"Don't worry, so did I. Any news on Frank?"

"Yes, he popped back in a few minutes ago for a change of clothes, but has headed straight back out again."

"At least he's safe. Has there been any loss of life?"

"Not that he knows of so far, which is a blessing, but there's untold damage to property, and folk's homes and businesses have been devastated. Have you been to look at the damage?"

"I've just had a peek at the yard and things don't look good. I've not yet seen what damage has been done to the house."

With a wide yawn, Marnie pushed the door open further. "There's no point putting it off, I suppose."

Annie coughed and covered her nose. "Goodness, this smell is really turning my stomach."

"It'll be from the water," said Marnie. "As well as the storm surge, it will have been coming up through the drains, bringing God knows what with it."

Annie sprayed some of Sally's perfume on a handkerchief and offered it to Marnie.

"Thank you," said Marnie, holding it to her nose.

Annie used another spray of perfume on one of Sally's scarves, wrapping it around her nose and mouth. She caught her reflection in the mirror, and couldn't help giggling, despite the seriousness of what they were facing.

Marnie's mouth was hidden, but the skin around her eyes crinkled in amusement. "Come on, let's see what we're dealing with."

"Look," said Annie as they reached the top of the staircase. "That line shows how high the water came when I was watching it last night."

"Good Lord," said Marnie, her hand reaching out but not quite touching the murky brown tide line stained on the floral wallpaper. "It reached waist deep."

The stairs carpet was ruined; brown, squelchy, and stinking, it took all Annie's resolve not to rip it up there and then.

"Be careful down here," said Marnie, "there's still plenty of water and goodness knows what's in it. Do you have any cuts on your skin?"

"No."

"Good, we don't want any of us picking up an infection." Marnie stopped on the second step and looked back up at Annie. "Can you fetch our wellington boots from my bedroom? I think the water level is low enough for them to be of some use."

Annie ran back up the stairs and returned moments later carrying two pairs of green rubber boots. They slipped them on and took tentative steps into the hallway. The smell caused them to cough, Annie swallowing down bile as it rose in her throat.

"Do we have any fresh water?" Annie asked.

"Only what we took upstairs last night. That's one thing Frank is seeing to. Folk from up in the town are already assembling to help. We'll be able to have a drink before too long."

The front door had been torn from its fastenings, and in its place was a gloomy portal onto the waterlogged street beyond. A man waded past, a young lad clinging to his back. When he saw Marnie and Annie, the man gave a solemn nod of the head.

"What a rum business," he muttered, before continuing on his way.

Annie and Marnie waded into the sitting room, silent as each took in the devastating sight. The front window had smashed, the curtains torn, their lower halves now black. A ball of wool still attached to a knitting needle floated around their legs. As they moved further into the room, the floor was soft underfoot, their boots clinging to the thick mud the tide had brought with it as one final, parting gift.

Brown slime clung two-thirds up each wall, and the floral fabric of the ruined three-piece suite had been transformed into ugly dark swirls. The surface of the water was oily, detritus floating languidly among larger objects.

"This isn't ours," said Marnie, picking up a straight-backed wooden chair, then letting it fall back into the water with a splash.

"Nor is this sideboard," said Annie, pointing and grimacing at the piece of furniture wedged halfway through the glassless window.

"It's like something from the bible," said Marnie. "Folk's lives will be ruined."

"But if there's one thing we know about people around here," said Annie, "it's that they stick together. It will take time, but we'll all get through this."

"I hope you're right," said Marnie. "Shall we see what's become of our kitchen?"

"Yes," said Annie, "but I think we know what we're going to find."

Marnie took Annie's hand and squeezed it. Still clinging to each other, with heavy hearts and deep breaths, they moved through the house.

Chapter 11

February, 1953

Annie smiled as Frank appeared at Sally's bedroom door. Stubble covered his chin, the skin around his eyes loose, dark pouches of skin betraying his sleepless night. "You look as bad as I feel," she said, and he laughed.

"When I was a younger man, I thought nothing of a sleepless night, but these days I'm not as sturdy as I was."

"Is it as awful as I'm expecting out there?"

Frank nodded. "But no loss of life as yet, so we must count our blessings."

"Have you come home to rest?"

"No, I've actually come to speak to Sally. Is she awake?"

"No," said Annie.

"Yes," said Sally, opening her eyes.

"How long have you been awake?" asked Annie.

"Long enough."

Annie reached across and felt her forehead. Whether from the shock of the flood, or the damp, cold conditions, Annie wasn't sure, but there was no doubt Sally had a fever, and the grey tinge to her skin worried her more than she could let on.

"Stop fussing," said Sally.

"You don't look too well, Nan."

"And who would, after all the excitement of the flood? Certainly not Frank, by the looks of him."

"Charming as ever, Sally," said Frank with a smile.

"What did you need to talk to me about?"

Frank sat himself in a chair beside her bed. "I wanted to ask for your help, but you are absolutely free to turn down my request, as I know it is a lot to ask."

"Go on."

"Christ Church Hall has opened its doors to locals, providing food and clothing to all affected by the flood."

"Was the church itself damaged?"

"Not too badly. Thanks to the position of the door, the water didn't have an easy way in, and they've been able to sweep out most of it already."

"That is good news. That church has been good to us over the years, seen us through a fair few weddings... and funerals."

"Yes, I know it holds a special place in your heart. Sally, this is a little delicate, but I know you still have all of Roy's old clothes hanging in the wardrobe. If you can't bear to part with them, I completely understand, but..."

"Take them," said Sally.

"Are you sure?"

"What use are Roy's clothes to me now? It's the man himself I miss, and no amount of shirts or trousers are going to bring him back to me. Take them and give them to those poor folk who've lost everything."

"Thank you, Sally, that's very kind of you."

Annie squeezed Sally's hand, grateful that she didn't seem to realise she was also one of those poor folk who'd lost everything. "Are you warm enough?"

"Oh yes, that fire's keeping me nice and toasty," said Sally, pointing to the small iron fireplace set in the far wall.

"Good, but, Nan, we need to think about moving you somewhere more comfortable."

"I'm quite comfortable here, thank you very much."

"I know, but we don't currently have any running water. Everywhere is soggy or covered in mud, and don't get me started on the smell."

"I'm quite comfortable here," said Sally, her voice resolute.

With a sigh, Annie gave up her attempts at persuasion and moved to the wardrobe to help Frank, who was carefully removing shirts and trousers from hangers.

"Don't take his smock, please, don't take that." Sally's voice was catching in her throat, her head turned away.

Annie pulled a faded blue smock from the wardrobe and laid it beside Sally. "Don't worry, Nan, you keep this."

Sally's hand reached out, pulling the smock to her and clutching it to her chest. For all her bravado, clearing out Roy's clothes was an enormous step, another down the path of widowhood, and one Annie knew Sally didn't really want to take. But Sally was also a pragmatist, and knew however much sentimental value they held, the clothes would be far more use to those with little left except the shirts on their backs.

"Do you think you could help me carry these to the church?" asked Frank once they had filled three cardboard boxes.

"I don't know," said Annie. "I don't really want to leave Nan here by herself."

"I'm not a child," said Sally crossly.

"Marnie will be here any minute," whispered Frank.

Annie nodded. "Alright, Nan, I'll go with Frank, but I won't be long."

Sally waved a hand to shoo them away and Annie and Frank left the room, boxes balanced in their arms. At the top of the stairs, they put their boxes down and pulled on their wellington boots.

"Are you sure you don't mind helping me?"

"Of course not. We all need to muck in, don't we? You're sure Mum is on her way, though? I don't want Nan left on her own for too long."

"Yes, she wasn't unpacking anything at Kitty's, just taking up a couple of suitcases."

"How long do you think we'll be there?"

"How long is a piece of string?"

Frank and Annie stepped out onto the street. Their boots kicked up a mixture of mud and brown water as they walked. A man slid past them in a canoe, a pile of framed paintings tucked in beside him. As they emerged onto Whapload Road, a group of uniformed men were manoeuvring what looked like a giant hosepipe.

"What are they doing?" asked Annie.

"They've sent fire crews from all across the country to help pump out the water," explained Frank. "This lot here is from Portsmouth. They'll be working day and night to get the water cleared."

"You've met them?"

"Yes, I took some tea and biscuits over to them when they arrived. They're a good bunch of chaps, but they'll have their work cut out for them. It's jolly good of them to come all this way to help."

"By the looks of it, their pumps will do a much better job than the brooms and mops we've been using so far."

It surprised Annie how busy the streets of The Grit were. Folk who'd made an escape to the higher ground of the town were returning in waders and boots to survey the damage to their homes. Women were hanging rugs and blankets from windows in a vain attempt to dry them.

Every home had swirls of smoke pouring from their chimneys as all the fires in every house were lit to dry out sodden walls.

In the church hall, women massed around trestle tables sorting through a mound of second-hand clothes under the watchful eye of Reverend Street, who, according to Frank, had been up all night playing his part in the rescue effort.

"According to the Reverend, he met some of his parishioners up in town earlier on their way to the Sunday service. They were oblivious to the flooding and couldn't understand why he wasn't in his dog collar and robes!"

"I wouldn't mind being in blissful ignorance myself," said Annie, as they handed over their boxes of clothes. "You said they're providing food here, too?"

"Yes, why, are you hungry?"

"No," said Annie, laughing. "But I'd like to help, so thought I could offer my services for a couple of hours."

"I'm sure they'd be delighted to have an extra pair of hands," said Frank. "I'd better head back to the house and check your mother is with Sally before I get stuck into the clean-up again. Will you be alright getting home by yourself?"

"Of course, but, Frank?"

"Yes?"

"You've been up all night, so how about you try to get a few hours' sleep before you go out again? You'll be no use to anyone if you fall asleep on your feet."

Frank laughed, but made no promises, just bid Annie farewell before heading back out onto the watery street.

Chapter 12

February, 1953

Annie crossed her legs and tried to distract herself from how desperate she was to use the bathroom. It was so kind of Kitty to take them in, but her house was not big enough to offer a long-term solution. Mornings were the worst, when everyone was trying to get out to work at the same time. They queued along the landing waiting for use of the bathroom, bumped into each other in the kitchen while trying to make toast, and spent an inordinate amount of time trying to find a matching pair of shoes from the mountain of footwear that had accumulated in the hallway.

"Bobby, are you going to be much longer?" called Annie, knocking on the bathroom door.

"Just coming."

"Good, my bladder's about to burst."

"That's not a very ladylike thing to say," called Bobby through the door, laughter in his voice.

"Be quiet and hurry."

"Yes, ma'am."

Annie could have hugged Bobby when he finally emerged from the bathroom. Instead, she rushed inside, used the toilet, washed her face and brushed her teeth as fast as she could, aware there would be others stirring and wanting to join the queue.

"That was quick," said Bobby, when Annie entered the kitchen.

"I knew there'd be others wanting to use it. Sorry to have hurried you. I am aware it is your home and your bathroom. It's so good of you to have taken us in."

"You know, Annie, I was your dad's best friend. He was like a brother to me. When we first started out on the boat together, we agreed that if anything happened to one of us, the other would look out for his family. I've tried to do that over the years the best I could."

"You have, and I'm sure Dad is looking down on us with a smile on his face."

"I still miss him, you know," said Bobby, surprising Annie with his candour. He coughed, turned his back on Annie, and filled the kettle.

Before Annie could reply, the back door opened and there stood Sam, smiling and handsome in his navy uniform.

"Sam, lad, whatever are you doing here?" asked Bobby, pulling his youngest son into a backslapping embrace.

"I was granted leave as soon as I told my superiors about the flooding. They felt my coming home to help with the clear-up was as much National Service as anything I'd be doing on base. I've only been granted three days, mind."

"Three days is better than nothing. Just wait till your mother finds out you've come home. In fact, I'm going to fetch her."

When Bobby had left the room, Sam turned to Annie. "How are you?" He reached out a hand and stroked her arm. "From what I've heard, things are bad down on The Grit."

For the first time since the flood, tears filled Annie's eyes. Sam stepped forward to hug her, but Annie pushed him away. "Don't, or you'll set me off," she said, smiling up at him. "I've managed not to cry this whole time and don't intend to start now."

"It's alright to be sad about what's happened."

"No, now isn't the time for tears. It's the time for action."

"Fair enough. How can I help?"

"Frank would be the best person to ask, but he's down at the house with Nan. She's refused to leave, so we're taking turns to stay there with her."

"Where are you sleeping when you're here?"

Annie pointed to the sitting room. "In there, on the floor, which isn't as uncomfortable as it sounds given the amount of blankets your mum has piled up for us."

"Still, it must be quite a squeeze with Stevie and Carol living here, too."

"The mornings are the worst," admitted Annie. "Every time I need to use the bathroom, someone else is in it."

Sam laughed. "Well, hopefully this is only a temporary measure. Why don't I walk into town with you and speak to Frank? Could you give me half an hour to unpack before we go?"

"Of course."

A squeal alerted them to Kitty's presence and Sam was almost knocked off his feet as she ran into the room and flung herself at her son. "Mum, you're acting as though I've been gone for months. It was only a few weeks ago I was last here."

Kitty pulled back, laughing. "It's felt like months to me. How long are you here for?"

"Three days."

"That's better than nothing. And you'll be helping with the clean-up?"

"Yes, they need all hands on deck, from what I've heard."

"Quite right. Do you know, I've missed The Grit since we moved up here, but since the flood, I've felt nothing but relief. All those poor families who've lost so much. Have you heard fire crews have come from all over the country to help?"

"I have. And I've also heard people are rallying worldwide to provide financial support. The whole of the east coast has been flooded. At least here there's been no loss of life. Those poor folk over in Holland didn't escape so lightly."

"I read about that in my newspaper this morning," said Bobby. "A terrible business."

"Listen," said Sam. "We'll catch up properly later, but I'm sure Annie is keen to get back to Sally and I need to receive my instructions from Frank, so we'd better get a move on."

"Of course," said Kitty. "I'll have your favourite dinner waiting for you when you get back."

"You spoil the lad," said Bobby.

"He's my baby," said Kitty, smiling at the six-foot-tall man in front of her.

While Sam unpacked, Annie went to find Marnie, who was folding up their bedding from the night before. The room was small but pleasant, with a bay window facing out onto the street and an old piano against one wall. Kitty had made it feel homely, but even so, Annie would be relieved when she no longer had to share a space with her mother and stepfather.

"Sam's here," said Annie, helping Marnie fold away the last of the blankets.

"So I gathered from Kitty's screaming," said Marnie with a smile. "I didn't expect him to be back so soon."

"He's come to help with the aftermath of the flood."

"That's good of him."

"We're heading to the house now, so I can take over from Frank and Sam can find out where he'll be most useful. What are your plans for the day?"

"I need to do some washing," said Marnie, "then I'm going down to the Steam Laundry to help the girls with the clear-up. The laundry boxes have been scattered all over the place, so our job today is to locate them and give them a good clean. I'll pop home once I'm finished to check on Sally. Are you sure you don't mind staying with her tonight? I imagine you'll want to spend some time with Sam while he's here?"

"There'll be plenty of time to spend with Sam later. For now, there's a mud-filled soggy house and a sick grandmother needing my attention."

Chapter 13

February, 1953

Annie looked out of the window to where Sam and Frank were scooping thick mud into wheelbarrows with large flat shovels. Despite the chill in the air, they had their shirtsleeves rolled up to the elbows and kept stopping to mop sweat from their brows.

The firemen from Portsmouth were still in town, but the night before the weather had taken a turn for the worse, petrol freezing in their carburettors, rendering one of their pumps useless. Locals had kept the firemen sustained with a steady stream of tea, biscuits, and hot soup in paper cups, and men from both The Grit and the town were working hard alongside the visitors to do all they could.

It had been three days since the flood came, and while there was still plenty of water around, it was the mud that was proving the greater problem. It was stickier than any glue Annie had come across, clinging to every surface with such determination it was hard to prise away. The smell of decay hung in the air, the bodies of both domestic and farm animals still being discovered as the water receded. Large mounds of damaged furniture had been piled on dry ground ready to be burned, and there were so many repairs needed to buildings, Annie feared it would be months if not years before they were back to anything resembling normality.

"How are they getting on?" asked Sally when Annie walked back into the room.

"They're working hard, that's for sure," said Annie. "They've pumped the worst of the water out, but it's the mud left behind that's now causing most of the problems. How are you?"

"Frustrated that I can't help."

"You just concentrate on getting yourself better," said Annie. "That's all anyone wants from you."

Sally smiled but didn't answer.

"I'm going to make Frank and Sam a cup of tea. Would you like one?"

Sally nodded, and Annie returned to her bedroom, where they had set up a rudimentary kitchen. With just one gas burner, a cold box, and bucket of water, it wasn't up to much, but it enabled them to make hot drinks and heat the soup Kitty had been cooking for them.

Keeping everyone on The Grit fed was a daunting challenge. Annie had heard that the landlords of The Gas House Tavern were busy cooking large vats of pea soup on their bogey stove. The women at Christ Church Hall were also churning out as much food as they could muster, and families from up in the town were busy cooking everything from casseroles to cakes to keep the Gritsters well nourished.

The kettle whistled on the stove and Annie poured it into the teapot Kitty had loaned them. They'd discovered their own smashed to pieces, along with the tea-set Marnie and Frank had received from Helen and Richard as a wedding present, not to mention the plates, cups and bowls that had suffered a similar fate.

Annie loaded up a tray with mugs and a pack of biscuits and carried it through to Sally's bedroom. "Here you go," she said, laying it down on the bedside table. "I'm going to take these to Frank and Sam, but I won't be long."

"Take as long as you like," said Sally, her eyelids already drooping with tiredness.

"I won't be long," Annie reiterated. At the top of the stairs, she slipped her boots back on and went out to find the thirsty workers. "I thought you could do with a break," she said, careful not to slip on the slimy pavement.

"You're an angel," said Frank, laying his shovel against a wall and taking a cup of tea.

"I quite agree," said Sam, doing the same.

"I was watching you from the window," said Annie. "You've got your work cut out here. It looks like Sally's about to doze off, and if she does, I'll come and give you a hand."

"There's no need for that," said Sam. "This isn't women's work."

Annie put her hands on her hips. "And what about all the land girls who worked on farms during the war? They dealt with their fair share of mud and dirt, and I didn't hear anyone complaining then."

Sam laughed. "Fair enough. Although you'll need to find a shovel."

"That can be arranged."

Annie walked through the house and out into the backyard. No attempt had been made to clear the muck and debris out there, and Annie's boots sank almost to their rims as she stepped outside. Twice she lost a boot crossing the yard, but kept her balance and made it across the yard to the shed.

Just as she was about to step onto the debris-strewn shed floor, Annie screamed. A mass of ginger feathers lurched towards her, the chicken screaming almost as much as she was. Annie stepped back, and skidded in the mud, her fall broken by the shed door that lay on top of other debris.

"There she is," called Mr Thompson, leaning over the fence. "I've been looking for that chicken everywhere. I assumed the water had taken her, but it looks like she found a dry spot to roost and wait it out."

"I'm glad I could be of help," said Annie, climbing to her feet, aware of a large streak of stinking brown down the left side of her coat.

"What you doing in the shed, anyway?" asked Mr Thompson.

"I was looking for a shovel to help Frank and Sam out front, but the shed's in such a muddle I don't expect I'll find anything of use in there."

"At least it's still standing," said Mr Thompson. "The only thing mine is any use for now is firewood, and even then it will be months before it's dried out enough to burn. I've got a shovel you can borrow if you need one."

"Yes please," said Annie, "as long as you don't need it yourself."

"I'm busy inside this morning," said Mr Thompson. "Got all the carpets to take up. Bloody plaster's already falling off the walls."

"Where are you staying?"

"In one room at my sister-in-law's up in town. It'll do for now, but I need to get this place ship-shape as soon as I can. How's Sally?"

"Not too well."

"Not still in the house, I hope?"

"She won't leave."

Mr Thompson shook his head. "Dear oh dear. Right, well, here's the shovel. I'd best be getting on. Give me a knock when you're done with it."

"I will, and thank you."

When Annie returned to the street, shovel in hand, Frank and Sam were still drinking their cups of tea.

"You sure about this?" asked Frank.

"Yes, I checked on Sally on my way through and she's sleeping."

"Roy's shed is still standing then," said Sam, nodding to the shovel in Annie's hand.

"Only just. I borrowed this from Mr Thompson."

"That's the one good thing to come out of this flood," said Frank. "All the community rallying together, it reminds me of the war."

"And that's a good thing?"

"The community spirit is, yes. Between us all, we'll return The Grit to its former glory."

Annie smiled. While she appreciated Frank's optimism, she felt strongly that things in The Grit would never be the same.

Chapter 14

February, 1953

Frank leaned his shovel against the wall and stretched his arms above his head. "I think we should call it a day."

"Thank goodness," said Annie, wiping a mud-coated hand across her forehead.

"I thought naval work was hard," said Sam, "but this mud's a beast to clear."

"Like glue."

"Exactly."

"Are you sure you don't mind staying here tonight, Annie?" asked Frank.

"You sound like Mum," said Annie. "Of course I'm alright staying here. It's what we agreed."

"Have you got enough to eat?"

"Yes, there's plenty of Kitty's soup left."

"Alright, if you're sure, then I suppose Sam and I will make our way home."

"Actually," said Sam, "I thought I may stay with Annie for a while. I could get us fish and chips from up in town?"

Annie's eyes sparkled at the thought, and her stomach growled. "Fish and chips sounds wonderful. I've certainly built up a hunger with all this shovelling."

"Shall I get some for Sally too?"

Annie shook her head. "No, she's lost her appetite. Get some for me and you, and I'll see if I can tempt her with a few chips."

"Alright then. I'll walk up the score with you, Frank." Sam turned to Annie. "I won't be long."

Progress through the streets was slow going. Sam and Frank slid their way along the path, frequently needing to step over debris that still littered the area. There was no distinguishing the pavement from the road, the mud still several feet thick in places.

"Whoa there," said Sam, as Frank lost his balance. He grabbed Frank's jacket, preventing his fall.

"Thank you. I've got enough mud on me already without lying in it. You've been such a help today, Sam."

"Just doing my duty," said Sam with a mock salute and a wink.

"I must say, you've turned from boy to man since you've been away, and I don't just mean the broadening of your shoulders. You've a confidence about you I've not noticed before."

Sam grinned. "Mum says the navy has been the making of me. I like to think she's right. Being the youngest, I think I was always a bit babied. Mum liked to spoil me, and I was next to useless when I first arrived on base."

"The navy certainly seems to do a good job of churning out fine young fellows, even if I say so myself. You must miss home, though."

"Yes, although in a way, since Mum and Dad moved up into town, I don't really have a home to miss, given I've never lived in their new house. I miss Lowestoft though, and the *Sally Ann*. I can't wait till I can come back and join the crew full time."

"So you've not been tempted by the delights of Portsmouth?"

"No," said Sam, shaking his head. "I'm a Lowestoft boy through and through. I can't wait to begin my adult life here and start a family of my own."

"And do these plans involve my stepdaughter, by any chance?"

Sam flushed. "I'd like to think so, but you never know with Annie. I sometimes wonder if Lowestoft is too small for her."

"I know what you mean," said Frank, "but I don't think her restlessness has anything to do with the size of the town. She found leaving Padstow harder than she let on, especially to her mother. When we think of the war, we think of the soldiers and civilians who lost their lives, but there's an entire generation of children who've been affected by evacuation in ways we'll probably never know. You must have felt it too, being sent up north?"

"Hmm, a little, but I had my brothers with me. When I came home, life carried on much as it ever had. It was different for Annie. With her dad gone and her house blown to smithereens, there was nothing familiar when she returned."

"And there was a stepfather added into the mix."

Sam slapped Frank on the back. "You've been nothing but a godsend to Marnie and Annie. I dread to think what their lives would have been like if Marnie hadn't met you."

"I like to think we've become a close-knit little family. Even so, my arrival on the scene was yet another change for Annie to contend with. When it comes to her future, she may have her doubts about Lowestoft, but from the way she looks at you, I'd be surprised if she has any doubts about you."

"Perhaps," said Sam, blushing again, "but me and Lowestoft come as a package. I just hope what I can offer Annie is enough."

The two men walked up Mariner's Score, then parted ways. Sam collected two parcels of delicious smelling fish and chips from the shop, then tucked them inside his coat to keep them warm. When he arrived back on The Grit, he made his way to the house and stepped inside.

"Annie?"

"We're up here."

Sam took the stairs two at a time, kicked his boots off on the landing, and followed the sound of voices.

As he walked into Sally's room, she sniffed the air and smiled. "This one's a keeper," she said, pointing to the parcels of food now in Sam's hands.

"Do you feel up to eating a little?" asked Annie.

"No, I'm exhausted," said Sally. "But save me a few chips, and I might fancy them later. You two go off and have your supper. I'll be alright here." She shuffled further down into the bed and Annie tucked the blankets around her.

"We'll be in my room if you need anything."

Sally yawned. "Off you go."

"Do you mind if we don't bother with plates?" asked Annie once they were in her bedroom-cum-sitting room.

"Not at all. Fish and chips taste better straight from the paper."

"I agree. Sit down and I'll put the kettle on."

"I'll sit on the floor, I think," said Sam, looking down at his mud-spattered trousers.

Annie laughed and waved her arms around. "Look at this place, Sam. I think a bit of mud on the chair cushions is the least of our worries."

Sam took up position on the floor, his back against the wall. They were hungrier than they realised, and for a while, the only sound to fill the room was the chewing of food and the bubbling kettle.

"That was delicious," said Sam as he popped the last chip into his mouth. He screwed up the paper, threw it in the bin, then sat back, rubbing his stomach. "We really worked up an appetite today, although walking around The Grit, you wouldn't think there's been folk out clearing and cleaning for days. The place is in a poor old state."

"I know. It's hard to imagine it will ever recover."

"True, but it survived the war, remember?"

"Only just." With a sigh of contentment, Annie finished her meal and poured two cups of tea from the pot. She handed them to Sam, then sat on the floor beside him, resting her head against his shoulder. "It's good to have you home," she said. "This flood has really pulled the rug out from under me. Goodness knows what will happen to this house, or to Nan. But you're a constant in my life I can always rely on, and I want you to know how much I appreciate you."

"Thank you," said Sam, his voice gruff. "I wish I could be home for longer and more often, but..."

"Annie?"

At the sound of Sally's call, Annie jumped up. "I'm sorry," she said, "but I'd better see what Nan needs."

"Of course," said Sam, "and I'd better be heading home." He pulled Annie into his arms and kissed the top of her head. "Everything will work out for the best," he said, smiling at her as she pulled away and went to see to Sally.

Chapter 15

February, 1953

"The fire's been going for a week now, and there's still water coming through the walls."

Annie stood beside Marnie, frowning at a wall whose plaster was bulging. She stepped forward and poked a finger in it. A torrent of brown water gushed out.

"Are you sure the fire's been going a week? It smells as damp in here as the day the water left."

"I know," said Marnie. "I hate to say it, but there's no way we can move back in properly soon. Folk are saying it could be months before the walls dry out and even once they do, there's no telling the amount of structural damage that will have been done."

"Have you spoken to Nan again about moving her somewhere more comfortable?"

"I have, but her answer hasn't changed."

"But it wasn't that long ago she was talking about how nice it would be to live in a new house."

"I don't think she was serious, or if she was, it was in an abstract way, not something she'd actually do."

"But staying here is making her ill."

"She was ill anyway, but I agree, staying in the house won't be helping, although her room hasn't been affected by the water, so as long as we keep the fire going in there, it isn't too bad."

It had now been over a week since Annie, Frank and Marnie began taking it in turns to stay in the house with Sally. For the first couple of days after the flood it had seemed the most sensible solution, for getting an immobile Sally out with all the debris strewn about would have been a tall order. But now, a week on, the arrangement was less than satisfactory. Plumbing had been restored and the toilet now flushed, but the bathroom itself was unusable and so Sally was reliant on a bedpan. And heating water was tricky with just one small gas stove, so Sally's washes had all been conducted with cold water, which wouldn't do her much good.

"I'll talk to her again," said Marnie. "But you know how stubborn she can be."

"A characteristic the females of this family share," said Annie with a grin. "I must say, I'm finding it a bit of a squeeze at Kitty's place."

"I know," said Marnie. "It was so kind of her to let us stay, but we need to find an alternative. Frank's back is playing up from sleeping on the floor, and it's affecting his work."

"What will we do?"

"Frank has arranged for us to look at some houses this evening."

"Where?"

"Up in town, mostly. And a couple in Oulton Broad."

"Oulton Broad won't be very handy for getting to work."

"You know what they say, beggars can't be choosers."

Annie sighed, picked up a mop, and began the futile task of clearing brown sludge from the floor. She stopped mopping and leaned against the handle. "Will we ever live here again?"

Marnie frowned. "The honest answer is, I don't know. Given the state the house is in, it would be wrong to make any promises, but I'm aware this is your home, and I'll do everything I can to make it habitable again."

"Then I'd better help with that," said Annie, returning to her mopping.

As her mop cleared mud from the floor, it revealed lino torn into thin strips below. Beneath the ruined lino, floorboards bulged, having soaked up so much water. They could clean away the mud, but even as no expert, Annie knew all the boards would need replacing. Even the houses whose boards were designed to be lifted and used as flood defences had been damaged beyond repair.

"Knock knock."

Annie and Marnie turned to see Sam in the open doorway, wearing his navy uniform with a canvas bag slung across one shoulder.

"Sam, this is a lovely surprise," said Marnie.

"I just popped in to say goodbye," he said. "The RAF chaps are here now, so I've been called back to base."

"Thank you so much for all you've done to help," said Annie.

"It's no more than anyone else has done. I just wish I could stay longer." He held Annie's eye and her stomach fluttered. "I've just spoken to one of the RAF chaps and apparently food parcels are arriving from Canada, along with rolls of carpet and other household items."

"Goodness, this flood really has brought out the best in folk," said Marnie. "To think provisions are being sent all the way from Canada! Right, I'll say my goodbyes, Sam, as I'd better head upstairs and check on Sally." Marnie walked over and kissed Sam on the cheek.

"So," said Sam, when Marnie had gone. "This is another goodbye." He stepped into the room, seemingly oblivious to the smell that still hung in the air.

"We seem to have had a lot of goodbyes lately."

"We have. You know, Annie, I'm not sure when I'll next be granted leave. It might not be for a while, so I'd like to leave with the two of us on a clearer footing."

"I'm not sure I understand."

Sam took another step towards her. "I think you do. I've loved you my whole life, Annie. Before I left for my National Service, I was thinking you felt the same, but now I'm not so sure."

Annie looked at the ground. When she spoke, her voice was quiet. "I love you, Sam, but the thought of any official arrangement between us scares me. I'm not yet eighteen and..."

"You don't want to be tied down yet? If it's a marriage proposal you're worried about, don't be. I wouldn't dream of proposing until I have more to offer."

"You have plenty to offer. It's not that..."

"Really? I'm not even living in the same town as you these days, let alone had time to prove myself as a crew member of the *Sally Ann*. I understand you'd need to see a more secure future before making a commitment like that."

Annie wondered how she could explain that however much security Sam provided, she needed to find her own sense of belonging and questioned whether that was possible in Lowestoft. Her heart longed for adventure, something to fill the restlessness she'd felt for as long as she could remember. "Sam, I..."

"I'm not about to propose," interrupted Sam, "but I think it would be good to have things clearer between us. Would you consider stepping out with me?"

Annie smiled at her old friend. She couldn't deny how handsome he looked in his uniform. He had inherited a toned-down version of Kitty's colouring, with wavy auburn hair and sparkling green eyes. His freckled skin covered a strong jaw and defined cheek bones. Yes, he was a very handsome man, and any girl would be mad to turn him down. Annie pushed down any reservations she felt. "Yes, Sam, I'll step out with you, whatever that means when we're living at opposite ends of the country."

They both laughed and Sam moved so close Annie could feel the warmth of his breath on her skin. Amid the stench and debris left by the flood, they shared their first proper kiss.

"I'd better go," said Sam, pulling away, "or I'll miss my train." He walked to the door, turned, and blew Annie one last kiss.

Annie stared at the doorway long after Sam had gone. The kiss had ignited feelings she'd never experienced before. Her desire to find a sense of belonging hadn't waned, but for the first time in a long time, Annie wondered whether it was a challenge she didn't have to face alone. And maybe, just maybe, Sam was the person to fill the longing and restlessness she seemed unable to shake.

Chapter 16

February, 1953

"Still no change?"

Marnie shook her head, brushing away a tear.

"Go and eat. Frank has bought fish and chips and is waiting for you in my bedroom."

"Are you sure?"

"Yes, I've got mine with me," said Annie, holding up a delicious smelling newspaper parcel.

"Alright then, but call me if there's any change."

When Marnie had left the room, Annie put her supper down on the dresser, unable to face eating anything. It wasn't just the rotten smell filling the house and seeping from the walls, but concern for Sally stemming her appetite. In the bed, Sally tossed and turned, her face creased, but whether from pain or nightmares, Annie wasn't sure. She rinsed out a cloth in a bowl and wiped it against Sally's forehead. For a moment she relaxed, her skin smoothing out, her limbs still. Her eyes opened and a faint whisper escaped her lips.

"I didn't hear you, Nan, say that again." Annie leaned over, her ear to Sally's lips.

"My boys," whispered Sally.

Annie sat up, wondering what she meant. With great effort Sally raised her arm, pointing to the far wall for a second before the effort became too great and her hand fell back down. Annie crossed the room and began removing photographs from their position on the wall.

"Is this what you wanted?" asked Annie, holding Sally's hand against the cool glass of a frame. Sally gave a tiny nod of her head. Annie propped the photographs around her on the bed. "I know you're feeling poorly at the moment, Nan, but we need to think about getting you out of the house. It isn't right for you to be lying here with the walls downstairs still full of water and the terrible smell the water brings with it."

"Not... leaving..." whispered Sally.

"I understand why you don't want to leave, Nan, but it might be time to think about hospital."

Sally shook her head with as much energy as she could muster.

Annie sighed. It was an impossible situation. It would devastate Sally to leave the house, and yet it wasn't practical for her to stay. And really, the only place she could go was the hospital. She needed proper care, greater than either Marnie or Annie could provide. "Why don't we see how you get on tonight, then decide in the morning?"

Sally didn't answer, but shuffled her arm, gathering the photographs of her children and husband closer. Her eyes closed and her breathing became heavier. Annie decided enough was enough. She crept out of the bedroom and went to find Frank and Marnie.

"What's happened?" asked Marnie when Annie walked into her old bedroom.

"Nothing, she's asleep."

"You shouldn't have left her."

"I won't be long, but we need to decide what to do. However much we all want it, Nan can't stay in this house."

"I agree," said Frank. "There's no room at Kitty's and most of the hotels are full. I've been inquiring about other properties, but there's such a demand for emergency accommodation it's near impossible to find somewhere. Sally isn't well enough to be camping out on someone's floor like we can."

"What about hospital?"

"That should be a last resort," said Marnie.

"Mum, you've seen how poorly she is. Someone that unwell should be in hospital, not in a damp, freezing, stinking house that could fall down around our ears at any moment."

"She made me promise," said Marnie, her voice thick with emotion.

"Promise what?"

"That she could die in her own bed."

"She's not going to..." Annie saw a look pass between Marnie and Frank and stopped talking.

"Annie, I had a doctor come round to see her this afternoon while you were taking more things over to Kitty's. He thinks she's reached the end of her life and may not survive the night."

"But she's strong. She's a fighter. Look at all she's overcome in her life!"

"Aye," said Marnie, "but I think the flood has proved one fight too many. Besides, I think Sally has been wanting to join her boys and Roy for some time now. She's lived a full life, and is one of the bravest women I've ever met. We could take her to hospital where they may keep her going for a few more days, maybe even weeks, but is that really fair? The doc has given her medicine to keep her comfortable, and told us to ring him if she gets any worse."

"Thank goodness for Bevan and his National Health Service," said Frank.

Marnie reached across and squeezed his hand. "Quite right."

"I'll go back to Nan," said Annie. Although her eyes were open, Annie felt as though she were sleepwalking. The thought of losing Sally was too much to bear, and she refused to let the knowledge sink into her heart. "Time for a story, I think," said Annie, picking up a book. She took a deep breath, swallowed down the emotion sticking in her throat, and started to read.

Sally looked so peaceful, and Annie was halfway through the second chapter when a sharp, faltering breath made her throw the book down and take her hands. She watched the intermittent rise and fall of Sally's chest, her nightdress barely moving as her need for air lessened.

"Mum," called Annie, "Mum, come here."

Marnie ran into the room and took up position on the opposite side of the bed. "We're here, Sally. You're safe. You can go to your boys."

Her eyes flicked. Annie felt a tiny squeeze of her hand, then Sally was gone. Marnie and Annie stayed where they were, pinned down not by grief but by a tangible peace filling the air. In Annie's mind's eye, she saw a newly invigorated Sally being embraced by Roy and her boys.

A tear slipped down Marnie's cheek. "Are you alright, Mum?" asked Annie.

"Aye, she was ready to go. Ever since Roy died, I knew it was only a matter of time, and she's at peace now. It's probably selfish of me to say, but Sally was my last link to Tom. Losing her feels a bit like losing your dad all over again."

Annie stood up and walked around the bed, wrapping her arms around Marnie. Their tears mingled as they looked down at Sally's still body and said their goodbyes.

Chapter 17

February, 1953

"Have you heard the news?"

"What's happened?" asked Annie, unable to bear the prospect of more bad news.

"Queen Mary has died."

"Oh no, that's very sad. We should add the royal family to our prayers today."

"Aye, I'm sure the vicar will be aware, but I'll mention it to him when we reach the church."

"Do you think they'll be up there together?" asked Annie.

"Up where?"

"In heaven," said Annie.

Marnie smiled for the first time that week. "You think Sally and Mary are up there together sharing a pot of tea?"

"Surely there's no hierarchy up there?" said Annie. "Perhaps they'll be enjoying a game of bridge."

"I'm sure there's some law against speaking in such terms," said Marnie, "but I like the thought. Although I can't imagine how Queen Mary will react to Sally's plain-speaking Lowestoft ways."

"It'll be an education."

Marnie laughed, then held a hand to her mouth as though moments of joy were forbidden. Annie crossed the room and pulled her mother into her arms.

"Nan would want us to laugh," she said gently. "She was never one for moping, was she?"

"I know," said Marnie with a sniff. "I just miss her so much."

"So do I."

In Christ Church, an army of parishioners determined to keep the church open had swept away all signs of the flood. The pews were full with a community out to remember, grieve and celebrate the life of one of their own. Sally had left clear instructions for her funeral service, and both Marnie and Annie were grateful for her thoughtfulness. Organising a funeral on top of all the work still to do to get their house habitable might have been a step too far.

After the coffin was carried in and the first hymn sung, the vicar stood to give his address.

"I met Mrs Hearn during my first week in this parish. I was young, new to the job, and if truth be told, a little lost. Sally took me under her wing, seeing to everything from introducing members of the community, to informing me of the best place to buy a loaf of bread.

"Sally's faith had been severely tested by the devastating loss of two sons during the Great War, and yet she refused to give in to hatred or blame. Through the stories of Jesus and his disciples, we are given a blueprint for how to live our lives. Sally embodied these Christian values as much as anyone I have met. The amount of mourners present today are testament to the respect for Sally in this community and the Christian love she showed to all those around her.

"Many of you will remember the tragic accident that claimed the life of Sally's youngest son, Tom. You will remember Sally's heartbreak, but also, I suspect, her resilience. The way the community here rallied around her during those dark days speaks of the remarkable bonds that bind those living on The Grit to one another. As a community, we are experiencing a time of significant challenge. Let the life Sally lived be a reminder that through hardship we can find strength, in grief we can find love, and when all seems lost, there is always hope."

The vicar then opened his bible and read from Corinthians. The church was so quiet you could hear a pin drop. Other than the dabbing of eyes with handkerchiefs, all were still.

"And so," the vicar said, "the passage ends: 'and now these three remain: faith, hope and love. But the greatest of these is love'."

The entire congregations responded with a collective, "Amen."

After the service had ended and they'd retired to the hall for the wake, Annie stood alone in the room's corner, staring through tear-blurred eyes at her surroundings as though in the middle of a dream.

"Come here, lass."

Annie's eyes refocussed, and she brushed away tears with her sleeve.

"Come here, lass," the voice said again.

"Oh, Kitty, it's you. Sorry, I was miles away."

"You need a break from all of this," said Kitty, waving a hand at the crowds of mourners. Without another word, she took Annie's hand and led her through the crowds and back into the church. Annie stumbled, and Kitty wrapped an arm around her, guiding her into a pew. From the pocket of her skirt, she pulled out a hip flask. "Drink," she said.

Annie did as she was told, wincing as the liquid burned her throat. "I'm sorry," she said. "I'm not sure what came over me in there."

"It's the shock of it all," said Kitty. "First the flood, then losing Sally. It's no wonder you're feeling topsy-turvy."

"I should go back and help Mum."

"There's no need," said Kitty. "Frank's with her and no one will begrudge you a moment to yourself. From what I've seen, all you've done is look after other people these past few days. Let's sit for a while. We don't have to talk, not if you don't want to."

Annie leaned back against the hard wooden pew and closed her eyes. Without a congregation to warm it, the surrounding air was bitter, but Annie welcomed the way it sharpened her senses. "I can smell the flood," she muttered, her eyelids too heavy to open.

"Aye," agreed Kitty. "Even Mrs Thompson's perfume couldn't drown out the smell."

Annie let out a chuckle, which turned into a choking sob.

"It's alright, lass," said Kitty, pulling her close. "Everything will be alright, mark my words."

"I want to believe you," said Annie, "but my life's been a series of disasters. Just when I feel settled, something always goes wrong. Dad dying, the war, the flood, losing Nan. Wherever I go, tragedy follows. Sometimes it feels like with each loss, a piece of me breaks away. I've left parts of my life all around the country, and I worry I won't belong or feel at home anywhere until I've put them back together again."

"Don't talk rot," said Kitty. "You belong here in Lowestoft, with the people who love you."

"Nan was my tie to Lowestoft, to The Grit. While I had her to care for, I had a purpose. Now there's nothing to keep me anchored here."

"What about your mam and Frank? Sam?"

"Sam's not here."

"No, but he'll be back. Don't the two of you have plans? I try not to pry, but I know my son and see the way he looks at you."

Annie shrugged. "Maybe. I can't think beyond today. The thought of going back to the house without Nan in it..."

"You can stay with us as long as you need."

"Thank you."

"And, Annie, after all that's happened to you, especially in the past few months, it's no wonder you're feeling out of sorts." The pew creaked as Kitty turned to her. She held Annie's face in her hands. "We're all here to help you, lass. You cared for Sally better than anyone, but you're young. The last thing Sal would want is you being drowned by grief and not grabbing life by the horns. You'll find your place in the world soon enough, and we'll all be with you on the journey to get there. Now, how about we go back to the hall? My toes are so cold I'm worried they'll drop off."

Chapter 18

March, 1953

"Thank you so much for everything you've done for us," said Annie as Kitty pulled her into a hug.

"Anytime. I'm worried about you all going back to that damp old house. You know you can stay here longer if needs be?"

"That's so kind of you," said Marnie, "but you all need your space back and we need a bit of normality. We won't be able to use the downstairs for some time, but we've set up a makeshift kitchen and sitting room in what was Sally's bedroom and, as temporary arrangements go, it could be worse."

"Hmm," said Kitty, folding her arms and frowning. "Alright, but if it turns out to be too uncomfortable, I want you all straight back here. Agreed?"

"Yes, ma'am," said Frank, kissing Kitty on the cheek, then turning to shake Bobby's hand.

Annie, Frank, and Marnie picked up the last of their belongings and said their goodbyes. Outside, a grey Morris Oxford was waiting, and the driver helped them store their suitcases in the boot before they climbed in.

"I'll take you as far as Christ Church," he said, "but you'll have to walk the rest of the way."

"Why?" asked Frank.

"Still a mud bath down there from what I've heard, not to mention all the broken glass and suchlike that could wreck my tyres."

"I'll have you know..." started Frank, but Marnie put a placating hand on his arm.

"Christ Church will be fine," she said.

"As soon as we're settled, I'm going to see about getting my own motor car," Frank muttered.

Annie could well understand Frank's annoyance with their driver. He and many others had been working tirelessly for weeks to clear the streets of The Grit and had done a fine job of it. A Lord Mayor's fund had been set up to help local families, but although Frank had accepted a donation of carpet from Canada, he had turned down the offer of financial support from the local fund, stating there were plenty of families in greater need than his. Not for the first time, Annie felt a rush of gratitude that Marnie had married Frank. He'd been a rock these past weeks, and she wasn't sure what they would have done without him.

"How are you feeling about moving home?" Frank asked Annie.

"I'll be grateful to get off Kitty's floor and back to familiar surroundings, but it will be so strange without Nan there."

"We'll make it homely in no time," said Marnie, rather optimistically, Annie thought. "Once the new carpet is laid, it will feel like a fresh start."

"Let's hope so."

"And if it doesn't, we can always look again at moving up into town," said Frank.

"Let's see how we get on, shall we?" said Marnie, casting an anxious glance at Annie, who hadn't been herself since Sally's death.

The taxi pulled up outside Christ Church, the driver true to his word. They hauled their suitcases out of the boot and began walking along Whapload Road. The smoke from chimneys and sounds of children playing suggested some families had already moved back, but there were still plenty of homes with their windows boarded up and with no sign their residents were eager to return.

"Let me carry that," said Frank, taking Annie's suitcase from her.

"Thank you. Mum, I'll take one of your bags."

"Good teamwork," said Marnie, handing over a canvas bag. "Thank you, both of you, for all the work you've been doing in the house. I know it's been a rough few weeks, but I want you to know how proud I am of you both."

When they reached the house, all three pulled their faces into smiles, determined to make the best of the situation. Frank turned the key in the lock and opened the newly fitted front door. A smell of lingering damp hit them, the stained walls and patches of mould an unwelcome reminder that it would be a long time before the effects of the flood were banished.

"The carpet arrives tomorrow," said Frank. "It will make a tremendous difference to how the house feels."

"And we'll keep the fires going until the walls are dry."

"We may run out of wood and coal before then," said Annie, poking a finger into sponge-like plaster.

"Come on now," said Marnie, "we all agreed we'd look on the bright side."

"You're right," said Annie. "I will certainly be grateful to be back in my own bed and away from both of your snoring."

"I don't snore!" said Marnie.

Frank hid a snigger behind his hand.

"I don't!"

"Whatever you say, dear." Frank escaped Marnie's scowl by carrying their suitcases upstairs.

"I'll make us a cup of tea," said Annie, "then we can unpack."

While Frank and Marnie busied themselves in their bedroom, Annie arranged cups and saucers on the dresser, which was currently in use as a kitchen worktop. She tried to push down the feeling of loss the room conjured in her. Each time she turned her head, she expected to see Sally, or Roy, sitting up in their bed with a cup of tea. Instead, where their bed had once stood was a second-hand sofa, donated by Kitty's son Simon, who'd insisted he'd been about to treat his wife to a new suite and had no use for the old one.

While she waited for the kettle to boil, Annie laid a fire in the hearth, holding out her hands as the flames took hold. She pulled an armchair closer and flopped down into it. Between her work at the factory and all the hours spent cleaning up the house, she was exhausted.

As her eyelids drooped, memories surfaced behind them; her dad, spinning her around in the kitchen downstairs when she was tiny, Granddad Roy snoozing in an armchair, a paper spread across his lap, and Sally, wonderful Sally, lying in her bed smiling as Annie read Jane Austen aloud. When Annie drifted off into a deep sleep, it wasn't just the fire's warmth soothing her, but the ghosts who clustered around her, surrounding her with their love.

Chapter 19

March, 1953

Marnie and Annie walked along the promenade, their arms linked. The sea glinted beneath a weak winter sun, a hushed lapping of waves against the sand. Both the flood and their recent bereavement had ignited a closeness between them that neither had felt since the early days of war.

"It's hard to imagine how something so benign could cause such damage," said Marnie, stopping to gaze at the sea.

"It's a changeable beast, alright."

"And we should know more than most. It took your father's life, after all. And Sally's, indirectly, not to mention all those lives lost in the flood over in Holland."

Annie nodded, swallowing down the lump in her throat. With thoughts of Sally too painful, she turned her attention to an older loss, one that remained a dull ache in her heart rather than the stabbing pain of losing her grandmother. Annie closed her eyes, but struggled to remember much about her father, Tom. When she pictured him, it was a blurred figure lifting her up and smiling. Yet, she remembered his laugh, and a feeling of warmth when she was with him.

"It's alright, you know, if you don't remember much about him," said Marnie, "you were so young when he died."

"I don't remember much from that time," said Annie, "not details anyway. Just feelings."

"What feelings?"

Annie screwed up her face, wondering how to explain things to her mother. "I don't know, unsettled, maybe? When I think of Dad, it's like there's a hole inside me, like something is missing. This will sound strange, but I wonder whether part of me will always be in Padstow, as that's where he is, or as good as. I wish there was a grave to visit. Losing him at sea, well, it's hard to say goodbye properly, isn't it?"

"It certainly is. Those were dark days. It's no wonder your feelings about those early years in Padstow are unsettled and confused."

"Hmm, I remember more from the war years, after you'd left to come back here."

"That makes sense, given you were that much older. In many ways, your years there without me were probably more settled. You knew you'd be there until the end of the war, and I know Helen and Richard did everything they could to create a calm, loving home."

Mother and daughter left the promenade, their feet kicking up plumes of golden sand as they walked across the beach. "It was here that I decided to bring you home," said Marnie. "Well, not this exact spot, but at Children's Corner. I was with Uncle Jimmy, and when we saw the beach finally reopened, I just knew it was the right time to bring you back to Lowestoft."

"I know from talking to my friends I was one of the lucky ones when it came to being an evacuee. You should hear the stories some of them tell, absolutely dreadful."

"Aye, I've heard a few tales, too."

"I think it leaves you restless, though," said Annie.

"Being an evacuee?"

"Yes. There's always this nagging feeling you don't quite belong anywhere."

"You don't feel at home in Lowestoft?"

"Sometimes, but not always. And since the flood, well, I suspect I'm not alone in feeling a little lost. Our home is damaged, neighbours moving away. The Grit is dying, Mum."

"It's suffered before. I'm sure the community will pull together and rebuild."

"You really think so? Even after all the destruction of the war? One disaster it could recover from, but two? And that's before you consider how factories are replacing the fishing industry. The need to live in The Beach Village seems less important without the draw of the fishing and all the jobs that came with it."

"Perhaps."

"But it's not only what's happened lately, Mum. I still have days when I hanker for Padstow, and going up to Holy Island for your wedding gave me a sense of going home. I know that must sound strange, given I'd never been there before."

"It doesn't sound strange," said Marnie. "You're a Watson from an island family. Island life is in your blood."

"I'd like to visit again."

"You know Uncle Jimmy and Aunt Clara would always welcome you should you fancy a holiday."

"I know. I'd like to go back to Padstow, too."

"Right," said Marnie, and Annie felt her mother stiffen.

"Would that be a problem?"

"No, not at all," said Marnie, a forced brightness to her voice. "It's just such a long way, that's all."

"So is the island."

"Aye, but expensive too. Two big journeys like that would cost a fortune."

"But I'm working now and saving hard."

"What about Sam? Does he feature in any of these plans?"

"Sam's still got another eighteen months of National Service. I'd like to find out a little more about myself before committing to settling down."

"You know," said Marnie, turning to her daughter. "I recognise this restlessness you're feeling, Annie. But, from my experience, I'm telling you it's not always about a place. You could travel to Padstow, or Holy Island and still not feel settled. You need to find peace inside yourself. Moving across the country won't solve a restlessness within."

"I'm not talking about moving anywhere," said Annie, frustrated by Marnie's lack of understanding.

"I know, but think about what I've said. You're on the verge of adulthood, and that can be an exciting time, but also daunting."

"Yes, I suppose you're right." As she gazed out to sea, Annie pictured herself as an incomplete jigsaw puzzle, with missing pieces scattered around the country. On them were questions about her past, people she had lost, hopes and disappointments. She longed to feel at home in Lowestoft, cocooned among people who loved her, but there were too many questions unanswered, too many nagging doubts to ignore. If she were ever to make a life here with Sam, first she'd have to leave. As mother and daughter walked back towards the harbour, Annie resolved to put travel plans in place as soon as possible.

Chapter 20

April, 1953

"You know, I'm really not sure about this," said Annie, as Beryl led her towards the Rising Sun pub.

"Annie, you only turn eighteen once."

"I know, but Mum will have planned a birthday supper and will be disappointed if I turn up late and half cut."

"We'll only go for one, I promise," said Beryl, linking arms with Annie.

"Alright, but I want to be home by six."

"I promise to get you home before you turn into a pumpkin. Ladies first," said Beryl, holding open the pub door for Annie.

"Surprise!"

Annie screamed and dropped her bag to the ground. Her hands flew to her cheeks, her mouth open. Around her, her family and friends struck up in song.

"Happy birthday to you, happy birthday to you, happy birthday, dear Annie, happy birthday to you."

"When did you arrange all this?" Annie asked as Marnie came and wrapped an arm across her shoulders.

"We've been planning it for weeks. I know you're off out to a dance with your friends at the weekend, but we couldn't let your actual birthday pass without a celebration, especially not your eighteenth."

"You were in on this too?" Annie asked Beryl, who stood beside her looking sheepish.

"Yes, your mum asked me to make sure you arrived on the dot of five-thirty."

"I'll never trust you again," said Annie with a laugh. "You were so convincing with your *one quiet drink, just the two of us* line."

"I know," said Beryl. "I think I would have made rather a good actress. Right, let me buy the birthday girl a drink. What are you having?"

"Do you know, I think I may push the boat out and have a port and lemon, seeing as it's my birthday!"

"Port and lemon coming right up," said Beryl, walking off to the bar.

"Happy birthday, love," said Kitty, pulling Annie into an embrace. "Eighteen, I can't believe it." Kitty held Annie at arm's length and looked her up and down. "You're the spitting image of your mother at that age. Now, Sam was so disappointed he couldn't be here to celebrate with you, but he asked me to give you this, and to tell you he'll buy you a drink the next time he's on leave." Kitty handed Annie a card and a small box-shaped parcel.

"Thank you. I'll save these for when I get home."

"You do that, love. And here's a little something from Bobby and me." Kitty handed a rectangular package to Annie. "Go on, you can open it now."

Annie carefully peeled back the newspaper wrapping to reveal a silver frame with a black-and-white photograph inside. Tears filled her eyes as she ran a finger across the glass.

"It was taken just before their last voyage," explained Kitty, pointing to the figures of Bobby and Annie's father Tom smiling aboard the *Sally Ann*. "We thought you'd want to have your dad with you on your special day."

"This is so thoughtful of you," said Annie, her voice catching. She hugged the photograph to her chest, noticing Marnie also had tears in her eyes.

"This is from Helen, Richard and Grace," said Marnie, handing Annie a small brown parcel. Inside was a card, a beautiful silk scarf, and a small watercolour painting of two girls standing beside Padstow Harbour. The blonde girl was the taller of the two, the shorter redhead holding the older girl's hand.

"Did Grace paint this?"

Marnie nodded.

"What a talented artist. I'll write to them as soon as I get home and thank them."

"This is from me and Frank," said Marnie, handing over a brown envelope.

"What? But you gave me that beautiful necklace this morning."

"I know. This is just a little extra."

Annie opened the envelope, her mouth falling open once more as she pulled out two train tickets. "To Padstow."

"It's a return," said Frank with a smile. "We don't want you getting there and deciding not to come back."

Annie hugged Marnie and Frank. "This is more than I could have dreamed of, thank you."

"There's one last gift," said Marnie. "From Uncle Jimmy and Aunt Clara." She handed over a second brown envelope.

"Oh my goodness," said Annie, opening the envelope to reveal another set of train tickets, this time to Northumberland.

"I told Jimmy you'd like to visit the island again and he thought this would be a useful gift. They're open tickets and valid for a year, so you can go whenever you feel ready."

"Anyone would think you're trying to get rid of her," laughed Beryl, appearing with a tray of drinks.

Marnie smiled at her daughter. "No, not trying to get rid of her, just allowing her to spread her wings."

"Oh, Mum, thank you. Thank you, thank you, thank you."

Later that evening, after one too many drinks in the wonderful company of her family and friends, Annie found herself alone in her bedroom. She kicked off her shoes and opened the card from Sam.

My dearest Annie,

Happy Birthday! You've beaten me to adulthood, but I shall join you there in a few months' time. I hope you have had a wonderful birthday and I wish I'd been able to celebrate with you. I wasn't sure what to get you as a gift, but I hope you like what I've chosen. My thought was it is something you can add to during your life and your many adventures, some of which I hope you will allow me to join you on. All my love, Sam.

Annie peeled back the paper surrounding a small square box. She opened the box and unwrapped layers of tissue paper to reveal a silver charm bracelet. Hanging from it was a single charm, a small sailboat. As she lifted the bracelet from its box, Annie saw a folded piece of paper underneath.

I took the liberty of choosing your first charm. It is not, as you may assume, to remind you of me, but of where you came from. I hope whenever you look at it, you will remember your dad and the fishing heritage you were born into on both sides of your family.

When I first saw the charm, it also reminded me of you, a little boat setting out to sea, ready to let the wind catch its sails. Go well, my dear Annie, and know that I shall wait for you whenever you return to port.

Annie fastened the bracelet onto her wrist and held her hand to her heart. Sam had given her the greatest gift imaginable: freedom. She was free to set off on her quest for belonging, safe in the knowledge he would be waiting for her on her return. Annie wished Sam was with her, for never had she loved him more, and she longed to take him in her arms and show him just how much he meant to her.

Chapter 21

April, 1953

Annie ran a finger along the map she had spread on her bed. Every spare moment she had, she used to plan her route. No firm dates had been put in place yet, but with her tickets safely tucked in her bedside cabinet, it was only a matter of time before she was on a train heading west.

The doorbell sounded, and Annie folded the map and ran to the mirror to check her lipstick. While she was still in Lowestoft, Annie had decided there was no point staying at home watching the hours slip past. She might as well make the most of any opportunities as they presented, and tonight was one such occasion.

"Oh hello, Mary love. Annie's upstairs getting ready. She should be down in a minute."

Annie heard Marnie greet her new friend from the factory and ran downstairs before she gave Mary the inquisition. "I'm here."

"Don't you look lovely," said Marnie, smiling as Annie spun around to show off her new olive green silk dress. It had just enough netting underneath to give it some volume and Annie knew it would twirl beautifully should a young man spin her around the dance floor.

Annie stopped twirling, giggling, as she struggled to regain her balance. "I love your dress," she said, eying Mary's cream silk gown. "Is it new?"

"Yes. It's made with parachute silk," explained Mary. "A seamstress on Victoria Road made it for me."

"You'll have to give me her details so I can get one, too."

"Do you girls want a lift to the dance?" asked Frank, looking up from the crossword he had spread across the kitchen table.

"No, we'll walk. You could pick us up later, though?"

"Ten o'clock suit you?"

Annie dropped her head, pouting her lips, her eyes downcast.

"That may have worked on me when you were a girl, but I'm not so soft these days. Ten-thirty is my final offer," said Frank.

"Deal."

Marnie sighed and shook her head, but Annie knew she'd be enjoying the exchange between daughter and husband. Annie and Mary said their goodbyes and promised to be waiting outside the Palais for Frank no later than ten-thirty.

"I think Frank is rather dishy," said Mary as they walked past the harbour towards the seafront.

"Urgh," said Annie, "that's my stepfather you're talking about. He's old enough to be your father, actually, he's old enough to be your grandfather."

"I've always gone for the older man," said Mary with a sigh. "They're so much more refined than boys our age."

"More available, you mean. We lost so many young men in the war there's not as much choice as there might have been."

"Speaking of war," said Mary, "have you heard sweets are no longer rationed? I went straight down to Delfs when I heard."

"Only you could move from talk of young men losing their lives to talk of sweets," said Annie, frowning at her friend and shaking her head.

“We don’t want to turn up at the dance all maudlin,” said Mary. “There will be plenty of chaps from Bentwaters there.”

“I thought you liked them older?”

“That’s English men. The chaps from Bentwaters Airbase are American,” said Mary with a roll of her eyes, as if that explained everything. “Is Beryl meeting us at the dance?”

“Nice change of subject,” said Annie with a grin. “Yes, her and Paul are going together.”

“She’s so lucky having a nice man to settle down with.”

“Don’t tell me you’ve got your sights set on Paul as well as my stepfather?”

Mary punched Annie on the arm. “I’m not a man-eater.”

The two women walked arm in arm past the harbour and the South Pier. Mary led Annie down a slope onto the lower promenade.

“Hold on a moment,” said Mary, perching on the concrete wall that separated the town from soft yellow sand. She began unfastening the buckle on her shoes.

“What are you doing?”

“These shoes pinch my toes. I’m going to have to put up with them all night, so thought I’d give my toes a brief respite before all the dancing.”

“But what about your...”

Before Annie could finish her sentence, Mary was peeling off her stockings and slipping them inside her leather handbag. “Don’t knock it till you’ve tried it,” said Mary, motioning for Annie to join her on the wall.

“Fine,” said Annie with a sigh, removing her own shoes and stockings and sinking her feet into the soft sand below. “Oh, that is wonderful.”

"Told you. Let's walk along the beach and pretend it's summer."

Annie laughed. "My toes have only been in this sand for seconds and they're already turning numb."

"We'd better get moving then, hadn't we?"

Together, they walked on along the beach. A few couples were out enjoying the clear, calm evening, and Annie and Mary attracted a few bemused looks as their high-heeled shoes swung in their hands as they walked. The sun was sinking low in the sky, throwing a pink tinge onto the sand. Gulls glided and swooped against the low orange sun, and the faint strain of a trumpet carried on the air.

"Do you know who's playing tonight?" asked Annie.

"Ken Macintosh. I really hope they play The Creep tonight. I'm longing for them to release it as a single."

"I don't think I remember that one."

"Of course you do. It was their finale the last time they were here."

Annie frowned. "Still not ringing any bells."

"I'll point it out to you tonight. Ah, can you hear the music? Come on." Mary grabbed Annie's arm and began running toward the sound of a big band playing.

"Slow down," said Annie. "It's hard to run on sand."

"You're right," said Mary. "Let's put our shoes back on and head up onto the esplanade."

Annie did as she was told, and soon she was struggling to keep up with Mary, who was half walking, half running past the Claremont Pier. "Slow down," said Annie. "We don't want to turn up out of puff and red in the face."

The path rose as they neared Pakefield, the Palais now coming into view. Groups were gathered outside, girls giggling as handsome American airmen leaned in close, offering cigarettes and the chance of a little excitement.

"There's Beryl," said Annie, waving as she caught sight of her friend.

"You took your time," said Beryl, glancing at her watch.

"Where's Paul?"

"Already inside getting our drinks."

"Then what are we waiting for?" asked Mary, linking arms with her two friends and dragging them inside.

Chapter 22

April, 1953

"There he is," said Beryl, returning Paul's wave. She took hold of Annie's hand, Annie took Mary's and they snaked their way through a sea of dancing bodies to the edge of the ballroom, where Paul was waiting at a round table covered in a crisp white tablecloth.

"I got gin for you ladies. I hope that's to your satisfaction."

"Perfect," said Annie, pulling out a chair and sitting down.

The room was noisy and the windows overlooking the sea were blurred with condensation from all the sweaty bodies jiving their way around the dance floor. Ken Macintosh and his band were in full flow, the saxophone taking central stage.

"There's already been a bit of bother," said Paul, nodding his head toward a group of local lads, one with a bloodied handkerchief clutched to his nose.

"What happened?"

"Some chap from Bentwaters asked a local fisherman's girl to dance. The Bentwaters chap wasn't to know she was spoken for, and it wasn't his fault she said yes, but that didn't stop the flying fists."

"Was he alright?"

"See for yourself," said Paul, pointing to an extremely handsome man twirling a girl around the dance floor. "The local lad didn't stand a chance."

Mary huffed. "Some of those fishermen give the rest of us a bad name. We don't want them putting the Bentwaters men off coming."

"They can more than take care of themselves," said Paul.

Annie gazed out at the groups of men around the room. There were very few airmen standing around the edges; after all, they never struggled to find a partner thanks to their exotic accents and good looks.

"Excuse me, ma'am."

Annie hadn't noticed the man walking towards her and jumped slightly as he appeared in front of her. "Good evening."

"Very formal," said the man with a chuckle. He held out his hand. "Would you like to dance?" His voice was like silk, his straight white teeth and full lips complementing his high cheekbones and pale blue eyes.

Mary jabbed Annie in the ribs. "What are you waiting for?" she hissed.

"That would be lovely, thank you," said Annie, climbing to her feet as Beryl raised an eyebrow.

The band had just finished a song, and the man led Annie into the centre of the dance floor. "My name's David," he said, wrapping an arm around her waist.

"Annie, Annie Hearn," she said.

"You local?"

"Yes, I am, but judging from your accent, you're not."

"No, ma'am. I've come up with my friends from Bentwaters."

"Isn't that a long way to come for a dance? Surely you have dances closer to the base you could go to?"

"Yes, but there's none so pretty as Lowestoft gals, and no one puts on a dance quite like the Palais."

"I wouldn't know," said Annie. "I've only ever been to a dance here."

"Then you've been spoiled," said David, "and don't need to go anywhere else."

The band struck up with a raucous shout of "A one, a two, a one two three four," from their leader, and conversation between Annie and David became impossible. He was an expert dancer. Annie could hold her own on the dance floor but allowed David to take the lead, enjoying the feeling of his capable hands on her waist and the way he somehow whisked her around the entire dance floor without ever bumping into another couple.

As he took her hand and lifted her arm aloft, spinning Annie beneath it, her charm bracelet glinted beneath the hall's lights. Despite being in the arms of a handsome American airman, Annie suddenly wished she was in Sam's arms, that it was him jiving and foxtrotting her around the hall. So when the second song ended and David requested a third dance, Annie declined, thanking him for his time and heading back to her seat.

"I think he wanted to dance with you all night," said Beryl when Annie resumed her place at the table. "He couldn't take his eyes off you."

"Maybe not," said Annie, "but I'm Sam's girl now, and no handsome American is going to change that."

"Is that so?" asked Beryl. "You're sounding far more sure of yourself than I've heard you before. Has something happened between the pair of you?"

Annie held up her wrist. "He got me this for my birthday."

"My, that is pretty."

"Yes, but it's the meaning behind it that makes it even more special. Sam wrote a note with it, telling me to have adventures and that he would be waiting for me when I got back. How could I not love a man who's prepared to give me so much freedom?"

"It probably depends what adventures he expects you to have," said Beryl.

"Alright here, ladies," said Paul, returning with a second round of drinks.

"Thank you," said Annie, taking her glass, "but I'm sure it was my round. Where's Mary?"

Beryl pointed to the dance floor, where Mary was being passed between two handsome men.

"She's in her element," laughed Annie. "I wouldn't be surprised if she leaves here with two marriage proposals by the end of the night."

"At the rate she's going, she'd better be careful she doesn't end up in the same condition as me," said Beryl, rubbing a hand across her stomach.

"Why aren't you two dancing?" asked Annie.

"My stomach couldn't cope with all that spinning around," said Beryl. "I've been sick as a dog since I fell pregnant."

"Would you mind if I pinched your fiancé for a quick dance?" asked Annie.

"Of course not. You'd be doing me a favour by taking him off my hands."

"Oi," said Paul, "it's not too late to withdraw my proposal."

Annie laughed and took Paul's hand. They found a space on the crowded dance floor and began moving to the music. Paul had a good sense of rhythm, though he wasn't a patch on David. But Annie didn't mind. Paul was a safer bet given there was no danger of her falling for his charms.

At half past ten, Annie went to find Mary, aware Frank would be waiting for them outside. She pushed her way through the crowds on the dance floor, but couldn't find her friend anywhere.

"Have you seen Mary?" Annie asked Beryl once she'd made her way back to the table.

"Last time I saw her, she was walking towards the cloakroom with an American on her arm."

"I'd better find her." Annie walked through the hall and out into a dark carpeted corridor. She turned a corner and almost bumped into Mary, who was locked in a passionate embrace with one of her earlier dance partners. Annie coughed, but neither half of the couple broke away. She cleared her throat louder and said, "Mary, we need to leave."

"Who's this?" drawled the man, pulling his head back from Mary's but keeping his arms wrapped around her waist.

"This is my friend Annie. Annie, this is Hank."

"Nice to meet you, Hank, but I'm afraid me and Mary need to leave."

"I'm not ready to go yet," said Mary.

"We have to," said Annie. "Frank will be waiting outside for us."

"Tell you what, ma'am, I've got a car of my own. How about you let your father drive you home, and I'll make sure Miss Mary gets home safe later, when we're done here?"

Annie sighed. "Come on, Mary, I don't want to leave you here by yourself."

"I'm not by myself."

"You know what I mean."

"Annie, I'm a free agent. Unlike you, I can stay or leave with whomever I choose."

Annie realised there was no point pleading with Mary, who she didn't know all that well but whose stubborn streak was becoming plain as day. "Alright, but be careful."

"I promise I'll take good care of your friend, ma'am."

"You'd better had," muttered Annie as she walked away. Before she left the dance, she went back to Beryl and Paul and asked them to keep an eye on Mary.

"Of course we will," said Paul. "We're waiting for the slow songs to start so I can finally have a dance with my fiancée."

"The slow songs won't make me feel too queasy," explained Beryl.

Annie laughed. "Do you think it may have been better to stay at home rather than waiting here all night for one dance?"

"Of course not," said Beryl. "Once this baby arrives, that will be the end of any dances for me. So sick or not, I'm going to pack in as many as I can before then."

"Alright then. Enjoy your slow dance. See you at work tomorrow. Night."

"Goodnight."

Annie left the Palais shrugging off her guilt at leaving Mary behind. If she wanted to get embroiled with a man she'd just met, who was Annie to stop her?

Chapter 23

April, 1953

"How was the dance?" asked Frank when Annie climbed into his new Ford Anglia. She kicked off her high heels, and he laughed. "It must have been good if your feet are sore."

"It was very good, thank you."

"Where's Mary?"

"In the back of the building kissing an American airman."

"Right," said Frank. "Well, I hope she won't be too much longer."

"She's not coming back with us," said Annie. "I tried to persuade her, but she insisted she wanted to stay. Beryl and Paul have promised to keep an eye on her."

"I don't like the thought of leaving her," said Frank with a frown. "Do you think you should go back in and have another go at persuading her?"

"There isn't any point."

"Alright. Well, I would offer to wait here a while, but we need to get home."

"Why?" asked Annie, studying Frank's face and realising his muscles were tense, his smile a little too forced.

"Your mother needs to speak to you."

"What's happened?"

"She'd rather tell you herself."

"Please, Frank, just tell me."

"It's best you wait to hear it from her."

Annie knew there was no point arguing, so they drove home in silence, Annie running through all the worst-case scenarios in her mind. Was Marnie ill? Had something happened to Uncle Jimmy or Aunt Clara? Surely there couldn't have been another natural disaster in the few hours she'd been out dancing?

The car pulled up outside the house and before Frank had turned off the engine, Annie was climbing out, then running towards the front door. She burst into the house and ran upstairs. She found her mother in the makeshift sitting room, a single lamp throwing shadows across the room, a pile of used tissues on the coffee table.

"Mum, what's happened?"

"Sit down," said Marnie, her voice sounding scratchy. Annie heard the front door close and Frank's footsteps on the stairs. As Annie sat down beside Marnie, he walked into the room and put the kettle on the stove.

"I think we could all do with a cup of tea," he said.

"Will someone please tell me what's happened? Is it Uncle Jimmy?"

"No," said Marnie, dabbing her eyes with a handkerchief. "I'm afraid it's Richard. Helen rang me while you were out. I'm so sorry, Annie. It seems Richard had a stroke earlier today. They took him to hospital, but he didn't survive."

"No," said Annie, her mind flooding with memories of the gentle man who'd seen her through the war years with a quiet, unassuming kindness that made a turmoil-filled world feel somehow safe. "No."

"I'm so sorry."

"When did Aunt Helen rang you?"

"Minutes after you'd left."

"You should have come and found me."

"What would have been the point? It wouldn't have changed anything."

"I know, but I was dancing and having fun while Helen and Grace..."

"You weren't to know. And wouldn't Richard have wanted it that way? He was such a selfless man. I never had the chance to thank him properly..." Marnie dissolved into sobs and Annie took her mother in her arms.

"Here," said Frank, laying two cups of tea down beside them. "If you both want to go down there for the funeral, I can make arrangements."

"No," said Marnie, blowing her nose and shaking her head. "Helen wants the funeral over and done with quickly, so there won't be time for us to travel down there. Besides, I think she needs time to get used to him being gone before welcoming any visitors."

"That sounds sensible. I never met the man, but from what you've both told me, he was a fine fellow."

"He was," said Annie. "I just can't believe this has happened, not so soon after losing Nan. Just when I think life is improving, something terrible happens. Will it never end?"

Marnie brushed a lock of hair from Annie's eyes. "Life is full of ups and downs," she said. "Of course we need time to grieve, but if Richard was here, I'm sure he'd be offering some wise words about finding the good in the world. There's plenty of it, if you know where to look."

"I should ring Grace."

"I'm sure she would appreciate that," said Marnie, "but best to leave it a few days. It will probably take a while for it to sink in for her. Does she have friends she can turn to?"

"I'm not sure. I've not done very well keeping up with my letters to her lately, but if she's still half the girl I knew in Padstow, she'll have plenty of friends who can support her."

"That's good. Give it two or three days, then ring her. I'm sure she'd appreciate hearing from you and having the chance to speak to someone who's been through something similar."

Annie nodded, wishing she didn't have such a broad experience of grief. First her father, then her grandparents, now Richard. She prayed every night that God would keep those she loved safe, but if there was a God up there, he appeared to have ignored her prayers.

"I think I'll go to bed now," said Annie.

"Yes, you do that. Why don't you take your cup of tea with you? And I know you're all grown up, but if you feel sad in the night, come and find me."

Annie hugged her mother and kissed Frank on the cheek. As she made her way to bed, she recognised the irony of hankering after adventure and discovery, while at the same time longing for things to stay the same.

Chapter 24

April, 1953

"Grace? It's Annie?"

There was a second's pause on the line. "Annie? Why are you ringing? It will cost you a fortune."

"Good God, Grace, of course I was going to ring. Mum spoke to Aunt Helen again yesterday, but I wanted to talk to you. I'm so very sorry about Richard. I couldn't believe it when I heard the news."

"I'm still not sure I believe it," said Grace, her voice quiet. "It came as such a shock."

"Of course it did. How have you been finding things?"

"I've not been doing all that well. Aunt Helen is being so strong, and I feel terrible that I can't pull on a brave face the way she can."

"You're young, and this is your first experience of grief. Of course you'll find it hard, anyone would."

"Out of everyone I knew you'd understand. I know Richard wasn't my birth father, but he's the only dad I've ever known and... and..."

Annie placed a hand over her mouth, her body wanting to join with Grace's sobs. But how would that help the girl who'd once been like a sister? "Do you have friends you can talk to?"

"I've a few good friends," said Grace, blowing her nose, "but none really understand."

"Well, as you said, I do. You can talk to me whenever you need a friend."

"Thank you. I just miss him so much, and it's so difficult being in the cottage with so many reminders of him everywhere."

"Perhaps you could come and stay with me in Lowestoft for a while, get away from everything?"

"I couldn't do that to Aunt Helen."

"Not now, just whenever you're ready. Or perhaps I could come to you? Mum and Frank gave me train tickets to Padstow for my birthday. I've been waiting for the right time to use them."

"Would you? Oh, Annie, it would be so wonderful to see you."

Annie smiled, despite the sadness of the conversation. "Likewise. I won't be able to come in time for the funeral, but perhaps I could come and stay next month, when things are a little more settled?"

"Yes, please do. I'll check with Aunt Helen, but I think she would love to see you as much as I would."

"Alright, but don't mention the idea to her yet. A visitor is the last thing she needs to worry about at the moment."

"It's the funeral I'm dreading," said Grace. "And I know it's such a trivial thing to say, but I have no idea what to wear. I don't own anything black except for my school skirt. Oh dear, what a selfish thing to worry about. I don't suppose anyone will care a jot what I look like, but I don't want people to think I'm being disrespectful, or that I didn't care about Uncle Richard. Everyone in Padstow knows I was adopted, and I worry people may think I loved him less as a result. Not that clothes should matter. Oh dear, I am getting in a muddle."

"Grace, hush. You say you have a black skirt?"

"Yes."

"And shoes?"

"Yes."

"Right, well, I have a rather nice black sweater that I shall put in the post tomorrow. It may be a touch on the large side, but you can tuck it in. And don't give a second thought to what other people are or aren't thinking. The funeral is your chance to say goodbye. Richard knew how much you loved him. You have absolutely no need to prove it to anyone else."

"I did love him," said Grace, her voice becoming swamped by tears. "I loved him so much."

"I know, I know." Annie longed to be with her young friend. To be able to take Grace in her arms and tell her everything would be alright. That was how it had been during those last years of war. Whenever Grace was scared, it would be Annie who comforted her. She was so young she probably didn't even remember, but the feeling of a trembling Grace in her arms was something that would stay with Annie forever. She had been there for Grace's first word, her first steps. Grace was more than a friend. She was like a sister, and Annie longed to help her.

"I'd better go," said Grace, blowing her nose once again. "I want to make supper tonight, look after Helen rather than the other way around for a change."

"That's very thoughtful of you," said Annie. "You're a strong young thing, Grace. The next weeks and months will be hard, but you'll get through them."

"Thank you. Goodbye, Annie."

"Goodbye, Grace."

Annie put down the telephone and went to find her mother. Marnie was in her bedroom, fixing a pole above the window to use in her net making. When she'd tried to use the one in the sitting room downstairs, large chunks of plaster had fallen from the wall, a sure sign the downstairs of the house was not yet ready to be used again.

"How was Grace?"

"As you'd expect, heartbroken."

"Richard was a wonderful man. His loss will hit them hard. I'll make sure I keep in regular contact with Helen. She'll need a friend and it's sometimes easier to talk to someone who's slightly removed from the situation."

"That's how I feel about Grace. In fact, I suggested she come here for a visit once things have settled down."

The colour drained from Marnie's face and she set down her tools. "I'm not sure that would be a good idea."

"Why not?"

"It's best she doesn't leave Helen alone."

"I'm not talking about now, in a few months, perhaps."

"I'm not sure the house will be ready for guests anytime soon, and besides, Grace is a little young to be travelling all this way by herself."

"She's not that young," said Annie with a frown. Her mother always acted so strangely when Grace was mentioned, and Annie could think of no reason she wouldn't want her to visit. *Perhaps, one day, the truth will come out, but until that day we are bonded not just by secrets, but by the love we all share for the child at the heart of them.* The words Annie had read three years earlier appeared in her mind. Could Grace be the child the author spoke of? No, thought Annie, that wouldn't make any sense at all.

"Annie? Are you alright?"

"Sorry, I was in a daydream," said Annie, shaking her head free of foolish notions. "I said I'd visit Aunt Helen and Grace next month."

"That sounds a better idea," said Marnie, her shoulders softening and a smile returning to her face. "But make sure Helen is ready for visitors before setting any firm plans. Grief is exhausting, and she may not be up to entertaining."

"I wouldn't need entertaining."

"You know what I mean."

"Yes, and of course I won't go until it's a good time. But I would like to be there to help. Grace has always been like a sister to me and..."

"I'm going to make some tea," said Marnie, cutting Annie off mid-sentence and almost running from the room. Annie put her hands on her hips and frowned. Sometimes, she really didn't understand her mother at all.

Chapter 25

May, 1953

When Annie arrived home from the factory, she was surprised to find both Frank and Marnie waiting for her upstairs.

"Oh, hello, Frank. I thought you'd still be at work."

"We have something we'd like to discuss with you, Annie."

"Oh goodness, not more bad news, please."

Frank gave Annie a sad smile. "I know you've had an awful lot on your plate lately." His demeanour brightened, and he clasped his hands in his lap. "What I have to tell you is, I hope, good news. A fresh start for all of us."

"Go on."

"I've found us a new house."

"What? But I thought we were going to stay here and repair the damage?"

"We've tried," said Marnie. "We've had every fire in this house burning for months now, and plaster is still falling off the walls, water still coming through. We've had a builder round to look, and he thinks the brickwork is damaged beyond repair."

"But surely there's something we can do? This is our home. This was Nan and Granddad's home. This was where my dad was born. We can't just abandon the house now."

"I'm afraid I don't think we have a choice," said Marnie. "No amount of new carpet can cover up the damage that's been done, and who's to say we won't be flooded again the next time a big storm hits?"

"But..."

"I know it's upsetting," said Marnie, "but I really think this is the best thing for all of us."

"I think you'll like the new house," said Frank. "It was built in the 1930s and has all the mod cons. There are three bedrooms and an indoor bathroom, not to mention a good sized garden where we can have our own veg patch."

"But how can we afford it?"

Frank's cheeks flushed slightly, and Marnie tapped his knee. "Frank is doing well at work, and has secured a mortgage at a very good rate."

"I can't believe you've decided this without me," said Annie, almost to herself.

Marnie crossed the room and perched on the edge of Annie's chair. "I know this will be a big change, but I really believe it's for the best. Once you see the new house, I'm certain you'll feel the same. You can have free rein on how you decorate your new bedroom, although I don't imagine you'll be needing it for long."

"What do you mean?"

"I had the impression things are getting more serious between you and Sam," said Marnie, pointing to the charm bracelet on Annie's wrist.

"He still has over a year left of his National Service."

Marnie laughed. "Please don't think we're trying to get rid of you, darling. Of course, you're welcome to live with us for as long as you like. I was merely pointing out that life is moving on in all sorts of ways."

"Where is the new house?"

"In Oulton Broad."

"Oulton Broad? But that's miles away."

Frank laughed. "A half-hour walk at most."

"What about your work at the Steam Laundry?" Annie asked Marnie.

"I'm going to give that up, but I'll still continue my work on the nets, and that work will be far easier without a pole that keeps falling out of the wall."

"So it's all decided?"

"I'm sorry," said Frank. "I truly thought you'd be happy about it."

Annie tried to untangle quite what she thought about this momentous piece of news. It wasn't that she was unhappy, after all, she could see as well as anyone that the house was crumbling around their ears. "I'm not unhappy," she said slowly, "but it's another big change, isn't it? Just as things were settling down."

"I understand your point," said Frank, "but in truth, the big changes have already happened; the flood, Sally, Richard. This is a chance to be more settled."

"When will we be moving?"

"We thought we could move most of our belongings while you are visiting Helen and Grace in Padstow. That way, you won't have to see this house in a sorry, empty state."

"It's already in a fairly sorry state," said Annie. "I can see the logic of a move. I suppose it just feels like another goodbye, severing our ties to The Grit."

Marnie reached across and squeezed Annie's hand. "Perhaps, but you won't be severing ties to family. They will come with us in our hearts. Your dad and grandparents wouldn't want to see you living like this," said Marnie, motioning to the space that still operated as a makeshift kitchen and sitting room. "This is no way to start adult life."

"Can I see the new house before I leave for Padstow?"

"Of course."

"Alright then."

"Alright?"

"Yes, alright. If this house is really beyond saving and you think this is for the best, then consider me on board with the plan."

"This calls for a celebration," said Frank, pulling a bottle of sherry from his bag. He poured out three glasses and toasted to fresh starts and a new home.

Later that night, when Annie was in bed, she tried to tap into the excitement her parents clearly felt about the move but found she couldn't, yet. Perhaps once she saw the new house, it would feel more real, but lying beneath her covers in the bed she had occupied ever since the end of the war, Annie struggled to imagine the new life. It felt as though the world around her was moving forward and, rather than being an active participant, she was being pulled along with the tide. A trip to Padstow would be well timed, a change of scenery just what she needed. Annie hoped that on her return, she would feel more settled and able to embrace the new life that would be waiting for her.

Chapter 26

May, 1953

Annie checked her appearance in the tiny bathroom mirror. She applied a touch of colour to her lips and teased out her curls with her fingers. Her dress was crumpled from the long journey, and she longed to stretch her legs and breathe in some fresh air.

She let herself out of the bathroom, closed the door behind her, and with careful steps began the jolting walk back to her compartment. She stopped briefly to admire the estuary spreading out across green fields, then entered the compartment, pulling her suitcase down from the luggage rack and hooking her coat over one arm.

It had been so long since she was last here. Had she left it too late? Would Grace even remember her? Annie waited by the door and as the train slowed, her heart raced. She pulled a handkerchief from her handbag and dabbed it against her warm forehead. It had been a tricky task applying makeup as the train rocked and stuttered its way along the tracks and she didn't want perspiration to mar her hard-won perfection.

With a groan of metal and a shrill whistle, the train pulled into the station. Annie held out a hand to steady herself as the train finally jerked to a stop. She took a deep breath, wound down the window, found the handle, and opened the door.

"Annie!"

Before Annie knew what was happening, a gangly girl with a shock of red curls hurled herself towards her. Annie just had time to drop her suitcase to the ground before Grace flung her arms around Annie's waist in a hug so tight it stole her breath. Annie looked up to see Aunt Helen walking towards her. She'd aged more than the eight years since she last saw her, but was recognisable from the warm smile Annie had loved so much.

"Annie's here," squealed Grace, turning to Helen.

"Yes, I can see that. Do you think you could bear to let go of her and let me say a proper hello?"

Grace grinned up at Annie, released her arms and stepped back.

"It's wonderful to see you, maid," said Helen, pulling Annie into an embrace.

"It's wonderful to see you, too. I was so sorry to hear about Richard. It must have been such a terrible shock." Annie's throat tightened as she fought back threatening tears. News of Richard's untimely death had hit her hard, compounding the grief over Sally and leaving her with a hollow feeling in the pit of her stomach.

Helen moved back to look at her, her cheeks damp, her eyes red-rimmed. "He would have been so delighted to see you, maid. I just wish he was here with me to greet you."

"And I'm so sorry I couldn't get down here for the funeral."

Helen waved a hand in the air. "Ah, maid, he wouldn't have wanted you here. What my darling husband would want is for you to remember him as he was, not stuck in some box buried in the ground."

"I wish I'd come down sooner. I never thought..."

"None of us did. He was fit as a fiddle until suddenly he wasn't. At least it all happened quickly. He would have hated to spend months as an invalid relying on other people's care."

"I miss Uncle Richard too," said Grace, stepping closer, "but I can't help feeling happy to see you."

"And nor should you," said Helen, reaching a hand across and stroking Grace's cheek. "We've done enough crying, haven't we, Gracie? Uncle Richard wouldn't want us being maudlin while Annie's here. Come on, I've got some fresh scones cooling at home."

"Of course you have," said Annie, smiling and taking Grace's outstretched hand in hers. "I can't wait to see the cottage again. It's been far too long since I was here."

"It was right taking time to make a life for yourself up in Lowestoft, and my, what a beautiful woman you've grown into. I knew you were a looker from the photos your mother sent, but they're not a patch on the real thing."

Annie felt her cheeks grow warm. She found compliments unsettling, however kindly they were meant. "How's Mr Potts?"

"Old," said Grace. "We've got a kitten called Mischief now to keep him company."

"And is Mischief very mischievous?" asked Annie.

Grace rolled her eyes. "Of course she is, why else would we have picked that name?"

Helen and Annie shared a smile. Grace might be almost as tall as them both, but there was still something of the little girl about her, and her enthusiasm for life was infectious.

"How's Marnie?" asked Helen as they walked beside the harbour.

"Very well. Sally's death knocked her for six, not to mention Richard's, but Frank's been a great support and Kitty's made sure she still gets out and about."

"And you get on well with your stepfather?"

"Yes," said Annie with a smile. "He's a good chap. He'll never replace my dad, but he's never tried to. And he makes Mum happy, which is all that matters."

"It's a shame we've not had the chance to meet him."

"You should come up to Lowestoft for a holiday. I know you have beaches here, but the scenery up there is so different."

"Richard and I always talked about coming to visit, but with the shop to run, there was never a good time."

"We don't have the shop anymore," said Grace.

"Really?"

"No," said Helen, "it was too much for me to run on my own. We lease the space to a local family now. It was Richard's pride and joy and with him gone, it seemed right to let someone else take the reins."

"So much has changed," said Annie.

The cottage came into view and Grace tugged on Annie's arm. "Hurry, or the scones will have gone cold."

"Welcome home," called Helen, as Annie and Grace ran on ahead of her.

Chapter 27

May, 1953

"Hello, Jack."

Jack turned, shielding his eyes from the sun. He took a step back, stumbling on a pile of nets. "Marnie?"

"No," said Annie laughing, "it's Annie. Surely I don't look as old as my mother?"

"You're the spitting image of her," said Jack, leaning against the gunwale to steady himself, "when she was younger, of course."

"Of course," said Annie with a smile. Jack's red hair had turned white, but his beard still held its colour. For the first time, Annie thought how strange it was that Jack had the same colouring as Grace, who was an adopted refugee and no blood relation. If Annie hadn't known better, she'd have said Grace and Jack were related. She pushed the fanciful notion from her mind. "Well, aren't you going to come up here and say a proper hello?"

Jack regained his composure, climbing up onto the harbourside and taking Annie's hand between both of his. "It really is good to see you, though to see you all grown is mighty strange."

"I'm eighteen now," said Annie. "It was my birthday last month."

"My goodness, an adult. That must mean I'm getting very old."

Jack flashed her the grin she remembered. It lit up his usually dour face and warmed her heart. Jack and Richard had helped fill the gap left by her father's death all those years ago, and Annie would always consider him a surrogate uncle. "How long are you here for?"

"A week. It was Mum and Frank's birthday present to me."

"Frank? He must be the chap your mother married?"

"That's right."

"And what's he like, this Frank?"

Annie frowned, wondering if Jack had once held a torch for her mother, for why else would he be so interested? "He's a wonderful man. Quiet, unassuming, but extremely kind. He's made Mum very happy."

"I'm glad to hear it," said Jack. "She's a strong woman, your mother, but I always hoped she'd find someone to take care of her. Especially after all her heartache. What are your plans while you're here?"

"The weather looks set to be fine, so I'm hoping for picnics on the beach, spending time with Grace and Helen, perhaps some walking. Goodness, I may even be persuaded to have a dip in the sea."

"A proper holiday then."

"Yes, and a much needed one after the start to the year we've had."

"Oh?"

Annie told Jack about the flood, Sally's death, and the damage to their home. He listened attentively, tugging on his ginger beard and frowning and nodding. Not once did he interrupt.

When Annie had finished her tale, Jack put an arm around her shoulders and pulled her into him, kissing the top of her head. "What a to-do," he said. "No wonder you needed to escape."

Annie laughed. "It's not as bad as it all sounds, and Mum's always encouraging me to look on the bright side. I'm sure the move to the new house will be good for us all, and by the end of her life, my nan was desperate to be reunited with Granddad and their boys. I picture them all up in heaven watching over me."

"You've got your mother's strength, that's for sure," said Jack. "I'm afraid I need to get out to sea now, but I'd like to spend some more time with you while you're here. Perhaps I could take you and Grace out on the boat one day? Not too far, obviously."

"Oh, I'd love that," said Annie, clapping her hands together.

"Looking at the tides, the day after tomorrow would be best. Would that fit with your plans?"

"I'm free as a bird this week," said Annie, "so yes, please. I'll head home now and tell Grace."

"You do that," said Jack, jumping back into his boat.

Annie waved a goodbye and walked back to the cottage. She found Helen and Grace in the small garden, doing some weeding.

"Did you find him?" asked Helen.

"Yes, he's invited me and Grace out on the boat on Friday."

"What a wonderful idea," said Helen.

"Do you need any help here?" asked Annie.

"You can help me weed this patch," said Grace. "The garden was Uncle Richard's pride and joy, so we're trying to keep on top of it in his memory."

"What a lovely thing to do," said Annie.

As they worked, Grace and Helen shared titbits of local gossip. They did their best to include Annie in their conversation, but despite the warm sun on her back and being in the company of two people she loved, Annie felt a sense of unease. She knew none of the locals they spoke about, and listening to their mundane chatter, she was aware of how removed she was from their everyday lives. She would do her utmost to enjoy her time in Padstow, but so far, her trip had done nothing to salve her restlessness. Padstow might once have been her home, but as she pulled weeds from the ground, the sound of gulls overhead and lapping waves in the distance, Annie knew it was home no longer. The question of where she belonged loomed as large as ever, and Annie's instinct told her the following few days would do nothing to answer that question.

Chapter 28

May, 1953

The wind rushed through Annie's curls, tugging them into a halo around her head. She smiled, tilting her head to the sun and letting its warmth bring a moment of peace.

"Here," said Grace, handing Annie tea from a flask. "You're not feeling seasick?"

"Not at all."

"Wasn't your father a fisherman?"

"Yes, he was."

"Then you must have seafaring in your blood."

"You don't look peaky either."

"No, Jack often brings me out on his boat. I'd be tempted to become a fisherwoman myself if Aunt Helen would allow it."

Annie laughed. Jack was busy in the wheelhouse and now seemed as good a time as ever to ask Grace the question she'd been wanting to ask since she arrived. "Do you ever wonder about your parents? Your birth parents, I mean?"

Grace's porcelain skin turned pink, and she turned her head away. "No, there seems little point as they're dead," she said eventually. "Why do you ask?"

"Curiosity, that's all. I'm sorry for prying."

Grace answered Annie's apology with a smile and took a sip of her tea. "Being at sea must remind you of your dad," she said after a few moments of silence.

Annie nodded, although it wasn't Tom on her mind. The mysterious letter had been occupying her thoughts, and although they might not share a secret, knowing there were also secrets in Grace's past made Annie feel less alone. But if Grace didn't want to talk about it, Annie couldn't make her. Instead, she tried a different tack. "Do you feel at home here living with Helen?"

"Of course!" said Grace. This time, there was no hesitation. "Why wouldn't I?"

Annie shrugged. "I don't know, I don't feel at home anywhere, and have always put it down to being an evacuee, but I suppose you were a newborn when you arrived here, so perhaps it's different for you."

"Exactly that," said Grace. "I've known nothing different. Padstow has always been my home. And look at it, why on earth would I want to live anywhere else?" Grace swept her arms out wide and Annie took in the surrounding scenery. "And to think, if things had turned out differently, I'd have been brought up in London. The thought of it makes me shudder. Not that I'd wish my birth parents dead, of course, but given the choice between London and Padstow, for me, there's no competition."

The boat cut through the calm water of the estuary, a plume of white streaming behind them. On either side, creamy dunes sloped down to ribbons of sand, turquoise water lapping against them. The sky was pure, brilliant blue, only a handful of candyfloss clouds to be seen.

"There's no doubt this is a special place," said Annie, leaning over the gunwale and staring into the water below. "I can understand why my dad loved being at sea so much."

"We're being spoiled on a day like today, though," said Grace. "Last month it rained every single day and you should have seen the storms we had over winter. Poor Aunt Helen was going out of her mind with worry over Uncle Jack."

"I'm not surprised. I remember that from when I lived here, Aunt Helen pacing the kitchen every time Jack was at sea, Uncle Richard trying to calm him down." Annie shared a sad smile with Grace as both girls remembered the gentle man gone too soon. "How has Helen been since Richard's death?"

Grace frowned. "When I say she's been alright, I don't mean she isn't terribly upset by his death. But in the past month I've realised how strong she is. I've heard her crying at night, but they are private tears. She's had to be strong for me, I suppose."

Grace's bottom lip wobbled and Annie moved closer, putting her arm around the girl who had once been like a sister. They stayed in their position until the boat reached open water. When it neared Puffin Island, Jack turned off the engine and joined them on the stern.

"Look," said Grace, pointing to where small black and white birds with bright orange bills bobbed on the surface of the water, periodically diving down.

"What are they looking for?" asked Annie.

"Sand eels," said Jack.

Annie squealed in delight as a handful of puffins took to the air, swooping past the boat close enough for them to see the stripes on their bills.

"You two alright? Not too bumpy for you?"

"We're both fine," said Annie with a smile. "Thank you so much for bringing us out here. It's so beautiful."

"That it is," said Jack.

"Can you show Annie how you catch the fish?" asked Grace.

"I catch mainly lobster and crab these days," said Jack. "If you look down there, you'll see my pots."

Jack and Grace leaned over the gunwale, concentration plastered across their faces. Annie watched them, her breath suddenly caught by a realisation. It couldn't be, could it? She squinted. Was she imagining things? They'd always had the same colour hair, but that could have been a coincidence. What Annie felt sure was no coincidence was the way both of their tongues poked out of the corner of their mouths in concentration, or the way both held curled fists to their hips, or the way their noses were exactly the same shape, their eyes the same colour.

Annie stumbled backwards, the world as she knew it turning on its head.

"Are you alright?" asked Grace.

"I think seasickness may get me after all," said Annie, her voice coming out as a weak croak. "I'll move to the bow for a while if that's alright."

"Whatever you need to do," said Jack.

Annie stumbled along the deck. When she reached the bow, she turned and looked back at Jack and Grace. Was her mind playing tricks on her? No, there was no way she could be wrong. Grace was Jack's daughter. But why had everyone lied to her? Why had they stuck to the story that Grace was an orphaned evacuee from London? Was Grace the child spoken of in the card she had found? Annie truly felt sick as thoughts swirled around her mind. If she was right, it meant all the adults she trusted the most had lied to her. What else in her life was a lie? Bile rose in her throat and Annie turned her face into the wind, hoping the fresh air would cleanse her. For the first time in a long time, she longed to have her father by her side. Tom would never have lied to her. He was honest, straightforward. "Oh, Dad," Annie whispered, "how I wish you were here."

Chapter 29

May, 1953

"Are you sure everything's alright?" asked Helen for the hundredth time.

"Yes, I'm perfectly fine," lied Annie. She knew she'd been quiet since she returned from the boat trip, but couldn't trust herself to speak, afraid some of the dark thoughts in her mind would fall out of her mouth.

"Are you still feeling poorly from the trip out on the boat?"

"Truly, Helen, I am fine." Helen flushed, and Annie regretted her sharp tone. "Sorry," she said, "I think I'm just overtired."

"No surprise there, given your long journey and all the excitement you've had since being here. Would you like to go upstairs and rest?"

"Yes, please, if you don't mind? I'm sorry, I don't seem to have much of an appetite."

"Of course," said Helen. "I'll let you rest for a while, then bring you a cup of cocoa in a little while."

"Thank you."

Annie cleared away her plate and trudged up the stairs. On the first landing, she paused, listening. The sound of easy chatter from Helen and Grace reached her, and Annie decided she'd not be disturbed for a while. With only the slightest twinge of guilt, she crept into Helen's bedroom.

The curtains were closed, and Annie switched on the light. She fought a wave of grief at the sight of Richard's pyjamas still neatly folded on a wooden chair. His reading glasses sat on top of them, a copy of *The Times* still open on the page he had been reading. Grace's assertions that Helen was coping with her loss didn't quite ring true. It seemed she had yet to fully come to terms with Richard's absence.

Being careful not to disturb any loose floorboards, Annie tiptoed to the dresser, where a row of photographs stood in silver frames. The first photograph was sepia, its edges curling within the frame. It was a portrait of a Victorian-looking family, husband, wife and their two children, staring unsmilingly at the camera. The neighbouring photograph was far more relaxed. Helen, dazzling in her white wedding gown, had her head thrown back in laughter, a bouquet captured mid-air as a suited Richard looked on.

Annie picked up a photograph on the end of the dresser. It must have been taken shortly before Marnie left Padstow to return to Lowestoft. Annie had no memory of the photograph being taken, but there she was, holding on to Marnie's hand. Beside them, Helen stood with her hands on what must have been an empty pram, as Richard had baby Grace clutched to his broad chest. Jack lurked in the back of the photograph, just visible behind Helen and Richard, as though wanting to disappear.

"If you wanted to look at my photographs, you only had to ask."

Annie jumped, dropping the frame she held and wincing as it clattered against the wooden dresser. "I'm sorry, Aunt Helen, I didn't mean to snoop."

"Then why are you in my bedroom?" Helen's voice was calm as she leaned against the door-frame, a cup of cocoa in her hand.

"I… I…"

With a sigh, Helen walked into the room and sat down on the bed. She patted the mattress and Annie came to sit beside her.

"Grace said you were asking about her parents earlier?"

Annie kept her head down, aware of the blush covering her cheeks. "Sorry."

"Annie, I'm not scolding you, I'm curious why you'd suddenly be asking such questions?"

Annie considered telling Helen about her revelation on the boat, then decided against it. If Jack was Grace's father, Helen must have been complicit in the subsequent cover-up. "I was trying to sort out the muddle inside my head."

"What muddle?"

"My memories from my time here are so confused. I remember Mum leaving me, but I also remember her being poorly for months. I wondered... well... I... oh, ignore me, it's just my mind playing tricks on me."

Helen reached across and took the photograph from Annie. "It was like herding cats trying to get this photograph taken," she said. "You wanted to be off playing, Grace had been grizzly all morning, Jack had to be dragged from his boat, and your mother was that worried about her return to Lowestoft, I gave up hope of getting a smile from her."

"Why did you take the photograph, if it was so difficult?"

"I wanted a souvenir of those years when your mother was with us. Despite all that happened with your dad and the war, it was a special time. Our lives had been so small before you and Marnie showed up at our door. Your being here changed me and Richard forever. I needed a permanent reminder of that, hence the photo."

"Grace can't have been here long when the photograph was taken."

"No, a matter of days, certainly not weeks."

"Wasn't it unusual for a baby to be sent so far from where it was born? I mean, London to Padstow is a hard enough journey to make as an adult. Who brought newborn Grace down here? I don't remember her arriving, just that I came home from a friend's house one day and she was here."

Helen took the photograph and replaced it on the dresser, keeping her back to Annie. "Those were strange times," she said. "The war changed everything. Normal life went out of the window, and if a baby could be saved from the Blitz, I don't suppose anyone cared how far they'd have to travel until it reached safety."

"You knew Grace's mother?"

"Yes."

Still, Helen didn't turn round, and Annie was sure she was keeping something from her. "I didn't realise you had friends in London."

"I don't. Not now."

"I see," said Annie, not seeing at all. She could understand Helen wanting to keep Jack's mistakes away from local gossip, but she could see no good reason it should be kept from her. She was eighteen now, an adult.

"I think that's enough talk of the past for one night," said Helen, turning and offering Annie a forced smile. "Why don't you take your cocoa up to bed and drink it before it gets cold?"

"Alright," said Annie. "Goodnight."

"Goodnight," said Helen.

Annie paused in the doorway and looked back into the room. Helen had the photograph in her hands, her thumb tracing the outline of all the faces. She didn't notice Annie watching, too lost was she in her memories.

Chapter 30

May, 1953

"Good morning," said Annie, finding Helen and Grace already at the table eating their breakfast. "Sorry, I must have overslept."

"Not to worry," said Helen, "there's plenty left. Tea's in the pot."

Annie made her way to the kitchen counter and poured hot tea into a mug. She marvelled at the show Helen was putting on this morning. Annie's own tiredness had been caused by the sound of Helen's late-night sobs filtering through the ceiling. And yet, here was the woman herself, fresh-faced and as if nothing had happened. Had Annie imagined the grief she'd heard?

"Do you have any plans today?" asked Helen.

"No," said Annie. "I thought I could help you if there are any jobs that need doing around the house."

"I can do better than that," said Helen. "I've been thinking about what you said last night, about your memories being confused."

"I'm sorry, I didn't mean to give you anything to worry about. It's not a problem, just frustrating sometimes that those years are such a jumble in my mind."

"I never said it was a problem," said Helen, "and I haven't been worrying, but I wondered if you fancied a trip down memory lane?"

"Memory lane?"

"Yes. I thought we could visit some places that were most important to you while you were living with us."

"Oh," said Annie, the suggestion taking her by surprise. She'd thought everyone had secrets to hide from those years, and yet here was Helen, offering to open up those years to full scrutiny.

"I'd like that too," said Grace. "I sometimes feel left out when you all talk about the war years as I was only a baby."

"That's decided then," said Helen. "We'll take a walk around the village this morning, come back here and pack a picnic, then go to the beach this afternoon. I might even persuade Jack to join us if he's not out on the boat."

Annie buttered a piece of toast and took a bite. "Where should we go first?" she asked when she had finished chewing.

"How about the school?" suggested Grace. "I'd like to say hello to my old teachers while we're there."

"Good idea," said Helen. "Are you still in touch with any of the Lowestoft children who were here with you, Annie?"

"No," said Annie. "I occasionally see the Clements, but by the time I arrived back in Lowestoft they had left The Grit and moved up into the town."

"From what your mother has told me, The Grit has had its fair share of challenges over the years."

"It certainly has."

Once they had finished breakfast and Annie and Grace had washed up, they pulled on jackets and left the cottage. It was a bright spring day, and Padstow was looking its best. Annie searched deep inside her for feelings of home, but whilst she adored the beauty and quaintness all around her, she couldn't shake off the feeling that she was a tourist rather than a local.

"Let's pop into the post office," said Helen. "Mary still runs the place and will be delighted to see you." Helen pushed open the heavy wooden door and smiled at the lady behind the counter. "Look who I've brought to see you, Mary," she said with a smile.

Mary peered through a pair of glasses perched on the end of her nose. She frowned. "Are my eyes deceiving me, or is this little Annie Hearn all grown up?"

"Hello, Mary," said Annie, reaching out a hand.

"Come here, maid," said Mary, stepping out from behind her counter and pulling Annie into a hug. "It's been a long time since we saw you around these parts. What brings you back down here?"

"I've missed everyone," said Annie truthfully, "and as I couldn't make it down in time for the funeral..."

"Yes, of course, of course. What a terrible business that was." Mary threw a sympathetic glance at Helen and shook her head sadly. "Well," she said, clapping her hands to signify a change of subject, "what a beautiful young lady you've become. How is life treating you in Lowestoft? Do you have someone special up there? I expect the young men are queuing down the street to take you to a dance."

Annie smiled as Mary launched into the customary gossip she remembered so well. She gave away enough details of her life to satisfy the woman's curiosity, but not enough to raise any eyebrows.

"And I heard your mother remarried?"

"She did," said Annie, "to a wonderful man named Frank." Annie was sure a flutter of disappointment crossed Mary's face. Happy families didn't make for interesting stories when chatting to customers.

"We'd better press on," said Helen, saving Annie from further interrogation. "We're taking Annie to see a few of her old haunts, starting with the school."

"What a wonderful idea," said Mary. "I know you're all grown up now, but why don't you girls take a sweetie from the jar to see you on your way?"

Annie and Grace accepted the offered jar of bonbons and each popped one into their mouths. For the rest of the morning they indulged Annie on her trip down memory lane, and as Helen had hoped, the visits to the school, shops and harbour brought back happy memories, but they didn't lessen the feeling that there were unanswered questions or secrets being hidden.

They spent a pleasant afternoon at the beach, paddling in the calm water and sharing memories of Richard. Jack didn't join them, and in a way, Annie was glad. After her suspicions on the boat, she no longer felt comfortable around him, distrust interrupting the easy friendship they'd once shared.

That evening, as Annie packed her suitcase ready for her return home, she decided she was glad she'd come. Helen and Grace would always be like family, and she would do everything she could to remain close to each of them. But there had been no sensation of a homecoming, no answers to the many questions still swirling around Annie's mind. Perhaps she had been looking in the wrong place all along, perhaps the answers she needed would be found closer to home?

Chapter 31

May, 1953

"Welcome home!" Marnie rushed towards Annie, her arms spread wide.

"Hello," said Annie, allowing herself to be scooped up into Marnie's embrace. "Hello, Frank." Annie waved over her shoulder to where her stepfather stood watching them, looking dapper in his waistcoat and tie.

"I want to hear all about it," said Marnie. "Shall we call in at a café for a cup of tea and a scone?"

"If you don't mind, I'd rather go straight home," said Annie.

"Of course, you must be exhausted after that long journey."

"Yes," said Annie. She was exhausted, and the journey had been long, but it was the strange fragments of memories jostling in her mind that left her tired.

"Let me take that for you," said Frank, stepping forward and picking up Annie's suitcase.

"Thank you. How has work been?"

"Oh, so-so," said Frank with his enigmatic smile.

He was a modest man and never enjoyed talking about himself. Annie knew he worked in some capacity for the council in their finance department, but couldn't picture his actual work. Perhaps he was embarrassed to be sitting behind a desk all day while other men went to work at sea or in factories, but Annie thought it more likely his job was challenging, his role important, and he didn't like to broadcast his success.

"How was Helen?" asked Marnie.

"Well, considering."

"Aye, Richard's death must have hit her hard."

"She puts on a brave face for Grace, but you can see the sadness in her eyes." Annie chose not to mention the weeping she'd heard each night. Helen was a proud woman and wouldn't want others knowing her distress.

"And... and Grace? She's well?"

Annie caught the note of hesitancy in Marnie's voice and added the information to the unformed jigsaw in her mind, ready to be slotted into place when she had a quiet moment. Why did the subject of Grace always cause Marnie to stiffen and fumble over her words?

"Grace is very well," said Annie. "She's almost as tall as me and has a shock of red hair."

"I bet she's a beauty."

"She is," said Annie. "You know, it's funny how much she looks like Jack." Annie watched Marnie from the corner of her eye, noticed her cheeks flush, her lids blink several times, and her tongue run over her dry lips.

"That's coincidence, surely?" said Frank.

Annie turned to him, surprised by this intervention. Given he'd met none of the people she spoke of, it was unusual for him to offer an opinion.

"Quite," said Marnie, regaining her composure and throwing a grateful smile Frank's way. "Next thing you'll be saying how much she looks like Kitty. Just because folk have red hair, doesn't mean they all look the same, Annie."

Marnie and Frank chuckled, but Annie didn't join in. She knew what she'd seen down in Padstow, and this forced joviality only confirmed she was right. But worse than being proved right was the realisation that everyone was in on the secret bar her, even Frank, for goodness' sake!

Frank unlocked the car doors, and they climbed in, Annie closing her eyes and pretending she was asleep to avoid further conversation. It still felt strange, the car heading away from the sea rather than towards it. Annie didn't want to see the rows of newly built houses or gangs of men laying bricks on raw patches of earth. It was another sign of change, another reminder that Annie didn't belong anywhere.

The car turned into a wide road, which would be tree-lined in a few years once the newly planted spindly saplings spread their roots. Frank pulled the car into the driveway and turned to Annie with a smile. "Home," he said, jumping out of the car and taking her suitcase from the boot.

As they walked towards the house, Frank seemed to grow taller. Annie could see how proud he was to have been able to provide them with a home. And it was indeed a fine house. But when Frank unlocked the door, and they stepped inside, it was the smell Annie noticed first. There was nothing unpleasant about it, it was the smell of new carpets, fresh paint, and meat roasting in the oven. What it wasn't, Annie decided, was the smell of home. Not her home, at any rate. In her mind's eye, she pictured Marnie and Frank being very happy in the new house, but she couldn't see herself in that image. Where would she be? Married and living with Sam? Or somewhere new, off on an adventure of her own?

"I'm going upstairs to unpack," said Annie, taking the suitcase from Frank.

"Why don't I give you a tour of the house? It will all seem different now we've got the furniture in it."

"I'd rather go straight to my room, if you don't mind."

"You remember which one it is?"

"First door on the left."

"Exactly. Have a think about what colour you'd like us to paint the walls while you're unpacking. We want to get it homely for you straight away."

"Thank you," said Annie, running up the stairs.

"Supper will be ready in about half an hour," called Marnie. "Make sure you don't fall asleep."

"I'll try not to." Annie kept her voice light and cheerful, but as soon as she was in her bedroom, she closed the door and slid down it onto the floor. The magnolia walls seemed to close in on her, and she closed her eyes and buried her head in her hands. Her mind couldn't fit the final puzzle pieces together, but Annie knew she'd stumbled upon a family secret that everyone knew but her. As she pushed herself to standing, she squared her shoulders and made a decision. She couldn't stay in here, not for any length of time, and she already knew where she would run to. It was a place which had been calling quietly to her ever since she'd first seen it. *You're a Watson*, Marnie had said. *That means the island's in your blood.*

"I'm coming," whispered Annie, "I'm coming home."

Chapter 32

May, 1953

Knives and forks clinked together in the quiet kitchen as the family tucked in to their roast dinner.

"This is delicious," said Frank, smiling at Marnie.

"Thank you."

Annie looked up and saw them both staring at her. "Yes, it's delicious, thank you."

Marnie put down her knife and fork and reached across to take Annie's hand. "Are you sure everything is alright? I know you're tired after your long journey, but it seems you have something on your mind."

Annie chewed her mouthful of potato, then set down her own knife and fork. "I've decided I'd like to use the tickets Uncle Jimmy and Aunt Clara gave me for my birthday and visit the island as soon as possible."

"What?" said Marnie, her mouth falling open. "But you've only just returned from one holiday."

"It seems our Annie has developed a taste for adventure," said Frank with a smile.

"That's as maybe, but I can't see the factory giving you any more time off, not for a while at least."

"I'm not talking about a holiday," said Annie, pushing green beans around on her plate with the end of her fork. "I'd like to go to the island for a few months, at least."

"But why?" said Marnie. "I thought we were going to decorate your new bedroom together. Don't you see yourself being happy here? I thought you were feeling positive about the move?"

"It's got nothing to do with happiness," said Annie. "And there's nothing wrong with this house." Seeing Frank's face fall, she added, "it's a wonderful house. You chose very well, Frank."

"Thank you," he said, "but there's no need for flattery. All that matters to me is you and your mother have somewhere comfortable to lay your heads each night."

"And I'm grateful," said Annie. "But this isn't about moving to a new house. You said it yourself once, Mum. I'm a Watson, an islander. I'd like to spend some time getting to know the place I'm from."

"You're from Lowestoft," said Marnie, "that's where you were born and bred."

"But it's not, is it?" said Annie. "I spent almost as much time in Padstow as I've spent in Lowestoft, and quite frankly, neither feels like home."

"Did something happen to you in Padstow?" asked Marnie. "Is that what's brought all this on?"

"Nothing happened in Padstow."

"What about Sam?" asked Marnie. "I can't see him being best pleased about you upping sticks and moving to the other end of the country."

"Sam has another year of his National Service to complete. Surely it's better I do this now than when he's home for good?"

"What about your friends? It's Beryl's wedding soon, and you seemed to get on nicely with that lass Mary."

"I'll miss my friends, of course, but I can come back for Beryl's wedding, and she and Mary will still be here when I get back. Besides, I'll make new friends on the island, I hope."

Marnie picked up the napkin from her lap and twisted it in her hands. "What do you think, Frank?"

Frank smiled at Annie. "I can't see what harm it could do. That's if Jimmy and Clara can offer Annie a job and accommodation. I'm not sure they were expecting a long-term resident when they sent Annie those tickets, but if she's happy to sing for her supper...Surely it's better Annie go somewhere where there's family? Jimmy and Clara will take good care of her."

"I don't doubt that," said Marnie. She turned to Annie. "I'd miss you."

"And I'd miss you too," said Annie. "But I really feel I need to do this before I settle down. Surely you understand?"

"Aye," said Marnie, "but I also know that wandering the country can leave you more restless than before, so be careful, won't you?"

Unsure quite what she was being warned of, Annie nodded and took another bite of mutton.

"I'll ring Jimmy tomorrow," said Marnie, "and see what he makes of this plan of yours."

"And once you've done that, I'd better speak to my boss at the factory. I can't imagine he'll be best pleased about me leaving the job so soon after I started it, but with all the new factories springing up, I'm sure I'll be able to find work when I return home even if Birds Eye put a black mark against my name."

After they had finished their dinner and washed up the dishes, Marnie announced she needed an early night, and Frank joined Annie in the new sitting room.

"Here you go," he said, handing her a small glass of sherry.

"What's this in aid of?"

"I thought we should toast the new house."

Annie clinked her glass against Frank's and looked around the room. The headrests of the green upholstered armchairs and sofa were covered in white lace antimacassars, giving the room a slightly old-fashioned feel. On the wall above the fireplace a large mirror reflected light into the room, and below it, Marnie had lined up a selection of family photographs. A small drinks cabinet sat beneath the bay window, and a large wooden box dominated one corner.

"Ah," said Frank, following Annie's line of sight. "I see you've spotted my pride and joy."

Annie frowned in confusion as he climbed out of his chair and crossed the room.

"This really is a bit of an extravagance," he said, "but with the Queen's coronation just around the corner I couldn't resist." He opened two wooden doors and Annie gasped.

"Oh my goodness, is that a television?"

"It certainly is," said Frank with a chuckle.

"Can we watch something?"

Frank checked his watch. "There won't be anything on now, but I'll fire her up tomorrow for you."

"Suddenly I'm tempted to stay here after all."

Frank sat back in his chair and studied Annie. "Is this trip north really about an adventure, Annie, or is there something more to it?"

Annie couldn't meet his eye. "I'd like to see the island again, that's all."

"You don't... I mean... I want you to know that this is your home. It will be your home for as long as you need it. I know it's a big change, but..."

"Frank," said Annie, meeting his worried frown with a smile. "This new house is wonderful. It's just time I spread my wings, that's all."

Frank seemed satisfied, and they sipped their sherry in silence. Annie cast a furtive glance at her stepfather and tried to fathom why and how he had been dragged into whatever secret surrounded Grace's parentage. He was such a good, honest man, Annie felt sure he wouldn't keep something from her without good reason.

Chapter 33

May, 1953

"I fancy an ice cream," said Annie.

Sam laughed. "An ice cream? Aren't you cold enough already?"

"It's almost summer."

"It feels like winter."

"Are you going to get me one or not?"

Sam gave Annie a soft punch on the arm and she gave him one back. This was how she liked things between them. They'd grown up like siblings, and the easy teasing and bickering felt like safe ground. "Go on then," said Sam, climbing up from the promenade and walking to the ice cream stand.

Annie watched Sam from the corner of her eye. He had changed since starting National Service. His shoulders had broadened, his cropped auburn hair showed off his strong jaw and jade green eyes. He was a handsome man, not the awkward boy he'd been only months earlier. Annie felt a flutter of butterfly wings in her stomach as she watched him.

"Here you go," said Sam, returning with two cones.

"You got one for yourself?"

"Of course."

"Then we need the full experience," said Annie, kicking off her shoes and pulling off her stockings. She buried her toes in the cold sand and tried not to shiver.

"You're mad," said Sam. "The next thing I know, you'll be suggesting a paddle."

"Naturally," said Annie, grinning at Sam before taking a bite of her ice cream.

"I miss this," said Sam.

"Sitting on the beach with a fierce north wind blowing any hopes of summer away?"

"Being with you."

Annie smiled. "I thought you were enjoying your National Service?"

"I am. But it doesn't stop me from getting homesick."

"We're all so proud of you," said Annie.

Sam held Annie's gaze, and she wondered if he might kiss her, but then their ice creams began to melt and they both giggled as they licked cream liquid from their fingers. "I can't believe the ice creams are melting in these temperatures."

"The sun is actually quite warm," said Annie. "It's the wind making it feel cold."

"Anyway," said Sam. "I didn't bring you here to talk about the weather. What's all this I hear about you heading north?"

"I told you Jimmy and Clara got me train tickets for my birthday."

"Yes, but what's prompted you to use them now? You seem desperate to rush off up there. Has something happened that I'm not aware of?"

Annie tried to organise her thoughts in a way Sam would understand. "I suppose I feel a little unsettled at the moment."

"You're bound to, what with the flood and having to move house."

"Yes, but it's more than that. When I went back to Padstow, I expected it to feel like home."

"And it didn't?"

"No. And also, I got the distinct impression there is something everyone is keeping from me."

"Like what?"

"Something to do with Grace. I've told you how she ended up living with us in Padstow?"

Sam nodded and took another bite of his ice cream.

"Don't you think it's strange? I mean, a newborn, sent all the way from Padstow to London? And then there's Grace's resemblance to Jack, and the fact my mother clams up every time I mention Grace's name. And do you remember the card I found a few years ago?"

Sam frowned. "I'm not sure..."

"You must do. It was sent to Mum and talked about a secret that had something to do with a child."

"Ah, yes, I remember you telling me about it. But what has that got to do with your trip to Padstow? I'm not entirely sure what you're saying, Annie?"

"I don't know." Annie threw the last of her cone down on the sand and a grateful gull swooped down to retrieve it.

"It's understandable folk don't want to talk about those war years. They were dark days for many. And if no one will talk about where Grace came from, it's probably because something particularly gruesome happened to her birth parents and people don't want to upset you with it."

"What about her resemblance to Jack, though? It's not just her physical resemblance, they share the same mannerisms."

"It's that old nature versus nurture argument," said Sam. "Jack has been a huge part of Grace's life, hasn't he?"

"Yes."

"Then isn't it possible she's picked up his mannerisms by mimicking him?"

"I suppose it's possible..."

"And the resemblance you see could just be down to their hair colour."

"That's what Mum said."

"There you go then. But, Annie, that still doesn't answer my question of why you need to go to the other side of the country for months. You'll be practically in Scotland."

Annie played with the bracelet on her wrist. "I'm not sure I can explain it. I suppose, in a way, it's a bit like your National Service. You've changed a lot since you've been away."

"Oh dear, is that a good or a bad thing?"

"Good," said Annie with a smile. "Not that there was anything wrong with you before, but you seem so much more grown up, so sure of yourself. I'd like to feel a bit of the certainty you do, and as I can't go running off and join the navy, the island seems as good a place to go as any."

"I understand," said Sam. "There's only one thing I need to know."

"What?"

"Can I visit?"

"Of course you can."

"Good. Sorry, I lied."

"About what?"

"There were two things I needed to know, not one."

"What else did you need to know?"

"Whether you're as brave as you make out." Sam grinned, swallowed the last of his ice cream, kicked off his shoes and socks and began running towards the water. "Catch me if you can!"

Annie leaped down from the promenade and began chasing Sam. Her feet sank into the yellow sand, throwing a veil of grains into the air with each step. Sam reached the water first, yelping and hopping from foot to foot as he tried to get used to the temperature. At the water's edge, Annie paused.

"What? Surely you're not backing out now?"

"Of course not." Annie took one tentative step forward and squealed. "It's so cold!"

Sam placed his hands on his hips. "Is this really the woman hankering after adventure I see before me? Surely someone as brave as she wouldn't fear a little cold water?"

"Fine," muttered Annie. She hitched up her skirt and marched into the water, screwing up her face as she tried not to cry out. The pain was excruciating as the icy water climbed up her calves. As she reached Sam, a wave caught her off guard and she stumbled. Sam caught her, holding her in his arms.

"I hoped that might happen," he said, holding her gaze, ignoring the discomfort of his feet growing numb.

"Was all this a ruse to get me in your arms?"

"It was you who suggested a paddle," Sam reminded her, his voice low.

Before Annie could reply, Sam's lips were on hers, his arms wrapped tight around her back. Instead of cold, all Annie felt was warmth. She would have her adventure, but safe in the knowledge that Sam would be waiting for her on her return.

Chapter 34

June, 1953

"So," said Marnie, "it will be like a leaving party crossed with a coronation."

"That sounds lovely," said Annie with a smile. Her feelings towards Marnie were all in a jumble since returning from Padstow, but with only twenty-four hours until she left for the island, Annie was attempting to behave as though nothing had changed. "Do you think Queen Elizabeth will mind sharing her big day with me?"

"I'm sure she'd be delighted."

"Will we all fit around Frank's television?"

"Of course." Marnie began counting on her fingers, "Kitty and Bobby, Beryl and Paul, Mary, me, you, and Frank, plus a few of the neighbours who heard we'd bought a television."

"Exactly how many neighbours have you invited?" asked Annie with a frown.

Marnie shrugged. "I'm not sure of exact numbers, but it wouldn't surprise me if word has spread."

"It's going to be bedlam in here."

"It will be fine. Now, can you help me with some food? We'll watch the coronation in here, then all head outside for a street party, so long as the weather holds."

The doorbell sounded, and Marnie went to answer it. "That'll be Kitty," she called. Moments later Marnie walked back into the kitchen, followed by Kitty, who was carrying several large tins.

"What have you got there?" asked Marnie.

"Fruit cake, scones, and a Victoria sponge."

"You have been busy. I'm about to prepare some cucumber sandwiches," said Annie.

"And I've had a go at Constance Spry's Coronation Chicken, although it tastes a bit strange, if you ask me." Marnie removed a tea towel to reveal a bowl of yellow slop and handed a spoon to Annie and Kitty. "What do you think?"

"It tastes better than it looks," said Annie.

"I agree," said Kitty, "although I might stick to cucumber sandwiches this afternoon."

Annie giggled, and Marnie sighed. "At least I've tried."

At ten o'clock, the neighbours began to arrive, keen to get a good position in front of the television. Annie stayed in the kitchen with Kitty while Marnie played hostess in the sitting room.

"I don't know any of these people," said Annie as yet another couple appeared at the door.

"It's a good chance to get to know them."

"True, but I leave for Holy Island tomorrow. I'll have forgotten all their names by the time I get back."

"How long are you planning on being away?"

"Until September, maybe October."

"As long as you come back," said Kitty. "From what I remember of the island, it's a charming place."

"Of course I'll come back," said Annie.

"Good, because it would break Sam's heart if you didn't."

Annie avoided Kitty's eye and continued to cut the crusts off her sandwiches.

"I know you're not officially engaged yet," continued Kitty, "but in all of our eyes, you're as good as."

"What? That's unfair, Kitty."

Kitty took a step back, surprised by Annie's strong reaction. "I'm sorry, love, I didn't mean..."

"You and Mum don't get to decide my future. Sam and I love each other dearly, but it will be our choice if we marry, not yours."

"Keep your hair on," said Kitty. "I didn't mean to upset you."

"Sorry." Annie's cheeks reddened, and she regretted snapping. Her mask had slipped, revealing some of the edginess she'd felt since returning from Padstow. Unsure who she could trust, Kitty's comment had hit a nerve.

"Sam really loves you, and I thought you felt the same."

"Of course I love him," said Annie, smiling at Kitty by way of an apology. "I just hate the thought that my life's been mapped out without anyone asking what I actually want."

"Sorry," said Kitty. "I'd better see if your mum needs any help."

"Wait," said Annie, holding on to Kitty's arm. "I'm truly sorry for the way I spoke to you."

"It's fine," said Kitty, hugging Annie and brushing a curl from her forehead. "You seem mighty rattled, love. Is this nerves about going away?"

Annie glanced into the hallway. Everyone was busy getting the television set warmed up, and this could be her last chance of finding out the truth before going away. Annie closed the kitchen door and turned to Kitty. "You've known Mum for years, haven't you?"

"You know I have. We've been friends since before she married your dad. Why?"

"So you'd know if she had any secrets?"

"Well," said Kitty, picking up a napkin and wringing it in her hands, "I'm not sure about that. We're best friends, but that doesn't mean there aren't things we keep from one another. What's this all about, Annie?"

"I know people are keeping secrets from me. Mum, Aunt Helen, Jack, maybe even Frank."

"What secrets?"

"I found a card once, in Mum's underwear drawer. Whoever sent it talked about a secret and a child. Then when I was down in Cornwall and saw how much Grace looks like Jack, I began wondering..."

"That's enough of this nonsense," said Kitty, her voice sharp. "I don't know what you're insinuating, but this needs to stop. Your mum and Frank are good people. If they're keeping something from you, it will be to protect you. Besides, parents are allowed a life beyond their children. You need to stop meddling in things that don't concern you."

With that, Kitty left the kitchen, leaving a stunned Annie staring open-mouthed. Kitty's speech had had the opposite outcome to the one she intended. Rather than allaying Annie's suspicions, they were now heightened. And Kitty had just had her name added to Annie's list of those involved in the deception.

Annie walked through to the sitting room and found it packed to the rafters with friends and neighbours. All attention was fixed on the small flickering screen, eyes glued to the moving image of the beautiful Queen Elizabeth looking resplendent in her regalia. Annie hovered at the back of the room, unable to share in the awe and wonder of the occasion. Instead of the television, she watched the hands of the grandfather clock, willing them to move faster around the face. For the moment of her departure could not come soon enough. She would leave Lowestoft, her family and all its secrets behind. This was the start of a new adventure, one she couldn't wait to begin.

PART TWO

Chapter 35

June, 1953

The island was as beautiful as Annie remembered. She had wondered whether some of its magic would have been lost seeing it through adult eyes, but she felt its impact just as fiercely as when a child.

"It's beautiful," said Annie, the words coming out with a sigh.

Jimmy turned and grinned. "I'm pleased you think so. Do you remember much from the last time you were here?"

"Everything."

Jimmy laughed, then turned his eyes back to the driver of the Austin 16, who for the princely sum of one pound was achieving the complicated task of navigating the vehicle across the sand. "You know they're planning to build a causeway onto the island?"

The driver let out a low growl to express his disapproval at the scheme. Annie pretended she hadn't heard.

"A causeway?"

"Yes, a road across the sand."

"That will make things easier, but I can't see how they'll manage it with the tide coming in and out."

Jimmy shrugged. "Thankfully, we're not the ones who need to worry about it. It will make it a darn sight easier getting across though, and those of us living there won't feel quite so trapped."

"Huh," muttered the driver, "no one's trapped with me here to guide them."

Annie ignored their driver once more. "Do you feel trapped, Uncle Jimmy?"

"No, not really," said Jimmy. "I won't pretend it didn't take a bit of getting used to when I moved back here. I'd lived away for so long, but as a place it's moved on, and living with Clara, well, nothing beats it."

"You old romantic."

"Less of the old please."

"I can't wait to see Clara again."

"The feeling is mutual. She's been like an excited child all week, counting down the days until you arrive."

"It's so kind of you both to let me stay for the summer."

"It's our pleasure and you'll be helping us out. There are more and more visitors coming to the island, and it's not always easy to find staff."

"I'll be happy to help in any way I can. I've not had any experience of hotel work, but I'm sure I can learn, and I enjoy hard work."

"You're so like your mother," said Jimmy, casting a sideways glance at Annie. "I keep catching glimpses of you and thinking it's Marnie sitting beside me. Do you think she'll come for a visit while you're here?"

"I think you'll have a hard time keeping her away. I've asked her to wait for a couple of months to give me time to settle in."

"I can't imagine she liked that."

"No, she'd have been on the train with me if she could. She said it makes her feel old having me leave home."

Jimmy laughed, and the driver guided the car up a sandy slope and onto the island. Annie wound down the window, letting in the smell of seaweed carried on a cool breeze. The sun hung low in the sky, turning the fields they passed golden, and reflecting on the windows of cottages and houses as they drew closer to the village.

The hotel came into sight, and Annie grinned. It was just as she'd remembered, set apart slightly, as though protecting its unrivalled view of the harbour and castle. The driver turned off the engine and thanked Jimmy as he handed over the payment. Jimmy jumped out of the car. His shoes crunched on gravel as he retrieved Annie's suitcase from the boot and opened the door for her.

Annie stepped out of the car, spinning round as someone screamed her name. Clara ran out of the hotel, skidding to a stop in front of Annie before pulling her into her arms and hugging her tightly.

"It is so, so good to see you," said Clara. "Let me look at you." She held Annie at arm's length, her eyes travelling from her head to her toes. "You must have grown another few inches since I last saw you, and what a beautiful young woman you've become."

"Thanks, Aunt Clara." Annie smiled at her aunt, who looked much the same, other than her auburn hair now being snow white, crow's feet around her eyes, and deeper lines forged into her cheeks from years of smiling.

"Are you hungry? You must be hungry. Come inside and we'll get some food for you. Your grandmother is asleep in her room, but she's been as excited to see you as I have. As soon as we've got you fed and watered, we'll wake her. She won't want to miss a second of you being here."

Annie laughed and linked arms with Clara. "Mum packed so much food for me I feel I may explode, so please don't force any more on me. We had so much left over from the coronation party and Mum couldn't bear to see it go to waste. But a cup of tea would be wonderful. And how is Grandma Rose?"

Annie noticed the look that passed between Jimmy and Clara. Eventually, Clara sighed and placed a hand on Annie's arm. "You'll see for yourself soon enough, I suppose. Poor Rose isn't too well these days. Not all that surprising given her age, even so, it's hard to see her so frail."

"How old is she now?"

"Eighty-three. Few on this island have ever lived so long."

"It's a miracle," said Jimmy, coming to stand beside them, "given the life she led."

"What do you mean?" asked Annie.

"Mam's got a few tales she could tell," said Jimmy. "My da, well, let's just say it came as a relief to everyone when he finally gave up the ghost."

"Mum never talks about him," said Annie.

"And with good reason. He was a nasty man, unkind, a brute, and that's putting it mildly. Poor Mam suffered for years at his hands." Jimmy's voice cracked.

Clara wrapped an arm around Jimmy's waist. "All that is true," she said, "but since your da died, she's found happiness, hasn't she?"

"Aye," said Jimmy, who had recovered a hint of his former accent since living back on the island.

"So instead of feeling sad about Rose's struggles, let's celebrate her freedom, the happiness she has found. Better late than never, as the saying goes."

"You're talking about her as if she's already gone," said Annie with a frown.

"Oh, ignore us," said Clara. "Rose is still here, and that's all that matters. Now, how about we get you settled into your new home?"

Chapter 36

June, 1953

"I've taken your case up to your room," said Jimmy, walking into the dining room.

"Thank you."

"Would you like some time to unpack?" asked Clara.

"No, that can wait. I'm happy to sit here with you for a while, unless you've something to be getting on with?"

Clara laughed and refilled all their cups with tea from the pot. "Our niece turns up here, having not seen us for two years, and you think we're going to abandon her the moment she arrives? Not likely. The work can wait. The birdwatchers have all been fed and watered and after a day of twitching they'll be wanting an early night. If anyone comes to the bar, they can ring the bell and one of us can serve them. Now, are you sure you don't want something to eat? Our cook, Steffie, made a delicious carrot cake this morning."

"Hmm, I think I could manage a small slice."

"I'll get it," said Jimmy.

The low evening sun spilled in through the windows. Annie sighed in contentment as she gazed across at a view of the harbour and castle. It felt wonderful to be away from Lowestoft and all the uncertainty and suspicion that had shrouded her recent weeks there. "I'm surprised anyone ever leaves this room. The view is wonderful."

"Aye, people tend to linger over their meals."

"How many staff work here?"

"Me and Jimmy, my assistant Olive, Steffie, our cook, two young sisters do the chambermaiding and a chap from Scotland fills in the gaps."

"That's not many people for a hotel this size."

"We hire an extra couple of locals on a casual basis when things get busy, but mostly we manage with a small team. That said, it will be a great help to have you here."

"I'm happy to do whatever you need."

"Wonderful, but there'll be plenty of time for that. While we're quiet, I want you to enjoy your time on the island. We didn't buy you tickets for your birthday so you could come here as our skivvy. They were supposed to be for a holiday."

Jimmy carried three plates of cake across to their table and sat down. "I checked on Mam on my way to the kitchen," he said. "She's still sleeping, so it's probably best you wait until the morning to see her."

"That's alright, I'll have plenty of opportunity to spend time with her. How is your family, Clara? I was sorry to hear about your dad's death."

"Thank you," said Clara. "It was difficult at the time, but he'd been poorly for a while and slipped away peacefully in his sleep with no suffering, so it was the best ending we could have hoped for. My stepmother Rachel still lives in my old cottage, along with my brother, Ben. They'll be joined by his fiancée Amy as soon as they're wed."

"Oh, when is the wedding?"

"August, so you should still be here to enjoy it."

Annie clapped her hands in delight. "I love a good wedding."

"We all do," said Clara. "It's been a long time since we had a wedding on the island. In fact, there hasn't been one since our own. But there must be something in the air, as three local couples will tie the knot this summer."

"Does your brother still fish?"

"Aye. There aren't as many fishermen as there once were, but there are still a core group of island men who fish these waters. And how about you?" asked Clara. "Do you have a young man on the go?"

Annie smiled and blushed. "I'm rather friendly with Sam Thorn these days."

"Kitty's lad?"

"Yes."

"How lovely. I bet Marnie and Kitty are over the moon."

"I think they've been planning our wedding since the day we were born," laughed Annie, "but we're taking our time. We're stepping out, but Sam still has a year of National Service left to complete, so we're not rushing into anything."

"Like mother, like daughter," said Clara, raising an eyebrow.

"And how long did it take us to finally wed?" asked Jimmy with a chuckle.

"Good point. I'll climb down off my high horse." Clara leaned over and kissed Jimmy's cheek.

"This is delicious," said Annie, biting into her slice of cake. "Please pass my compliments to the chef."

"You can tell her yourself when you meet her tomorrow," said Clara. "I know time is getting on and you're tired from your journey, but would you like a tour of the hotel before you go to bed?"

"Yes please," said Annie. "I can't remember much about it from when I was last here."

"It will probably all seem much smaller given how much you've grown. Come on, let's begin with the bar."

As they left the dining room and walked back into the oak-floored lobby, they met a group of men coming in through the front door.

"Oh dear, here comes trouble," said Jimmy.

A tall man with broad shoulders, jet black hair and a thick beard carrying a hint of grey stepped forward and slapped Jimmy on the back. "Best not insult your best customers, brother."

"Stop it, Ben. Annie will think she's arrived at a madhouse."

"Annie? Oh my, surely this isn't the little mite I met all those years ago at the weddings. Mind you, there's no mistaking whose daughter you are. You're the spit of Marnie."

"So I keep being told," said Annie, smiling and shaking Ben's hand. "Congratulations, by the way. Clara tells me you're to be married this summer."

"Aye, that I am. I'd given up hope of finding myself a good woman, then Amy came here for a holiday and I never let her leave." Ben laughed, and ornaments rattled on their shelves. "These are my crew-mates, David, Pete and Andy. Lads, this is my cousin, Annie."

The men took it in turns to shake Annie's hand. She noticed how calloused their palms were, their skin like leather. Their faces were ruddy, cheeks pink, hair held at all angles by salt water.

"Sorry," said Andy. "We've come straight from the boat, so don't judge us too harshly by our appearance."

"I wouldn't dream of it," said Annie.

"I'm guessing you fellows would like a drink?" asked Jimmy.

"It's why we're here," said David.

"Then let's go to the bar. We were on our way there as part of Annie's tour. She only arrived this evening."

"Then please," said Ben, "if you're not too tired, join us for a drink. You too, Jimmy and Clara."

Annie glanced at Clara, unsure whether it was appropriate to drink with customers, even if they were family.

Clara smiled. "Go on then, you've twisted my arm. Do you know," she said, turning to Annie, "me and Ben live on an island less than ten miles in circumference, but with him out on the boat and me working here, we rarely get the chance to sit down together."

Jimmy took up position behind the bar and poured everyone a drink. Annie watched Clara and Ben, marvelling at their ease with one another despite the age and gender gap. Not for the first time she longed to have a sibling, someone she could share her life with, her worries, her happiness. But she didn't dwell on those thoughts, for in the company of her family and Ben's crewmates, with a glass of wine in hand, there was space for nothing but happiness.

Chapter 37

June, 1953

Annie did up the clasps on her empty suitcase and slid it under the bed. She walked to the window, staring out at the harbour and castle beyond. The view was constantly changing with the light, as though an artist was adapting, adjusting, switching out blues for crimsons, then back again. The previous evening, by the time Annie had been shown to her room, the light was milky, fading before her eyes. Cool tones of creams and blues had filled her vision.

Now, the castle rose as a black silhouette against a pink sky, streaks of orange lying across the horizon. *Red sky in the morning, shepherd's warning.* Annie hoped the old saying didn't prove true, for she was looking forward to exploring as much of the island as she could. She opened the window and took a deep gulp of island air. A feeling of peace crept over her. She had been on the island for less than twenty-four hours, but with tears of relief, Annie identified the feeling within her. It was a feeling of home, of belonging.

Turning her back on the view, Annie surveyed her new bedroom. It was up in the eaves, and the ceiling sloped down on one side, leaving little headroom above the narrow single bed. In the room's corner was a washstand, a thin wardrobe leaning against the wall beside it. The walls were covered in pink floral paper which matched the linen on the bed.

A knock on the door startled Annie. She opened it to a smiling Clara.

"Your grandmother is awake," said Clara, "she's asking to see you, but I thought you might be hungry so brought you this." Clara handed Annie a tray containing a piece of toast and a cup of coffee.

"Thank you," said Annie, "but I could have made something myself."

Clara laughed. "Steffie won't let you anywhere near her kitchen, but feel free to sneak in there whenever she's not around, and Jimmy and I have a kitchenette in our flat that you're very welcome to use."

Annie sat at the small writing desk in the window and ate her toast quickly, aware her grandmother was waiting.

"Don't worry," said Clara, noticing Annie's speed. "Rose isn't going anywhere. You don't want to give yourself indigestion. How is the unpacking going? Do you need more time to get yourself settled?"

"No, I'm all done here," said Annie.

"The room is alright for you?"

"I love it," answered Annie honestly. "The view is spectacular." She cradled her coffee cup and stared out of the window.

"It certainly is. The sad fact is I'm so used to it now I barely stop to notice the beauty. It's nice having a fresh pair of eyes here to remind me what's on my doorstep. Right, shall I show you to your grandmother's room? She's on the ground floor as stairs are a bit much for her these days."

Annie followed Clara down a carpeted staircase. The hotel was quiet, but they passed a few guests, who Clara greeted by name.

"Do you have many people staying here this week?"

"Only a handful of birdwatchers," said Clara. "We were very busy at Easter, but things tend to die down a little and ramp up again come the summer holidays. In a few weeks' time, we'll be full to the rafters. This way."

Clara pushed open a heavy door which opened onto the hotel's reception area. Clara introduced Annie to her assistant Olive, then led Annie down a narrow corridor, pausing outside a room with a gold number 1 nailed to the door. She knocked gently, then eased the door open.

"Rose? Are you awake?"

"Of course I'm awake, lass. Is that granddaughter of mine here yet?"

"She's right here beside me."

Annie followed Clara into the dark room. Clara walked to the window and pulled open the curtains.

"Don't open them too much," said Rose. "I don't want all them nosy buggers you've got staying peering in through my window."

"They're more interested in the local bird life than what goes on in your bedroom, Rose."

Through the gloom, Annie saw Rose slumped against the headboard of her bed. Her curly white hair poured down across her shoulders and chest. The skin on her face was loose and wrinkled, but she still had the broad-shouldered, sturdy frame Annie remembered.

"Come here, lass." Rose held out a hand and Annie walked over and took it. "Sit," said Rose, nodding her head to the bed. "I canna see much these days. Is it alright if I touch ye?"

Annie cast a nervous glance at Clara, who gave her a reassuring nod. "Of course, Grandma," said Annie.

Rose's hands scrabbled in the air for a moment, before settling on Annie's cheeks. With her fingertips, she moved around Annie's features, tapping on her nose, eyes, mouth and cheeks. With a calloused thumb, Rose stroked a line along Annie's skin. "I see with my hands these days," said Rose, "and I can tell ye are a beauty. Just like yer mam."

"And like you, Rose," added Clara.

Rose let out a bark of a laugh. "Nae need for flattery, Clara. I gave my bairns their curly hair and sharp minds, but their good looks were all Alex. He was a monster, aye, but a handsome one, until the drink took his looks at any rate."

"Goodness," said Annie, "I'm not sure I want the looks of a man like that."

"Ah, dinna fret, lass. The greatest blessing in my life is that none of my husband's character passed down to my bairns. Some of them turned out bitter, aye, but nothing as bad as their father. Others, like yer mam and Jimmy, turned out better than I dared hope."

A smile creased Rose's face even more, a single tear slipping from one eye and getting caught in a papery fold of skin. Annie wanted to reach across and catch it with her handkerchief, but decided Rose was too proud for that level of intervention.

"Do you get out and about much?" asked Annie.

"I've that darned contraption," said Rose, waving a hand in the vague direction of her wheelchair, "but I canna get out on my own these days."

"Perhaps I could take you out while I'm here?" suggested Annie.

"That would be lovely," said Clara. "Jimmy takes Rose to church each Sunday, but the pair of us are so busy we don't have as much time for Rose as we'd like."

"Dinna listen to that nonsense," said Rose, scowling at Clara. "If it weren't fer yer aunt and uncle, I'd have been dead and buried years back. They look after me better than I deserve."

"Do you feel up to going out this morning?"

"This morning?" asked Rose, an eyebrow raised.

"Only if you're not too tired."

"Would that be alright, Clara? The lassie taking me out?"

"Of course," said Clara with a laugh. "You don't need my permission, Rose."

"Maybe not, but it's ye that will have to get me washed and dressed, so it's only right I ask. I've nae forgotten my manners in my old age."

From Clara's stifled laugh, Annie guessed Rose hadn't been known for manners at any age.

"I can help get you ready. Clara, if you show me what to do, I can help Grandma while I'm here."

"If you're sure, that would be wonderful, thank you."

Annie picked up Rose's hand and kissed it. Despite how frail her grandmother looked, Annie hoped they'd have plenty of time together while she was on the island. After the shock of losing Sally, she was determined to make every second she spent with Rose count.

Chapter 38

June, 1953

The wind tugged Annie's curls around her face as she bent over the wheelchair, tucking blankets around Rose. "Are you sure it's not too cold for you, Grandma?"

"Too cold? This is practically tropical compared to some of the weather I've seen," said Rose. "Nae need to fuss, lass. I'm tougher than I look."

"I thought we could walk through the village, then down to the harbour," said Annie.

"Makes no odds to me, lass, I canna see a thing these days. It's enough that I can feel the breeze on my face and know you're beside me. Go where ye want, I'm at your mercy." Rose tapped the arm of the wheelchair to emphasize her point, then tilted her wizened face to the sky. "Smells like there'll be rain coming in later."

"Then we'd best get going while we still can."

The wheelchair was heavier than it looked. Annie's muscles strained until she gathered enough momentum and then it became a battle to stop it rolling too fast down the natural gradient that led from the village to the harbour.

"We must be passing my old cottage by now. Tell me what you see."

Annie looked around her. "To the right of us there's a large stone house with a small cottage tucked in beside it, and on our left is a row of four single-storey cottages, some whitewashed, others stone."

"Ah, well, my old cottage will be the third in that row. Your aunt and uncle lived there after I moved to Clara's, but both of them are dead now, so it's your cousin Philip who's taken over the rent."

"Would I have met him at Mum's wedding?"

"Aye, probably. He's a dour chap, and it's hard enough getting him to wish ye a good day, never mind an entire conversation. Not once have any of Sally and Robert's children called round to the hotel to see me."

"Do they all live on the island? I'd like to get to know my cousins."

"Only Philip these days. The rest scarpered to the city as soon as they could. I've nae idea what they're up to down there. They showed their faces for their parents' funerals, so I'm told, but they're nae ones for family. Not like Jimmy and Clara."

"Uncle Jimmy and Aunt Clara are wonderful."

"Aye, they are. Poor Jimmy had it rough when he was a lad. He was nothing like his da, and that put him in the firing line, but he's done well for himself. Aye, the lad's done well."

Annie smiled, amused at her grey-haired uncle, who was now in his sixties, being referred to as a lad. "You must be very proud of him."

"I am, not that I can take any credit. I was never the best mam."

"I'm sure you tried your best."

"Aye, maybe."

"I can see the sea," said Annie, sensing a sadness cloaking Rose and keen to change the subject.

Rose barked out a laugh. "Seeing the sea isn't much of a surprise given yer on an island, lass."

"I suppose not," said Annie.

"What colour is it?"

"What?"

"The sea, of course."

"It's bright blue. It's chilly for June, but the sun is shining and making everything sparkle."

"Lovely."

They walked the rest of the way to the harbour in companionable silence, it taking all Annie's concentration not to lose control of the wheelchair. When they reached the grassy bank hugging the water, Annie wheeled the chair to a wooden bench, then secured the brake. "We're by the harbour now," she said.

"Aye, I can hear the water lapping on the shore. Tide must be in."

"It is. Would you like to go further to the castle?"

"Nah, this chair must be heavy with me in it."

"I think this chair would be heavy without you in it," said Annie with a laugh. "It's like something from before the war."

"Will you manage pushing it back up the hill?"

"Let's hope so," said Annie. She sat herself on the bench beside Rose and took in the view. A handful of small pleasure boats bobbed on the lumpy water, the wind catching its surface and sending spits of water into the air.

"Do you see those buildings behind us?" asked Rose, sticking up her thumb and pointing in what she hoped was the right direction.

"Yes, I do. Stone buildings with a courtyard in the middle."

"Aye, that's them. They're the herring houses. When I was a lass, they'd be one of the busiest places on the island as that's where herring were prepared and oak-smoked, though you probably guessed that by the name." Rose chuckled to herself. "My, the fun I had working with the herring lassies who came here. I only managed a couple of seasons, mind."

"Why was that?"

"Because I ended up saddled with a bairn, that's why. Whatever ye dee, lass, dinna rush into motherhood. There'll be plenty enough time for that." Rose shook her head and tutted to herself. "Tell me what else you see. What's gannin' on around the harbour?"

By the long harbour wall, a group of fishermen were preparing to head out to sea. Annie shielded her eyes from the sun to get a better look at a tall figure striding along the beach.

"There are a group of fishermen at the far side of the harbour readying their boat to go to sea, and a tall man is walking across the beach, coming our way."

"What does he look like?"

"It's hard to see with the sun in my eyes," said Annie, "but he's tall and slim with a long overcoat and a scarf. No, wait, I think he has long hair."

"Humph," said Rose, crossing her arms over her ample chest.

"You know him?"

"There's only one man around here who dresses like that."

"Who is he?"

"His name is Blaine McCloud and ye'd do well to steer clear of him."

"Why?"

"Because I dinna trust the man as far as I could throw him. Reminds me of a chap I met once, Tam, his name was. All charm and no substance, as my Jimmy would say. Goodness knows what yer aunt was thinking, employing a man like that."

"He works at the hotel?"

"Aye. Clara thinks the lad can dee nae wrong. Thinks the sun shines out of his backside. Pardon my French."

"And what about you? Why don't you like him?"

"He calls himself an artist, that's why."

Annie spluttered with laughter. "What's wrong with that? I can't see why you'd hold that against him. Shush now, Grandma, he's walking over."

"Morning, Mrs Watson."

Rose gave a gruff greeting that came out more like a grunt.

"Beautiful weather we're having. Blaine McCloud," he said, holding out a hand to Annie.

She took his offered hand, vaguely aware of the roughness of his skin, but it was the man's eyes that captured Annie's attention. Icy blue, they gazed at her from beneath thick black lashes, their colour even more pronounced against his olive skin. His hair hung loose across his shoulders, black, but with an occasional streak of grey. Annie had never met someone so striking.

"Cat got your tongue, lass?" called Rose from her chair, "or are you gannin to introduce yerself?"

"I assume this young lady is a friend of yours, Mrs Watson?" asked Blaine, without taking his eyes off Annie.

"My granddaughter, Annie."

"A pleasure to meet you, Annie."

Annie realised she was still gripping on to the man's hand, and dropped it, her cheeks flaring red. Blaine chuckled.

"We were just heading home, weren't we, Annie?"

"Um, yes," said Annie, who didn't think Rose had had any intention of leaving until this strange man appeared.

"How fortunate," said Blaine. "I was just going back to the hotel myself. I'll push the wheelchair for you."

"There's nae need." "Thank you" said Rose and Annie simultaneously.

Blaine laughed, clicked off the brake, and wrapped his hands around the wheelchair handles. "Homeward bound," he announced, setting off as if the wheelchair was light as a feather. Annie followed behind, feeling all at odds around this most unusual man.

Chapter 39

June, 1953

"I see you've met Blaine," said Clara, standing up from the flowerbed she had been weeding and stretching out her back.

"I could have done that for you," said Blaine, pointing to the trowel in Clara's hand.

"What *is* your job here?" asked Annie, who had finally recovered her voice.

"General dogsbody," said Clara with a laugh.

"Some days I'm a gardener, some days a handyman, other days I run the bar or work as a waiter in the restaurant."

"A man of many talents," said Annie, blushing as she caught Blaine's eye.

"Shall we have a cup of tea out here in the garden?" asked Clara. "It would be a shame to be inside on such a lovely day and we're sheltered from the wind here."

"Are you warm enough to sit out here?" Annie asked Rose. "You're not too tired?"

"All I've been doing is sitting down, lass. I'll take a cup of tea with ye all, then retire for a rest."

"Would you like me to help you out of your wheelchair?" asked Blaine.

"No!" Rose barked the word, surprising Annie and, it seemed, Clara, who looked at her mother-in-law through narrowed eyes.

"Fine," said Blaine with a laugh, brushing off the comment.

Annie was embarrassed on her grandmother's behalf. She understood how frustrated Rose must be stuck either in a wheelchair or her bed, but that didn't excuse her rudeness. Perhaps, Annie thought, she was glimpsing the true Rose, before old age and disability mellowed her.

"Did I hear the mention of tea?" called Jimmy, walking across the lawn carrying a tray housing a teapot and china cups.

"You're a mind reader," laughed Clara.

"No, I just saw you all gathered out here and decided tea was called for."

"Morning, Mr Watson."

"Blaine." Jimmy greeted his employee with a nod and brief smile, and although he was not as rude as Rose, Annie sensed mother and son shared a dislike for the man. "I see you've met my niece."

"Only briefly," said Blaine, "but I'm looking forward to getting to know her better." With this, he gave Annie a piercing stare, and she felt a tide of heat spreading from her neck to her cheeks.

Jimmy set the tea tray down on a wooden table and positioned Rose's wheelchair before taking a seat himself.

"I'd better get back to work," said Blaine, hovering with his hand on the back of a chair.

"Good idea," said Jimmy, avoiding Blaine's eye as he poured tea into cups.

"Don't be silly," said Clara. "Sit down and join us."

"I wouldn't want to intrude on a family occasion."

"Sit," said Clara with a smile.

"Yes, ma'am."

Blaine sat in a chair beside Annie who felt unsettled, not just by his proximity, for their knees were touching, but also by the strained atmosphere. In all the years she'd known them, she'd never heard a cross word pass between Jimmy and Clara, yet Blaine seemed to have brought disharmony to the couple and Annie couldn't work out why.

"Ye kna, Blaine, ye remind me of my husband, Alex," said Rose.

"Thank you," said Blaine, as Clara spat out her tea and looked at Rose with horror in her eyes. "What?" asked Blaine, glancing between the two women with a mischievous glint in his eye. "Is Mr Watson senior not a favourable comparison?"

"Um..." said Clara.

"Well..." said Jimmy.

"Ah, I just meant the way ye speak," said Rose. "There's a confidence to ye I've nae come across in a while."

Jimmy and Clara exchanged a look that Annie couldn't decipher. Relief? Surprise? Mistrust?

"I see no point being a shrinking violet," said Blaine. "You only get one life, so may as well grab it with both hands."

"Well said," said Clara, clinking her tea cup against his. "But I have a bone to pick with you, Blaine."

"Is that so?"

"Yes, you've been promising to show me some of your paintings ever since you got here, and I've yet to see any of them."

Blaine laughed. "They're works in progress."

"Perhaps, but I'd like to buy a piece of your artwork for the hotel. It's not every day you employ a famous artist."

Annie noticed Jimmy roll his eyes and Rose let out a sigh.

"I'm certainly not famous," said Blaine with another laugh.

"No, but you may be someday. I consider purchasing a painting a fine investment."

"It's probably best not to make any promises before you've actually seen Blaine's work," said Jimmy.

"Quite right," muttered Rose. "His paintings may be dreadful."

"Wise words, Mrs Watson," said Blaine. "And, Clara, I promise I'll show you my paintings as soon as they're ready. Then you can make your own assessment of my artistic ability."

"Very well," said Clara.

As the conversation moved on, Annie let her mind drift to the last time she'd sat in this garden. It had been the day her mother and Frank, and Jimmy and Clara, married in a joint ceremony. The day had stuck in Annie's mind as one of the happiest she'd experienced. Would she celebrate her wedding on this island, or would it be back in Lowestoft? Her thoughts turned to Sam, and she realised it was the first time she'd thought of him since she arrived. She should write and let him know how she was getting on, but sitting beneath the warm summer sun, sheltered from the breeze, it felt as though Sam belonged to a different world, a different life.

"More tea, Annie?" asked Blaine, offering her the pot.

"Thank you." Annie returned her focus to the present moment. When she thought of Sam, it was like thinking of someone else's life. Lowestoft seemed far further than its three hundred miles. She might have only been on the island one day, but sitting in the sunshine looking over the harbour, Annie couldn't imagine she'd ever want to leave.

Chapter 40

June, 1953

Rose had been right, and the appearance of a large black cloud and the whipping up of the wind had cut short their tea in the garden. Now, rain pummelled the window of Annie's attic bedroom, streaking the glass and blurring the view beyond.

The excursion down to the harbour had tired Rose. As Annie and Clara had helped Rose back to her bedroom, Annie had studied the way Clara handled her mother-in-law, determined that she would take over some of the caring duties while on the island. It was clear Rose hated being mollycoddled and insisted on being as independent as her fading eyesight would allow.

"I told you there'd be rain," Rose had said as the first few drops slapped against her windowpane.

After losing Sally so recently, Annie was determined to spend as much time with her one remaining grandparent as possible, and was disappointed when Rose said she needed some time alone to rest. Clara and Jimmy both had chores to attend to and had insisted Annie enjoy her first full day on the island free of work.

So Annie found herself alone in her bedroom, the rain trapping her inside. With everyone else busy and too restless for reading, Annie pulled out her pen and notebook to write to her parents. With a telephone in the hotel, Annie could have rung them to let them know she had arrived safely, but she didn't want to set a precedent. This time on the island was hers and hers alone.

Dear Mum and Frank,

I have arrived safely (which you've probably heard from Jimmy), and am settling in to life at the hotel. This morning I took Grandma Rose down to the harbour, which was just as beautiful as I remembered. I can see right across to the castle from my bedroom window and look forward to waking to that view each morning.

There is plenty of work for me here, but Clara and Jimmy are insisting I take a few days' holiday before getting stuck in. To be honest, I'd rather be busy, but they are being so thoughtful, I don't want to appear ungrateful.

I don't have much news yet, but will write again next week when I shall hopefully have more to share. I hope you are both well and enjoying the new house, yours, Annie.

Annie knew she should write to Grace, but couldn't bring herself to. Since the visit to Padstow, she'd not been able to see Helen and Grace in the same way and each time she sat down to write, she found no words came. She stood and pressed her face to the window, closing her eyes and picturing Grace looking out of her own window. They now had harbour views in common. Perhaps she could send a postcard rather than a letter? It would reduce the scope of words needed, and Grace would be pleased to see where Annie was spending the summer.

With her decision made, Annie grabbed her trench coat from a hook on the door and made her way downstairs. Clara was standing at the front desk beside her assistant Olive, hunched over a large hardback book.

"Oh, Annie, you're not going out in this weather, are you?"

"Yes," said Annie. "I want to buy some postcards from the post office."

"I see. If you don't mind waiting for a while, I can come with you. We've got a problem with one of our bookings I need to help resolve, but once that is done, I could spare some time."

"There's no need for you to come with me," said Annie. "I remember seeing the post office earlier when I took Grandma out."

"Alright then, if you're sure. But don't stay out too late. The rain is bad enough, but there's a storm approaching and we don't want you catching a chill in your first week here."

"I'll hurry back," said Annie. She said goodbye to the two women and let herself out of the hotel. The rain fell like spears, whipped up by a wind that blew in violent gusts. It was hard to imagine the sunshine of hours before as Annie screwed up her eyes and stepped out onto the village streets.

There was no one else out in the village but lights were on in several cottages and as she struggled against the weather, Annie wondered if they had the right idea staying inside. Annie passed a small chapel, its doors closed firm against the weather. She walked on past a row of cottages, picking up her pace as the post office came into view.

The door banged behind her as Annie entered the small shop, pulling down her hood and shaking rain from her hair.

"You'd nae think it's summer, would ye?" called a young woman from behind the counter.

Annie smiled, pulled out a handkerchief and wiped rain from her face. "It was brilliant sunshine this morning. I can't believe how quickly the weather has changed."

"Ye get used to it when ye live here. Are ye here for a holiday or are ye one of those pilgrims?" The girl wrinkled her nose at the word 'pilgrim' and Annie smiled.

"Neither. My aunt and uncle run a hotel here, so I've come to work for them for the summer."

"Who's your aunt?"

"Clara Watson."

"Oh, ye're a Watson, are ye?"

"My mother was a Watson before she married. My name is Annie Hearn, my mother is Marnie, Jimmy Watson's sister."

"That makes you an islander in my eyes." The girl smiled and held out a hand. "Genie Guthrey. My family has been here for donkey's years and I'm the latest recruit into the family business."

Annie shook the girl's hand. "Nice to meet you, Genie."

Although Annie judged Genie to be a similar age to her friends in Lowestoft, she dressed in a far younger, more old-fashioned way. Her hair, rather than set or coloured, hung in two long brown braids down her back. She wore what looked like a home-made woollen cardigan over a simple cotton blouse and the hem of her pleated brown woollen skirt hung around her calves. As she stepped out from behind the counter, Annie noticed her stockings were wrinkled and her sensible Mary-Janes were scuffed on the toes. But when she smiled, her face lit up, and Annie realised that despite her dowdy outfit, the girl was a beauty.

"So what can I get for ye today? Need a letter posting?"

"Actually, I've come to buy some postcards."

"Over there," said Genie, pointing to a stand beside the door.

"Thank you."

"I hope you dinna think me too forward, but there aren't many other lassies my age living here. Would you join me for a cup of tea?"

Genie's cheeks had reddened slightly, but Annie met her awkwardness with a smile. "I'd be delighted. Clara and Jimmy don't want me starting work yet, and what with the weather, I'd found myself at a loose end."

"Grand. You pick out your postcards and I'll make us a cuppa. Give me a shout if anyone comes into the shop, though I doubt we'll have any customers on a day like this."

As Genie retreated into the back of the building, Annie spun around the display of photographs, pleased she'd braved the weather. If she arrived home having made a new friend, the soaking would be worth it.

Chapter 41

June, 1953

"Did ye watch the Queen's coronation?"

"Yes, my stepfather bought a television set especially for the occasion and all the neighbours came round."

"Didn't the Queen look muckle barey?"

"Pardon?"

"Oh, sorry, it means she looked *very nice*." Genie put on her best attempt at a southern accent and Annie laughed. "Have you ever been to Buckingham Palace?"

"No."

"Have you been to London?"

"Only when I had to catch the train to Padstow and back. I took a bus through the city but couldn't see much other than grime and lots of people. To be honest, I can't see what all the fuss is about. If I was Queen Elizabeth, I'd spend all my time at Sandringham or Balmoral, not London, with all its smog and noise."

"Aye, ye may be right there. Although I'd love to visit London one day. The furthest I've ever been is Berwick."

"Is that your nearest town?"

"Aye. There's a train goes up to Edinburgh, but I've never had reason to visit."

"Perhaps we could go together while I'm here?"

"Really? That would be wonderful. I'd have to give Mam plenty of notice mind, so she could find someone to cover me in the shop, but that shouldn't be a problem."

"That's settled then," said Annie with a smile. "If you don't leave the island much, how do you fill your spare time? Do they have dances here?"

Genie laughed. "Not often enough. They'll put on a dance in the village hall from time to time, if someone gets wed and such like. I spend most of my time here in the shop these days. I'll be lucky to find myself a husband."

"There aren't any local men you've got your eye on?"

"Not likely. Most of the lads my age have either left the island to find work in the city, or have joined their da's out fishing, and I canna see myself marrying and becoming a fishwife. Do they have lots of dances in Lowestoft?"

"Yes, me and my friends often go to two a week down at the Palais."

"You lucky devil. Are there lots of nice young men to dance with?"

"Yes, plenty," laughed Annie. "We get a lot of American airmen coming to the dances. Their base is over an hour away, but they say nothing beats the Palais. The girls go wild over them, so no wonder they enjoy themselves."

"Goodness," said Genie, practically swooning at the thought of American airmen. "You're so lucky. Why on earth did ye choose to leave all that and come to this tiny island?"

Annie shrugged. "I suppose I knew the island was an important part of my family history and wanted to experience it for myself." She wanted to confide her feelings of discontent, but wondered if Genie would understand, having lived in the same place her entire life. "You're not tempted to leave the island yourself?"

"Na, I couldn't do that to Mam and Da. This post office has been in our family for generations and neither of them are in the best of health, so mostly it falls to me to keep things going. I'll probably die here, an old spinster."

Annie laughed. "Let's hope not." She downed the last dregs of her tea and placed the paper bag filled with postcards in her trench coat pocket. "I'd better be getting back, or Aunt Clara will send out a search party."

"Thank you for joining me for tea. It's a breath of fresh air having a lass my age to blether away to."

"Blether?"

"Chatter. Ye'll get the hang of these words soon enough."

"I'm sure I will. It was lovely to meet you, Genie. Perhaps we could have a drink together at the hotel one night?"

"That sounds like a wonderful idea."

"Great. I'll see you soon."

The storm had hit the island with full force and Annie felt panic rise in her as she bent her head low and tried to force her way along the street, the wind trying to thwart her attempts by pushing her backwards. By the time she finally made it back to the hotel, Annie was out of breath, sweating, and rainwater had seeped through gaps in her trench coat and dampened her clothes.

"Where have you been?" asked Clara, rushing into the lobby as soon as she heard the door bang.

"Sorry," said Annie. "I got chatting to Genie in the post office."

"Ah, I see," said Clara. "She's a lovely young thing. I've known her family for years, and you could do far worse than befriending a Guthrey. Sorry if I sounded alarmed. This weather is wild for the time of year and I was worried about you being out in it. Did you get your postcards?"

Annie pulled the paper bag from her pocket, relieved it had survived the downpour. She took them out and showed them to Clara.

"Very nice," said Clara. "You know you're also welcome to use the hotel telephone whenever you like?"

"Thank you," said Annie, "but I prefer writing letters to speaking on the telephone."

"Well, the offer's there if you need it. Now, why don't you go upstairs and have a leisurely soak in the bath? There's plenty of hot water and I don't want you catching a chill."

"You really don't need to worry about me, Aunt Clara. I'm an adult now."

"I know, but as I never had children of my own, I enjoy having a niece to spoil." Clara's smile was warm, but Annie detected a hint of sadness in her voice. She'd heard the tale of Clara and Jimmy's romance many a time, but knew there would be more to it. No relationship was sunshine and roses all the time, and Annie suspected Clara's lack of children caused some sadness.

"I invited Genie Guthrey here for a drink one night this week. I hope that's alright?"

"Of course it is. It's good you're making friends your own age. Now go and have that bath."

"Yes, ma'am."

Chapter 42

June, 1953

For all the grandeur of the hotel, Jimmy and Clara's living quarters were modest. They lived in a small flat on the ground floor comprising a bedroom, bathroom, and kitchenette. When Annie had asked why they didn't take more of the building for themselves, Jimmy had laughed and said they had all they needed.

It had been over a week since she arrived on the island and Clara and Jimmy had insisted Annie use that time to settle in, forbidding her to undertake any work other than light caring duties for her grandmother. On her eighth day on the island, Annie stood outside Jimmy's front door and knocked.

"Come in."

Annie stepped into the room, which acted as both a lounge and dining room. At the far end were two armchairs, a doily-covered coffee table sitting between them, and they faced a fireplace, family photographs positioned on the mantel above. Despite the jug of fresh flowers on the coffee table spilling their scent into the room, the overwhelming smell was one of coffee and baking, and Annie's mouth watered.

Jimmy and Clara were sitting at a small wooden table, a paper spread between them. They each had a plate of toast, Jimmy's spread with marmalade, Clara's with jam, steam rising from a pot of coffee.

"Good morning, Annie. Would you like to join us for breakfast?"

"I don't want to intrude."

Clara laughed. "I wouldn't have invited you if I felt you were intruding. Get yourself a cup from the cupboard over there and I'll pour you a coffee."

"Thank you," said Annie.

"Shall I make you some toast?"

"No, thank you. I've already had breakfast with Grandma."

"How is she this morning?" asked Jimmy.

"She seems well. She didn't eat much, though."

"No," said Clara. "Rose doesn't have much of an appetite these days."

"It's wonderful to see how well the two of you get on," said Jimmy.

"She's a lot of fun."

Jimmy threw down his toast and laughed. "I wouldn't let her hear you describe her as fun. She prides herself on her battle-axe persona."

"Don't be mean," said Clara. "Your mam has led a hard life. She had to be tough. What are your plans today, Annie?"

"I'd like to start work."

"Are you sure you wouldn't like longer to settle in?"

"Quite sure. I heard Olive talking about a party of ramblers arriving today. I thought you could do with some help."

"We could," said Clara, sitting at the table and pouring coffee into a china cup. "Here you are," she said, handing the cup to Annie.

"Thank you."

"Is that Lowestoft?" asked Annie, walking across the room to where a large oil painting hung above a plump peach sofa.

"Yes," said Jimmy. "One of my former pupils painted it. I think it's rather wonderful."

"And it reminds us of our years living there," said Clara, "and how lucky we are to be together now."

Annie saw a private smile pass between her aunt and uncle. She thought the story of their complicated path to love was one of the most romantic things she'd heard. She wondered if her own life story would ever be as interesting.

"I hope you're not too homesick," said Clara.

"No, not at all," said Annie with a smile. "I love it here."

"And we love having you here," said Jimmy. "Although I can't quite believe the civilised young woman who turned up on our doorstep. You were such a little tearaway when you were small. Your poor mother had quite the run-around with you."

"I wasn't that bad!"

Jimmy laughed. "No, you weren't, but you've always known your own mind."

"I wish I knew my mind now," said Annie. "I never seem able to feel at home anywhere. Sam is keen for us to settle down as soon as he's finished his National Service, but..." Annie stopped talking, aware she'd said far more than she intended.

"You'll have plenty of time to think things through while you're here," said Clara, coming to stand beside her. "And you're still so young. There's no rush to launch into adult life just yet."

"Thank you. I'm so glad to be here. What would you like me to do today?"

"How about a spot of chambermaiding? I've seven rooms to prepare for our guests."

Annie drained the last of her coffee and washed her cup in the kitchenette. "I'm at your service," she said.

"Right then, no time like the present. I have a spare uniform in my wardrobe. Come through to the bedroom and you can get changed in there."

Once Annie was suitably dressed in a blue gingham dress and white apron and armed with a bucket of cleaning materials, the morning sped by in a blur of fresh bedding and furniture polish. By the fourth bedroom, Annie's arms were aching, but she enjoyed the chance to lose herself in a task, and Clara kept her occupied with a steady stream of conversation about the island and its residents.

The rooms at the hotel were simply furnished, with a bed, dresser, wardrobe, and a sink in the corner. The walls were painted magnolia and needed little in the way of decoration, given the spectacular views. Even those facing away from the harbour enjoyed views of the priory and church, with the mainland just visible in the distance.

Annie plumped up the pillows in the last bedroom and stood back to admire her handiwork. Clara came to stand beside her and put an arm around her shoulder.

"You've done a grand job there," said Clara. "It took me a long time to master making beds to a hotel standard."

"You must have been so brave," said Annie, "buying this hotel and running it by yourself."

"There's a fine line between brave and foolish," said Clara with a laugh. "It was a steep learning curve."

"Do you ever wish you'd married Uncle Jimmy sooner? It must have been hard coming back here and leaving him behind in Lowestoft."

Clara folded a towel and propped it on the bed. "That's a tricky question. Part of me regrets the years we lost out on, but you can't turn back time. I'm very grateful for all the years we've had, and there'll be plenty more to come, I hope. Some people never meet the love of their life. I have. If that love comes with sacrifices, so be it. Everything turned out for the best in the long run."

"How did you know?"

"How did I know what?"

"That Uncle Jimmy was the love of your life? That you wanted to come back here?"

"Oh, returning to the island was something I'd always wanted to do. Things with your uncle were a little more complicated. We were friends for a long time before any romantic feelings developed. I think that friendship gave us a bond strong enough to see us through difficult times. When we met again as adults, we had that friendship to fall back on. But, truth be told, I'd always loved your uncle, for as long as I can remember. We weren't that different from you and Sam. You've been friends since you were bairns, haven't you?"

"Yes, we have."

"You must miss him."

"I do. He's promised to come and visit me here as soon as he gets more leave. If that's alright with you?"

"Of course it is. Now, how are you at cleaning bathrooms?"

"Good, I think. If I can clean our old bathroom free of layers of mud brought by floodwater, I'm sure I can clean the bathrooms here."

"Wonderful. There are four shared bathrooms spread between the ground, first and second floors. It's fortunate you're here to help me with them as the two girls who usually clean for me are away visiting relatives on the mainland."

"I must say, I'm surprised how much work you do here yourself," said Annie.

Clara laughed. "So you've been picturing us up here living a life of leisure, have you?"

Annie flushed. "I didn't mean to imply you're lazy. I suppose I thought your role would be more managerial."

"It is, but we muck in with everything around here, especially in the winter when we take on less staff, and at times like this, when some of our staff members are away. Now we're coming into the season I shan't have to spend as much time cleaning, but there's always something to be done. Your role will be very varied, so you shouldn't get too bored. When Jane and Mary are here, they'll do the lion's share of cleaning, so you'll mostly be waitressing and serving drinks if that's alright with you?"

"I'm happy to do anything."

"You're a grafter, that's for sure, just like your mother," said Clara with a smile.

"And like you," said Annie.

"I think we'll make an excellent team. In fact, I'm not sure we'll ever let you leave." Clara grinned at Annie and threw a duster her way. Annie caught it, thinking she'd be quite happy to live with Clara forever, no matter how many toilets she had to clean.

Chapter 43

July, 1953

Annie glanced at the clock. Ten p.m. Were the last guests ever going to leave? She longed to go up to her bedroom, kick off her shoes, and lie on her bed listening to the 78 record of 'I Believe', that Sam had sent her as a surprise. Jimmy had loaned her his precious record player, and Annie had already listened to the record about twenty times. When Frankie Laine's crooning vocals filled her small bedroom, Annie could close her eyes and imagine herself lying in Sam's arms. Tonight she wanted Frankie to lull her to sleep where she could dream of Sam, but as another burst of laughter erupted from the hotel guests, Annie knew any plans for listening to music were a long way off.

When Annie had heard a group of ramblers were coming to the hotel, she'd pictured middle-aged men in waxed jackets and corduroy trousers. While the dress code was as she'd expected, the behaviour of the guests was not. They enjoyed a tipple, several in fact, their voices growing louder, their language cruder with every glass refilled.

Annie leaned against the polished wooden bar, longing to take the weight off her feet. Four men and one woman sat around a round table, its white tablecloth stained with red wine and gravy, napkins crushed and discarded among a plethora of empty glasses.

In a bid to move the revellers on, Annie had cleared all the empty tables, added their tablecloths to the laundry and stacked the chairs.

Rather than taking the hint, the remaining group seemed more entrenched than ever.

"Another round of drinks, please, waitress."

"I'll get these."

Annie jumped as Blaine McCloud appeared at her shoulder. She'd only seen him in passing over the past few weeks and was curious to know more about him. "I thought this was your evening off?"

"It is, but I saw that group through the window and thought you might need some help."

"I can manage, really."

"I'm sure you can, but they look like they could be here for a while and you look dead on your feet."

"Thanks," said Annie, her hand going to a stray curl which had escaped the bun that held the rest of her hair in place.

"You know what I mean," said Blaine, placing a hand on Annie's arm. "Sit down for a minute."

"Alright." Annie perched on a bar stool, her skin still warm from Blaine's touch. There was something about the man that sent her thoughts haywire. Annie still wasn't sure whether the effect Blaine had on her was more pleasure or pain. She watched as he took the guests' orders, charming them into agreeing this would be their final round.

"What did you say to them?" whispered Annie, as Blaine poured a round of drinks and the guests began pulling on their jackets and standing up.

"I suggested they'd be more comfortable drinking in the guest lounge beside the fire."

"Why didn't I think of that?" said Annie.

"Because you're tired. What's your tipple?"

"Pardon?"

"What do you like to drink? You look like you could use one."

Annie weighed up her options. Listening to 'I Believe' and dreaming of Sam was tempting, but so was a drink with Blaine. His appearance and manner aroused her curiosity, and the record player would still be there after one drink.

"Well?"

"Gin, please. On the rocks."

Blaine made her a drink and slid it across the bar. He filled a tray with the group's order and called for them to follow him through to the lounge. By the time he returned, Annie had cleared their table and was stacking the chairs.

"I told you to sit down and have a drink," said Blaine, frowning at Annie.

"I know, but I'm here to work, not drink."

Blaine laughed. "I was trying to be nice."

"Hmph," said Annie, Blaine's overfamiliarity leaving her wary.

"You remind me of your grandmother."

"I'll take that as a compliment."

Blaine laughed again. "Tell me about yourself, Miss Annie Hearn."

Annie watched Blaine through narrowed eyes as he poured himself a measure of whisky and tapped the stool beside him for her to sit down. "What would you like to know?"

"Everything."

"I'm not sure there's much to tell."

"There's always something to tell. Let's start with why you came to the island."

"Aside from its beauty and the chance to spend time with my aunt and uncle, I suppose I wanted to see if I felt at home here."

"At home? Now you've piqued my curiosity. Why didn't you feel at home in Lowestoft?"

Whether it was the gin loosening her tongue, or the hypnotic effect of Blaine's gaze, Annie found herself pouring out her worries and troubles to a man who was as good as a stranger. When she mentioned the card she had found all those years earlier, his eyes widened.

"You know what I've learned, Annie? It's best to trust no one but yourself."

"That doesn't sound like the makings for a happy life."

Blaine shrugged. "I'm just giving you my tuppence worth. Perhaps it's not just your experience as an evacuee making you feel unsettled, but your instincts about your family. I always believe in trusting one's instincts. From what you've told me, it sounds as though none of your family can be trusted. And if you've had to run away up here to be rid of them, they can't make you that happy."

"I'm sure they have their reasons for keeping things from me."

Blaine laughed. "You think they're protecting you, is that it?"

Annie flushed, for that was precisely what she'd been thinking.

"In my experience," said Blaine, topping up his glass with whisky, "folk keep secrets for selfish reasons, nothing more, nothing less."

Annie frowned and swirled the gin around her glass.

"But don't listen to me," said Blaine. "I'm just a jaded old fool who's been lied to and tricked one too many times."

"By whom?"

"My father, mostly. That's how I learned to rely on no one but myself. But let's not dwell on that. Tell me something more about your life. What's your happiest memory?"

When Annie next glanced at the clock, it was almost midnight. They'd been talking for hours and yet she still knew very little about the man beside her. "It's late," she said. "I should get to bed."

"Are you working tomorrow?"

"No, I have a day off."

"And what do you intend to do with your free time?"

"Spend it with Grandma, write a few postcards, perhaps go out for a walk."

"Could I join you for that walk?"

"Don't you have to work?"

"I'm on breakfasts, then not back on shift till the evening, so I'll have all afternoon free."

"Alright then," said Annie.

"I'll meet you by the harbour at two."

"The harbour? Why not here?"

Blaine gave Annie a lazy smile. "I get the feeling your uncle is a little overprotective of you. I'm not sure how keen he'd be on us spending time together."

"I don't see what harm a walk can do?"

Blaine fixed Annie in an intense stare. What did that look mean? Her palms grew sweaty, and she wiped them on her skirt. "I really must get to bed."

Blaine leaned over and kissed Annie's cheek so lightly it almost tickled. "Goodnight, Annie."

"Goodnight, Blaine."

"Oh, and, Annie?"

"Yes?"

"I was wrong earlier when I said you can't trust anyone but yourself. You can trust me, and I hope I can trust you. In fact, I think we're going to become great friends."

Annie nodded, unsure how to respond. She left the bar and walked up to her attic bedroom, slightly unsteady on her feet after all the gin she'd consumed. In her bedroom, she went to the writing desk, where a postcard to Sam lay unfinished. She twirled the postcard around in her fingers, feeling more confused than ever.

To clear her mind, Annie walked to the record player and turned the volume dial down to its lowest setting, then lifted the needle and closed her eyes as 'I Believe' crackled into life. But try as she might, she couldn't imagine herself in Sam's arms.

A surge of guilt filled her, but she pushed it away, telling herself she'd done nothing wrong. There was no law against talking to other men, forming friendships with other men. Annie leaned against the desk and squeezed her eyes shut, trying to picture Sam's face. The only image playing on her eyelids was Blaine, and the look he had given her. What had it meant?

Annie opened her eyes, turned the postcard to Sam face down on the desk, kicked off her shoes, and climbed into bed fully clothed. The alcohol had left her body drowsy, but her mind buzzed with an excitement she couldn't pin down. When she finally drifted off to sleep, Blaine's image was still at the forefront of her mind.

Chapter 44

July, 1953

"This isn't fair," said Annie, turning to Blaine with a smile. "You know everything there is to know about me now, and yet have revealed nothing of yourself." She paused to catch her breath and admire the view. In the distance the castle squatted against the sky, beyond it the harbour. In front of her stretched a large expanse of water, the dark outline of the Farne Islands the only blot on the landscape.

"There's not much to tell," said Blaine, taking Annie's hand as if it was the most natural thing in the world and tugging gently to get her moving.

"How did you end up on this island?"

"I saw an advertisement in the local newspaper for a job in the hotel."

"But why here?"

"Because accommodation was included, and I need to save as much money as I can."

"What for?"

Blaine laughed. "So many questions."

"No more than you've asked me."

"Fair enough. You want to know the truth?"

Annie nodded.

"It's embarrassing."

"I don't care."

"Fine," said Blaine with a sigh. "I ran away to escape my father. He hated the fact I wanted to pursue my art, but I'd rather be a penniless artist than an arthritic carpenter. We argued, I left, and we've not spoken to each other since."

"What's embarrassing about that?"

"Take your pick. That I'm still chasing my dreams at my age, or the fact I still care what my father thinks of me?"

"And how old are you, exactly?"

"Thirty-seven."

"That is old."

"Thanks."

"In all seriousness, though, wanting to be an artist in your thirties is only embarrassing if you're not very good. Are you a good artist, Blaine?"

"You can judge for yourself later if you come to my cottage."

Annie paused and studied his face. "What about my Uncle Jimmy? I thought you were worried about him seeing us together?"

"You can come once he's gone to bed. He and Clara are usually tucked up with a hot cocoa by nine."

"I thought you were working tonight?"

"The ramblers leave today, so it's likely to be quiet in the restaurant. You don't have to come if you don't want to."

"I want to," said Annie, without a second's hesitation.

"Wonderful." Blaine leaned over and planted a kiss on the top of Annie's head. It was the kiss a brother or father might give, and yet it sent Annie's pulse racing, and she hoped the hand Blaine still held hadn't become clammy. "Would you like to continue on, or head back to the village?"

"I'd like to walk further, if that's alright? I want to soak up every inch of the island while I can."

"You won't be here for long?"

"I honestly don't know. My plan was to come here for the summer, help Aunt Clara during the busy season, then return home to Lowestoft."

"And have your plans changed?"

Annie thought about the question. "It's still early days here, but I feel so at home and that's not something I've felt before."

"Would your mother mind if you extended your stay?"

"I don't think so. My mum and stepfather just want me to be happy. But I'm an only child, and this island is about as far from my family as I could get. My parents aren't getting any younger. Oh, I don't know. I suppose the answer is my plans are up in the air." Annie smiled at Blaine, and he returned it. "How about you? How long do you intend to stay here?"

"As long as it takes."

"For what?"

"To save enough money to head to Paris."

"Why Paris?"

Blaine's eyes widened, and he gasped. "Why Paris? Because it's the artistic capital of the world, that's why."

Annie laughed. "I'm sure the Italian masters would have something to say about that."

"Perhaps, but it's certainly where all the greats have trained; Picasso, Monet, Van Gogh, Matisse... need I go on?"

"Fair enough. What will you do in Paris?"

"The same as I do here probably, work hard to fund my artistic passion. But I'll be doing that in Paris, not on some rock stuck out in the North Sea."

Annie felt a moment of disquiet and wondered whether *a rock stuck in the North Sea* was as offensive as it sounded.

"Don't look like that," said Blaine. "I'm not insulting your island, just stating facts. There's not a lot goes on around here and whilst the natural beauty is breathtaking, I like a little more excitement in my life. Your arrival is the most exciting thing to happen since I moved here."

"Oh." Annie flushed as Blaine fixed her with an intent stare. "Come on," she said, letting her curls fall around her face to hide her blush, "let's keep walking."

After a further half an hour of walking, Annie had blisters on her heels and her calves were aching. She kept quiet about her aches and pains, not wanting to spoil the time with Blaine. Once she'd prised open his shell, he'd talked with enthusiasm about his art, his childhood on the outskirts of Edinburgh, his father's disappointment that his son hadn't joined the family carpentry business. Each mention of his father brought creases across his forehead, and Annie sensed there was more to their relationship than he was letting on but was sure he'd tell her everything in good time.

"This is beautiful," said Annie, as they reached a sweeping horseshoe of sand bordered by towering mounds of dunes and marram grass.

"It's my favourite spot here," said Blaine.

"Have you painted it?"

"I did a quick watercolour once, but I'm more interested in people than places."

"Can we walk on the beach?"

"Of course. I'll go first as the sand is quite loose and I don't want you to fall."

Annie followed Blaine, keeping hold of his outstretched hand. Her feet sank into the soft sand, her progress unsteady as she descended the steep bank. When she'd almost reached the beach below, Annie stumbled, falling forward into Blaine who caught her in his arms. Rather than set her upright, he held her close, so close she could feel his heart beating beneath his shirt.

"Thank you," said Annie, pulling away and turning to hide her rosy cheeks. "I must have lost my footing."

"You're welcome. This way." Blaine strode off across the beach and Annie ran to keep up with his long strides. "We may see some seals if we're lucky," he said, gazing at rocks in the distance. "Yes, there. Can you see them?"

"I don't think so."

Blaine moved behind Annie, lifting his arm in the direction she should look while holding his free hand on her waist. Annie could feel his breath on the back of her neck and tried to keep her own breathing steady. "What are they doing?"

"Sunbathing by the looks of things."

"I wish we could get closer."

"We'll bring binoculars with us next time."

Next time. Annie's heart fluttered at the thought that this walk wouldn't be a one-off, but told herself her excitement was everything to do with the scenery and nothing to do with the company. She told herself she was doing nothing wrong. Where was the harm in making a new friend? She felt no guilt about spending time with Beryl, or Mary, or Genie. But as she stood beside Blaine gazing out to sea, Annie couldn't shake the feeling she was standing at the edge of a dangerous new world. One she was excited to explore.

Chapter 45

July, 1953

Annie slung a tea towel over her shoulder and arranged glasses on a shelf. She covered her mouth as a yawn crept out. The restaurant had been busier than expected, a local family turning up to celebrate a fortieth birthday. Annie had been like a cat on hot bricks waiting for them to leave. When they finally said their goodbyes and she could clear up, nerves appeared in her stomach.

"Was everything alright this evening?" asked Jimmy, walking into the bar.

"Yes, not too bad."

"Where's Blaine?"

"He went down to the cellar to change a barrel."

"As long as he's been pulling his weight?"

"Blaine's worked just as hard as me this evening. I told him he could go to bed once the barrel has been changed, as I'm almost finished here," said Annie, smiling and pointing to the polished glasses.

"Wonderful. Thank you so much for stepping in this evening, I know it was your day off."

"It's really no trouble. I'd much rather be busy."

Jimmy smiled. "If you don't need any help to clear up, Clara and I will turn in for the night."

"I'm fine here. You get your beauty sleep."

"Goodnight then," said Jimmy, leaning over to kiss Annie's cheek. "Don't stay up too late."

"I won't," lied Annie. She waited until Jimmy had left the room, then sat watching the clock for ten minutes before she dared make her move. Jimmy was a mild-mannered man, but Annie didn't want to test his temper if he found out where she was going.

Annie stood in the empty lobby of the hotel and listened. She heard the hiss of a pipe, a door slamming on one of the upper floors, but other than that, the hotel was quiet. The front door needed its hinges oiling, so Annie crept along the corridor and through the large kitchen. At the back door, she paused and listened again. Nothing. She unlocked the door, slipped the key into her pocket and stepped out into the night.

Blaine's cottage was tacked onto the side of the main building, and Annie crept her way along the back wall of the hotel, ducking down as she passed Jimmy and Clara's windows. To call his home a cottage was generous. The building had once been a stable big enough for the two horses the owners needed to bring supplies across from the mainland. Annie had never been inside, and was curious to see how someone lived in such a small space.

Annie knocked gently on the wooden front door and waited. Through a gap in the curtains, a thin shard of orange light spilled out. Smoke rose from the chimney and the muffled sound of Duke Ellington crept out into the night. Given Blaine had only left the hotel fifteen minutes before her, he must have been busy.

"Annie. You came."

Blaine was wearing an old navy smock, full of holes and covered in colourful splodges of paint. His hair was tied up against the back of his head, and a cigarette drooped from his lips.

"You weren't expecting me?"

"I wasn't sure you'd be able to sneak out. I heard Jimmy come through to the bar and thought he may hang around. Please, come in."

Annie followed Blaine into the cottage, which was, in fact, one small room. A wooden bed had been pushed against one wall, a small dresser beside it. A few feet from the bed were two armchairs positioned either side of a low wooden table housing a pile of well-thumbed books. Easels, pots of paints and canvases took up the rest of the space.

"I'm sorry about the mess," said Blaine. "This is more of a work space than a home, I'm afraid."

"Can I see some of your paintings?" asked Annie, walking to where a stack of frames leaned against a wall. Blaine rushed past her, positioning himself between her and the paintings.

"Those aren't finished."

"I don't mind."

"Maybe not, but I do. Here," he said, taking her hand and leading her towards the armchairs. "This is a finished example of my work."

Hanging on the wall was a painting of an old woman. Her white hair hung in a rope-like plait across one shoulder, striking brilliant blue eyes peering out from a face creased by laughter lines. Even in her old age, the woman was a beauty. Blaine had captured her in oil paints, the bright colours he'd used giving her the vibrancy of someone far younger.

"This is incredible," said Annie. She walked over to the painting and had to fight the urge to stroke the thick layers of paint. "Who is she?"

"My mother."

"She's beautiful."

"She was, indeed."

"Was?"

"She died three years ago." Blaine's voice was hard and brittle.

"I'm sorry," said Annie. "I understand how it feels to lose a parent."

"Thank you," he said, his voice softening.

"Do you have other paintings I can see?"

Blaine reached under the bed and pulled out a large wooden crate. "Some of these are a little rough around the edges," he said.

Annie took her time leafing through the paintings. All were portraits, mostly of older people, both men and women. "Is there a reason your paintings are mostly of the elderly?"

Blaine smiled. "Yes, there is. You see more of their life etched on their faces and in their eyes. Some radiate wisdom, others loss, but every person I've painted has a unique story to tell, and that's what I hope to capture with my images."

His words entranced Annie, spoken in his soft, slightly husky voice and cloaked in a gentle Lowlands burr. Annie daydreamed of being read to by that voice, just as she had read to Sally all those months ago. It was the kind of voice that felt like velvet being draped over your skin. Annie shook her head, flushing as she realised Blaine was staring at her.

"Sorry," she said. "I was thinking about my grandmother." She tried to force back her blush, for this wasn't a complete lie.

"Rose?"

"No, Sally, my grandmother on my dad's side. I wish I'd met you sooner, for I would have loved to have her image captured on canvas."

"Your grandmother had stories to tell?"

"None most would consider exciting. She was a very ordinary woman, but in others, extraordinary."

"How?"

"She suffered so much loss in her life, but navigated it with strength and grace. I never realised it when she was alive, but looking back, I think she's one of the strongest women I'm ever likely to meet."

"I expect your grandma Rose might give her a run for her money."

Annie smiled. "Yes, she probably could."

"And what about you? Do you consider yourself strong?"

Annie's eyes widened at the question. She'd never considered herself anything but confused, lost, and unworldly. But, now she thought about it, hadn't she weathered plenty of storms in her young life? She jutted out her chin and looked Blaine straight in the eye. "Yes," she said, "I suppose I do."

Blaine grinned. "Then, in that case, I'd like to paint you. But for now, how about a cup of coffee?"

Annie sat down in an armchair as Blaine busied himself with a kettle. Had he just offered to paint her? She shuddered with excitement.

Chapter 46

July, 1953

Rose let out a contented sigh as warm water met her skin. "It's not too hot?" asked Annie, checking the flannel against the inside of her wrist.

"It's a perfect temperature," said Rose.

"Good." Annie continued sponging Rose's wrinkled skin. She'd chosen a bar of soap that smelled of lavender, and could see the muscles in Rose's back relaxing each time the soap and water met her skin.

"We used to take baths once a week, and that was only if we were lucky. Sometimes it would be once a month." Rose chuckled at Annie's look of horror.

"Once a month?"

"Aye, that's right, lass. And it was always the eldest first. Alright for me being the eldest, but nae so good for my poor brothers and sisters."

"Are your siblings still alive?"

"I've nae idea. They left the island when I got married and moved to the Highlands."

"But you've seen them since?"

Rose shook her head slowly. "They left the island on my wedding day and that was the last I saw of them."

"That's terrible!"

"Ah, lass, it was the way things were back then. My da had died at sea, and there was no way we could keep the cottage on. It wasn't easy to travel in those days. Not like now, with ye gallivanting up and down the country."

"That's another thing we have in common, isn't it?" said Annie. "We both lost our fathers to the sea."

"Something I wish we didn't share," said Rose. "I would have been older than ye, mind, but the pain is the same. It's nae something I'd wish on anyone, losing a parent like that."

"I had nightmares for months afterwards. I still do from time to time."

"So did I." Rose's voice was quiet, and Annie wondered if this was the first time her grandmother had spoken of such things. "My da wasn't perfect. Sometimes he could be cruel to my mam, but goodness me I loved him. I was his favourite, everyone in the family knew it. It would have been easy to fall apart once he died, but my mam did that, so I had no choice but to be brave."

Annie put down the flannel she was holding and took Rose's hand. "You don't get nightmares anymore?"

"Do you know, they stopped for years, but lately they've returned? I think it's because my end is drawing near, so my thoughts have returned to Da. It won't be long till we're reunited."

"Don't talk like that," said Annie.

Rose chuckled. "Nowadays folk are scared to talk about death, but it's a fact of life, a sad one, but a fact nonetheless. I've been given more time on this earth than most, so I count my blessings that I've had this long instead of mourning the shortness of time I have left."

"Shall I wash your hair?" asked Annie, hoping to move the conversation away from the overwhelming sadness she felt.

"Aye, if it's nae too much bother. You have such kind fingers. Clara is a kind lass, but she's always in a bit of a rush and often my curls end up tangled. Dinna tell her I said so, mind. I'd hate her to think I'm nae grateful for all she does for me."

"My lips are sealed." Annie filled a jug with warm water and poured it over Rose's scalp. She filled her palm with a drop of shampoo and massaged it in. As Rose relaxed, her skin smoothed out and Annie could see the young girl who'd lost her father so many years before. "Is your father buried on the island?"

"Aye, in the churchyard."

"Would you like to lay some flowers on his grave this morning? I know my dad isn't there, but perhaps I could take some flowers too, as a sort of joint remembrance."

"What a wonderful idea," said Rose, her eyes filling with tears. "It's been too long since I visited the grave since I canna get myself there and it's nae the kind of request ye want to ask of someone."

With Rose washed and dressed, Jimmy helped her into her wheelchair and pushed it onto the street beyond the hotel. "Are you sure you don't want me to come with you?" he asked Annie.

"Thank you, Uncle Jimmy, but we'll be fine."

"You know," said Jimmy, lowering his voice, "to my knowledge Mam has never told anyone what happened to her father. She must think a lot of you to have shared such private memories."

"We think a lot of each other," said Annie with a smile. "And it's sometimes easier to talk to someone who has experienced the same thing as you."

"You are far wiser than your years, Annie."

Annie smiled, thinking how far from the truth that was. She hadn't been able to stop thinking about Blaine McCloud, and knew that was far from wise. "We won't be long," she said.

"I'll have lunch waiting for you when you get back."

It wasn't far from the hotel to the churchyard, and although navigating the narrow path with the bulky wheelchair was tricky, they found the grave of Peter Macintosh without too much difficulty.

"Here," said Annie, placing the posy Clara had helped her pick into Rose's hand. "Shall I leave you alone for a moment?"

"Would ye mind?"

"Not at all. I won't be far away, so call me if you need me."

Annie walked as far as the church gate, crossed the path and leaned on a wall that shielded a field sloping down to the beach. From her position she had a clear view of Rose, and could see her lips moving as she spoke words that had most likely lain dormant for years.

"Annie?"

"Coming." Annie retraced her steps. "Are you alright, Grandma?"

"Aye, thank you, lass. It's been such a long time since I thought of Da. It was good to remember. Would you mind laying the flowers on the grave for me?"

"Not at all." Annie leaned forward and placed Rose's posy, then her own, down on the grassy mound. She thought briefly of her own father, spoke a few silent words to him, brushed a tear from her eye, and turned her attention back to Rose. "Homeward bound?"

"Homeward bound."

Chapter 47

July, 1953

"There's a letter for you," said Olive, as Annie came down to breakfast.

"Thank you." She picked up the letter, expecting to see a Lowestoft postmark. Instead, the postmark was Cornwall and Annie felt a rush of guilt when she considered how long it had been since she last wrote to Grace. Being on the island had allowed her the space to push concerns about Grace to the back of her mind, but she owed it to her to be a better friend.

Dear Annie,

I hope you don't mind, but I got this address from Aunt Helen, who got it from your mother. It has been a little while since I last heard from you, so I wanted to check you are well. How exciting that you're spending the summer on an island! I wish I could have joined you. Is it very beautiful? I loved the postcard you sent when you first arrived, and Aunt Helen showed me a picture of the island that she found in a book, but I expect it's even more magnificent in real life.

How are things going with Sam? Is he going to visit you while you're on the island? You are so lucky to have found a good man that you like. There are no boys at my school, but those on the bus are rude and silly. I can't imagine ever wanting to be friends with them, never mind anything more.

Life here has returned to normal, or as normal as it will ever get without Uncle Richard. I still hear Aunt Helen crying at night sometimes, but those occasions are less frequent, and I heard her laughing at something on the radio the other day, which was a joy. We are finding new rhythms without Uncle Richard. I have been tending to his vegetable patch and besides the constant struggle of keeping the cats away, the plants are growing well and we ate my first crop of carrots yesterday. I also take the bins out each week, another job that was once Richard's. Slowly we are filling the gaps he left, but we will never forget him, and both think of him and miss him every day.

In case you are wondering, I continue to do well at school in all subjects other than mathematics, which I find impossible to understand. My teacher shouted at me after our last exam and questioned how I ever passed the eleven plus. I have no idea myself, but somehow I did. I came top in the class in our last English test and have a knack for learning French. What were your favourite subjects when you were at school?

It is now the summer holidays here and I am grateful for a few weeks away from the classroom. The village is full of families on holiday and some days it's a job walking along the street without bumping into someone. The weather has been fine and I've been spending most days out with my friends on our bicycles. We know a few secret beaches where we can get away from the crowds and sunbathe and swim in peace, so have been making the most of our local knowledge. The next time you come and visit, I will show you some of our favourite spots.

I shall sign off here, as I expect you are very busy, but if you find the time to write, I should very much like to hear from you, your friend Grace.

Annie folded the letter flat on her bed and reread it. From the sounds of things, Grace was doing well, but still, Annie felt terrible at her own lack of contact. Whatever the secrets around Grace's parentage, she was an innocent victim in it all, and as much in the dark as Annie. Annie shook her head and berated herself for her actions. She would reply to Grace and make sure the letter made the next post.

Dear Grace,

Please accept my apologies for my tardiness in writing to you. My only excuse is I have been caught up in all the excitement of arriving on the island, but there have been times I could have written, and I should have done so.

I am very much enjoying living in the hotel. Clara and Jimmy keep me busy and there is always some job to be done. So far I have turned my hand to everything from cleaning toilets to working behind the bar, but I think my favourite job is waitressing. The hotel chef, Steffie, is a wonder so the customers are always cheerful and I even sometimes get left a tip.

Aside from my work, I have been taking every chance I get to explore the island. It isn't all that big (about nine miles in circumference) but the scenery is so varied there is always something new to explore. My favourite place to go is the sand dunes. In fact, when I'm among them, they remind me of the dunes you can see across the estuary from Padstow. The beaches here rival Padstow too, although the harbour isn't anywhere near as busy.

I have made friends with the girl who works in the post office. Her name is Genie, and she's never travelled more than ten miles from the island! I intend to broaden her horizons while I'm here, although I don't imagine she'll ever venture too far. We had a drink together in the hotel bar on my day off last week. It is wonderful to have made friends with someone my age. Clara and Jimmy are excellent company, but they are getting on a bit and our interests are quite different.

Speaking of getting on in years, I've been spending a lot of time with my grandma, Rose. She's a bit of a battle-axe, but excellent company. She has told me some wonderful stories from the good old days, although her life when she was my age sounds dreadful. Can you believe, by the time she turned eighteen, she already had a husband, two children and another one on the way? I can't imagine anything worse!

I'll sign off now, but thank you for your letter and I promise not to leave it so long before I write to you again, Annie

Annie sealed the letter inside the envelope, then picked up a fresh piece of paper. Grace wasn't the only friend she'd been neglecting. Sam's last two letters had gone unanswered and there was no excuse.

With a pen in hand, Annie began sharing her news, and was filled with the warmth of writing to a man she knew better than anyone. Her recent foolish thoughts of Blaine pushed aside, she wrote of her explorations on the island, shared funny stories of hotel guests, and spoke of the varied tasks she undertook daily at the hotel.

When she had finished, Annie had filled six sides of writing paper and felt closer to Sam than she had in a long time. She sealed the letter in an envelope, addressed it, and held it to her heart. Eyes closed, she found she could picture Sam, imagine his arms around her, his reassuring voice in her ear. She raised the envelope to her lips and kissed it, vowing to be better, and stop all the foolish thoughts filling her mind.

The island might feel like home, but so did Sam and Grace. As she collected the letters to take to the post office, Annie made a silent promise to herself and her friends that she wouldn't be so quick to forget them again.

Chapter 48

July, 1953

Annie was trying to tame her unruly curls when a knock came on the door.

"Come in."

Clara poked her head around. "Only me."

"Is everything alright?"

"Aye, everything's grand. I wondered if you fancied joining me for a spot of shopping?"

"Shopping? On the island?"

"Don't sound so surprised," said Clara with a laugh. "This is 1953 and us islanders need clothes on our backs, too."

"But I didn't think there were any shops like that here?"

"There aren't, but every few months James Pringle the draper turns up at the Castle Hotel for the day. They bring all sorts from their shop; ladies' and children's dresses, underwear, hosiery, you name it, they'll have it. Some island women go into Berwick between times, but as we're so busy here, these sales are my only chance to replace worn out items or treat myself."

"In that case, I'd love to come with you," said Annie. "But won't you need me to be working?"

"No, the sisters are back from their mainland trip, so they can see to the bedrooms and bathrooms. I could do with your help in the restaurant later, but that will leave us plenty of time for dress shopping."

"Dress shopping? I've only seen you wear slacks since I got here."

"Don't you start about that," said Clara. "I have enough disapproval coming from your grandmother."

"She doesn't approve of your slacks?"

"Men's clothes, she calls them."

"They suit you," said Annie.

"To be honest, Annie, at my age, I couldn't care a jot whether they suit me. What matters to me is they're comfortable. It's much easier changing beds or doing the gardening in a pair of slacks. You should try them."

"Perhaps," said Annie, who was quite comfortable in her dresses, but secretly admired the bravery of her aunt's fashion choices. She might claim them to be more comfortable, but Annie could see style was also a consideration where Clara was concerned. The high-waisted, wide-legged style suited Clara's height, and paired with a silk blouse and dash of red lipstick, the outfit gave Clara a film-star aura. "I'm not sure I'd be brave enough to wear slacks," she admitted.

"What? A beautiful young thing like you? You could wear a sack and still look glamorous. And what has confidence got to do with anything?"

Annie laughed. "Perhaps I'll be persuaded to purchase a pair of slacks at the clothes sale."

"Not likely," said Clara. "James Pringle's selection is far too conservative. If you wanted to, I could buy some fabric and make you a pair?"

"Thank you, but I think you have enough to be getting on with."

Clara linked arms with Annie as they walked through the village. She stopped to greet other island women who were heading in the same direction, grateful for the chance to get away from their housework for a while.

"Do other women on the island work?" asked Annie.

"Work?" asked Clara with a laugh. "You've never met a more hard-working bunch of ladies. As well as their housework, those connected to fishing families will collect bait just as they've done for generations and there will still be nets to make and mend."

"Oh look," said Annie, "there's Genie."

Genie spotted Annie's wave and rushed over to her. "Are you two on your way to the clothes sale?"

"We certainly are," said Clara. "How are you, Genie? I missed you when you came to the hotel the other week."

"I'm very well, Mrs Watson, thank you."

"I hear you've taken Annie under your wing."

"More like the other way round," laughed Genie. "She's broadening my horizons beyond this island."

"Is she now?"

Annie laughed. "Don't worry, I'm more likely to never leave the island than drag Genie away from it."

"I'm glad to hear it," said Clara. "Here we are."

As they walked into the Castle Hotel, they were greeted by a wall of heat and the excitable chatter of ladies not granted the chance to go shopping in quite some time. Trestle tables had been placed around the edge of the room, James Pringle's wares laid out in neat displays.

"What are you looking for?" Annie asked Genie.

"Not a lot, but I could do with a new blouse. How about you?"

"I'm not sure, nothing really, but it's nice to have a browse."

"Not as exciting for you as it is for me," said Genie. "You must have hundreds of dress shops on your doorstep back home."

As they took an initial walk around the room, Annie told Genie about Chadds and how Marnie had once been supervisor of the women's department.

"You know that's how I found Jimmy again?" added Clara. "I bumped into your mam in Chadds when I went to buy a vase. The rest, as they say, is history."

"So romantic," said Annie.

Clara smiled. "Well, enough of my reminiscing. I'll leave you girls to your browsing, but, Annie, if you find something you like, I'd like to treat you."

"You don't need to do that."

"I do," said Clara, squeezing Annie's arm. "I don't get many opportunities to treat my favourite niece."

Clara wandered off, and Genie let out a long sigh. "You're so lucky to have Clara as your aunt. She's the most glamorous woman on this island. Her mother was a beauty too, according to my grandmother."

"I'm named after her," said Annie, "but never met her."

"You should ask Rose about her. They were living on the island at the same time."

"Good idea. Oh, look at this blouse," said Annie, holding up a garment of sky blue silk. "This matches your eyes perfectly."

Genie took the blouse from Annie and checked the price. "It's not too expensive. Perhaps I could wear this to Ben and Amy's wedding?"

"Oh, yes, you'd look lovely in it."

"Annie," said Clara, walking over with a petite brunette by her side. "This is Amy, Ben's fiancée."

"Lovely to meet you," said Amy. "I'm sorry we've not met until now. Ben has been off on his boat most days, and I've been busy looking after Rachel. Would you like to come back to the cottage for a cup of tea once you've finished here? You'd be welcome too, Genie. Rachel doesn't get out much these days and would love to see some friendly faces in the cottage. I could do with a natter too. Poor old Rachel's getting a bit deaf these days, so conversation can be tricky."

"I'd love to join you, as long as I wouldn't be intruding," said Annie.

"Me too," said Genie.

"Wonderful. The more the merrier. There's all sorts of gossip I've been dying to share, including a rumour about someone you'll know well." She winked at the girls, and they shared a look of confusion, wondering who on earth Amy was talking about. They hurried after her, keen to find out.

Chapter 49

July, 1953

"This is where I spent the first few years of my life," said Clara when they arrived at the cottage, "although it's very different now. Ben has added two extra rooms on the back, so there's now an indoor bathroom, and he's built a bedroom up in the eaves."

They stepped into a small kitchen that looked as if it hadn't changed in a hundred years. The only hint of modernity was a gas stove sitting against one wall. The stone walls crowded in on them and the cottage was so small, Annie struggled to imagine how anyone could have lived there without the extra rooms on the back.

"Rachel?" called Amy. "I'm home and I've brought some visitors with me."

An old lady shuffled into the room with the aid of a walking stick. "This is your mam and Jimmy's sister, Rachel," said Clara. "Perhaps you remember her from the wedding?"

"I think so," lied Annie.

"My, haven't you grown," said Rachel. "You were only a wee lass when yer mam came up here to wed. Hello, Genie, lovely to see you again."

"And you, Mrs Robson."

"Rachel, please, there's no need for formalities in this home."

"I'll put the kettle on," said Amy.

"Ben has all sorts of plans for this room," said Rachel, pulling out a wooden chair and indicating for her visitors to do the same. "Bill, my husband, used to store all his fishing gear up in the rafters, but Ben's built a bedroom up there now. He says he's slowly dragging the place into the twentieth century. Not that I'm complaining. I don't miss the days when we had a privy in the yard."

"This kitchen needs a little updating," said Amy. "A refrigerator would be a good start."

"What did ye say, lass?"

"I said a refrigerator would be a good start," said Amy, speaking slowly and loudly before patting Rachel on the arm.

"Ye can do whatever ye want to the place when yer living here," said Rachel. "Mind, the lass practically lives here already, what with all the help she gives me."

"You and Ben met when you came here for a visit?" asked Annie.

"Yes," said Amy. "I came here on holiday, met Ben and never left. I live and work at the Lindisfarne hotel and will continue working there once we're married."

"I can't wait for your wedding," said Genie.

"Yes, I'm told it will be the first the island's seen in quite some time," said Annie.

"Aye," said Rachel, "there are nae that many young couples on the island these days."

"And next to no eligible bachelors," said Genie with a sigh.

"That'll be the war for you," said Rachel. "Such a waste of those fine men's lives. Speaking of men, how's that new chap getting on up at your place?" asked Rachel.

Clara frowned.

"She means Blaine McCloud," said Amy.

"Oh, he's not that new anymore, Rachel. He's been working for us for several months now."

"Word has it he's a bit of a cad."

Annie's ears pricked up, and her heart beat faster. *Stop it*, she told herself. *It makes no difference to you if he's an old rogue.*

"Well, if he is, I've seen no evidence of it," said Clara. "He works hard, and when he's not at work, he's painting, from what I gather."

"Have you seen any of these so-called paintings?" asked Rachel.

"No," said Clara.

"Yes," said Annie, the word slipping out of her mouth before she could stop it. Four faces turned to her, their eyes wide.

"When have you seen his paintings?" asked Clara.

"I... um... well..." Annie stopped and pinched herself to focus her mind. "I was passing his cottage the other day, and the door was open. I popped my head in to say hello and he let me see some of his work."

"I'm a little envious," said Clara. "I've been asking to see his paintings ever since he arrived. What are they like?"

"Very good. Mostly portraits of ordinary people. I think you'd like them."

"Oh," said Clara, a hint of disappointment in her voice. "I was hoping he might have painted a few landscapes of the island that I could put up in the hotel."

"I'm sure he could if you commissioned one especially," said Annie.

"Aye, perhaps I'll ask him to do just that."

Amy set a pot of tea and a selection of cups and saucers down on the table. "Goodness me, I can't hold it in anymore. Blaine was the person I was talking about when I said I'd gossip to share." She stared wide-eyed at the assembled women, and they stared back.

"What did she say?" asked Rachel, holding a hand to her ear.

"Nothing," said Clara, then turning back to Amy asked with a frown, "what have you heard about Blaine? I've done nothing but sing the man's praises since he arrived. He's been a godsend."

"Well, all I'll say is I'd be careful of getting too close to Blaine McCloud," she said. "The staff at my hotel don't have a lot of time for the man."

"He's always seemed pleasant enough when he's come into the post office," said Genie. "But then again, I've not paid him much attention given he's so old."

"Old?" said Clara with a laugh. "If you think Blaine McCloud's old, I dread to think what you think of me."

"Or me," said Rachel with a cackle.

Genie flushed. "Sorry, I didn't mean he's really old, just far too old for me to be interested."

"Don't worry," said Clara, "we knew what you meant. We're only teasing. What do your colleagues have against Blaine, Amy? I've always found him to be a real gentleman."

"Everything I've heard is rumour and gossip and there's no evidence for any of it." Amy's eyes twinkled and Annie could tell she was dying to spit out whatever gossip she'd been holding in.

"We won't pass on anything you tell us," said Genie.

"Genie's right," said Clara. "Anything you say will stay between these four walls, but if you'd rather not tell us, please don't feel pressured to do so."

"Well," said Amy, trying not to look too gleeful, "the others at the hotel seem content to gossip, so I suppose there's no harm passing on what I've heard." She sat down, leaned forward, and lowered her voice. "Blaine came for a drink in the hotel one night, and that one drink turned into several. From what my colleagues said, he became quite rude and some of the hotel guests complained, but that wasn't the worst of it."

"Go on," said Clara.

"Please understand there is no evidence of this, no proof, but, well, one of the hotel guests had his wallet stolen that evening."

"And they pointed the finger at Blaine?" said Annie. "But that's ridiculous."

Amy shrugged. "Perhaps, but the hotel guest was there with a group of friends. I hardly think one of his pals would have swiped his wallet. The only other person not in their group was Blaine McCloud."

"What about the bar staff? Surely it was just as likely to be them?" asked Annie.

"There were two members of staff on that night, each able to vouch for the other. Like I said, there's no proof Blaine McCloud was involved, but out of everyone, he was the most likely candidate."

Annie felt as though she had a stone wedged in her stomach. How could they think such things of her friend? He wasn't a thief, she was sure of it. Why would people make up such horrible rumours?

"I've got a bit of a headache," said Annie, standing. "I'm afraid I need to go home and have a lie-down."

"I'll come with you," said Clara.

"No, you stay here and finish your tea. I'll be fine to walk home by myself." Before anyone could protest further, Annie thanked Amy and Rachel for their hospitality and let herself out of the cottage. What had begun as a lovely day had quickly turned sour. She refused to believe the rumours about Blaine, despite what her friends might think.

Chapter 50

August, 1953

Still angered by the gossip her friends had shared about Blaine the previous week, Annie didn't hesitate when he asked her to sit for a painting. To have a secret of her own for once felt powerful, rebellious, exciting. But as she stood in front of a ruined building in a deserted corner of the island, the first doubts entered her mind.

"What is this place?" asked Annie, as Blaine tried to push open a rotten wooden door attached by only one rusty hinge.

"It used to be someone's home, by the looks of things."

"And now?"

"As you can see, it's been derelict for a long time."

"Yes, I can see that, but why are we here?"

"I was drawn to the concept of old and new. You have the island in your blood, and yet you represent a new generation. This place is the past, you are the future."

"Very poetic," said Annie.

Blaine put his shoulder against the door and it finally gave way, expelling a cloud of dust into the air and groaning in protest. As they stepped into the abandoned cottage, it took a moment for their eyes to adjust to the gloom. Blaine went outside again and tugged at a patch of ivy covering the window. Light flooded in, and Annie shivered at what was revealed.

"It's like someone walked out one day expecting to come back, but never returned."

"Perhaps it's haunted?" said Blaine, walking to an old rocking chair and checking the wood was sound before risking sitting down.

"I don't believe in ghosts," said Annie, "which is just as well." She walked to a dust-covered wooden table and picked up a rusty pair of spectacles. Beside them was a chipped mug and a small dinner plate with a crack running along the middle.

"I suppose it must have been very lonely living all the way out here," said Blaine. "Perhaps the owner had enough one day and moved into the village?"

"You'd have thought they'd have taken their belongings with them, though, wouldn't you?"

"Alright then, maybe the owner died and had no heirs to inherit the cottage. Whatever the reason, it's clearly been empty for years."

"How did you find out about it?"

"I came across it on one of my walks and asked one of the local lads about it. No one seems to remember who it used to belong to."

"It's a shame to see it going to rack and ruin," said Annie, pulling a candlestick from the mantel and blowing dust away.

"Yes, but it's handy for us. It makes the perfect backdrop to the painting I have in mind. Can we get started now?"

"Alright, but I'm not entirely sure what you need me to do."

"Very little," said Blaine with a chuckle. "But I will need you to get changed. Here, put this on." He pulled a cream silk slip from his bag and threw it at Annie.

"I'm not wearing this!"

"Why not?"

"It's little more than underwear!"

"Lucky I brought this too then, isn't it?" said Blaine, throwing Annie a cream woollen shawl.

"I'm not sure about this..."

"You seemed excited at the thought of a painting when I first mentioned it."

There was a change in Blaine's tone. Gone was the free-spirited artist, and in its place was a man who sounded irritated and frustrated.

"Sorry," said Annie, "it's just..."

"Perhaps this was a bad idea. I should have chosen a different model, someone like Clara, or Rose, even."

"No, no, please don't. I'll wear the dress and the shawl."

"Are you sure? I don't want to make you do anything you're not comfortable with. I thought our friendship was built on trust, but if you're having second thoughts..."

"I'm not," said Annie, taking the shawl from Blaine's hand. "Where can I get changed?"

Blaine threw his hands out. "Here. Don't worry," he added, "I'll turn around."

When he had his back to her, Annie slipped off her clothes as fast as she could, letting them fall to a heap on the ground and not bothering to pick them up and fold them. She pulled on the silk slip and wrapped the shawl around her. "I'm ready."

"You look like you've just stepped out of a magazine," said Blaine, running a hand through his long hair and fixing his blue eyes on Annie.

"Where should I sit?"

"In the rocking chair."

"Like this?" asked Annie, sitting down and crossing her legs.

"No, more like this." Blaine moved Annie's limbs as though she were a mannequin in a shop. "Elbow resting on the arm of the chair, please. Tuck this ankle beneath this one. Head tilted slightly to the left. Perfect."

"Should I smile?"

"No, but keep your lips open slightly, please. Right, give me a moment to set up, then we're all ready."

By the time Blaine had set up his equipment, Annie's shoulder was aching from the unnatural position he had put it in.

"Keep still," Blaine said as he began stroking a pencil across the paper.

"I'm trying."

"Don't talk."

"Fine," hissed Annie under her breath. She distracted herself from her discomfort by watching Blaine work. He had tied his hair away from his face and his blue eyes flicked between her and his page. His tongue stuck out slightly from the corner of his mouth, lines appearing on his forehead as he frowned in concentration.

"You're so beautiful," he murmured, his hand sweeping back and forth across the page.

Annie tried to control her breathing, the knowledge that her cheeks were reddening only increasing the process until her skin felt as though it were on fire. She noticed Blaine's top lip curl, amusement sparkling in his eyes, and thought how powerful he must feel with her at his mercy.

"There's no need to feel self-conscious," he said. "You're doing really well."

I'm not doing anything, thought Annie, trying not to scratch the itch on her cheek.

An hour later, Blaine threw his pencil down onto a dust-covered table and announced, "that's enough for one day."

Annie stretched, feeling returning to her limbs. "Can I see?"

"Not yet. Here, come and sit." Blaine gestured to the rickety table and chairs in the centre of the room.

Annie pulled the shawl tighter around her shoulders and joined Blaine at the table.

"You look like you've stepped out of a 1920s silent film," he said, reaching into his bag and pulling out a bottle of wine. "You look like a star."

Unsure how to reply, Annie stayed silent, watching as Blaine filled two glasses with wine.

"To celebrate your first sitting," he said, handing Annie a glass.

"Isn't it a bit early for wine?"

"It's never too early for wine," said Blaine with a grin. He held Annie's gaze as he lifted his glass to hers. "Here's to a wonderful portrait of a beautiful girl."

Their glasses clinked and while Annie took a delicate sip, Blaine gulped down half the contents of the glass. He was left with a line of red above his top lip and Annie had to fight the urge to lift a finger to his lips and rub away the stain. The intensity of the moment left her legs like jelly, her stomach squirming as though packed with earthworms. Never had another person had such an effect on her, and Annie couldn't decide whether the sensations Blaine evoked were closer to pleasure or pain.

"We'd better be getting back," said Annie, her voice coming out as a croak.

"Yes, you're probably right. Shall we pick this up at the same time next week?"

Annie nodded, wondering what on earth she was getting herself into. Spending time with Blaine felt dangerous, but it was a danger she was powerless to resist.

Chapter 51

August, 1953

The stone skimmed across the calm surface of the water, finally sinking and sending ripples in its wake.

"I need to tell you something," said Annie.

Genie turned around, and noticing the serious expression on her friend's face, came to join her on the sand. "What's happened?" she asked, sitting beside Annie and taking her hand. "Is it something bad? Only, the look on your face is scaring me."

"I don't know if it's bad. I feel like I'm going mad."

"What happened?"

"Blaine McCloud is painting my portrait."

"Is that all?" Genie laughed.

"All? Genie, this is serious."

"An old man is painting your portrait. So what?"

"He's not old."

Genie frowned and studied her friend's face. "Oh no, Annie. Ye're not. Please tell me you're not."

"Not what?"

"Falling for Blaine McCloud, that's what."

"Of course not."

"Good, because that would be madness."

"Why?"

"Why? Well, for starters, there's the lovely Sam you keep telling me about. But even if there was no Sam, Blaine McCloud is old enough to be your father."

"No, he's not."

"He is. And there's something about him I don't trust."

"You're just taking what Amy said as gospel. There's no evidence he stole that man's wallet."

"It's not just that."

"Then what?"

"Don't you think it's strange that a man of his age is working odd jobs in a hotel supposedly so he can fund his artistic career? What about his responsibilities? Why doesn't he have a wife and children like other men his age? And if he was really such a great artist, why does he need to work in a hotel? He's living the life of a deluded twenty-year-old. And why here, on this island? Doesn't it strike you as strange that he's ended up here?"

"No, not at all. He came here for the work."

"And there were no jobs he could do where he's from?"

"Not with accommodation. He's explained it all to me."

"Hmm," said Genie. "I don't know, Annie, something about the man doesn't add up."

"Just because he's different doesn't mean he's untrustworthy. Long hair doesn't make you a criminal."

"True, but..."

"I don't know what everyone has against him." Annie stood up and in her frustration began throwing stones out into the sea.

"Calm down," said Genie, moving to stand by Annie's side. She took hold of her arm. "Stop that for a moment and sit back down."

Annie did as she was told, burying her toes into the gravelly sand. "Sorry, but it upsets me when people speak badly of Blaine."

"So I see, and that's what is worrying me."

"What do you mean?"

"Just that Blaine McCloud seems to mean an awful lot to ye. Listen, I can understand why ye may be keen on him, but truly, Annie, please don't throw your future away on a man who doesn't deserve ye."

"Who said anything about the future? Blaine's painting my portrait, that's all."

"Aye, but you know it's more than that else you wouldn't have told me. Come on, let's walk for a bit."

Genie stood up and brushed sand and shingle from her skirt. She held out a hand and pulled Annie up beside her and began following the line of the tide. Genie pointed out landmarks as they walked; the prayer caves, Guile Point in the distance, the Fenham Flats.

"Help me understand," said Genie. "What's the draw of Blaine McCloud? I can't see it myself."

"He's my friend," said Annie. "He understands me, he sees me for who I really am. We trust each other. I can tell him anything and he'll listen, truly listen. Do you know how long I've wanted to feel at home, and have people I can rely on? I feel so at home here on the island, and one reason for that is my friendship with Blaine."

"So it's just a friendship between the two of ye?"

"Yes! Nothing romantic has happened between me and Blaine. I wouldn't do that to Sam."

"I'm pleased to hear it. Let's climb up here," said Genie, pointing to a rocky outcrop that acted as steps up onto the Heugh. "When is Sam coming to visit you?"

"In a couple of weeks."

"That's good. I understand you've struck up a friendship with Blaine, but please be careful, Annie. He is so much older than you, and there's something about the man..." Genie shook her head and sighed. "Seeing Sam will do you good. From what you've told me, he's a real gentleman."

Annie stopped walking and turned to face the mainland. "What if I want more for my life?"

"More than what?"

"More than marrying a man I've known all my life and living in the same town where I was born. More than living with people I know keep secrets from me and who I no longer trust. I trust Blaine, and the life he leads is more exciting than anything I've known. Why shouldn't my life be exciting, too?"

"If it's excitement you're after, I'm not sure why you're friends with me. I must seem the most boring girl in the world to ye." Genie continued up the rocky slope, her steps faster than before.

"Don't be like that, Genie. You know what I meant."

Genie turned and stared at Annie, her hands on her hips. "Do ye know, Annie, I really don't. I have no idea what all this secrets and trust business is all about. Especially not if ye're placing your trust in Blaine McCloud over your own family." Genie stopped to take a breath and shook her head. "Of course I understand wanting a little excitement in your life, but from where I'm standing, you already have plenty. You're here, aren't ye? Miles from home, living away from your parents. Finding a good man who loves you isn't boring. It's a privilege not afforded to everyone. I'd say ye have plenty of excitement in your life and to say otherwise makes you sound like a spoiled brat."

Annie's eyes opened wide. "You think I'm a spoiled brat?"

"No, I said you sound like one."

"I should get back," said Annie, pushing past Genie and half walking, half running towards the field that would lead back to the hotel.

"Annie, come back. I didn't mean to upset you," Genie called, but Annie ignored her, breaking into a run.

Annie brushed a tear from her eye. It had been a foolish idea to confide her thoughts to Genie. How could her friend possibly understand the dilemma Annie was facing? Genie had barely left the island. Her world was so narrow. Annie almost envied the simplicity with which Genie viewed the world. *If only things were that simple for me*, thought Annie. She had lied to Genie about her feelings for Blaine. He had bewitched her and Annie couldn't imagine how she would get through Sam's visit without giving her feelings away. But what good could come from breaking things off with Sam? Blaine hadn't tried to move their friendship to anything more. All the feelings involved were on her side. If she left Sam for Blaine, all she would have achieved was breaking one man's heart for another who wasn't even interested in her.

As she drew closer to the hotel, Annie's footsteps slowed. She would do her best to avoid Blaine in the run-up to Sam's visit. That way, by the time Sam arrived, Annie would have pushed away all the foolish thoughts she was having. But when she glimpsed Blaine working in the hotel garden, Annie realised that was easier said than done.

Chapter 52

August, 1953

"Sam, good to see you," said Jimmy, taking Sam's hand in a firm shake as soon as he stepped out of the taxi. "How was the journey?"

"Long," said Sam with a smile. "But worth it to be here. How long has it been since you were down our way?"

"Three years or thereabout, and by the looks of things, you've changed from boy to man in that time."

Sam puffed out his chest, grinned at Jimmy, and gave a mock salute. "That'll be the navy for you, sir."

"Come on, sailor," said Jimmy, "the only person giving orders around here is Clara and I'm under strict instructions to show you to your room, then to take you down to the harbour."

"The harbour?"

"A picnic has been arranged in your honour."

"Is Annie already down there? I'd rather hoped she'd be here when I arrived."

"She's waiting for you with the others. She and my mother have been as thick as thieves since Annie arrived here and Mam didn't want anyone else pushing her down there."

"I see," said Sam, trying not to let his disappointment show. Jimmy was a straightforward man, but Sam couldn't shake the feeling he was making excuses for Annie. Why hadn't she been there to greet him? Much as he liked Jimmy, it wasn't quite the welcome Sam had been hoping for. Annie was looking forward to seeing him, wasn't she?

Sam followed Jimmy into the hotel. In the lobby, a family was trying to squeeze buckets, spades, a cricket set and a picnic into a large canvas bag. A couple of old boys propped up the bar, and from the back of the building came the sound of clattering pans and cheerful conversation from a busy kitchen.

"I'm sorry to descend on you at your busiest time," said Sam. "I'd hate to take the space of a paying customer, so will cover the cost of my room, of course."

"We won't hear of it," said Jimmy. "You're practically family. Besides, there isn't as much call for our single bedrooms at this time of year. Birdwatchers and ramblers avoid the busy family times."

"If you're sure, but I'd like to pay my way somehow. Perhaps there are some maintenance jobs you could throw my way?"

Jimmy laughed. "Serving your country for the past year is enough for us. Are you enjoying it, or counting the days till your time is up?"

"A bit of both," said Sam. "I've made some wonderful friends and on the whole enjoy navy life, but I'm desperate to get out on the boat with Dad, and he could use the help."

"How is Bobby getting on?"

"He's doing his best to keep things going, but he's a dying breed these days. Especially after the flood. So many fishing families have given up their boats as there's not the money in it there once was. But if anyone can make a go of it, it will be Dad. He always says he's keeping things going for Tom's sake as much as his own."

"He's a good man, your father. But I'm sure Tom wouldn't have wanted him to carry on if there isn't a livelihood to be had."

"Dad will never give up the *Sally Ann*. I'm sure what you say is true, but Dad feels he still owes it to Tom to keep the boat going."

"Perhaps, but Tom's been dead a long time and the last thing he'd have wanted was to see your family struggling for the sake of a boat."

"If I wasn't interested in fishing, Dad may feel differently," said Sam. "But knowing I'm keen to carry on the tradition gives him something to fight for."

"Good for you," said Jimmy. "I'm sure you'll be an asset to your dad's business. Here you are." He unlocked the door to a small room housing a single bed, chest of drawers, and an armchair positioned by the window.

"What a view," said Sam, walking to the window and looking out over the harbour and castle.

"Yes, this is one of our smallest rooms, but arguably has the best view. Would you like some time to unpack and settle in?"

"No, I'd like to head straight to the harbour if that's alright? I can't wait to see Annie."

"Of course," said Jimmy. He handed Sam the room key. "I'll just get my walking stick, as I'm afraid old age hasn't been kind to my gammy leg. Shall I meet you in the lobby in five minutes?"

"Perfect."

It was a further fifteen minutes before they finally set out for the harbour, by which point Sam was ready to burst with frustration. He'd been longing to see Annie for weeks, and would have run to the harbour were he not being slowed by Jimmy and his limp.

"I can see I'm slowing you down," said Jimmy. "Why don't you go on ahead?"

"Sorry," said Sam. "Is my impatience that obvious?" He laughed and slowed his steps. "I feel like a child on Christmas Eve at the thought of seeing Annie, but we'll have plenty of time, so I'll walk with you. It must be frustrating for you, not being as mobile as you once were?"

"Aye," said Jimmy, "although in truth I used to drag my feet going down to the harbour as a young lad, but for quite different reasons."

"Oh?"

"I used to fish with my da, just like you plan to do with yours. The difference being, my da was an evil man, and yours is a gentleman."

"Would you have taken over your dad's boat if you'd stayed on the island?"

Jimmy shook his head. "No, he made it clear what he thought of me and would never have passed the boat down to me. You know he tried to drown me once?"

"What?" Sam stopped walking and stared at Jimmy. "Your own father tried to drown you?"

"It was the main reason I left this place," said Jimmy. "It took me years to summon the courage to return, even after Da was long dead and buried."

"Do you regret coming back?"

They had reached the far corner of the harbour. Jimmy lifted his walking stick and pointed to a group of women sitting on a rug spread across the grass. "How could I have regrets? Look at all I have now."

Chapter 53

August, 1953

Annie watched Sam and Jimmy walking towards them. She should have been waiting at the hotel to greet Sam when he arrived. She'd been a coward not to. As they drew closer, Annie stood. Sam was wearing a pair of navy slacks with a short-sleeved white shirt tucked into the waistband. A jacket hung over one arm and his hair had been teased from its neat Brylcreemed side-parting by the breeze. He looked as handsome as a film star and Annie could have kicked herself for letting her eye wander.

"Annie," said Sam when he reached her, leaning over and kissing her cheek.

"It's lovely to see you," she said. "We've prepared a welcome picnic for you, as it's such a beautiful day. Please, sit down." Sam smiled at Annie and sat on the rug. "You remember my Aunt Clara and Grandma Rose?"

"Of course," said Sam. "It's lovely to see you again after so long."

"How is your mam?" asked Clara.

"Very well, thank you. She told me to send her love and tell you to pay a visit to Lowestoft so you can see her new house."

"Oh yes, I heard she'd moved up to the town. Just in the nick of time, too, given what happened with the flood."

"Yes, she was certainly relieved to be on higher ground that night."

"Give the lad a bite to eat," said Rose. "He must be hungry after his long journey."

"That I am, Mrs Watson."

"Rose. Call me Rose."

"Very well then, thank you, Rose. Would you like me to put together a plate of food for you?"

Rose smiled. "That would be very thoughtful of ye. Thank ye, Sam."

Clara raised an eyebrow at Annie, who tried not to laugh. It was strange hearing the brusque Rose so easily charmed. Few people managed it these days, particularly not men.

Annie opened the wicker picnic basket and began serving out the food Steffie had prepared for them. She'd thought of everything from home-made pork pies to fruit cake, and several gulls swooped overhead, drawn by the feast below.

"This is a rather fine welcome," said Sam as Annie handed him a plate. She caught his eye and smiled.

They were coming to the end of their meal when a shadow was cast over them. Annie looked up to see Blaine blocking the sun. An intense blush swept across her skin as Blaine looked from her to Sam.

"This looks like a fine picnic you're having."

"Good afternoon, Mr McCloud," said Jimmy, his voice devoid of its usual warmth.

"I thought you were helping Steffie in the kitchen this afternoon?" asked Clara.

"That's why I'm here," explained Blaine. "She asked me to come and see if the fishermen can supply another lobster for tonight's meal. More bookings have come in and she's worried there won't be enough to go around."

"I see," said Clara. "It's a shame you won't have time to join us for a piece of cake."

Blaine checked his watch and glanced around the harbour. "It doesn't look as though the chap I need is here yet, so I'm sure I could spare a few minutes."

As he lowered himself down onto the grass, Annie noticed Jimmy pull a face at Clara and receive a shrug in return.

"I don't think we've met," said Blaine, extending a hand out to Sam. "I'm Blaine McCloud. I work up at the hotel."

"So I'd gathered. I'm Sam, Annie's... Annie's..."

"My friend," interrupted Annie. "Sam is one of my oldest friends from Lowestoft and he's come for a visit."

"And his mam is one of my best friends," added Clara, "so that practically makes him family."

"I see. And how long are you staying on the island, Sam?"

"Only a few days, unfortunately. I'm in the middle of my National Service and leave is limited."

"That is a shame," said Blaine, the tone of his voice suggesting otherwise.

"Sam's in the navy," said Jimmy. "And a fine job he's doing too if what I hear is to be believed."

"Then I thank you for your service to our fine country," said Blaine, his voice dripping with sarcasm.

"Thank you. Did you serve during the last war?"

"Oh, look, there's the chap I was coming to meet," said Blaine, ignoring Sam's question and jumping to his feet.

"Don't you want to finish your cake?" asked Clara.

"No, you have it. I'd best be off."

Blaine set off to the far side of the harbour and the others watched him go.

"I'd nae be surprised if he shirked his duty during the war," muttered Rose. "Fellows like him care for none but themselves."

"Grandma, that isn't very kind," scolded Annie.

"I'm sure if Blaine didn't serve, he would have had his reasons," said Jimmy before adding under his breath, "perhaps he didn't want to cut off his long locks."

Clara clapped her hands. "That's enough meanness, thank you very much. We're here to celebrate Sam's arrival, not slander our staff members. Have another slice of cake, Sam."

"Thank you."

"Are you alright, Mam?" asked Jimmy, as Rose gave a wide yawn.

"Aye, it's all this sea air making me tired."

"Why don't we pack up and get you home," said Jimmy. "Annie and Sam, there's no need to come with us. I'm sure you have plenty to catch up on."

"We could have a walk to the castle?" suggested Sam.

"I really don't mind helping clear up," said Annie.

"No, you two go off and enjoy yourselves. We'll see you back at the hotel."

"Alright."

Annie and Sam said their goodbyes and began walking towards the castle. The sun was sinking in the sky, the surrounding light soft, the air warm. It was one of the most beautiful evenings Annie had witnessed since she arrived. Sam took Annie's hand, and they walked in silence.

"That chap Blaine seemed a little strange," said Sam, breaking through the serenity of the evening.

"Strange? In what way?"

"Well, he wasn't very friendly."

"What are you talking about? He was perfectly friendly."

"Why are you defending him?"

"I'm not, but he's my friend and I don't like hearing him spoken about like that."

"Your friend? What could the two of you possibly have in common?"

"You know nothing about the man and have spent less than five minutes in his company, so I'm not sure how you feel able to judge."

Sam stopped walking, took Annie's hands, and smiled. "Let's not argue when I've only just arrived. It's you I'm interested in, not some long-haired chap who interrupted our picnic."

Annie smiled back at Sam, feeling foolish for sticking up for Blaine. He was a fantasy, not a reality. Her future was staring down at her with his wide green eyes, and she'd be a fool to feel anything but love for him.

Chapter 54

August, 1953

"Annie."

The whisper that came out of the darkness made Annie jump and drop the bag of rubbish she was carrying. "Who's there?" she whispered back.

Blaine stepped out from the shadows and smiled at her.

"What are you doing lurking around in the dark?"

"I could hardly come and knock on your bedroom door, could I? I wouldn't want that jumped-up cadet boxing my ears."

"If you're talking about Sam, he'd do more than box your ears if he heard you describing him like that."

Blaine grinned. "Please accept my apologies for insulting your friend."

"What do you want, Blaine? It's late, I'm just finishing up for the evening and I'll fall asleep on my feet if I don't make it to my bed soon."

"I thought you might like to see how your painting is progressing."

"You've done more to it? But I haven't had another sitting yet."

"I've finished the rough sketch. I'll tidy it up and start adding some colour during our next sitting. You seemed keen to see it the other day, but if you're not interested, I shan't be offended."

"I'd love to see it," said Annie, "but do I have to see it now?"

"It's now or never," said Blaine. "But like I said, if you're not interested..." He began walking away.

"No, wait, I'll come and see it."

"Wonderful." Blaine picked up the bag of rubbish Annie had dropped, flung it into the nearest bin, then took her hand and walked with her to his cottage.

The inside of the cottage was pitch black. Blaine pulled a box of matches from his pocket, struck one and held the flame to a lamp. "They've not installed electric light into the cottage yet," he explained.

"I see. When I last came here, I thought all the candles were for effect."

"No," said Blaine with a laugh. "They're a necessity. Take a seat on the bed and I'll bring the picture over."

Annie did as she was told, slipping her tired feet out of her shoes and curling her legs beneath her. Blaine laid a large leather folder on the table and unzipped it, pulling out a sheet of thick paper. He carried it over to Annie, but rather than show her, he held the paper behind his back.

"Are you sure you want to see it before it's finished? It might be better to wait."

Annie covered her mouth with her hand to hide a yawn. "As you've dragged me over here in the middle of the night, I may as well take a look."

"Alright, but remember, this is only a sketch."

Blaine sat down on the bed beside Annie and placed the paper on her lap. Annie stroked a finger across the rough pencil lines, the beauty of his work stealing words from her mouth.

"You don't like it," said Blaine, snatching the drawing away.

"It's beautiful," said Annie, pulling the paper back and staring down at it. "It's like me, only better, prettier."

"No," said Blaine. "I never lie in my drawings or paintings. What is on the paper is what I see, no better, no worse. You are a very beautiful woman, Annie."

"Thank you." Annie's breath caught as Blaine brushed a handful of curls from her shoulder and stroked a finger along the skin of her neck. "What are you doing?" asked Annie, her voice catching.

"Don't you like it?" Blaine took her silence as affirmation, leaned forward and began placing feather-light kisses from her ear to her collarbone.

"Stop it," she said, jumping up from the bed and folding her arms around herself.

"I'm sorry," said Blaine, walking up to her and placing a hand on her shoulder. "I mistook your silence for an invitation."

Annie shrugged off Blaine's hand. She turned to look at him, her heart full of conflict. "We can't. It wouldn't be fair to Sam."

"So it's not that you don't want to?"

Annie looked down at the floor. "It wouldn't be fair to Sam," she said again.

"I thought your little sailor chap was just a friend? Wasn't that how you introduced him to me?"

"It's more complicated than that." Annie's fingers felt for the charm bracelet she had worn on her wrist every day since Sam had given it to her.

"I see," said Blaine.

"You see what?"

"That there's some sort of arrangement between the pair of you. You're waiting until he's finished his National Service, is that it?"

"Whatever is going on between me and Sam is none of your business."

"Whatever you say," said Blaine. "Only that letter you told me about, that secret... how do you know your precious Sam isn't in on it too? He could be lying to you, Annie, just like all the others." He took a step towards Annie and stroked her cheek, his fingers resting on her lips as he stared into her eyes. "I'm the only person you can truly trust, and I think you know it."

Blaine took another step forward and Annie felt her heart hammering inside her chest. She could feel his whole body against hers, causing her skin to tingle and burn like it was on fire. "Stop it." Her voice came out as a whisper. "Please."

Blaine cupped Annie's face with his hands and leaned forward to kiss her.

"No!" Annie found her voice and pushed hard against his chest. He stumbled backwards, looking at her not with anger, but with something more akin to amusement. Not trusting herself to spend another moment in Blaine's presence, Annie turned and ran from the cottage, only slowing as she reached the front door of the hotel.

"Annie?" The cook, Steffie, was coming out of the kitchen having finished for the evening. "What were you doing out there?"

"Taking out the rubbish."

"You've been gone quite some time."

"I was looking at the stars."

Steffie frowned, wished Annie goodnight and made her way to the door. When she stepped outside, Annie noticed her glance up into the murky darkness, the sky full of clouds. "Looking at the stars, were you?" Steffie raised an eyebrow, then gave a little chuckle. "Don't worry, lass. What you get up to or with who is none of my business. My lips are sealed."

"I wasn't..." began Annie, but Steffie was already walking away.

Chapter 55

August, 1953

"Just these please," said Sam, placing a handful of postcards down on the shop counter.

"Certainly, sir," said Genie. She slipped the postcards into a paper bag and twisted the corners. "That will be fivepence, please."

Sam handed over the coins with a smile. "I don't suppose you're Miss Guthrey, are you?"

"Who's asking?"

"Sam Thorn, I'm a friend of Annie Hearn's."

Genie's smile widened, and she took Sam's outstretched hand and shook it. "Genie Guthrey. It's a pleasure to meet you. How are you finding the island?"

"It's a wonderful place," said Sam. "I have visited before, but I was a lot younger and it's different viewing it through adult eyes."

"I expect Annie's been showing you all the sights?"

A frown crossed Sam's handsome face before he forced his features into a smile. "Actually, Annie's been busy with her work. So we've not had as much time to spend together as I would have liked."

"What a pity. I know she's been so excited about your visit."

"She has?" Sam heard the hope in his voice and cursed his obvious desperation.

"Oh, aye," said Genie. "She'll be as disappointed as you are not to have had much time together."

"Thank you," said Sam as Genie handed him the paper bag. "And I hope you don't think I'm complaining?"

"Not at all," said Genie, bidding Sam farewell with a smile.

Sam stepped out of the post office onto a busy street drenched in sunlight. The inaccessibility of the island hadn't put folk off, and there were even a couple of motor cars parked along the street. Jimmy had mentioned the plans for a new causeway to be built, and Sam wondered how it would change the feel of the place. He suspected he was witnessing the end of an era, and that by the following summer the place would be overrun with day-trippers able to access the island in the motor cars, which were becoming so popular among the middle classes.

The conversation with Genie had left him feeling brighter, and he hoped she'd been telling the truth about Annie looking forward to his visit. Before arriving on the island, Sam had imagined Annie rushing to embrace him upon his arrival, moonlit walks, stolen kisses, talking late into the night. He'd hoped she would notice the change in him that others saw; the confidence, maturity, and reliability his time in the navy had instilled in him.

Instead, Annie seemed too busy to spend any meaningful time with him. She spoke to him as if he were still a boy rather than the man he knew he had become. If only he could open her eyes to who he really was, rather than the past version she knew from childhood.

Other women noticed the recent changes in him. He was never short of a girl to dance with down in Portsmouth and had several propositions lately from young ladies with dubious morals. The women he met while in uniform didn't see him as a boy, if their appreciative looks and muttered comments were anything to go by.

And it wasn't just the women. The chaps he worked with day after day respected him and saw him as a leader. So, why did Annie seem unable to recognise any of those changes?

"Are you alright there? You look a little lost."

"Oh, hello, Jimmy. No, I'm not lost, just contemplating which pub to acquaint myself with. I don't suppose you'd like to join me? Annie's chambermaiding and I've found myself at a loose end."

"Ah, yes, I'm sorry you've not had much time together. We've been run off our feet this week and without Annie's help, I'm not sure how we'd have managed."

"I completely understand. It's no one's fault. So, how about that drink?"

Jimmy glanced at his watch. "I think I can find time for a swift one. Let's go to the Ship Inn."

"Lead the way."

The pub was busy. Locals crowded the bar, the looks they cast to visitors a mix of curiosity and disapproval. Jimmy walked up to the bar and introduced Sam to the assembled men. As soon as they learned he was from a fishing family, they welcomed him as one of their own. In fact, the welcome was so warm, it took fifteen minutes before they could extricate themselves to find a table.

"Fishing's a universal language," said Jimmy, taking a sip of his pint.

"That's true enough. If it weren't for the men's accents, I could well be in the Rising Sun."

"So, how are you getting on in the navy?"

Sam smiled and wiped the froth of beer from his top lip. "I'm getting on very well, thank you. Did Annie tell you about my promotion to Able Seaman?"

"No," said Jimmy, "she must have forgotten. That's wonderful news."

"Thank you," said Sam, hiding his disappointment that the news hadn't been exciting enough for Annie to share. "And I heard last week I'm being promoted again, this time to Leading Seaman."

"Congratulations," said Jimmy, giving Sam a hearty clap on the back. "Your family must be so proud, and Annie, of course."

"I haven't actually told Annie about this latest promotion. I was planning to as soon as I got here, but there hasn't been the right time."

"My lips are sealed until you've had the chance to share your news."

"Thank you. There was mention of officer potential, but I've always made it clear to my superiors that while I'll give National Service my all, fishing is where my heart lies, not the navy."

"It's good to know your own mind," said Jimmy. "You're an impressive young man, Sam Thorn."

"Thank you," said Sam, appreciating the compliment, but wishing that rather than coming from Jimmy, it was coming from his niece.

Chapter 56

August, 1953

"I would have thought we'd have had some more time together, that's all."

Annie sighed and ran her hands through her hair. This was the closest to an argument she and Sam had come since the day he arrived, and she knew it was all her fault. "I told you before you came that I'd need to work while you were here."

"Yes, but I didn't expect you to be busy every minute of every day. I'm sorry, Annie, but it feels as though you are actively avoiding me."

"Avoiding you? For goodness' sake, Sam. It was you who came at the busiest time of year."

"It was when my leave fell! You can't blame me for that."

"And you can't blame me for working."

"Perhaps I should speak to Jimmy and Clara, explain that I've only got one full day left and it would be nice to spend some time with you."

"No! It wouldn't be fair to bother them. They're flat out and exhausted."

"Fine." Sam turned and stomped out of the restaurant.

"Wait," called Annie. "I'll see whether I can take tomorrow off. Even if I can't take the full day, we could spend a few hours together."

"Thank you. I'll leave you alone now. Goodnight."

"Goodnight. I'll see you in the morning."

After finishing work, when she was finally tucked up in bed, Annie reflected on Sam's anger. Whilst his visit hadn't been a disaster, it could hardly be characterised as a success. And although it pained her to admit it, it was true she had been avoiding Sam. How could she not? Blaine had placed a kernel of distrust in her mind and it nagged at her every time she was with Sam.

In her rational moments, Annie knew she could trust Sam with her life. She'd spoken to him enough about the letter and her suspicions concerning Grace, and was sure he was as much in the dark as she was. He was so sweet and kind, but the only man occupying her thoughts was Blaine. *I'm a horrible person*, thought Annie, a wave of self-pity washing over her. When she finally fell asleep, dawn was already breaking on the day Annie was dreading.

Over breakfast the next morning, Sam kept casting glances at Annie that she did her best to ignore. Given it was Sam's last day on the island, the whole family had gathered in the dining room for breakfast, even Rose making an unusually early appearance.

"What are your plans for the day?" asked Jimmy, cracking a hard-boiled egg with his spoon.

"A walk, I think," said Annie, knowing her voice sounded flat.

"I don't wish to interfere in your plans," said Clara, "but if it's of interest to you, my brother Ben would be happy to take you out on his boat. Please say if that sounds too much like a busman's holiday."

Sam's eyes lit up, a wide smile spreading across his face. "That sounds absolutely wonderful. Are you sure it's no bother?"

"He'd be delighted to have you aboard, and you, Annie."

"Oh," said Annie, "wouldn't you prefer to go just the two of you? I thought it was bad luck having a woman on board."

"These men and their superstitions," sighed Clara. "I don't see why it would be a problem. Ben would take you to see the sights, it wouldn't be a usual working day."

"Don't you want to come?" asked Sam, his voice quiet, his eyes downcast.

"No, it's not that," said Annie, trying to force a brightness she didn't feel into her voice. "I just thought you'd like some time to talk about fishing, and that's not a subject I'm well versed in."

"Ye should take an interest, though," said Rose. "Ye may not be out fishing yourself, but it's part of yer heritage. Fishing's been in both sides of yer family for centuries."

"Well said, Mam," said Jimmy with a smile.

Annie placed her discarded napkin down on her plate. "I should probably go upstairs and put on some warmer layers if we're heading out to sea."

"Perhaps ye could help me back to my bedroom first," asked Rose.

"I can do that," said Clara.

"I'd like Annie to help me, if that's alright?"

"Of course," said Annie.

Annie stood and took control of Rose's wheelchair, pushing her back along the corridor to her bedroom. "Would you like me to help you back into bed?" asked Annie when they reached the room.

"No, not today. Can ye help me into the chair by the window?"

"Of course."

"And open it, too. I feel the need to smell the sea today."

"Have you ever been out on a boat, Grandma?"

"Not likely. I'm far happier on dry land."

"Then why were you so insistent I should go?"

"Sit," said Rose, pointing in the vague direction of a spare armchair.

"Is everything alright?"

"Nae."

"What's wrong? Do you feel unwell?"

"It's nothing to do with me, lass," said Rose. "It's ye that needs yer head examining."

"What are you talking about?"

"Ye and that lovely chap of yers."

"I don't understand."

Rose sighed. "Ye canna see what's right in front of ye, can ye? I may be blind, but I can see better than ye can."

"Grandma..."

"Nae," said Rose, holding up a hand. "Ye need to listen to me, lass. It's plain as day yer mooning after that scoundrel Blaine McCloud. Nae good can come of that match, believe me. He's nae good enough for ye."

"I don't..."

"Enough!" Rose's voice was sharp, and Annie felt tears spring to her eyes. "Ye have nae idea how lucky ye are. I loved a good, kind man once, but he dinna love me back and I ended up saddled with Alex Watson more's the pity. Blaine reminds me of Alex, and ye'd do well to stay clear. Unlike me, ye have the chance to end up with a good man. I dinna need eyes to know that chap Sam loves ye. Ye can hear it in his voice. Throw that away and ye'll never forgive yerself."

"What about love?" asked Annie, her voice quiet.

"Love?" Rose spat the word, as though it tasted foul on her tongue. "What do ye kna about love? Ye've had yer head turned by charm and a handsome face. If ye think that's love, yer mistaken, lass. Open yer eyes and see what's right in front of ye. If ye canna do that, there's no helping ye."

Annie bristled. Who was Rose to be dishing out advice? She'd admitted to being a poor mother and living with an unhappy marriage. She was the last person Annie should take advice from. "Thank you for your concern, but I can assure you I can look after myself. Now, if you're comfortable, I need to get ready for our boat trip."

Rose said nothing, just closed her eyes and waved Annie away. Only as Annie was leaving the room did Rose speak. "Ye'd do well to heed my words, lass, or ye'll find yerself in a fair bit of bother."

Annie let the door close behind her, thinking how little Rose knew about romance.

Chapter 57

August, 1953

Sam climbed over a low stone wall and reached out his hand for Annie.

"Thank you," she said, knowing she could have negotiated the wall without his help, but deciding it would be churlish to refuse.

Annie jumped down onto the springy grass, the wide harbour stretching out before them. They crossed the field, a flock of curious sheep watching them from a distance.

"What's Clara's brother like?" asked Sam.

"I don't know him very well. He works hard and is out at sea most days and even some nights. From the little I've seen of him, he seems a nice enough chap. He's getting married next week."

"Good for him. Do you know, I can't wait to get out on the water. Obviously I'm at sea a lot with the navy, but a boat is very different from a ship, and there's nothing quite like being out on the open water feeling the movement of every wave beneath you, the wind in your face."

"Have you always wanted to follow in your dad's footsteps? You've never seen anything different in your future?"

Sam laughed. "Fishing on the *Sally Ann* is all I've wanted to do since I was a boy, you know that."

"Yes, but I always wondered whether that is what you truly wanted to do, or whether you wanted to please your dad."

"I'd not go into fishing if I didn't want to. Not the way the industry is going."

"I suppose that's my point. It's a completely different way of life from when my dad and yours started out. Times have changed. There are different paths your life could take."

"Oh yes, like what?"

"Well, there's the new Birds Eye factory for starters, and those types of businesses are only going to increase. You could get a position there and work your way up."

"Are you sure this is about me?" asked Sam, frowning.

"What do you mean?"

"You've been behaving strangely since I arrived. Is this about my future as a fisherman? Is it too lowly a profession for you?"

"Not at all."

"Are you sure? Because it sounds like you want a factory supervisor on your arm rather than a simple fisherman."

"That's not what I meant. There's nothing simple about fishing. It's a skilled, dangerous job. I, of all people, know that. I was just wondering whether taking over the *Sally Ann* was the extent of your ambitions." Annie cringed, aware of how pompous she sounded. It wasn't as though she had any grand ambitions of her own. But Blaine McCloud and his talk of Paris had opened her eyes to a different way of living, possibilities she couldn't un-see.

"The extent of my ambitions? My father is as astute a businessman as any chap working in an office. Fishing may be manual work, but these days, more than ever, to make a success of it, you need brains as well as brawn. I'll be able to bring that to the *Sally Ann*. With my help, we'll turn things around. I would have thought you would have had more faith in me, in my desire to make a success of what was once your dad's boat."

"I do, it's just..."

"Just what, Annie? Forgive me if I'm wrong, but it feels as though you're trying to find fault. Do you want to argue? Is that it?"

"Of course not."

With a heavy sigh, Sam stomped towards the harbour, and Annie had to jog to keep up. She could tell he was angry, that her questioning had upset him, but couldn't, or didn't want to make amends. Why shouldn't she ask questions of the man everyone assumed she would marry? Surely, if she was to spend her life with Sam, she had every right to know how far his ambitions extended.

"Annie!"

Annie was relieved to see the bear-like form of Ben leaning against a rickety-looking shed. Sam reached Ben first, introducing himself and turning pale as Ben extended a finger-crushing handshake.

"Good to meet you," said Sam, removing his hand from Ben's and giving it a surreptitious shake behind his back. "Thank you for agreeing to take us out on your boat."

"You're very welcome. I rarely get to mull over the industry with fishermen from other waters. Long gone are the days when island boats travelled south in search of herring."

"The glory days," said Sam with a smile. "Dad's told me about them, even though he was very young at the time."

"Aye," said Ben, "and Jimmy's told me all about the famous year of 1913. I'm so envious of him experiencing that, even if he stopped fishing soon after."

"Dad's got some wonderful photographs and newspaper cuttings from those days. I'll send you some copies if you like?"

"Aye, if it's nae bother, I'd love to see them."

"I'm sorry to interrupt," said Annie, "but if you pair would like to spend the day comparing notes on fishing grounds, I really don't mind sitting the trip out."

"Of course not," said Ben. "Besides, me and Sam can meet up later for a pint to talk fishing, if ye'll have time?"

"I'm sure I can find a spare hour or two," said Sam, who was grinning like a cat who'd got the cream.

"So, Ben," said Annie as he took her hand and helped her climb aboard, "where are you going to take us?"

"I thought we could visit the Farne Islands," said Ben. "They're famed for their wildlife. We'll nae go ashore, but from the boat you'll be able to see puffins, kittiwakes, shags, guillemots, and that's just for starters."

"How exciting," said Sam, grinning at Annie and following Ben into the wheelhouse with the enthusiasm of a small boy in an ice cream parlour.

"Do you want to join us in here?" asked Ben, "or are you happy out on deck?"

"I'm happy out here," said Annie, walking to the bow and enjoying the breeze on her face as Ben started the engine and steered the boat beyond the harbour and out into open sea.

The breeze grew stronger, teasing the water below into bumpy mounds, white horses spraying plumes into the air as the bow cut across them. Annie held tight to the gunwale, her heart lifting as brilliant white gulls ducked and dived around the boat, wispy cotton clouds scudding across the deep blue expanse of sky that stretched from island to island.

The boat drew closer to a cluster of islands and Annie heard the engine's roar drop a tone as their speed slowed. Ahead of them was a sheer cliff of jagged rock, a tricolour of white, grey and brown jutting out into navy water. Birds of all varieties perched on the rocky outcrops casting a few curious glances at the boat before getting back to their preening and hunting for food.

"Isn't this spectacular?" said Sam, joining Annie on deck and slipping an arm around her waist.

"Yes, it really is."

"We'll go around this island and on to the next," called Ben. "Keep an eye out for puffins and seals. The puffins will be getting ready to leave, so there'll nae be as many as earlier in the year, but we're bound to see a few."

"Where will they go when they leave here?" asked Annie.

"Out to sea. They spend most of their lives at sea, just like me and Sam here," said Ben with a chuckle.

Ben disappeared back into the wheelhouse and moments later, Sam's arm shot out, pointing in the distance. "Look, I see some puffins."

"Oh yes," said Annie. As she watched the little birds, she was transported to a time earlier in the year, many miles away when she'd seen the same birds, but in very different company.

"Are you alright?" asked Sam.

"Yes," said Annie, unable to drag her mind away from Jack and Grace and into the present moment.

Before Sam could quiz her further, Ben turned off the engine, dropped the anchor and joined them on deck. "I brought some refreshments," he said, grinning and pulling three bottles of beer from a canvas bag.

"Good man," said Sam, taking a bottle and clinking it against Ben's.

"Annie?" Ben held out a bottle, but she shook her head and politely declined. "All the more for us then," he said, clinking his bottle for a second time against Sam's.

Annie sat down and leaned against the hull, enjoying the sound of birds screeching around her, waves tapping against wood, and the feel of the warm sun on her face. She pushed away thoughts of Padstow and resolved to focus on the present moment. It was the least Sam deserved.

Chapter 58

August, 1953

"Are you drunk?"

"What? No," said Sam, stumbling into a chair as he staggered through the bar.

"I knew it was a bad idea when you and Ben headed off to the pub. How much did you have to drink?"

"Only three pints."

"And the rest," muttered Annie, scowling.

Sam flung himself down on a barstool, which wobbled precariously for a moment. "Have I upset you?"

Annie sighed. "No."

"It sounds like you're upset."

"I'm not."

Sam raised an eyebrow and burped. "Excuse me."

"Why don't you get to bed and sleep it off? You need to be up early tomorrow."

"It's our last night together."

"Yes, but you've come home drunk, so clearly spending time with me wasn't a priority."

"What?" The word was slurred, but there was no mistaking the anger in Sam's voice. "How dare you!"

"There's no need to raise your voice."

"I'd say there's every need." Sam climbed off his stool, walked behind the bar, poured himself a measure of whisky and downed it in one gulp. He slammed his empty glass down on the bar and stared hard at Annie. "You haven't wanted to spend any time with me since the moment I arrived. I've used all my leave and spare money to come and visit you, and you've repaid me by avoiding me."

"That's not fair. I went out on the boat with you today."

"Only because you didn't have a choice. Just admit it, Annie."

"Admit what?"

"Whatever it is you've not been brave enough to say. Don't you love me anymore, is that it?"

Annie shook her head.

"Have you met someone else?"

Annie shook her head again, but felt her cheeks warming.

Sam took a step back. "I know you too well, Annie. It's written all over your face. Who is he?"

"I've not betrayed your trust, I promise you that."

"You haven't answered my question."

"Please, Sam, don't do this."

"Do what? All I'm asking for is a name."

"Nothing has happened."

"But you've wanted it to. Who is he?" Sam's face was a similar colour to his hair as he leaned over Annie, gripping hold of her arms.

In what couldn't have been worse timing, at that moment in walked Blaine, looking as handsome in person as in the dreams Annie had each night.

"Annie? What's going on? Get your hands off her, now!" Blaine stormed through the bar, grabbing Sam by the scruff of the neck and dragging him into the room. "Customers are not allowed behind the bar, especially not the type who'll threaten the staff."

"Blaine, please stop." Annie rushed over to the two men, grabbing hold of Blaine's raised fist. "Me and Sam were talking, that's all."

"It didn't look like talking to me," growled Blaine, his face set in a scowl.

"Please, Sam wasn't hurting me, I promise."

Blaine looked from Annie to Sam, then set Sam straight on his feet and patted him on the arm. "I shouldn't have tried to play the hero, but you must understand what it looked like when I walked in. Are you alright? Did I hurt you?"

Sam ignored Blaine, his eyes wide with sadness as he turned to Annie. "I see what's going on here." His voice was quiet, his shoulders slumped. "Yes, I can see things clearly now. I'd better get to bed. Goodnight."

"Sam..."

"Goodnight, Annie."

Annie watched a defeated-looking Sam trudging out of the bar and felt a rush of self-loathing. She'd just hurt one of the kindest men she knew. And for what? A fantasy that could never be reality? What was wrong with her?

"Sam!" she called, running after his departing back. Before she caught him up, he had reached his bedroom, and without turning around, he stepped inside, locking the door behind him. Annie tried knocking, but Sam refused to answer, and not wanting to disturb the other guests, she gave up and walked back to the bar.

Blaine was waiting for her on the bar stool recently vacated by Sam. "I'm so sorry, Annie. I can see I've put my foot in it, but the way Sam was behaving, well it just proves my point, doesn't it? He can't be trusted.

Surely you see that now? Goodness knows what he would have done to you had I not stepped in when I did."

Annie shook her head. Sam wouldn't have hurt her... would he? "I thought you were visiting friends on the mainland and not back till tomorrow?" she said quietly, pouring herself a measure of gin.

"I came back early."

"Why?"

"I missed you."

Annie looked up, surprised. Blaine had known Sam was visiting. Had his premature return been an act of chivalry to fight for her affections, or a calculated move to disrupt her relationship with Sam? Blaine's piercing blue eyes bored into her own, the rush of emotions his gaze provoked only confusing Annie further.

Blaine reached out across the bar and took Annie's hand in his. "I know your situation is complex. I know that I'm not deserving of you. You need time, I see that. But I wanted you to know that should you choose me, I will be ready and waiting." He lifted Annie's hand to his lips and kissed it. "Goodnight, Annie Hearn," he said softly, before climbing off his stool and walking away.

Annie stood watching his departing back, feeling stunned. Her life had just shifted course in a new direction, and she wasn't sure she could keep up with the rapid change. After wiping down the bar and stacking the glasses, Annie made her way to her bedroom, knowing she was unlikely to get a wink of sleep.

When Annie came down for breakfast the next morning, there was an empty seat at the table. "Where's Sam?"

"He's already left," said Jimmy, handing Annie an envelope. "He asked me to make sure you got this."

"Thank you." Annie took the envelope and slipped it into her pocket. "I'm not hungry this morning, so if you don't mind, I'll get ready for the day upstairs."

"Of course," said Clara. She reached out and squeezed Annie's hand. "It's alright to be sad Sam has gone."

Annie smiled at Clara and left the room. Once back in the quiet of her bedroom, Annie tore open the letter and flopped down onto the bed to read it.

Dear Annie,

I'm sorry I didn't wait to say goodbye, but I didn't want to risk the tide, and under the circumstances, I don't think there's much left to say. I'm very hurt by what has happened between us, but I still consider myself your best friend, and I have loved you for as long as I remember. At the moment, I can't imagine my life without you in it, but in time I shall have to get used to the idea, and I'm sure I will. But, Annie, my greatest wish is for you to be happy. It's all I've ever wanted. I see now that the only way I can make you happy is to let you go. I'm sorry I wasn't enough for you, but wish you all the best for your future. Yours, Sam.

Tears streamed down Annie's face as she read Sam's note. Her grandmother was right. Rose was the one who could see clearly, and it was Annie who had been blind. The kindest man she'd ever known had just walked out of her life and it was all her fault. Annie walked across to the window and looked out onto the hotel lawn. Blaine was pushing a lawnmower, creating parallel strips of bowling-green, neat lawn as he went. Annie had given up her future for him, a decision she hoped with all her heart she wouldn't live to regret.

Chapter 59

August, 1953

"Good morning, Grandma."

"Blimey, is it morning already?" asked Rose, yawning and rubbing sleep from her eyes.

"It is, and I've strict instructions to get you up, dressed and presentable."

"Oh, aye? And why is that?"

"Your daughter arrives today, that's why."

"What?" said Rose, heaving herself up against her pillows. "Which daughter? You don't mean Marnie?"

"I do."

"Thank God," said Rose with a cackle. "I'll be delighted to see that one, nae so much the others."

"Grandma, you can't speak like that about your own daughters!"

"If ye'd met them, ye'd agree with me. Bunch of old crones they are, but I've only got myself to blame."

"What about Rachel? I thought she was very sweet when I met her?"

"Aye, Rachel's a canny enough lass, I'll grant ye. Wouldn't say boo to a goose that one. Marnie has more about her, a bit of my spirit without the hardness."

"Grandma, you shouldn't speak badly of yourself."

"I kna what I'm like, lass. Anyway, what time is that daughter of mine arriving and why did none of yous tell me she was coming?"

"We thought you'd enjoy the surprise, but also realised you'd be cross if we hadn't let you prepare for her arrival."

"Quite right too. I dinna want Marnie to find me in bed like I'm about to cark it."

"And that's why I'm here. Come on, let's get you into your chair."

Annie pushed the wheelchair up against the bed and helped Rose shuffle into it. Once they were in the bathroom, Rose placed her arms around Annie's neck. Annie heaved Rose up, slipped a towel onto the chair and lifted Rose's nightdress over her head. Whereas at first the sight of her grandmother naked had embarrassed Annie, now she felt no unease. She lowered Rose down and filled a bowl with warm, soapy water.

A bath had become a step too far for Rose. Getting her in was easy enough, but Annie had learned from bitter experience that to get Rose out was too great a challenge for one person. The last time she'd tried it, she'd had to enlist the help of both Clara and Jimmy, resulting in mortification for both mother and son. A sit-down wash in the wheelchair was far easier and saved a lot of blushes.

Annie rinsed a cloth and stroked warm water across Rose's face, then down to her neck. Rose let out a soft moan, closing her eyes as her features relaxed. As Annie worked her way down Rose's body, a calmness filled the room, the only sound the ringing out of a cloth in water and the gentle stroking of cotton against skin.

"Would you like me to wash your hair?" asked Annie, once Rose was clean and wrapped in a dressing gown.

"Aye, if it's nae too much bother."

"Of course it's not. I enjoy washing your hair."

"Ye've got a fine, caring nature about ye, lass. Ye must get it from yer mam. Have I ever told ye about how Marnie cared for Jimmy after his accident?"

Rose had told the story many times, but she let her tell it again, her words of pride filling the room as Annie tilted Rose's head back against the sink, poured warm water over her and began massaging shampoo into her hair.

"And then… when he got that job… in the… school…"

"Grandma? Don't fall asleep. I need you to hold the towel to your eyes while I rinse out the shampoo."

Rose let out a snore and Annie gave her shoulder a gentle squeeze. "Sorry, lass, where was I?"

"You were about to hold the towel up so I can rinse your hair," said Annie with a laugh.

With Rose's hair free of shampoo, Annie towel-dried her curls and wheeled Rose back into her bedroom. By the time a knock came on the door, Annie had Rose dressed and was pulling on her stockings.

"Only me," said Clara, poking her head around the door. "Are you decent?"

"Aye," said Rose. "The lass has done a grand job."

"Wonderful. Would you like to come to the flat and have breakfast with me and Jimmy?"

"That I would, lass. We'll be with you in a tick."

"Wonderful. We'll see you shortly."

Clara closed the door and Annie slipped Rose's shoes onto her feet. As she was fastening the final buckle, Rose reached down and grabbed hold of Annie's wrist. "There's something I need to say to ye, lass."

"Oh?"

"I want ye to understand why I spoke so harshly to ye the other day. It was nae meant to sound unkind, but I fear it did."

"Don't worry, Grandma, I know you were trying to help."

"The thing is, lass, I think an awful lot of ye. I was once like ye, trying to find my way in the world, a head full of confusion, a heart full of dreams. But dreams can blind us worse than old age. I lost half my life to a man who lied and cheated and treated other folk like dirt, and I canna bear to have the same happen to ye."

"It won't, Grandma. I'm not as daft as you seem to think I am."

"I'm nae saying ye are daft, but ye've lived through a lot, and it can make life very confusing. Ye won't have known if yer coming or going half the time and that changes a person. I remember growing up being confusing enough, without a war and being dragged here, there and everywhere across the country. Ye kna my feelings about that chap Sam, but it's nae up to me who ye step out with. But, lass, if ye've broken things off with him as I think ye have, then can ye dee one small thing for me?"

"What?"

"Dinna go jumping straight into another fellow's arms. Give yerself time to learn what it is ye truly want and where ye truly want to be. And remember, it's better to have nae man at all than the wrong man."

"I'll bear that in mind," said Annie, making no promises.

Chapter 60

August, 1953

"When is your mother arriving?"

"This afternoon."

"You've got the day off?"

"Yes."

"Fancy a walk?"

Annie looked up at the bright blue sky, not a cloud in sight. "Aren't you in the middle of something?" she asked, pointing to the secateurs in Blaine's hand.

"I don't actually begin work until noon. I was filling my time until then."

"Alright."

"Wonderful. I'll just run and get my jacket. You'll wait for me here?"

Annie nodded, walking to the end of the garden and leaning against the stone wall, admiring the view.

"Everything alright out here?"

Annie turned and saw Jimmy limping towards her. "Yes, fine. What about you? Is your leg playing up?"

"It will loosen up as the day goes on. What a beautiful day. I'm so pleased the sun will be shining for Marnie's arrival."

"Yes, the island's certainly looking its best. In fact, I'm about to go for a walk to make the most of it."

"Really? Perhaps I could join you? It's better for my leg to keep moving."

"Um, well..."

"Ready," called Blaine, striding across the lawn. "Morning, Jimmy."

"You're going for a walk together?" asked Jimmy, his forehead creased.

"I don't start work till midday."

"Jimmy said he'd like to join us," said Annie.

"On second thoughts, it would probably be more sensible to rest as I'm sure Marnie will be keen to go out exploring later."

"Are you sure?" asked Annie. "You'd be very welcome to come with us."

"No, I'm better off staying here. I'll see you later on."

"Alright."

Annie and Blaine set off into the village. "There's something different about you," said Annie, giving him a sideways glance.

Blaine puffed out his chest a little. "Could it be my jacket?"

Annie stopped walking. "It's new?"

"I got it when I was on the mainland last week." Blaine smoothed a hand across the fine linen fabric and squared his shoulders. "Do you like it?"

"It's very nice, but it must have cost a fortune. Is it tailor made? It fits like a glove."

"Yes, I treated myself. Why not, hey?" Blaine grinned and continued walking through the village streets.

Annie followed him, wondering how Blaine could afford such fine clothes on a modest wage, as he was meant to be saving. With a start, she remembered the conversation several weeks ago about a missing wallet and how all the women had suspected Blaine. Surely there could be no truth in the rumours?

Annie jogged to catch Blaine up. “How did you afford it?”

“Pardon?”

“The coat. How did you afford it?”

“That’s a very personal question.”

“Sorry, it’s just...”

“Don’t worry, I don’t want there to be any secrets between us,” said Blaine, giving Annie a piercing look. “The truth is, I’ve spent barely any of my wages since I arrived. I probably shouldn’t have blown so much of my savings on a jacket, but I work hard, and there’s no crime against splashing out once in a while.”

“What about Paris? I thought you were saving your money for that.”

“I am, but I’ve got plenty of time to accrue the funds I need, and if I want to be respected over there, I need to look the part.”

“When do you intend to go?”

“Late October or early November. The hotel will enter its quiet season, and Jimmy and Clara won’t have any work for me.”

Annie felt a wash of sadness at the thought of being separated from Blaine.

“Don’t look so sad,” he said.

“I’m not,” lied Annie. “I’ll miss you, that’s all. You’ve been a good friend to me.”

By now, they’d left the village behind and were walking along a track that cut between two fields belonging to the local farmer. Blaine took Annie’s hand and led her to a low stone wall. He lifted her up onto it and stood so close his face was inches from hers. “Come with me.”

“What?”

“You heard. Come with me.”

"To Paris?"

"Yes, to Paris."

"But we hardly know each other."

"I know I love you."

"Love me?" Annie's voice was a whisper, her head spinning, Rose's earlier warning ringing in her ears.

"I heard things ended badly with your friend Sam, and I'm sorry to say this, Annie, but I'm glad. You deserve so much more than to be a fishwife to a man you can't trust in some parochial town. You deserve more, and I could give it to you. I've loved you since the moment I first saw you. You're a free spirit, like me. Imagine all the fun we could have together in Paris."

"What would we do for money? I can't even speak French."

Blaine's mouth spread into a wide grin. "That sounds more like a yes than a no to me."

"It's neither. This is all too much to take in." Annie jumped down from the wall and continued along the path. The future she had imagined for herself had crumbled with Sam's departure, and now here was Blaine, suggesting a future she hadn't dared dream of. Was she really going to turn down the adventure of a lifetime, even if it meant leaving all she knew and loved behind for a man she didn't know? And what if Rose was right? That rushing into a new romance could lead to disaster?

"Annie, wait. I'm sorry, I seem to have upset you."

"You haven't upset me, Blaine. If anything, you've confused me. We aren't even stepping out and yet here you are talking of running off to Paris together. Talking of love!"

"I'm sorry, I can see this is all moving too quickly for you."

"Perhaps we should spend a little more time getting to know one another before committing to something so huge?"

"Very sensible," said Blaine. "But can I ask you one thing?"

"What?"

"Would you mind awfully if I were to kiss you?"

"I… I…" Before Annie could form a coherent sentence, Blaine's mouth was on hers, his arms around her waist, pulling her close to him. It was at once the most exciting and terrifying moment of her life so far. The feelings of pleasure were intense, and yet so was the sensation that her future was spinning out of control, that she'd just handed over all the power to a man who most of the people she loved didn't even like.

Blaine pulled away and planted one last kiss on Annie's lips. "I love you, Annie Hearn. You don't need to say it back to me, not yet. Just know that I'm yours, and I'll wait as long as it takes for you to be mine."

"Do you mind if we walk back to the hotel now? I've so much to think about."

"Of course. Just tell me this, have I scared you off?"

Annie shook her head. "No, Blaine, you haven't. But you have given me plenty of food for thought."

Chapter 61

August, 1953

Annie paced the length of her small bedroom, periodically stopping to gaze out of the window and check the hotel's driveway for cars. The arrival of Marnie and Frank was already bringing with it mixed feelings and that was before Blaine had made his startling proposition. By now, her parents would know she'd broken things off with Sam, and Annie was dreading their reaction.

The crunch of tyres on gravel caused Annie to rush to the window, and she watched as Frank climbed out of the taxi, then held out a hand for Marnie to take. Annie watched her mother stand up straight, then turn a full circle, taking in her childhood home. Marnie looked up at the hotel and Annie stepped back from the window. With a sigh, she pulled on a cardigan and went downstairs to greet the new arrivals.

"Annie, so good to see you," said Frank, holding out his arms to Annie. She stepped into his embrace, feeling a moment of calm.

"How was your journey?"

"Not too bad, although that drive across the sands is a little hairy. That new causeway can't come soon enough."

"Do I get a hug?" asked Marnie.

Annie embraced her mother, though it was with less warmth than Frank had received. "Island life suits you," said Marnie, stepping back and holding Annie at arm's length.

"Thank you. Is it good to be back?"

"Wonderful. Oh, there are Clara and Jimmy." Marnie waved at her brother and sister-in-law.

"It's wonderful to see you both. Thank you for making the long journey up here."

"We wouldn't miss Ben's wedding for the world," said Marnie, "and I was going to come and visit Annie anyway, so this way we kill two birds with one stone."

"You're in the same room as last time," said Clara, linking arms with Marnie.

"Are you sure? You must be busy at this time of year."

"We've closed to the public for a couple of days. Amy was keen to have her wedding reception here, so it seemed the most sensible solution. Her family will also stay with us, but they're not arriving until tomorrow, so we've got you to ourselves this evening."

It wasn't until late afternoon that Annie found herself alone with Marnie and Frank. They had all been walking around the ruins of the old priory, but Jimmy's leg was hurting, so he and Clara had gone home ahead of the others.

"Let's sit for a while," said Marnie, perching on a wall of red stone with views out to the harbour. "It really is so good to be back."

"It was good to see your mother again," said Frank, "she seemed very pleased to see us and was singing your praises, Annie. Clara says she's had a new lease of life since your arrival."

"I'm pleased to hear it," said Annie. "I love spending time with Grandma Rose, although I've been so busy working lately I've not had as much time with her as I'd like." She didn't mention that any free time she had was more often than not spent with Blaine.

"Have you thought about when you'll be coming home?" asked Marnie. "I asked Clara about it and she said the season is ending in a month or so, so there'll be less need for an extra worker."

"Yes, I spoke to Clara about it last week. She said I'm welcome to stay as long as I want, but it wouldn't feel right staying here if I couldn't pay my way."

"Well," said Marnie, squeezing Annie's hand. "I know you'll miss this place, but it will be good to have you home."

Annie gave a strained smile. Now was not the time to tell Marnie about her plans to follow Blaine to Paris. In fact, there might never be a good time.

"I bumped into Beryl the other day," continued Marnie. "She's Mrs Smith now. It was a shame you couldn't make it to her wedding."

Annie shrugged. "It fell during one of our busiest weeks. I couldn't leave Clara and Jimmy in the lurch like that."

"I understand, and so does Beryl. She told me there are plenty of jobs going at the Birds Eye factory, so I don't think you'll have any difficulty finding work when you come home."

"That's good."

"I can call in and ask about a position, if you like?" said Frank. "Then you could hit the ground running as soon as you get back?"

"No, thank you. I think it's best if I talk to them when I get back."

"Quite right," said Frank, "though I daresay you could find some more hotel or restaurant work in Lowestoft now you have the experience of working here."

"I'll think about it." Annie couldn't look at her parents for fear guilt and deceit would show on her face. Would they understand when she disappeared off to Paris? Annie hoped they'd be excited for her, but feared the most likely reaction would be one of disappointment and hurt. But then again, if they could keep secrets, why shouldn't she?

"We'd better get back to the hotel," said Marnie. "There'll be plenty of preparations needed for tomorrow, and I'm sure they could do with all hands on deck."

"I think I saw Amy going towards the church with baskets of flowers."

"Then let's see if she needs an extra pair of hands."

"I'll leave you ladies to it," said Frank, turning toward the hotel and giving them a wave as he strode away.

It was a short walk from the priory to the church, and as they stepped beyond the porch, the scent of summer flowers hit them. Sunlight streamed through the stained glass, clouds of dust particles dancing in the air.

"Amy? We thought you might need some extra pairs of hands. This is my mother, Marnie, Ben's aunt."

Amy set the flowers in her hands down on a pew and walked over to meet them. "It's a pleasure to meet you. Ben has told me all about you. You were married here yourselves, weren't you?"

"Aye," said Marnie. "This church has seen a fair few weddings of both Watsons and Robsons over the years."

"Then I'm pleased to add our names to that long history," said Amy. "Now, if you'd like to help, there are plenty of flowers to tie into bunches and secure onto the ends of the pews."

"We're at your service," said Marnie with a smile.

"Me too," said Clara, walking in from the porch. "Jimmy's resting his leg, so I thought I'd come and help."

"Wonderful," said Amy, clapping her hands. "All the flowers are in buckets in the porch. Marnie and Clara, could you arrange them into posies, and Annie and I will attach them to the pews?"

"Good plan," said Marnie.

The four women made a good team and soon had a production line going. "I think we're almost ready for more posies," said Amy. "Could you fetch some?"

"Of course." Annie walked towards the back of the church. The door to the porch was slightly ajar, and as she approached, the sound of Marnie and Clara's conversation reached her.

"I don't expect it will be long until Amy and Ben start a family," said Clara.

"I don't know them well," said Marnie, "but I'd say they'll make fine parents."

There was a lull in conversation, and Annie was about to push open the door when Clara spoke again. "Do you have any regrets about Grace?" Clara's voice was quiet, conspiratorial, and Annie froze.

"Aye, sometimes."

"And what about Annie? Do you ever wonder if telling her the truth would have been for the best? Sometimes she seems so lost, and I wonder if she knew the truth..."

"No!" The word was loud, clipped, and Annie heard Clara's sharp intake of breath. "Sorry," Marnie continued, "I didn't mean to snap. But Annie can never know. She's been distant with me ever since she returned from Padstow, and I fear if she knew what happened down there, our relationship would never recover, not when I've kept the truth from her for so many years."

Annie staggered back, knocking into a table and causing a metal collection plate to tumble onto the stone floor with a clatter. The porch door swung open and Marnie and Clara stared at her. Annie forced a smile onto her face. "Are there any more posies ready? Me and Amy are ready for some more."

Clara smiled, and Annie noticed a flicker of relief cross her face. "Of course, here you are."

"Thank you," said Annie, offering another smile before walking away. As soon as her back was turned, her smile dropped, her legs turning to jelly. Blaine was right. He was the only person in the world she could trust.

Chapter 62

August, 1953

Annie sighed and flung off her bedclothes, giving up on sleep. She crossed the room and stared out over the gardens and harbour view beyond. Silhouetted against the early morning sky was a figure sitting on a bench. Annie screwed up her eyes and pressed her forehead against the glass. A long white nightdress stood out against the grey and Annie watched as Clara pulled up her knees and hugged her arms around them.

With her dressing gown pulled on, Annie left her room and crept through the silent corridors of the hotel, grateful for the thick carpet which muffled her steps. As she crossed the lawn, dew found its way into her slippers and Annie silently cursed herself for not wearing boots. Clara had her body turned towards the harbour, and clutched a handkerchief in her fist.

"Clara?"

Clara jumped and rubbed her eyes.

"Clara, is everything alright? What are you doing out here so early?"

"Couldn't sleep, and besides, the guests are coming across the sands at seven, so I needed to be up and ready to greet them."

"Have you been crying?"

"Oh, don't mind me," said Clara, patting the bench beside her for Annie to sit down. "It's just this wedding brings up an awful lot of memories." In the early morning light, Clara's tears glistened like jewels against her skin.

"Sad memories?"

Clara smiled through her tears. "Some sad, some happy."

"Would you like to talk about them?"

This time Clara laughed. "If I did that, we'd be here all day. There's something about that church... oh... I'm probably being silly."

"No, go on."

"I was in the church last night checking everything was ready, and being there always reminds me of my mother. It was as though I could hear her singing to me, taking me right back to when I was a wee bairn. My mam sang in the church choir and my, did she have a beautiful voice. She also helped arrange the flowers for special services and weddings... and that church is where we held her funeral. It's been so long since she died, but the pain is no less than the day she went."

"What was she like?" asked Annie, who loved hearing about her namesake, and hoped the topic would cheer Clara up.

"Beautiful, kind, brave."

"Brave?"

"Oh, aye. She gave up everything for love, to be with my da. Left behind a life of luxury for the work of a fishwife on an island she knew nothing about. That takes no small amount of courage."

Annie smiled, thinking how her own situation mirrored one from all those years ago.

"I love being back on this island, but to live here means sharing my life with plenty of ghosts. Anyway, that's enough maudlin talk. My mother would have loved you, Annie."

"And I her, I'm certain."

"Aye. Look, I can see the bride-to-be stirring." Clara pointed up to a window on the first floor of the hotel. Amy was opening the curtains, her profile highlighted by lamplight as she gazed out to an approaching dawn. "We should take her breakfast up to her and see if she needs help to get ready. This wedding is mighty early, thanks to those blasted tides. Come on." Clara stood and pulled Annie up from the bench.

Ten minutes later, Annie and Clara were knocking on Amy's bedroom door, a plate of toast, boiled egg, and a pot of coffee on a tray beside them.

"Oh, good morning," said Amy, stifling a yawn.

"We brought breakfast."

"You didn't need to do that."

"It's your wedding day. Of course we did."

"Come in. I was about to have a bath, but I'll eat breakfast first, although I'm not sure how much I'll manage with my stomach churning." Amy laughed and sat at her dresser, her tray of breakfast in front of her.

"I'll start that bath running," said Clara.

"Would you like me to leave you in peace?" asked Annie once Clara had left.

"No, you can take my mind off my nerves," said Amy with a chuckle.

"Are you unsure about marrying Ben?"

"Good God, no. I've loved that man from the second I laid eyes on him."

"Goodness, you knew that quickly he was the man for you?"

Amy waved a teaspoon in the air. "If you know, you know," she said.

Annie smiled. She'd felt a strong attraction to Blaine from the moment they met, and if what Amy was saying was anything to go by, it could well be love. "Are your parents pleased you're marrying Ben?"

"Delighted. They were sceptical at first. Ben's quite a bit older than me, and the difference in age worried them. But as soon as they met him and saw us together, all their worries disappeared. They should be here soon. I think the sand is clear from seven this morning. I hope they don't mind the early start. When I pictured my wedding day, it was never at eight in the morning, but that's island life for you."

"I'm sure they don't mind what time you wed so long as they're here to see it. It will be lovely to meet them."

Clara rushed back into the room, her face shiny from the steamy water. "The bath is almost ready."

"I'll get in now," said Amy. "I've eaten as much as I can manage. Feel free to finish off the coffee."

"No, we'll leave you to get ready, but if you need any help, you know where to find us."

At half past seven, Annie walked to the church with a bleary-eyed Jimmy, Marnie and Frank. After finishing their flower arranging, Annie had kept up her pretence of hearing and knowing nothing about any secrets, and despite a night of little sleep, the prospect of a wedding had lifted her mood.

The hour was early but everyone was in good spirits, the bright morning and bunting streaming between buildings adding to the celebratory feel. They were almost at the church when Blaine caught up with them.

"Morning," he said. "It's a fine day for a wedding."

"Indeed it is," said Annie, giving her best attempt at nonchalance. Blaine looked so handsome in his navy suit and burgundy tie. His hair was slicked back away from his face and secured by a band at the nape of his neck.

"Marnie, Frank, this is Blaine McCloud," said Jimmy. "He works at the hotel and will serve the wedding breakfast later on."

Annie frowned at Jimmy, wondering if his words were a deliberate reminder that Blaine was staff, not family.

"Nice to meet you," said Frank, reaching across and shaking Blaine's hand.

At the church, they parted ways, the family walking to the front two pews, while Blaine took up position at the back. Annie stole occasional glances behind her, wondering if Blaine was thinking the same as her, that St Mary's church was a fine venue for a wedding, should they ever need one.

Chapter 63

August, 1953

Annie dug her toes into the pebble-strewn sand. The tide was in, the setting sun throwing pinks and oranges into the clear, calm water. Across the stretch of sea, the mainland rose against the horizon, a dark mass of land that could've been a different planet as far as Annie was concerned. She leaned her head so it was resting on Blaine's shoulder.

"Are you happy?" he asked, pouring a glass of wine and handing it to her.

"Now I'm alone with you, I am."

"It's been a fine day, but I agree it's nice to get away from it all."

The wedding party was still in full swing back at the hotel. Although the mainlanders had long since departed with the encroaching tide, the dance-floor was full of islanders as the band played on, showing no sign of tiring. It had been Blaine's idea to slip away while everyone was distracted, and Annie had been all too happy to oblige.

"Amy looked beautiful in her white dress, and you could tell Ben was as pleased as punch."

"Those traditions were something special too, the gunfire, the petting stone. And when they smashed those plates of cake over Amy's head, well, I'd seen nothing like it."

"I remembered it from Mum and Frank's wedding."

"And is that what you would want, a wedding like that?"

Annie stared at him. "Blaine McCloud, is that a proposal?"

Blaine gave an uneasy laugh, his usual confidence deserting him. "No, I'm afraid it wasn't. I love you, Annie, but I'm not the marrying type."

"Oh." As she'd sat through the earlier wedding ceremony, Annie hadn't been able to stop herself imagining what it would be like to marry Blaine. Would he whisper, *you look beautiful*, just as Ben had? What hymns would they choose? Would his family she had yet to meet be sitting in the front row, pleased with the match?

"Don't look like that. Just because I don't fancy getting married doesn't mean we can't be together."

"And live in sin?"

"It's 1953."

"So?"

"Things are different in Paris. People there don't have the same old-fashioned attitudes of folk in this country."

"So the Paris idea is serious?"

"Of course it is."

"Only, I was wondering about the logistics of it."

"Like what?"

"Like when would we go?"

Blaine waved a hand in the air. "We'll go when and where the wind takes us, my love."

"But..."

Blaine quietened Annie with a kiss and her questions melted away. "If you'd prefer a more conventional arrangement like you'd have with Sam, I'll understand."

"It's you I want."

"Even if being with me means sacrificing the big white wedding?"

"Yes, even then." Annie turned her head and smiled at Blaine, pushing her disquiet away. He kissed her nose, her cheeks, her forehead, and finally her lips.

"I never thought I'd meet anyone as wonderful as you," he said, kissing her again.

"I'm nothing special," said Annie.

"No," said Blaine, taking her hands in his, his voice earnest. "Never say that. You are a princess in my eyes, Annie, and I'll hear nothing to the contrary."

Annie flushed, then shivered as a cool breeze teased her cotton dress.

"It's getting cold. Why don't we go back to the cottage for a while before re-joining the party?"

"Alright then."

Blaine stood and held out his hand to Annie. She took it and he pulled her up off the sand. They linked arms and walked along the beach, the rising moon casting cream ripples into the navy water. Swept up in the evening's romance, Annie ignored the niggling voice in her head, asking why she'd accepted Blaine's terms so readily. The adventure-filled future she had imagined had always included a marriage. The two didn't have to be mutually exclusive. Annie smiled, Blaine would come round to the idea of marriage in time, she was sure of it.

When they reached the cottage, the air was filled with music and laughter. Several wedding guests were clustered in groups outside the hotel, so Blaine and Annie kept to the shadows, determined to keep their romance a secret.

The cottage was dark and Blaine set about lighting candles. Annie ignored the mess and dirt, concentrating on the romantic soft light the candles threw out across the room and the warmth coming from the embers in the hearth.

Without speaking, Blaine took Annie's hand and led her over to the bed. They stood beside it, and without taking his eyes from hers, he began loosening the pearl buttons that held her dress in place.

"What are you doing?" Annie whispered.

"Do you love me?"

"You know I do."

"Don't you want to enjoy the ultimate expression of love?"

"Yes, but..."

Blaine's fingers paused on the fifth button. "I won't make you do anything you don't want to. We can stop and return to the party. I know you're still very young. If you're not mature enough for this, it's better that you speak up now."

Without being sure what *this* meant, Annie shook her head. "I am mature enough. I want to show you how much I love you."

"I'm not sure," said Blaine, dropping his hands to his side and turning away. "I think this was a bad idea."

"No," said Annie, grabbing hold of his hand and pulling him to face her. "No. It's a wonderful idea."

"I suppose, if you really want to..."

"I want to."

Annie let Blaine take the lead. She wasn't sure what was happening. She'd heard whispers from friends about what happened between a man and a woman when they were married, but hadn't realised it would involve the removal of all their clothes. As Blaine peeled off her layers of cotton and silk, Annie kept glancing to the door, afraid someone would come in and discover them in a state of undress.

When Blaine unfastened the hooks of her brassiere, Annie clasped her arms around herself, her cheeks flaming red with embarrassment.

"You're beautiful," said Blaine, pulling her hands away from her chest. "So very beautiful."

Tears burned in Annie's eyes. She suddenly felt very unsure of what was happening. Did she really want to do this? There would be no going back. "Can I lie beneath the covers?" she whispered.

"Of course, my love," said Blaine, stroking her cheek.

Annie climbed beneath sheets which smelled musty, as if they were long overdue for a wash. She wrinkled her nose and swallowed a cry as Blaine removed all his clothes and stood gazing down at her. She had never seen a man naked before and couldn't decide if she wanted to scream or giggle. Blaine seemed proud of his physique, and as he climbed into the bed beside her, Annie's laughter faded.

"Ready?" Blaine asked. Before Annie could reply, his mouth was on hers, and he was climbing on top of her, his weight squeezing the breath from her lungs.

After, when she was back in her clothes and ready to leave, Annie brushed away the tears which were rolling down her cheeks. Blaine had described the act as beautiful, and he must have been satisfied, for he was now snoring gently beneath his covers. But for Annie, the entire experience had been one of confusion, embarrassment, and no small amount of pain. She carried a candle to the far side of the room and studied her reflection in the mirror. Would everyone be able to tell she was changed? Would they guess what had occurred while they were dancing merrily just feet away from the cottage? The thought of Marnie and Frank caused Annie to stifle a sob. If they knew, they would be so disappointed in her.

Annie crept back to the bed and gave Blaine's shoulder a gentle nudge. "Blaine? Blaine, I'm going back to the party."

Blaine let out a little snort, then rolled over onto his side, his back to her. Shoes in hand, Annie crept over to the door, slipped her shoes back on her feet, and headed back to the hotel.

Chapter 64

August, 1953

Annie ran a hand over her stomach, which still ached from the night before. All night she had lain awake waiting for the euphoria Blaine had promised to hit her, but she was yet to experience it and couldn't shake the feeling she had just made a terrible mistake. Sun streamed into her room through a gap in the curtains, causing Annie to squint against the light.

After deciding sleep would not be forthcoming, Annie gathered up an armful of items and made her way to the bathroom. The hotel was quiet, only the faint sound of snores coming from behind the bedroom doors. The wedding party had gone on long after midnight, and its weary participants were unlikely to make an appearance soon.

Annie slipped into the bathroom and closed the door. She turned the taps of the bath just a fraction, not wanting the sound of pummelling water to wake anyone in the rooms below. While the bath ran, Annie stood by the sink dealing with the mess from the night before. The amount of blood was both unexpected and worrying. Annie had always associated blood with injury, pain and the regular nightmare that was her uncomfortable monthlies. It didn't sit right that bleeding could result from an act of pleasure, especially one which had lasted less than ten minutes.

With her scrubbing done, Annie peeled off her clothes and climbed into the half-filled bath. She sank down beneath the water, holding her breath and letting the warm water wash her clean. When she emerged, she squeezed water from her curls and looked down at her body. The warmth of the water soothed her aching stomach, and she felt her limbs relax. Did she look any different from before? As she studied the body she knew so well, Annie couldn't see any discernible difference.

"Am I a prude?" Annie wondered out loud. She'd never thought of herself in those terms, but her discomfort with what had happened the night before made her question herself. If she loved Blaine as much as she thought she did, why had sleeping with him felt so very wrong? Was it a hangover from her days going to Sunday school, or an intuition that shouldn't be ignored?

"Stop this," said Annie. In one swift movement, she stood, grabbed a towel from the hook, and banished the water from her skin. She needed to see Blaine, then all her doubts and worries would melt away. He loved her. They were going to run away to Paris together. Everything would be alright.

To cheer herself up, Annie had chosen to wear her favourite dress. Short-sleeved with a V-shaped neckline and delicate blue and pink flowers, the dress swung gracefully just below her knees and never failed to lift her spirits. Annie pulled on the dress, slipped her feet into her low-heeled peep-toe sandals and collected her belongings inside a towel.

Annie opened the door and almost bumped into Marnie, who was walking down the corridor, covering her mouth as she yawned widely. Marnie was the last person Annie wanted to see after learning of her betrayal of trust, but with only twenty-four hours until Marnie and Frank left the island, Annie felt sure she could keep up the pretence that everything was fine for that long.

"Late night?" asked Annie with a smile.

"Urgh," said Marnie. "I didn't even have much to drink. It's the tiredness that's done me in. I don't suppose you could direct me toward a cup of coffee?"

"If you wait here a moment, I'll drop off my things in my bedroom and we can have a coffee together."

"That would be lovely."

Annie ran up to her bedroom, threw her towel and its contents on the bed, and went to find her mother.

"That was quick," said Marnie.

"I'll do something with my hair later," said Annie, shaking out her damp curls. "Coffee takes priority."

"Were you up late as well? I don't remember seeing you?"

"I came to bed at a reasonable time but couldn't sleep."

"It must have been all the excitement of the day. Didn't Amy look beautiful?"

"She certainly did, and Ben looked pleased as punch with his new bride. Do you think it matters that she's so much younger than him?"

"Love's love," said Marnie. "Frank's older than me, but it's made no difference to our happiness. Besides, it's not like the island is teeming with women of Ben's age. And Amy's very mature. I think they make a wonderful match."

"I agree. Have you ever loved a man besides my dad and Frank?" Annie kept her tone light.

Marnie laughed. "What sort of question is that? Of course I haven't."

"Here we are." Annie led Marnie into the dining room and walked over to a table where Steffie had already laid out a pot of coffee, a pot of tea, and a jug of orange juice. She poured the coffee out into two cups and handed one to Marnie. "Shall we take these outside? It's a beautiful morning."

"Good idea."

They walked slowly across the lawn, careful not to spill a drop of the precious nectar in their cups. The bench at the end of the garden glistened with the hint of dew, but mother and daughter ignored the dampness and sat down to admire the view.

"So," said Marnie, after a few minute's silence. "We've not yet had the chance to talk about Sam."

"There's nothing to talk about." If her mother expected honesty, she had another think coming. Trust worked both ways.

"Of course there's something to talk about," said Marnie. "The poor lad returned from the island heartbroken. Kitty was so worried about him when he went back to his base. While he was with her, he refused to eat anything and barely left his bedroom."

Annie shrugged. "It was his choice to break things off."

"That's not the impression he gave Kitty. According to her, he felt he had no choice."

"Did he say why?"

"No. Annie, what's going on? You and Sam were happy the last time I saw you. What's changed?"

"I'm not sure how happy you can be with a man you see for a few days every few months."

"Perhaps, but it's not Sam's fault he's doing his National Service. Besides, didn't he write to you?"

"Religiously."

"Then why did you break things off with him?"

"I don't know, Mum. Perhaps being here has changed me."

"Is there someone else?"

Annie felt her cheeks redden and turned her face away.

"You can tell me if there is."

Could she, though? Marnie had lied to her for years about Grace, for reasons unknown to Annie. Why should she be expected to be open with her mother when it didn't go both ways? "I promise, there is no one else."

"Alright," said Marnie, though she didn't look convinced.

Chapter 65

September, 1953

Annie cried out as she walked into the restaurant and a hand reached out and grabbed her.

"Shush," said Blaine, covering Annie's mouth with his hand. He pressed up close against her back and kissed her neck. "I've missed you."

Annie removed his hand from her mouth and turned to face him. "Blaine, we see each other every day."

"I know, but I've not had the chance to be alone with you since the wedding."

"Hmm," said Annie, glancing around the room to check no one was watching. Whilst the lack of time with Blaine had given her some breathing space, Annie resented the interference she suspected had come from Jimmy. Ever since the wedding, Annie and Blaine had been rostered onto opposite working hours. Besides this, the hotel had been busy with older couples, birdwatchers, pilgrims and ramblers who preferred the quiet of the island once children had returned to school. The heavy workload left little time or energy for romancing.

"Are you working this afternoon?"

"No, I'm on breakfasts and lunches, then I've got a four-hour break before I'm needed again for the evening meals. How about you?"

"I'm not working until five, then I'll be stuck behind the bar until closing time. Do you think we could snatch a couple of hours together later?"

"At your cottage?"

"No, I was thinking we could go to the shack. I've not worked on your portrait for weeks and I'd like to get it finished before we leave the island."

"Alright. Shall I meet you beside the farm at two?"

"I'll be there." Blaine risked a quick kiss on Annie's lips, pulling away just before Jimmy walked into the dining room.

"What are you doing in here, Blaine? Your shift doesn't start for hours."

"I ran out of milk for my coffee and thought I could scrounge some from the kitchen."

Jimmy scowled. "We provide you with staff accommodation. We're under no obligation to feed you."

"It's only a bit of milk," said Annie.

"Stay out of this, please, Annie. This is a management decision. If we loosen the rules for one member of staff, it's not fair to the others."

Annie raised her eyebrows. Her uncle was generous to a fault, but now she was seeing a completely different side to him.

"Very well," said Blaine. He turned on his heel and left the hotel, heading toward the village shop.

The rest of the morning dragged. Annie was filled with a mix of nerves and anticipation at the thought of time alone with Blaine. She hoped he meant what he said and just wanted to paint her portrait, as she had decided she would rather slow things down between them. After reflecting on their last encounter, Annie realised she wasn't ready to go that far again. Aside from the fact Blaine's kisses were much more pleasant than the other things he did, she hated how much deception their relationship involved. It was one thing sneaking kisses in dark corners, and quite another lying in a state of undress when Clara or Jimmy could come knocking at any moment.

"I'm off out for a walk," Annie told Clara at half-past one.

"Would you mind taking Rose her dinner before you go?"

"Not at all," said Annie, glancing at her watch. As long as she was quick, she would still be with Blaine by the agreed hour.

Annie collected the tray of food from the kitchen and carried it to Rose's bedroom. She knocked gently on the door and stepped into the gloomy room.

"Only me, Grandma."

"Ah, my lovely Annie. I've not seen enough of ye lately."

"I'm sorry, Grandma, we've been so busy with guests, by the time I've finished of an evening, you're usually asleep."

"Never mind, lass, ye're here now. Come and sit beside me and tell me all ye've been up to."

Annie cast a glance up at the clock on the wall, then sat down beside Rose. "We've been nonstop since the school holidays ended. Clara says things will quieten down towards the end of this month."

"Have you heard anything from Sam?"

"No, and I don't expect to."

"I hope that Blaine McCloud hasn't been sniffing around since Sam's departure?"

"No, not at all," lied Annie.

"Good. Now, did I ever tell you about my last summer working as a herring lass?"

Rose had far more energy than usual, and by the time Annie felt able to leave her bedroom, the clock had already chimed two. She took the stairs two at a time to her bedroom, changed out of her uniform and slipped on a dress and cardigan. She checked her appearance in the mirror, and after pinching her cheeks to add a little colour, she made a hasty exit.

As she walked through the village, Annie kept her head down, determined not to be delayed further.

"Annie!"

Annie cursed silently, let out a sigh of frustration, then turned around. "Genie, how lovely to see you."

"How've you been?" asked Genie, linking arms with Annie.

"Fine, thank you," said Annie, wishing Genie would pick up the pace of her steps. "And you?"

"Busy. What are you doing now? Do you have time to come round for a pot of tea and a gossip? I was hoping to see you at the wedding, but you disappeared."

"No, I'm afraid I don't. I don't have long before my next shift begins, so I'm getting some fresh air while I can."

"Do you fancy some company?"

"No, if you don't mind, I'd quite like to walk alone."

Genie's face fell and Annie felt terrible for her rudeness. "I see."

"If you want to know the truth, I'm meeting Blaine. He's keen to finish my portrait today."

"Won't he be in his cottage?"

"No." Annie didn't know what else to say. If she told Genie they were spending time alone at the old ruin, her mind would undoubtedly leap to conclusions.

"Well, I can see ye've secrets to keep," said Genie, sounding affronted. "I'll not bother ye any longer."

Genie strode away, and Annie groaned. Things had been tense between the pair of them since their disagreement weeks before, and now she'd rebuffed Genie's renewed attempt at friendship. But there was no time to worry about Genie, for her watch told her she was terribly late for her assignation with Blaine. As she left the village behind, Annie broke into a run.

Chapter 66

September, 1953

Blaine had his back to her. His hair hung loose in long waves down the back of his jacket, tangled in places by the intermittent breeze. Back straight, he was staring out to the horizon, where a flock of birds gave an aerial display against a sky which was turning from blue to grey. His hand rested on the low stone wall and Annie could see his fingers tapping against the stone.

When Blaine turned, Annie was not greeted with the smile she was expecting, but with a frown. He made a pointed show of looking at his wristwatch, then back to Annie. "We said we'd meet at two."

"Yes, I know, but I got held up, first with Grandma then with Genie."

"We said two." Blaine enunciated his words slowly, as though speaking to a simpleton.

"As I explained, I got held up, but I'm here now."

"You know, Annie, if you didn't want to spend time with me this afternoon, you could have just said."

Blaine began striding along the grass path. It had rained for the previous few days and the path was now more of a bog. Not that Blaine seemed to notice. Mud and water sprayed up onto his trousers as he marched on.

"Wait," called Annie, wishing she had worn more sensible shoes. Her wedge heels were wonderful for wearing to dances, but they were not designed for mud. Instead of waiting for her, Blaine picked up his pace. Annie ran to keep up, her progress slowed each time she had to cling to the wall and pick her way around the edge of large puddles.

Annie cupped her hands around her mouth. "Blaine, please wait for me."

Perhaps he hadn't heard her, thought Annie as she watched his figure departing into the distance. At least she knew where he was heading. Annie reached another puddle that was more like a pond. There was no way around it. She clambered up onto the stone wall. It was too narrow to walk along, but she hoped the other side of the wall would be drier. It looked alright, springy green grass nestling up against the stone.

With one last desperate look at Blaine, Annie swung her legs over the wall and jumped down onto the other side. Two things happened in that moment. First, the skirt of her dress caught on a jagged stone and tore. Second, rather than landing on bouncy tufts of grass, Annie's feet sank up to the ankles in mud. "Appearances can be deceptive," she muttered to herself, pulling her way along the wall. Now that her shoes were ruined, Annie saw little point in avoiding the mud. She clambered back over the wall and began wading her way toward the ruined cottage.

Annie could see the cottage in the distance, the figure of Blaine leaning against its rotten door-frame. She was about to wave when a drop of water landed on her cheek. Annie tilted her eyes to the sky, alarmed to see that the blue had turned to grey and then to black. Another drop of water landed on her nose, then seconds later, a torrent met her skin. Annie screamed, lifted her cardigan over her head, and began sprinting towards the abandoned cottage.

Pain tore through her ankle as her foot caught on a stone and twisted at an uncomfortable angle. Then the tears came. Tears of self-pity, tears of anger that Blaine had abandoned her, tears of guilt that she had upset him, but mostly, the tears resulted from the terrible pain she found herself in.

Blaine was no longer in the doorway and must have moved inside the cottage when the rain came. Annie limped towards the small building, caring more about finding shelter than Blaine's reaction to her presence. Each time any weight went on her ankle, Annie yelped in agony. By the time she reached the cottage she was drenched from rainwater, her clothes were sticky with sweat, and pain had caused her face to drain of all colour.

"Oh my Lord," said Blaine when Annie stumbled through the doorway. "What on earth has happened to you?"

Rather than answer, Annie burst into tears, collapsing against a small wooden chair, her fingers rubbing her now swollen ankle.

"I'm such a fool," said Blaine. "I should never have left you."

"I was only twenty minutes late," whimpered Annie.

Blaine dropped to his knees in front of her and took her hands. "Please forgive me, my love. My pride was hurt, and I reacted like a jilted schoolboy. It's only because I love you so much. I thought you'd decided not to meet me and I couldn't bear the thought of being without you. You should have been met with my relief, not my anger. What can I do to make amends?"

"You may need to carry me home," said Annie, meeting Blaine's concerned look with a small smile.

"Let me see that ankle," said Blaine. He lifted Annie's leg onto his knee and began running his thumbs up and down the skin. "I don't think it's broken. It looks like a bad sprain to me. You'll need to rest it, let that swelling go down."

"But I need to work this evening."

"There'll be no work for you today."

Annie sniffed and dabbed her eyes with a handkerchief. "I know you wanted to work on the painting, but I need to get back and let Clara know she needs to find someone to cover my shift." She frowned at Blaine, praying this news wouldn't anger him further. To her relief, his earlier anger had been replaced by nothing but concern.

"Of course, my love. I'll carry you as far as the village, but then we had better part ways. I'm already on thin ice with your uncle. If I turn up with his injured niece in my arms, it might be the final straw."

"It wasn't your fault."

"Perhaps not, but us turning up together will raise too many questions. I'm sure we'll find a stick on our way back that you can use to support you."

"Alright," said Annie. After all, she had little choice in the matter.

Chapter 67

September, 1953

Annie clung to Blaine's neck, his arms supporting her legs. If she weren't in so much pain, she might have laughed at the ridiculous sight of being carried on his back like a sack of potatoes. Instead, she took comfort from the warmth of his skin beneath his shirt. He had given her his jacket to wear, but the rain had soaked through it, leaving goose pimples on her skin.

Fat drops of rain hammered relentlessly from the sky, blurring the surrounding fields. A flock of sheep huddled beside the stone wall for shelter, heads down, woollen coats soaked. Streaks of water flowed down Annie's face, her hair slick against her scalp, the rain too great a foe even for her bouncy curls.

Conversation was impossible, water flowing into their mouths each time they opened them, the surrounding air filled with the rhythm of rain hitting hard surfaces below. Through blinking eyes, blurred shapes of buildings formed amid the sheet of grey.

As the village came into view, Blaine slowed his steps. "I think this is as far as I can take you without folk noticing," he said, crouching so Annie could sit on the stone wall. "Wait here and I'll find you a walking stick."

Annie pulled Blaine's soaked coat tighter around her and waited. She closed her eyes but could hear the slopping sound of mud sucking and pulling on Blaine's boots as he climbed over the wall and began searching the edges of a nearby field. A few minutes later he reappeared with a long branch he had broken off one of the few island trees.

"I'll go ahead," he said, "and prepare to be as surprised as everyone when you arrive back at the hotel. I wish I could carry you all the way, truly I do." He leaned forward, cupped Annie's chin in his palm and planted a kiss on her lips.

Without another word, Blaine marched off towards the village. Annie gingerly climbed down from the wall, testing her weight on her sprained ankle and finding it just as sore as before. She leaned on the branch, making slow, tentative steps towards the village.

The deluge had emptied the village streets of both islanders and visitors alike. The pubs were all full, their windows steamed up, and the island cottages all had their lights on. Annie limped along, stopping every few paces to catch her breath. A dark figure, head wrapped in a scarf, was walking towards her. Only when they were a few paces from each other did Annie recognise the figure as Genie.

"Oh my goodness," said Genie, dropping the basket she was carrying and rushing to Annie's side. "What happened? Has that Blaine McCloud hurt you?"

"No. No! I think I've sprained my ankle. I was hurrying on uneven ground and landed a step badly."

"Can you put any weight on it?"

Annie shook her head.

"I presume you were with Blaine when this happened?"

"Not exactly." Annie didn't want to retell the earlier events, knowing Genie's reaction would not help.

"But he knows you're hurt?"

"He carried me most of the way, but said it was best we arrive separately at the hotel."

"How gentlemanly of him," muttered Genie. "Right, put your arm around me. I'll help you back."

"Are you sure? You'll get soaked."

"I'm already soaked," said Genie with a laugh. "Mam had errands to run, but her chest has been bad lately so I offered to go out instead. The weather's really taken a turn for the worse."

Somehow Genie helped Annie as far as the hotel gardens before stopping. "One thing before I take you in there," she said.

"What?"

Genie looked Annie up and down. "I don't think it would go down very well if you turn up wearing Blaine McCloud's jacket."

"Oh no, I forgot I was wearing it."

"Don't worry," said Genie. She helped Annie out of the jacket and hid it beneath a nearby bush. "You can let Blaine know of its whereabouts later."

"Thank you."

They limped together across the driveway, and Genie put her shoulder against the front door to open it. When they stumbled into the foyer, Clara looked up in surprise from her position behind the reception desk.

"Annie fell and twisted her ankle," explained Genie, pushing streaks of hair heavy with rain from her eyes.

"Rose said you'd gone walking," said Clara, rushing across the foyer. "If I'd known, I'd have told you not to. Ben was here earlier warning of a weather front pushing in."

Annie shivered and rubbed rain from her face with a damp sleeve.

"We need to get you out of these clothes and into a hot bath," said Clara. "Once you're warm and dry we can see to that ankle of yours. Can you help me get Annie upstairs?"

"Of course," said Genie.

"You're almost as wet as Annie," said Clara, looking Genie up and down with a frown. "Jimmy has lit the fire in the bar. Once we've helped Annie upstairs, why don't you sit beside the fire and have a hot cocoa?"

"That sounds wonderful, thank you."

Between them, Clara and Genie inched Annie up the stairs. By now, she was shivering uncontrollably, her teeth clacking as they chattered in her jaw.

"In here," said Clara when they reached the first floor bathroom. "You get yourself warmed up now, Genie. I'll be alright here."

"Are you sure?"

"Yes, off you go."

Genie left the room and Clara turned on the taps, then began peeling off Annie's sodden clothes. She wrapped a thick towel around Annie's shoulders, and another around her head, then began rubbing her arms. "Feeling better?"

"Y... yes... th... thank you."

"You must have walked an awfully long way to get such a good soaking. Where were you heading?"

"To the north shore," lied Annie, unable to look Clara in the eye.

"It's funny," said Clara. "Blaine turned up here not fifteen minutes ago just as wet as you. It's a shame he didn't see you or he could have helped."

"Yes," said Annie.

Clara frowned and stared at her, then shook her head and gave Annie's arms one final rub. "I'll leave you to your bath and find you some clean, dry clothes. Then we'd better get a hot cup of tea inside you and something cold on that ankle. There'll be no work for you this evening, or the next few days, by the looks of things."

"I'm so sorry."

"Don't you worry. We'll manage. The important thing for you to do is rest that ankle. I'll leave you in peace, but will wait outside the door with your clean clothes when you're ready."

"Thank you," said Annie, feeling undeserving of such kindness from a woman she'd just lied through her teeth to. Annie was grateful when Clara left the room and she locked the door behind her. She limped to the bath and climbed in, waiting for the water to wash away yet more of her sins.

Chapter 68

September, 1953

"What on earth is going on?" asked Annie, as a group of finely robed men began a solemn march from the church back through the island streets. After four days laid up with a swollen ankle, it felt wonderful to be out and about again.

"They're from the Knights Templar," explained Jimmy. "Over one hundred men from as far south as Yorkshire and as far north as Scotland. How's your ankle?"

"Much better, thank you. I'm sorry for all the days' work I've missed. It's still a little sore if I stand on it for too long, but I think it's good to build up some strength. Anyway, enough about me. Who are the Knights Templar?"

"Freemasons, I think."

"Right," said Annie, still not understanding.

"Not something you'd have come across living at The Grit," said Jimmy, his eyes twinkling.

"Not something I expected to come across living here," said Annie with a smile.

"They've come for a pilgrimage," said Jimmy. "There was a service held in the church. Now they're on their way back to the village hall to disrobe before going for lunch."

"What's all this then?" asked Blaine, sauntering up to Annie and Jimmy. "Come to watch the toffs prancing around in their fancy dress?"

Annie's heart rate quickened. Blaine had stayed out of her way since the day of the injury, and despite her mixed feelings, she had missed him.

"You don't approve?" asked Jimmy, his voice less than warm.

"It's just a pompous club to sustain the grip of elites on this country," said Blaine.

"I wouldn't say that too loudly. There are Masons on this island too."

"I don't care if they hear me," said Blaine. "I speak for the ordinary man."

A look of distaste flickered across Jimmy's face. Annie still couldn't work out his dislike for Blaine, but it was there, clear as day on his face and in the tone of his voice. "I'd better get back. I'll leave you to it."

"Don't you want to stay to watch them parade past?"

Jimmy glanced at Blaine. "No, I've work to do."

"Alright."

When Jimmy had left, Blaine stepped closer to Annie, placing a hand on her waist. She tried to move away, worried an islander would see and report back to Jimmy or Clara, but Blaine's grasp was strong.

"Are you sure you want to watch this fiasco?" he asked. "I could think of better things to be doing back at my cottage."

"I'm sure you could," said Annie, blushing, "but I've seen nothing like this, so would like to stay."

"Suit yourself. They off to the church?" asked Blaine.

"No, they're coming from there. They've had their service and are going for lunch once they've disrobed. I expect without all their finery, they look like ordinary chaps. I doubt we'd be able to single them out from all the birdwatchers and ramblers. This procession though, well, it's like something from a historical novel."

"They are getting changed in the village hall?"

"Yes, that's right, then they're off somewhere for lunch."

Blaine's eyes flickered, and he chewed on his lower lip in a gesture Annie now knew meant he was thinking. "I just remembered Clara asked me to run an errand for her. I'll see you back at the hotel later."

"Are you sure you can't stay for the rest of the procession?"

"No, I'd best get going."

Blaine disappeared into the crowd, and Annie turned her attention back to the procession. Through the throng of robed men, she spotted Genie standing on the other side of the street. She lifted a hand in a small wave, which Genie returned. A gap formed in the processing men, and Genie made a dash across the street, gaining frowns and tuts from the pilgrims.

Annie giggled. "You were lucky you didn't get swept along to the hall with them."

"They don't allow women in their ranks," said Genie, raising an eyebrow. "How have you been? How's the ankle? Sorry I've not been in to check on you. Things have been so busy at the post office."

"Don't worry," said Annie, "Clara's been fussing over me, and not being able to work has had the benefit of being able to spend more time with Grandma Rose."

"How is the old girl?"

"She's well at the moment, thank goodness."

"Tell her I said hello. Was that Blaine I saw standing with you a moment ago?"

"Yes, he had to run some errands for Clara, so couldn't stay."

"I see. Listen, Annie, I doubt we'll ever see eye to eye over Blaine McCloud, but I'd hate for a man to get in the way of our friendship."

"Likewise," said Annie, giving Genie's hand a squeeze.

"I need to get back to work, but would you like to come with me? I can make us a pot of tea and we can catch up on each other's news?"

"That sounds lovely. To be honest, I've seen enough of old men in robes for one day. Tea with you sounds far more interesting."

The two women linked arms and turned off down a side street. Annie kept an eye out for Blaine, but their paths didn't cross. As they walked past the village hall, Annie thought she saw a shadow darting around the back of the building.

"What is it?" asked Genie.

"Nothing, I thought I saw someone, but it must have been my eyes playing tricks."

"There's no one there yet, but soon the place will be full of portly men de-robing, so I suggest we move on quickly, as I for one would rather not witness that."

Any tension over Blaine forgotten, Genie filled Annie in on all the latest gossip she'd picked up in the shop. Annie told Genie stories of the various guests who'd stayed at the hotel over the past few weeks, some kinder than others.

"I struggle with the children," Annie said. "They leave sticky handprints everywhere and the dining-room floor is disgusting after they've been eating in there."

"Ah, they're just kiddies being kiddies. I love it when families come here for their holidays. It breathes life back into the place. I can't wait to have a horde of bairns of my own."

Annie shuddered. "I just hope when I have my own children I don't find them as repulsive as other people's."

"You'll find your maternal streak soon enough," said Genie. "All you need is the right man."

Annie smiled. She longed to tell Genie that rather than children, her future held the promise of adventure, beginning with Paris, but she knew she would disapprove. If Genie hadn't left her alone to make the tea, the momentous news might have slipped out. But then Annie remembered Blaine's warning, that she could trust no one but him. Annie squeezed her lips together and swallowed down the news she was bursting to share.

Chapter 69

September, 1953

"Annie, we need you in the dining room," said Clara.

"Shall I finish polishing these glasses first?" asked Annie, checking a wine glass before housing it on a shelf behind the bar.

"No, we need you now. The police are here. They've come over to the island from Berwick."

"Police? What's happened?"

"It seems there's been a rather large theft. You saw the members of the Knights Templar processing yesterday?"

"Yes, I was watching it with Genie."

"Right, well, it seems while they were having their lunch, someone broke into the village hall and stole several items belonging to two of their members."

"That's awful. Surely the police don't suspect anyone on the island?"

"From what they've said, at this stage they're just gathering information. They'd like to speak to everyone who was on the island yesterday afternoon."

"I see." Annie folded the cloth in her hand and followed Clara into the dining room, where she found all the staff assembled, waiting with bated breath for the latest news. Blaine caught Annie's eye and smiled, but she looked away, scared that someone would notice the effect he had on her.

There were two uniformed officers standing with their hands clasped behind their backs, their eyes moving across each staff member sitting before them.

"Thank you for your time. As I'm sure most of you will have heard, yesterday afternoon a serious theft occurred in the island village hall. We will take statements from each of you, ascertaining where you were at the time of the theft, and whether you have any information which could help with our inquiries. Mr Watson has kindly provided his private sitting room for these interviews. You are welcome to get on with your work in the meantime, but please do not leave the hotel grounds, and make yourselves available when your name is called."

"We'll proceed in alphabetical order, so if we could begin with you, Mrs Armstrong."

Steffie turned to the rest of them and said, "this won't take long. I was in the kitchen all afternoon and didn't get home till gone ten." She followed Jimmy and the two officers out of the dining room. The rest of the staff breathed a collective sigh of relief, then the speculation began; what had been stolen? Had anyone seen anything suspicious? Who could be to blame? Was it a visitor to the island, for surely it must be?

"My worry," said Clara, "is the effect this will have on our community. In all the years I've lived here, no one has ever locked their doors. Something like this can cause suspicion to grow between neighbours, distrust of unfamiliar faces, and a general sense of unease."

"I'm sure the police will have the matter tied up quickly," said Annie, "then the island can move on just as before."

"I hope so," said Clara, staring out of the window.

"If it's alright, I'll go back to my glass polishing. I'll be in the bar when it's my turn."

"Of course," said Clara, waving a distracted hand in Annie's direction. "I'd better check on Rose, let her know what's going on."

Annie walked through to the bar and jumped as Blaine appeared behind her, grabbing her waist.

"Shush," he said, putting his finger to his lips and closing the door behind him.

"Now really isn't the time, Blaine," Annie said, glancing over his shoulder.

"I've not come in here for that. I need your help."

"My help? What for?"

"I need you to say you were with me yesterday afternoon."

"What? But I was with Genie after the procession."

"I know, but if you could be vague on your timings, say you spent a little while with her, then came round to my cottage for a cup of tea, or something along those lines."

"But that would mean lying to the police. Why can't you just tell them where you were?"

"Because I was on my own so have no alibi."

"Why should that matter if you've done nothing wrong?"

"It shouldn't, but there are those on this island who take against *interlopers,* as they like to call them. Some of the local men have been trying to get rid of me ever since I arrived. Just because I dress differently and would rather be painting than fishing. They don't trust me and have spread all sorts of rumours about me since I arrived."

Annie flushed as she thought of the chatter the day of the clothes sale. "But surely if you explained all that to the police..."

"You think they'd believe a long-haired artist? Those bastards won't trust a word that comes out of my mouth."

"But..."

"I can see you don't want to help me. I thought you believed me when I told you I'm the only person you can trust, but obviously not." Blaine turned, his hand reaching for the door.

"Wait. Tell me again what you need me to say."

By the time Annie's name was called for her interview, she was a nervous wreck. She had been muttering the story Blaine told her for the past half-hour, terrified she would slip up and say the wrong thing. However much she wanted to help Blaine, lying to the police seemed a bad idea. What if Genie contradicted her story?

"Good morning, Miss Hearn," said one of the policemen as Annie walked into Jimmy's sitting room.

"Good morning."

"Please take a seat."

Annie sat in an armchair, the two policemen opposite her on the sofa. One had a notebook open on his lap, a pen in his hand.

"Is it alright if I stay? Annie is my niece."

"I'm sorry, Mr Watson, but your niece is eighteen, so no longer a child. We wish to speak to her alone, if we may."

"I'll be just outside," said Jimmy, squeezing Annie's shoulder.

"Right, Miss Hearn, let's start with where you were between the hours of noon and four p.m. yesterday afternoon."

Annie took a deep breath, clutching her hands firmly in her lap to stop them shaking. "At noon I was watching the Knights Templar process through the village streets."

"Were you alone?"

"No, at first I was with my Uncle Jimmy, Mr Watson, then I was joined by Blaine McCloud, and later by Genie Guthrey."

"I see. How long did you stay watching the procession?"

"Probably around ten or fifteen minutes. I can't be certain."

"You weren't wearing a wristwatch?"

"No, it was my day off yesterday, so I wasn't tied to any schedule."

"I see. So, after watching the procession, what did you do next?"

"I went and had a cup of tea with my friend Genie at the post office, then I came back to the hotel and went to Blaine McCloud's cottage."

"On your own?" asked the policeman, his eyebrow raised.

"Yes, on my own. I have commissioned a painting from Mr McCloud as a thank-you for my aunt and uncle's hospitality while I've been on the island. It's a surprise, so I didn't want them knowing I was going to see Blaine, I mean, Mr McCloud."

"And what did you do in his cottage?"

Annie fought against the blush threatening to expose her lie. "He made me a cup of tea and we looked through a selection of photographs of my aunt and uncle, trying to decide which one he would turn into a portrait."

"And how long did all this take?"

"I can't be sure, I'm sorry."

"Take a rough guess."

"An hour, possibly longer."

"And what time did you leave Miss Guthrey and arrive at Mr McCloud's cottage?"

"As I said, I wasn't wearing a wristwatch, so I'm afraid I can't give you any specific timings."

"I see. Well, thank you, Miss Hearn, you have been most helpful."

"Is that it?"

"Yes, you're free to leave."

"Thank you." Annie stood on shaking legs and bid the policemen goodbye.

Chapter 70

September, 1953

"Did they ever find out who stole all those jewels?"

"It wasn't all those jewels, Grandma," said Annie. "It was two suede pouches, a gauntlet, gloves, spurs, and a single jewel. And no, they never found the culprit."

"Humph, things like that would never have happened in my day."

"No, but I doubt you had many visitors to the island in your day."

"We had plenty of fishermen and herring lassies."

"But I don't suppose any of them brought jewels with them."

"Nae need to be so contrary, lass. What's got into you today?"

"I don't know," said Annie, pulling Rose's stockings up her weak legs. "I suppose I'm feeling a little unsettled. Clara and Jimmy have made it clear there'll be no work for me beyond October."

"So you're worried about leaving, is that it?"

"Yes, I suppose so." What Annie didn't mention was that however exciting Blaine's talk of Paris was, no firm details had been mentioned, and when pressed, he kept changing the subject.

"You'll be alright, whatever you do next. It may not be a bad thing for ye to get away from this place for a while."

"Why do you say that?"

"Because you dinna seem happy."

"I'm perfectly happy," insisted Annie.

A knock at the door interrupted any further questioning by Rose. Annie looked up to see Genie standing in the doorway, a gun slung over her shoulder.

"Whatever have you got there?" asked Annie.

"What's going on?" asked Rose. "Who's there?"

"It's my friend Genie," said Annie. "Genie Guthrey, and she appears to have a gun with her."

A smile spread across Rose's face. "Off rabbiting, are ye?"

"Aye, Mrs Watson, I am, and I thought I'd see if Annie would like to join me."

"Oh aye, ye should take Annie with ye. If she's anything like her grandmother, she'll be a fine shot." Rose's face was now creased into a wide grin, and she seemed lost in her memories.

"Could one of you explain what you're talking about, please?" said Annie.

"I'm off rabbiting, shooting rabbits. Mam wants to cook rabbit pie for supper."

"That sounds very cruel."

Genie shrugged. "Aye, maybe, but there's so many rabbits around now, their numbers need managing else it'll be bad for other wildlife."

"How I wish I could come with ye," sighed Rose, a wistful look on her face.

Annie grinned at her grandmother, a vivid image of a young Rose wielding a gun coming to mind.

"Off ye go then, lassies, and shoot one for me."

"Will do, Mrs Watson," said Genie.

"So," said Annie when they stepped out of the hotel, "where are we going?"

"To the dunes, but the path, as you'll know, is still muddy, so I brought you these." Genie grabbed a pair of wellington boots she'd stashed by the front door. "You'll thank me later," she said as Annie discarded her own shoes and put them on.

Two hours later, Annie flopped down against a large dune, exhausted. Much of their time had been spent hunched over or lying on their stomachs waiting for their prey, but they had still covered a large distance, and climbing up the crumbling sandy hills had taken its toll on Annie's calves and her ankle which wasn't yet fully healed.

Genie had three rabbits tied together by string, two of which she'd shot, and one which Annie had reluctantly caught. "Rose was right," said Genie, "we'll make a fine marksman out of you."

"I'm not sure I'm cut out for this," said Annie, pointing to the gun. "I've always fancied having a rabbit as a pet rather than for my supper."

"That's a shame," said Genie. "With your eye, they could have rabbit pie on the menu at the hotel every night."

Annie shuddered.

Genie stood up and stared out into the distance, a hand held up to shield her eyes. "Isn't that the ruined cottage Blaine McCloud takes you to?"

Annie sighed, wishing she'd never let that piece of information slip out. "He's only taken me there twice, and it's not nearly as seedy as you make it sound."

"I implied nothing of the sort," said Genie, raising an eyebrow. "I'd like to see it. Let's go."

Annie groaned, her legs and ankle protesting as she climbed to her feet. "Alright, but we'll have a quick look and then we're heading back. I'm gasping for a cup of tea."

"Deal."

The two women trudged across the sand, Genie dragging Annie up inclines when she protested about her sore legs. By the time they reached the cottage, Annie would have welcomed not only a cup of tea but also an afternoon nap. Genie shoved open the door and coughed as a cloud of dust filled the air.

"Goodness me, this place has seen better days."

"Yes," said Annie, "but there's something rather charming about it when you get used to it."

Genie crossed the room and flopped down in an old rocking chair. "I wouldn't want to be here after dark. I bet there are all kinds of ghosts lurking in the shadows."

"Let's hope not." Annie pulled out a chair beside the table, sat down and laid her head on her arms, yawning loudly. She was about to close her eyes, when, from the corner of her eye, she spotted something glinting in a narrow patch of sunlight. "What's that?"

Genie leaned forward in her chair. "What can you see?"

"I'm not sure." Annie walked to the far side of the room and crouched down in a dark corner. "Oh, my goodness."

Genie leaped out of her chair and knelt beside Annie. They both stared at an old wooden box, which would have been well hidden had the top not come loose, exposing a sliver of gold within it. "You'd better open it," said Genie quietly.

With one finger, Annie knocked the lid of the box free. She rocked back on her haunches, staring open-mouthed at the objects inside. "Don't," she said, as Genie reached out to touch them, but it was too late. Ignoring Annie's protests, Genie laid a pair of gloves, a gauntlet, spurs, suede pouches and a single jewel onto the dirty cottage floor. "You shouldn't have done that," whispered Annie.

"Why ever not?"

"Because if I'm not mistaken, those are the stolen items the police were searching for, and now your fingerprints will be all over them."

"The thief's fingerprints will be on them, too."

"Not if he or she wore gloves."

"We'll have to take these to the police," said Genie.

"But what if they suspect us? We were each other's alibi. They might think we were both in on it."

"Well, we can't just leave them here."

"Why not?"

"Because then whoever stole them will get away with it."

"They can't be worth all that much," said Annie, picking up the pair of pure white gloves and turning them over in her hands.

"I thought you were worried about fingerprints?"

"In for a penny..." Annie picked up each item, marvelling at the quality of materials, but still not believing they held any real value. "Surely, if these items were valuable, they wouldn't have been left unattended in the village hall?"

"You may have a point there. Even so, they shouldn't have been stolen. Do you remember that time Amy told us about the stolen wallet?"

"What has that got to do with anything?" asked Annie, bristling at the implication.

"Don't you think it's strange? First those rumours, and then the stolen items turn up here, and you and Blaine are the only people I know who use this cottage?"

Annie threw the items back in the box and, with the toe of her boot, shoved it back into the corner of the room. "This is just what Blaine was worried about," she said. "You islanders have it in for him, and someone will have planted these here to set him up."

"Us islanders?" said Genie, rising to her full height and placing her hands on her hips. "It wasn't that long ago you were counting yourself as an islander, if I remember rightly. And besides, don't ye think we've more to be getting on with than causing trouble for Blaine McCloud?"

"It's the only rational explanation."

"No, Annie," said Genie, gripping Annie's wrists. "Listen to yer-self. The only rational explanation is Blaine McCloud stole from the Knights Templar, then hid the items in this deserted cottage."

"No," said Annie, her voice raising, "it's not true." She wrenched her hands free from Genie and fled the cottage, her earlier exhaustion forgotten. As she ran, she tried to ignore the voice inside her head reminding her of Blaine's request for an alibi. "It's a coincidence," she told herself, "nothing more." For the alternative was too awful to contemplate, and if true, would spoil every plan she had made for her future.

Chapter 71

September, 1953

A week had passed and Annie had neither seen Genie, nor had a visit from the police, so deduced from this that her friend had kept quiet about what they'd found. Twice Annie had seen Blaine in passing, but had found excuses not to spend any length of time with him. He was growing frustrated, but the only way Annie could carry on as normal was to bury her head in the sand and pretend the excursion to the cottage had never happened.

That morning, Annie was carrying a tray of dirty dishes through from the kitchen when she heard a scream. She put down her tray and ran toward the commotion. Just outside the main entrance, Clara was leaning over the prone figure of Jimmy, a ladder beside him.

"What happened?"

"I told him not to clean those windows himself. His leg isn't strong enough to be climbing up and down ladders."

Clara was crying, her hands held to Jimmy's head. When Annie stepped forward, she realised there was blood everywhere, on the gravel, running down Jimmy's face, and covering Clara's fingers.

"Jimmy? Jimmy, can you hear us?" Annie crouched beside her uncle and could have cried with relief when he opened his eyes and let out a groan.

"Thank God," said Clara. "Annie, can you fetch some cloths from inside please, and a bowl of warm water, and before you do any of that can you telephone for an ambulance?"

"I don't need to go to hospital," muttered Jimmy.

"You can't see all this blood," said Clara. "If you could, you'd agree with me. You've a nasty gash on the back of your head and it needs seeing to."

Jimmy groaned again, his face twisting in pain. "Everything hurts."

"I'm not surprised. What were you doing up there in the first place?"

"The windows urgently needed a clean. I've been asking Blaine to do it all week but..."

"That's enough talking," said Clara. "You just lie still for me. Annie? I know this looks bad, but you need to move and do as I say."

Annie blinked, her body obeying Clara's instructions even if her mind was a step behind. It was the shock of seeing her capable uncle like that. Would he be alright? Annie ran to the telephone and dialled the emergency services. At least the tide was out and an ambulance could get across. When she had fetched all the supplies Clara needed, Annie ran back outside.

"Thank you," said Clara. "Is an ambulance on its way?"

"Yes, but I wondered if I should ask a taxi driver to wait on the mainland and help guide it across. It will be here a lot quicker if it doesn't have to creep across the sand."

"Good thinking."

Annie ran through the village and banged on a cottage door.

"Is everything alright, lass?" asked Mick, the friendliest of the drivers Annie had encountered.

"No, it's my Uncle Jimmy." Annie explained the situation, and Mick gathered up his coat and car keys.

"I'll head out now. It shouldn't be too long before Jimmy has the medical attention he needs. Is there anything else I can do for you before I leave?"

"No, thank you."

"I'll be seeing you then," said Mick.

Annie ran back to the hotel and found Jimmy sitting against a wall, holding a pad of gauze to his head.

"He insisted on sitting up," said Clara. "I told him not to, but he wouldn't listen."

Annie gave Clara a reassuring squeeze on the shoulder and crouched down in front of Jimmy. "How are you feeling?"

"Apart from the headache, not too bad."

"That's good. I should probably ring Mum and tell her what's happened."

"No," said Jimmy. "Don't do that. You'd worry Marnie over nothing. At least wait till the doc has checked me over, then you can explain what happened without concerning her."

"Alright," said Annie.

"Will you be able to mind the hotel if I go with Jimmy to the hospital?" asked Clara.

"Of course."

"There shouldn't be too much to do. The group of pilgrims that were here left this morning, and the next guests aren't arriving until tomorrow afternoon. You may get the odd local wanting a drink later, but we'll close the restaurant, so you don't need to worry about that."

"Don't worry about this place," said Annie. She turned back to Jimmy. "Would you like something to eat or drink?"

"A cup of tea would go down nicely."

"Put some sugar in it, please," said Clara, "it will help with the shock."

"You look like you could do with some sugary tea too," said Jimmy, reaching out and taking Clara's hand. "I'm sorry for all the worry I've caused."

"Don't be ridiculous," said Clara. "We only worry because we care. You're the most important person to me, seeing you lying on the ground covered in blood, well, it's no surprise I'm a little pale and pasty."

"I'll get the tea," said Annie.

They were draining the last from the teapot when the ambulance finally arrived. A nurse climbed out, rushing over to Jimmy and checking his head wound. "How many fingers am I holding up?" she asked.

"Three, and one thumb."

The nurse rolled her eyes. "I've heard that one before. Can you tell me your name?"

"Jimmy Watson."

"And what year is it?"

"1953."

"Good, that's very good."

"Is he going to be alright?" asked Clara.

"It seems so, but we'll need to get him properly assessed at the hospital."

"There's really no need."

The nurse stood and placed her hands on her hips. "I've seen enough head injuries in my time to know it's always better safe than sorry. Let's get you into the ambulance, and can someone pack an overnight bag for Mr Watson, please?"

"I will," said Clara. "Please don't leave without me."

"You're Mrs Watson?"

"Yes, I'm Jimmy's wife."

"Very well, you can come with us, but please hurry."

Clara ran inside the hotel, reappearing minutes later with a leather bag in hand. "Are you sure you can manage?"

"I'm certain. You save your worrying for Jimmy. Will you ring me later so I know how you've got on?"

"Of course."

Annie gave Clara a brief hug, then waved as she and Jimmy departed in the ambulance. Despite the circumstances, Annie felt proud that Clara had trusted her enough to look after the hotel in their absence. She turned and walked into the lobby, hoping that after all the excitement of the day, it would prove a quiet evening.

Chapter 72

September, 1953

"So," said Blaine, walking behind the bar and wrapping his arms around Annie, "I hear we have the hotel to ourselves for the night."

"Yes, and any paying customers who turn up," said Annie.

"Look at it," said Blaine. "The place is dead."

"Clara said she thought it would be quiet."

"I hope you don't mind, but I've got a few friends on the mainland who are keen to come over this evening."

"What?" asked Annie, confused. She thought Blaine had been suggesting a quiet evening with just the two of them.

"Like I said, just a few friends. They're all artists too, and very sweet. I lived with them for a few months on the mainland before I came here."

"Right, well, they won't be able to come for long. The tide closes in a couple of hours."

"I thought they could stay here. It's not as though we don't have the space."

"The rooms are ready for the next guests who are arriving tomorrow. They can't stay in the hotel. Besides, Clara left me in charge. I don't want her to think I've gone behind her back. I'm guessing these friends of yours wouldn't be paying to stay here?"

"When did you become so prim and proper?" asked Blaine, frowning. He leaned forward and began massaging Annie's shoulders. "You're only eighteen. You should be keen for a party."

"No one mentioned anything about a party," said Annie, her pulse racing.

Blaine laughed and shrugged. "Party, gathering, reunion, call it what you like. My friends have wanted to visit me here for such a long time, but the right moment has never presented itself."

"By the right moment, I assume you mean when Jimmy and Clara are away?"

Blaine grinned, but for once, Annie was immune to his charm.

"Blaine, Jimmy is in hospital with a head injury. Clara says he'll be alright, but it must have been serious for them to keep him in overnight. Surely you're not suggesting going behind their backs while they're spending the night in hospital?"

"Like you said, it's nothing serious. Jimmy will be fine by the morning. Anyway, it's too late, I've already invited my friends and they're on their way."

"How did you even know Jimmy and Clara weren't here? I've not seen you all day."

"I saw the ambulance driving off the island and asked a local lad what had happened."

Annie was lost for words. Blaine must have telephoned his friends as soon as he knew Jimmy and Clara were driving to the mainland in an ambulance. But why would he do it? It was a breach of trust.

"Hey," said Blaine, cupping Annie's face in his hands. "Don't look so worried. I'm not about to throw a mad party, it's just a few friends, that's all. There's no one about, so we can close the bar to customers and this can stay between ourselves."

"I suppose," said Annie. "But no one can sleep in the hotel."

"Fine, they can stay with me."

"Good."

Two men walked in and the conversation ended, and with it the idea of closing to the public, as the locals took up position at the bar.

"Evening, Dougie, Ted. What can I get you?"

"A pint of ale to wet my whistle, please, lass," said Dougie, heaving his ageing body onto a bar stool.

"And the same for me," said Ted.

"Of course. Busy day?"

"Aye, the herring are on the move now, so we've been busy preparing the long lines. Quiet in here tonight."

"Yes," said Annie. "There's another group arriving tomorrow, so we'll enjoy the peace while we can."

"Terrible about your uncle. Jimmy's a fine fellow. We were all worried when we heard what happened. Is there any news about how he is?"

Annie smiled. "Yes, I spoke to Clara not long ago, and he's going to be fine. They're keeping him in overnight to be on the safe side, but he should be home in the morning."

"That is good news. So they've left you in charge, have they?"

"They have."

"Well, we'll cause you no trouble, will we, Dougie?"

"None. You know, you're the spit of Marnie when she was a youngster."

"You know my mum?"

The old man chuckled. "Everyone knows everyone here. She was a good lass, was Marnie. Of course, she left when she was little more than a bairn, but who could blame her, living with Alex?"

"My grandfather?"

"Aye, he was a nasty piece of work."

"I thought Mum left the island to care for Jimmy after his accident."

"Oh aye, that's right enough. But getting away from Alex was a bonus. I dinna remember him well as I was only a lad, but I've heard enough stories to know he was a wrong 'un."

Annie would have liked to hear more about her family, even the less flattering recollections, but at that moment a group of long-haired, dirty looking men burst into the bar. From the way they walked and the volume of their voices, Annie guessed they'd already had a fair amount to drink. The islanders at the bar bristled, setting down their pints and straightening their backs.

"Can I help you?" asked Annie.

"Evening, gentlemen," said Blaine, throwing the group a wink that only Annie noticed.

"Jock's old bus almost got stuck on the sand," one man said. "We had to get out and push." They all roared with laughter, slapping each other on the back.

"Get some drinks for these gentlemen, Annie. Whisky all round?"

"Aye, and the rest," laughed one man.

While Annie poured out drinks, the men drew chairs around a table and sprawled out, throwing coats onto the carpet and kicking off their shoes.

"You know them?" asked Ted, nodding towards Blaine's friends, his voice low.

Annie shook her head.

"Looks like your colleague does," said Ted, as Blaine took up position at the table.

"Huh," said Dougie. "That explains a lot." He scrunched up his face as though a foul smell had wafted in front of him.

"He's just being friendly," said Annie, but her protest was ignored.

Over the past few weeks, Annie had come to realise Blaine was far more popular with women than men. She couldn't understand why men took against him, but wondered if they felt threatened by his good looks and charm. What other explanation could there be?

"Here," said Annie, passing a tray of drinks across the bar.

"Thanks," said Blaine. "You're an angel." He blew her a kiss and Annie's cheeks reddened as she saw the frowning faces of Dougie and Ted.

When Blaine placed the tray of drinks on the table, cries of delight filled the room. Shots of whisky were poured down necks in one gulp before the men picked up their pint glasses, clinking them together with accompanying shouts of 'cheers'. Annie rubbed her neck, trying to dispel some of the tension held within her muscles. She didn't like the attitude of the men who'd invaded the hotel, and had a bad feeling about how the night was going to progress.

Chapter 73

September, 1953

"I canna take much more of this," grumbled Dougie. Ted whispered something in his ear and the two men nodded. Dougie climbed off his bar stool, placing his half-drunk pint down on the bar.

"Are you off home?" asked Annie, trying to hide the hope in her voice.

"No."

Annie looked on in panic as Dougie strode from the room. She suspected where he was going, and it didn't bode well. As the drinks flowed in an endless stream from the bar to Blaine's friends, the mainlanders' behaviour had become increasingly worrisome. One man had already vomited over the carpet, his friends laughing as Annie appeared with a mop and bucket to clean it up. Another had climbed up onto the table and recited a poem in something between a shout and scream. Worse than everything, though, were the loud, disparaging comments about the island and its residents.

"Bunch of inbreds."

"Thick as two short planks."

"Have to marry their sisters as no other women will look at them."

So far, Dougie and Ted had sat stony-faced, pretending not to hear, but Annie could feel the tension rising. It was obvious Blaine's friends were spoiling for a fight. From the look of them, fighting was a mainstay of their Saturday nights, several ageing bruises visible beneath their dirty skin.

"Ted, where has Dougie gone?"

"For reinforcements," said Ted, taking a sip of his pint.

"Please, I don't want any trouble."

"You shouldn't have let that bunch through the door then," he said, cocking his head toward Blaine's table.

"Oh, and how was I meant to stop them?"

"Dinna worry, lass. They won't be here much longer."

"Please, Ted, Clara left me in charge. If she comes back to find men have been brawling in her absence, she'll never trust me again."

"It's nae you she shouldn't be trusting. Goodness knows what Clara was thinking, employing that scoundrel from the mainland."

"Blaine?"

"Aye, that's the one."

"Perhaps if you got to know him, you'd realise he's not as bad as you think?"

At that moment Blaine stood up, lifted a pint to his lips and downed it in one, to roars of laughter and cheers from his friends. Ted turned to Annie and raised an eyebrow.

Colour drained from Annie's face as the doorway to the bar filled with the unsmiling faces of island men. One by one, they walked in, gathering together in an ominous silence.

"Looks like word of a party has spread," said one of Blaine's friends. "Have you come to join us, lads?"

The only movement from the islanders was the folding of arms, the deepening of frowns and narrowing of eyes.

"Doesn't seem like our new friends can talk," said a mainlander.

"The rumours of backward islanders must be true," said another. No one laughed, the tension in the room having a sobering effect.

Blaine stepped forward. "Alright, Dougie? Your friends fancied a drink, did they?" Blaine's voice was light, friendly, and he gave Dougie a jolly tap on the arm.

Dougie looked down at his shirt to where Blaine's hand was resting. He slowly lifted his eyes. "Did ye think yer friends could talk us islanders doon and there'd be nae consequence?" His accent had thickened, his words dripping with menace.

"There's no need to be like that," said Blaine. "These chaps were just joking around."

"Where did ye find these friends of yers? They look to me like someone pulled them out of a gutter."

A chair fell to the ground as one mainlander stood up too suddenly. "You're not going to let him talk about us like that, are you, Blaine?"

"Dougie here is right, we have been a little rude, but I promise you, it really was in jest. How about I buy you chaps a drink by way of an apology?"

"That sounds a good idea," said Annie. "What would you like, gentlemen?"

"There'll be time for drinking later," said Dougie. As he stepped forward, the other island men joined him, moving as one mass towards the mainlanders, who were all now standing poised beside their chairs.

Annie wasn't sure who threw the first punch. All she knew was that within minutes of Dougie's reinforcements arriving, the bar was a blur of fists, spatters of blood flying and landing on walls and tables. Chairs were thrown across the room, or smashed directly into men's heads. Annie screamed at the men to stop, but no one paid any attention.

"Blaine, Blaine, please stop this!" shouted Annie, but he either couldn't hear her, or chose to ignore her. As she stepped out from behind the bar, two men stumbled into her, an elbow catching her nose. Annie screamed. She lifted her hand to her face, and it came away covered in blood. Tears joined the blood running down her face. The men hadn't even noticed she was injured, too distracted were they by the fight at hand.

Annie made a dash for it, running to the nearest toilet to grab a handful of tissue for her bloody nose. Once she had stemmed the bleeding, she ran to the only person on the island who stood a chance of stopping the brawl.

In stark contrast to the hotel bar, the island streets were quiet. Orange light spilled from pubs and homes, but there wasn't another soul out. As soon as she reached the cottage she needed, Annie began hammering on the door.

"What is it?" asked Ben, flinging open the door and staring in surprise at Annie. "My God, Annie, what's happened? You're covered in blood!"

"It's the hotel," said Annie, unable to hold back a sob. "Some mainlanders started drinking in the bar and they were being rude about the island and its people. Dougie Solomon heard what they were saying and fetched a group of island men to teach the mainlanders a lesson."

"How many are there?"

"About twenty men. They're destroying the place, Ben. I don't know what to do."

"Where's Blaine with all this going on? I thought he'd be there to help you."

Annie paused. As angry as she was with Blaine, if she admitted the role he'd played in the evening's events, Ben was sure to tell Clara and he'd get the sack. She couldn't risk it. "He tried to stop the fighting but ended up getting caught up in it."

"I see," said Ben, his voice doubtful. "Come on then, we'd better get going."

Chapter 74

September, 1953

The sight that greeted them when they entered the hotel was even worse than when Annie had left. The fight had spilled out into the lobby. A huddle of men were wrestling on the floor, a vase lay splintered against tiles speckled with blood. Ben took Annie's hand, sidestepping the brawling men on the floor.

"What in God's name!" he said, his mouth falling open as they stepped into the bar area. A blood-covered Blaine stood in the middle of the room, a broken bottle in one hand. Around him, the air filled with shouts and the sound of fists against flesh and bone.

"Enough!" shouted Ben. When no one listened, he pulled a whistle from his pocket and blew a long, piercing note. The men stopped fighting and turned to him. "You have all of five seconds to leave the premises," he shouted, "or I shall pass your names on to the constable, and that includes islanders and mainlanders."

A sheepish-looking Dougie limped across the room. Bruises were already forming around one eye and his hair was matted with blood. "I'm sorry, Ben, but you should've heard what these animals were saying."

"I dinna care what they were saying," said Ben, his voice cold. "There is nae excuse for what has happened here tonight. After all Jimmy and Clara do for this community, this is how you repay them? Look at the place. You've caused hundreds of pounds' worth of damage."

"I think the lads thought they were helping," said Ted, emerging from behind the bar.

"Helping?" said Ben. "You lot." He pointed to where the mainlanders had gathered in a group, nursing their wounds. "I want you off this property now, and if I ever see your faces on this island again, there'll be hell to pay."

"Blaine, are you going to let this chap talk to us like that?"

Blaine slowly turned, his eyes not meeting his friends. "I'm sorry, but you heard the man. You need to leave."

"It sounds as if these men know you, Blaine."

The broken bottle Blaine was holding dropped to the ground. He took a deep breath, then turned to face Ben. "No, not at all. I must have told them my name while I was serving them. You know what fellows are like when they get drunk. You either become a best friend or an enemy. Thankfully, I became the former to them."

Annie's mouth fell open. She expected someone to contradict Blaine, but cowed by Ben's anger, they kept quiet.

"What are you all waiting for?" shouted Ben. The men trooped out of the hotel, Blaine following them. "Not you," said Ben, holding his arm out to stop him.

Annie saw something flicker in Blaine's eyes. Fear? Anger? Defiance? Ben left Blaine and Annie standing in the bar, making sure all the men were not just out of the building, but walking away back into the village.

"I told him you weren't to blame for the fight," whispered Annie, her eyes flicking to the door to check Ben wasn't coming back. "What were you thinking, inviting them here?"

"It was the islanders who started the fight."

"What?" asked Annie, incredulous. Before she could speak again, Ben strode back into the room.

"The men who came here tonight," Ben said, addressing Blaine. "Are you certain you'd never met them before?"

"Of course not."

"You couldn't have made them leave before this got out of control?"

"They seemed harmless enough at first."

It shocked Annie how easily the lies fell from Blaine's lips. She almost believed him herself, despite knowing the truth. He was utterly convincing, even summoning tears as he spoke of how ashamed he was.

"You'd better get yourself cleaned up," said Ben. "I'll help Annie get this place sorted out."

Blaine nodded and threw Annie a secret smile before leaving the room. She couldn't see what there was to smile about. It was already gone midnight, and she had hours of cleaning up to do if she were to make the hotel presentable before Clara and Jimmy arrived home. As she crossed the room, her feet crunched broken glass into a carpet stained with spilled pints of beer. Several chairs had broken legs, and one table had a large crack running from one side to another. A window's glass had been destroyed by a man falling through it, and there was no way she could do anything about that before the morning.

"I'll fetch some cardboard for that window," said Ben. "We'll have to pray it doesn't rain tonight. I'll fix some wood across it in the morning, but we'd better hope Jimmy can get the glass replaced soon, as it will give a terrible first impression to arriving guests."

Annie's tears returned. "Poor Jimmy, this is the last thing he needs. I'm so sorry, Ben. I should have managed the whole situation better."

"Annie, you were one small lass surrounded by a horde of drunken louts. You've nothing to be sorry for. I'm just relieved the worst you suffered was a bloody nose, and I'm sure Jimmy and Clara will feel the same."

"Still, I feel partly responsible. I'll pay for the window out of my earnings."

"What about Blaine? He was here too, and I don't see him offering to pay for any damage or help clean up."

"He was injured. You told him to go home."

"Aye, that I did, but you seem able to clean with tissue stuck up each nostril. Still, I suppose there's time for him to return and redeem himself."

Much as Annie hoped Blaine would return and help them, in her heart she knew he wouldn't. He was too selfish. The realisation shocked her. She had pinned all hopes for her future on a man who enjoyed a pub brawl and accepted no responsibility for the consequences.

Chapter 75

September, 1953

Annie rubbed her eyes as she descended the staircase. It had been gone three before she'd finally made it into bed. Between her and Ben, they'd restored the hotel bar to as good a condition as they could. There was no hiding the broken window, or missing chairs, but at least the carpet was clean, the air smelled fresh, and there was no danger of anyone cutting themselves on broken glass.

"Morning," said Annie, smiling at Olive, Clara's receptionist and longest serving member of staff.

"Good morning, Annie. I heard there was a bit of a to-do last night. I've rung a glazier on the mainland who can come and fit a new window this morning."

"Thank you," said Annie.

"Your grandmother has asked to see you."

"When?"

"Now. She was quite insistent about it."

Annie sighed, smiled at Olive and walked the short distance to Rose's bedroom.

"Come in," called Rose, when Annie knocked.

"Good morning," said Annie.

"You sound tired. Sit."

Annie pulled up a chair beside Rose's bed. "Is everything alright, Grandma?"

"Nae, it isn't, and I think ye know why."

"I'm not sure I do."

Rose rolled her eyes. "Dinna play the fool, Annie. I had my window open last night and heard the commotion. If I'd been able to get myself out of bed, I'd have rung the police, or better still, dragged them off the island by the scruff of their necks. What happened? It sounded like a riot."

"It wasn't as bad as that, but it was bad," admitted Annie. "A group of men came over from the mainland. They were already drunk when they arrived, and didn't slow down. They were being rude."

"Rude about what?"

"The island. Islanders. Dougie and Ted were in having a quiet drink and took offence."

"Quite right too."

"Yes, I can understand why they were upset, but that doesn't justify what happened next. Dougie went out and gathered a group of island men to confront the mainlanders."

"I gathered as much. What was the damage?"

"A broken window, smashed glasses, quite a few chairs need repairing. We cleaned the rest up without too much trouble."

"And where was Blaine McCloud when all this was happening?"

"He was there in the bar."

"But he couldn't get control of the situation?"

"He got a little carried away."

"I understand he was friendly with the mainlanders."

Annie wondered how on earth this information had reached Rose.

"I heard them talking outside my window," said Rose, answering Annie's unspoken question. "Blaine was inviting them back to his cottage. It didn't sound like the first time they'd met."

"What are you going to tell Jimmy?"

"It's nae my place to tell Jimmy anything." Silence stretched between them, Rose fixing Annie with a stare despite her lack of vision. "It's nae my place, but it is yours."

"What? No. There's no reason to drag Blaine into this."

"For goodness' sake," said Rose, slamming her palm down on her bedside cabinet. "I thought ye were more intelligent than this. He's taking ye for a fool, Annie Rose Hearn. Open your eyes!"

"Blaine is doing nothing of the sort," said Annie, unable to keep the irritation from her voice despite her own misgivings.

"He's been a blight on this place ever since he arrived. Jimmy should have put his foot down about him. Oh, he charmed Clara alright, but nae Jimmy. Nae, not my lad. He's enough experience of men like Blaine to know it's always best to steer clear."

"I need to get back to work," said Annie, standing. "Is there anything I can get you before I go?"

Rose reached out for her hand. Annie paused, then stepped forward, taking Rose's hand in hers. Rose squeezed so hard it was all Annie could do to stop herself from crying out. "I've nae much time left on this earth," said Rose, "so please, listen to me while ye still can. Ye need to stay well clear of that man. Dinna make the same mistake I did. Annie, it would break my heart if ye became trapped in a life ye dinna want, tied to a man who only thinks of himself. I spent half my life living under the threat of violence, and it would break my heart were the same to happen to ye."

"Blaine would never hurt me."

"Maybe not with his fists, but there's more than one way to hurt a person."

"Thank you for the warning, Grandma, but I can look after myself." Annie let go of Rose's hand and walked out of the room. As she was closing the door, she heard what could've been a sob, but she didn't hang around long enough to find out.

"Annie, there you are."

Ben stood in the lobby, ready for a trip to sea in waterproofs and wellington boots.

"I didn't expect to see you today. Thank you for all your help yesterday."

"I wanted to come by and see if you were alright? I've spoken to Clara. They are hoping to come home as soon as the tide opens at midday, providing the hospital allows it."

"I'm fine, and thank you for letting me know when they'll be returning."

"No problem. You need help with anything else?"

Annie shook her head. "No, thank you. You've done more than enough, and besides, you look as though you're about to head out on the boat."

"Aye, that I am. Very well, tell Clara I'll pop in this evening to check on Jimmy."

"I will do. Ben, before you go... what did you tell Clara about last night?"

Ben sighed and ran a hand through his hair. "Nothing. I told her nothing. I'll leave it to you to break the bad news. Sorry." Ben waved a hand and headed off towards the harbour.

"Annie."

Annie turned and saw Genie rushing through the gate. "What are you doing here?"

Genie took Annie's arm and pulled her across the lawn, away from the hotel. "The entire island's abuzz with what happened here last night. What was Blaine McCloud thinking inviting those chaps over here?"

"Blaine didn't..."

"Oh, dinna try that on me, lassie. Dougie Solomon told Mam all about Blaine's denials. He thinks he can keep lying and get away with it, but Dougie has other ideas. As soon as your uncle's better, he'll be over here to speak the truth."

To Annie's shame, she burst into tears.

"Oh, lass, I dinna mean to upset ye."

"I've been such a fool, Genie, and now I don't know what to do."

"Come here." She pulled Annie into her arms. "It will all be alright, lass. Let's sit over there on that bench and ye can tell me everything."

Chapter 76

September, 1953

Annie stared up at the ceiling and let out a loud sigh. After noticing the bags under her eyes, Olive had told her to get some sleep, but Annie had been lying with her eyes closed for the best part of an hour and still sleep wouldn't come.

Ever since she'd poured out her worries to Genie, she'd known what she had to do. The only sensible course of action was to break things off with Blaine, and return to Lowestoft. She'd been a fool to think a man like Blaine could solve her inner restlessness. And as for trust? Perhaps she couldn't trust her family, but after recent events, Annie doubted she could trust Blaine either.

A clinking against her window caused Annie to sit upright on her bed. Wood rattled against glass as a ladder shook. Annie walked to the window and saw Blaine climbing towards her. She eased open her window an inch.

"What are you doing?"

"What does it look like?" asked Blaine, holding up a bucket of soapy water. He was dressed in faded blue overalls and had his hair pulled back from his face. "This is what I should have done days ago. If I had, Jimmy wouldn't have been up that ladder in the first place."

Annie frowned, more confused than ever.

"I can tell from the look on your face you're cross with me," said Blaine, "as you have every right to be. I was an idiot last night. The truth is, all those chaps have made successful careers from their art, and I wanted to impress them. I was like a child in school, trying to make the popular bairns like me. It's pathetic behaviour for a man of my age. I'm sorry."

"They didn't look very successful to me."

Blaine laughed. "Just wait till we get to Paris. If you thought those chaps were a little rough around the edges, you'll be shocked to see the artists in Montmartre. Some of the best artists in the world walk around looking like they're the starving homeless. Anyway, I really am sorry, Annie. I behaved like a fool."

Annie's frown deepened. "Thank you for your explanation, but why lie about knowing them?"

"Because I'm a coward. I'm sorry, Annie, you deserve a better man than me."

Blaine's eyes filled with sadness, and Annie's heart melted at the sight. "We all make mistakes," she said, allowing him a small smile.

"I can't change what happened," said Blaine, "but I can try to put things right. The glazier is arriving soon, and I'll cover the bill for the new window, and throw in some free labour to get the job done quicker. Olive just told me they're keeping Jimmy in hospital for a second night as a precaution, so by the time he and Clara arrive home, everything should be as good as new."

"Will you tell them what happened?"

"It's the first thing I'll do when I see them."

"Good, because Dougie Solomon will tell them if you don't."

Blaine winced. "He's another person who deserves an apology from me. I'll go down to the harbour and see if I can find him once I've finished here."

"Do you need some help? I'm no good on ladders, but could help with the ground-floor windows."

"Really? You'd do that for me?"

"I'd do that for Clara and Jimmy."

"Of course."

Annie gave Blaine another smile and pushed her fingers through the gap in the window. He leaned forward and kissed them. "I'll change into some old clothes, then meet you out there."

Annie turned to her wardrobe, but Blaine called her back. "Annie?"

"Yes."

"I love you."

Annie hesitated only a moment. "I love you too."

Blaine blew her a kiss, then disappeared behind a fog of soapy water, his sponge attacking the marks left by birds and the recent bad weather.

"I can only spare an hour or two," said Annie later, as she walked over to Blaine.

"It's more than I deserve. Let me make things up to you properly later?"

"I'll be serving the next residents in the restaurant later."

"I mean after that, at my cottage."

Blaine fixed Annie with an intense stare, and her heart skipped. "I'm not sure that's a good idea."

"Please. Besides, we've plans to make... if you still want to come away with me, that is?"

"I'll come and find you once my shift's over. For now, let's concentrate on getting this place ship-shape for Jimmy's return."

*

"I can't stay long," said Annie, as Blaine let her into the cottage later that evening. "I'm dead on my feet, me and Ben were up till three last night trying to put things right."

Blaine looked at the floor. "I should have been there to help."

"Why weren't you?"

"Because I was drunk, and fearful of what Ben might do should we cross paths. As I said, Annie, I'm a coward, a filthy, pathetic coward." Blaine marched to his bed, sat down, and threw his head in his hands.

"Oh, Blaine," said Annie, rushing over to him and wrapping an arm across his shaking shoulders. "Please, don't cry."

"I let you down," he said, sniffing and wiping his eyes on his sleeve. "All the exciting plans we have, and I went and risked it all for drams of whisky with chaps I barely know. I'm a fool."

"You are, but you're my fool."

Blaine turned to look at Annie, his eyes shining. "Do you mean that?"

"You know I do."

Blaine clasped Annie's hands in his. "I meant what I said. I don't deserve you."

"Of course you do, but I should warn you, I have my limits. You put me in a terrible position last night, and if that were to happen again..."

"It won't, I promise you that. I blame the whisky. I shouldn't touch the stuff. My father was a terrible drunk, and I always swore I'd never follow in his footsteps."

"He was a drunk? I thought he was a carpenter with his own business?"

"The two aren't mutually exclusive."

"I suppose not."

"He never thought I was good enough and always made his feelings plain. I thought if I could get in with those chaps I might get a leg up in the art world and finally be able to make him proud."

"Oh, Blaine."

Annie took Blaine's face between his hands and their lips met. He pushed Annie onto the bed and began unbuttoning her blouse.

"Blaine, I'm sorry, but I really am tired."

He sat up and hung his head. "Of course, this was too much to ask after the way I behaved."

"No," said Annie, "it's not that."

"Really? Because it feels to me all I ever do is let people down. I'm not surprised you want to get away from me."

"Come here," said Annie, hating to see the sadness in his eyes. She pulled down the sheets and climbed into the bed, hoping that this time would be better than the last, and forgetting all about the plans they were supposed to be making.

Chapter 77

September, 1953

"Uncle Jimmy!" Annie rushed over to the car and hugged a tired-looking Jimmy. A white bandage covered his head, and he winced with every movement. "How are you feeling?"

"There's no lasting damage," said Jimmy, "but I'll be glad when the blasted headaches have stopped."

"The doctor sent us home with some aspirin," said Clara, "and a lie-down should help."

"I'm fed up of lying down," said Jimmy.

"Annie, would you mind helping Jimmy to the flat? I want to pop round to Ben and Amy's and let them know the walking wounded have returned."

"Of course," said Annie. She linked arms with her uncle and guided him at a snail's pace towards the hotel.

"How have things been while we've been away?"

Annie hesitated, then decided the truth could wait until he was feeling stronger. "Fine," she said, "nothing I couldn't handle."

"Difficult guests?"

"Something like that."

Olive clapped her hands when she saw Jimmy cross the threshold. "Thank goodness you're alright. Steffie has made a Victoria sponge to celebrate your return. Would you like me to fetch you a slice now?"

"Perhaps in a little while. My wife has ordered me to have a lie-down. She's worse than any of the nurses in that hospital," said Jimmy.

"Quite right too," said Olive. "You need looking after."

Jimmy groaned and waved to Olive as they made their way to the flat. Annie unlocked the door and led Jimmy to an armchair beside the window. "Will this do, or would you rather get into bed?"

"No, I'd like to sit and look out at the view."

"I'll fetch you a blanket."

Jimmy laughed.

"What is it?"

"I'm getting a terrible sense of déjà vu."

"To when?"

"To the last time I had a hospital stay and your mother came to look after me. You're so like her, the way you move, the way you speak. No wonder the two of you are so close."

A shadow passed across Annie's face.

"Annie? What is it?"

"Nothing."

"I may have a headache, but I'm not blind. Has something happened between you and your mother?"

Annie sat down in a chair beside Jimmy. "Not exactly. But I'm not sure she's always honest with me."

Jimmy laughed, then winced. "Is that all?"

"What do you mean, is that all? It's part of the reason I wanted to come here. I hate feeling like people are keeping secrets from me."

"And you have no secrets of your own?"

The way Jimmy fixed Annie with a piercing stare caused her cheeks to redden. Did he know more about her relationship with Blaine than she'd first thought?

"I'll take that as a yes," said Jimmy with a knowing smile. "Everyone has secrets, Annie. But if there's one thing I know about Marnie, it's that if she's kept something from you, it will be to protect you."

"Maybe."

Jimmy's eyelids fluttered, and he gave a slight jolt. "Sorry, Annie. It's all the painkillers I'm on. I keep dozing off like an old man."

"It's alright. Would you like me to stay with you while you sleep?"

"No, you get on. I'm sure you've far better things to be doing than listening to me snoring away."

"Alright, but I'll come back and check on you in half an hour." Annie didn't wait for Jimmy to reply, for he was already asleep.

When Annie walked out into the lobby, she found Clara hunched over the reception desk with Olive. "Oh, Annie, come here for a minute."

"Is everything alright?"

"Yes. Olive and I have been looking through the bookings, and as they're very sparse, we've decided to close early this season."

"Really? Are you sure?"

"Yes. It will mean a couple of cancellations, but I'd rather Jimmy be able to recover without guests tramping around the place. Obviously, you're welcome to stay as long as you want."

Annie didn't know what to say. Without guests, there would be no work, and she still hadn't pinned Blaine down about their Paris plans. "Is there anything you need me to do?"

"We'll need to wash all the soft furnishings before closing for the winter, but there's no need to start that today. Oh, that reminds me, I was going to do a boil wash if you have anything to add to the laundry? I'd just gathered everything up when Jimmy had his accident."

Annie's cheeks flared red. The only items of hers that went into a boil wash were her monthly rags. Her stomach turned. When was her last monthly? "I'll check," she said, trying not to look panicked as she ran up the stairs to her bedroom. As soon as she'd closed the door, she rushed to the writing desk and opened her diary. She'd not had a monthly in at least six weeks. Six weeks? How was that possible? It should have started two weeks previously.

Annie's stomach turned, and she swallowed down the bile rising in her throat. Surely she couldn't be expecting a child? She'd been fit as a fiddle the past few weeks. There had been no tiredness, no sickness, none of the usual signs women complained of. But there was no getting away from the fact that her monthly was late. There was only one thing for it. She would have to speak to Blaine.

Chapter 78

September, 1953

Annie had pleaded tiredness, and told Jimmy and Clara she would have an early night, but instead had sneaked out through the back door. Dishonesty never sat comfortably with her, and now the reality of her romance had hit her like a sledgehammer, she wondered how much longer she could keep up the subterfuge. Wasn't it time to admit the truth to Jimmy and Clara? If she was expecting Blaine's child, it wouldn't be long before someone noticed her changing figure.

For now, there were more important things to worry about and Annie prayed Blaine would be happy about the bombshell she was about to drop. Sneaking off to meet Blaine after dark paled in comparison to the announcement of a pregnancy, and as Annie walked, it was on shaking legs.

Blaine was later than usual and Annie prayed he hadn't gone drinking in one of the island's many pubs. She paced the floor, willing him to arrive. He would know what to do. Perhaps he would reconsider his views on marriage? Annie took a deep breath and tried to calm down. There was no need to panic. A late monthly could be put down to all sorts of reasons, even if it had never happened to her before.

With a sigh of impatience, Annie stood up from the bed and walked over to a desk piled high with paperwork. Most of the papers contained pencil drawings, sketches of what would go on to become his impressive oil paintings. Annie began flicking through, feeling a rush of pride at the talent she held in her hands. A section of handwriting caught Annie's eye, and she picked up what turned out to be a letter. Annie glanced towards the door. It would be terrible if Blaine walked through the door and found her rifling through his personal correspondence. Annie knew she should put the letter back where she had found it, but curiosity got the better of her. Blaine kept so much of himself private, this was an opportunity to find out more about the man she loved.

Annie unfolded the letter and spread it out across the desk.

To my dearest Blaine,

Thank you for the most recent package you sent. It was a relief to pay the rent and stop Mr Fuller fussing and turning up at ungodly hours demanding payment. I know how hard you are working over there, and that by supporting us, you are leaving yourself in a precarious position. We are truly grateful.

Have you found any time to paint? From what you've said, your employers sound like hard taskmasters. The way they treat you makes me so angry. If I wasn't so far away, I'd travel over there and give them a piece of my mind. Surely by now you should be able to demand a higher wage? There are youngsters around here earning more than those scoundrels are paying you. I know how hard you tried to find work here, but perhaps if you came home, there might be an opening for a job that pays more? We all appreciate the sacrifice you have made leaving to find work, but you are missing so much of the children's lives, I can't help feeling there must be a better way.

On the subject of the children, Amelia is flourishing at school. She is a firm favourite with her teacher, and besides her academic work, her artistic talent has also been remarked upon. You can imagine her pride in telling everyone she has inherited that talent from you.

In contrast to Amelia, William is a little rascal. He is always getting under my feet, but it is hard to be angry when he smiles his dimply smile. He lost another tooth last week, and is growing so fast I worry you'll not recognise him when you next return home.

In other family news, I saw your father in town last week. He said little, but I got the impression he regrets accusing you of stealing from him. Everyone but him knows you would never do such a thing, and from the shifty look in his eyes, I suspect he is coming round to the same conclusion. I'm sure when you return home, you will make things up with him.

I shall pause my letter here, as I know how busy you are. If you have time to respond, the children (and I) would be delighted to hear from you. They talk of your island as though it is a mythical place. If you could find any time to do a quick sketch of your surroundings, we would be very grateful.

We miss you, but are all so proud of how hard you are working.

Your loving wife,

Cecily

The thin paper shook in Annie's hand. Footsteps sounded on the path outside the cottage and in a panic, Annie shoved the letter into the pocket of her skirt. Blaine burst through the door, his lazy smile and fumbling movements suggesting he'd availed himself of the bar, as well as serving his customers.

"Annie, my love." He stumbled towards her, reaching out and pulling her into his arms. His breath held a stale combination of whisky and cigarette smoke, and Annie pulled away. "Is everything alright? You look a little pale."

"Actually," said Annie. "I'm not feeling all that well. I think I had better get myself to bed."

"There's a bed here," said Blaine, running his hand down Annie's back, his fingers dipping into the waistband of her skirt.

"Not tonight," said Annie, pulling away. "I've a dreadful headache and wouldn't be very good company. I'll see you tomorrow." Before he could reply, Annie almost ran out of the cottage. At the hotel, she slowed her pace, creeping through its corridors and hanging her head in shame.

As soon as she arrived in her bedroom, Annie kicked off her shoes and flung herself down onto her bed. She shed no tears at the dreadful revelations contained within the letter. Instead, anger burned deep inside of her, not just at Blaine, but also at herself. How could she have been so stupid? It wasn't as though she hadn't been warned. Rose had seen straight through Blaine's charm, and had predicted the liaison would end in tears. How could she have been so blind?

Annie smoothed out the letter and read it again. The news that Blaine was married felt like a hammer blow, but it was all the lies he had told that spurred her anger. And what was all the nonsense about his employers being hard taskmasters offering stingy pay? Annie had seen the hotel books and knew Jimmy and Clara paid above the odds. Was Blaine lying to his wife and squirreling away money for himself? His wife. The thought of the poor woman somewhere on the mainland waiting to hear from her husband caused tears to rush to Annie's eyes.

A third reading of the letter highlighted quite a different issue. Blaine's father had accused him of stealing. Like a jigsaw, everything slotted into place. What were the chances of someone being falsely accused three times? Wasn't it far more likely that the saying *there's no smoke without fire* rang true in Blaine's case? He was a thief, and an adulterer, and Annie had let him turn her against everyone she loved. Suddenly any secrets her family might or might not be harbouring lost all significance. So what if they were keeping things from her? They loved her, and that was what mattered. As the full weight of Blaine's deception and her own foolishness sank in, she dropped to her bed, put her head in her hands and cried.

Chapter 79

September, 1953

Annie had not slept. Dawn was breaking, and she was surprised not to have worn a hole in the carpet from all her pacing. Sadness had turned to anger, the letter still clenched between her fingers. Deciding she could bear it no longer, Annie left her bedroom, padding as quietly as she could through the hotel and out of the back door.

At Blaine's cottage, she knocked on the door, but there was no answer. Given how much he'd had to drink the previous night, Annie wasn't surprised. She clicked open the door that she knew was never locked, and walked into the dark room. Blaine's clothes were strewn in a heap on the floor, a bare leg sticking out from a mass of tangled sheets. A shard of sunlight pierced a gap in the curtains, pointing a spotlight into the thick dust hanging in the air.

"Blaine."

Blaine didn't stir, other than a twitch of his toes.

"Blaine!"

He grunted, then pulled the sheets up over his head. Beside his bed was a glass of water. Annie picked it up, pulled down his covers and threw the water at his head.

"What on earth?" Blaine scrambled to his knees, blinking as he looked around the room, his hands scrabbling to brush water from his hair. His eyes opened wider, and he stared at Annie, the empty glass in her hand. "Well?" he said, "aren't you going to tell me what's going on?"

Annie threw the glass to the floor, ignoring the sound of it breaking. She pulled the letter from her pocket and held it just beyond Blaine's reach. "I found this," she said, her voice unsteady with anger.

"What is it? I can't see."

"It's a letter from your wife."

Blaine's face drained of colour and he gathered a sheet around him, trying to stand. Annie pushed against his chest and he slumped back onto the bed. "Annie, there's an explanation for this."

"Blaine, according to this letter, not only do you have a wife, you are also a father. Were you ever going to tell me?" By now, her entire body was shaking.

"It's not what it seems. Yes, I was married, but Cecily and I divorced some time ago."

"Really?" Annie scrunched the letter back in her pocket, grabbing her hair and trying not to scream. She took a series of deep breaths, and through clenched teeth said, "the letter is addressed here, and dated last week. Either your divorce is very recent, in the past few days, or this is another lie to add to your collection. All that nonsense about wanting to make your father proud, and all along you had stolen from him! No wonder he wants nothing to do with you! And what about Jimmy and Clara? They've shown you nothing but goodwill and you repay their kindness by spreading slurs against their name? I can't believe I was such a fool as to fall for your lies."

"You seemed to enjoy it at the time." Blaine raised himself to full height, letting his sheet drop to the floor.

Annie turned her eyes away, the sight of him naked making her want to throw up. "And Paris?" she said. "Was that a lie, too?"

"Not entirely. I intend to go to Paris, but not with you. Why would I want some snivelling little girl on my arm when there is a city full of beautiful women waiting for me?" Blaine laughed, and tears burnt the backs of Annie's eyes.

"I don't understand why you chased after my affections if you think so little of me?"

"Chased you?" Blaine laughed. "I saw the way you looked at me when we first met and decided I could have a little fun with you. All that snivelling about not being able to find your place in the world? It wasn't hard to get you eating out of my hand." Blaine widened his eyes, peered up from beneath his lashes and in a voice which made Annie's skin crawl said, "You can't trust your family, only me." He blinked, his eyes narrowing, his mouth curling into a sneer. "Ha! You were putty in my hands. A chap has needs, and with my wife so far away, I was more than happy for you to step into the breach."

For a moment, Annie was stunned into silence, then her fingers tightened around the letter. "I'll take this letter to my uncle. I'll tell the police it was you who stole from the Knights Templar."

For the first time, Blaine looked uncomfortable. He pulled on a pair of trousers, frowning. When he turned back to face her, his frown had been replaced by a smile. "You will, will you? I'd like to see what evidence you have."

"I'll tell them I gave you a false alibi."

"And get yourself into as much trouble as me. Besides, go running to Uncle Jimmy, and I'll be delighted to tell him all about our night-time antics. I wonder how he'll take the news that while he slept soundly, we were…"

"You wouldn't."

"Oh, my darling, I would."

Annie stared at Blaine, finding no evidence of the attractive face she'd grown to love. He was ugly, inside and out, and she wanted to scrub the memory of him from her skin. She turned to leave, but he grabbed her arm.

"I'd think carefully before telling tales, little Annie Hearn. Pick a fight with me, and I think we both know who'll win." He released her, and Annie crossed the cottage floor. At the door she paused, glancing at a pile of canvases propped against a wall. She flicked through, finding the one she was looking for.

"Really?" asked Blaine, his voice full of amusement. "You'd really do something so juvenile?"

Annie let out a roar of despair, flinging the canvas onto the ground and stamping as hard as she could. Her foot went through the carefully drawn lines of her face. The eyes were still intact, and she couldn't bear to see the misplaced trust that shone from them. With a final cry, Annie pressed down on her heel until the image was in tatters, then turned and fled.

She didn't stop running until she reached the beach. The tide was on its way out, but was still high enough to act as a barrier between her and the tiny St Cuthbert's island beyond.

Annie began stumbling across sand and rock, salt water spraying up around her, soaking her feet, the hem of her dress. The tiny island represented isolation, and that was what she needed now. How could she face anyone after what she had done? She had placed all her trust in a stranger, and now it had come back to slap her in the face.

Strings of water tugged at Annie's legs, the power of the tide making itself known. She pressed on. Her foot caught between two stones and she had to reach down to tug it free. Salt water seeped up the arms of her blouse, the hem of her skirt, her stockings were soaked through and her shoes ruined.

When she finally reached the island, Annie collapsed onto a grassy mound, then on hands and knees crawled to the remains of an old building, leaning against the crumbling stone, pulling her knees up to her chin and letting the tears fall.

Chapter 80

September, 1953

By the time Annie felt able to leave her place of refuge, it was midmorning, the sun rising ever higher in a clear sky. A stiff breeze had dried out her sodden clothes, and apart from the squelch of her boots, there was no outward sign to suggest anything untoward had happened.

Annie crossed back to the beach, the tide now so low she could use large flat rocks as stepping stones and avoid any further water getting into her shoes. At the beach, she placed her hands on her hips, stared up toward the village, and took a deep breath. Yes, Blaine had humiliated her and yes, he had broken her heart, but she had suffered worse in the past and if she could survive losing her father, she could survive losing the man she had pinned hopes of the future upon.

When Annie entered the hotel, the lobby was silent. She walked across to the door of Jimmy's flat and knocked. No answer. She poked her head around the doors of the restaurant and bar, but found them empty.

Annie stood in the middle of the lobby and listened. Somewhere a door creaked open, and she heard the sounds of footsteps against the wooden floor. Jimmy appeared, a hand rubbing through his hair. "Jimmy?" He jumped, his eyes blinking as he spotted her.

"Sorry, Annie, I was away with the fairies."

"Where is everyone?"

"We've sent Steffie and Olive home for the day and Clara is in with Mam. She's not well, not well at all."

"Oh no. Is there anything I can do to help?"

"Aye, you could see if Clara needs help washing Mam, if you don't mind? I would have helped myself, but Mam would be mortified for me to see her in a state of undress."

"Of course. I'll go through now."

Annie left Jimmy and walked to Rose's bedroom. She knocked, then walked in, finding the bed empty and the sound of running water coming from the bathroom.

"Clara?"

"In here."

Annie found Clara sitting on the edge of the bath, Rose slumped in her wheelchair as the room filled with steam. Rose's eyes flicked up to Annie, and her lips turned in a smile. She held out a hand, and Annie took it.

"Jimmy said you're not feeling too well, Grandma?"

"Huh," said Rose, "I'm grand. Grand, I tell ye."

But from the huskiness of her voice, she didn't sound grand. She seemed to struggle for breath, and sweat glistened on her skin. Clara caught Annie's eye and grimaced. "Rose is in a lot of pain. Her sheets are sodden, as are her clothes. I thought a nice warm bath may make her feel better."

"Good idea. Would you like me to help in here, or shall I change the sheets?"

"If you could help me lift Rose into the bath, then I'll keep an eye on her and you could take care of her bedding."

"I'm nae a bairn," barked Rose, before pulling in a rasping breath.

Annie smiled and perched on the toilet seat beside her grandmother. "No one's saying you are. But right now you need our help, so accept it and quit your blethering."

Amusement sparkled in Rose's eyes. "Hear that, Clara? I've trained the lass well. She's even starting to sound like me."

"One of you is more than enough," said Clara, with a wink to show she was joking.

Rose smiled, then her head flopped back and she let out a snore.

"She keeps dropping off," whispered Clara. "She's putting on a show for you, but she's not well at all. I've rung the doctor, but he's busy with patients all morning and then the tide will be in until this evening. Where have you been? You don't look too good yourself."

Annie wiped away a circle of steam from the mirror and checked her appearance. Her face was puffy, her eyes bloodshot, the skin around her nose chapped and sore. "I'll explain everything later," said Annie. "For now, let's concentrate on Rose."

"Alright," said Clara, "but I'll hold you to it."

Annie nodded. "I'll fetch the clean bedding while the bath's still running." Before Clara could reply, Annie escaped the stuffy bathroom, making her way to the laundry cupboard and enjoying a moment of solitude. At least Rose's condition put her own problems into perspective. Unlike Rose, Annie had had a lucky escape. She still had no idea what to do if she was pregnant, and her heart was broken, but whereas Rose had found herself trapped in a terrible marriage, Annie had found out the truth just in time. Things could be worse. Annie just wished losing her future with Blaine didn't hurt so much.

By the time Rose was washed and sitting in a clean nightie with her bed freshly made, she seemed to have perked up a little, her breathing easier. Clara placed the back of her hand against Rose's forehead, relieved to find the skin cool to the touch.

"Can we go for a walk?"

"A walk?" said Annie. "Grandma, I don't think that's a good idea."

"Ah, lass, there's nae such thing as a bad idea when you reach my age. Just a short walk, even to the end of the garden, would be grand. I want to feel island air on my face."

Annie looked across at Clara, unsure what to do.

Clara placed her hands on her hips and stared at Rose. "I suppose a short walk can't do much harm, but you're not to be gone longer than fifteen minutes."

"Yes, ma'am."

Annie and Clara helped Rose into her chair, layering blankets across her legs and tucking them tight around her. Annie questioned the wisdom of taking her outside, but Rose was set on the idea, and Annie knew once her mind was made up, there would be no changing it.

"Ready for the off?" asked Annie.

"Aye," said Rose, her eyelids heavy.

Annie pushed the wheelchair through the hotel and out of the front door. As soon as they were outside, Rose took a big gulp of air, and her face softened into a dreamy smile. Her eyes closed and her head lolled to one side. Not wanting to stray too far, Annie followed a path that led to the ruined priory. Once between the red sandstone walls, she fixed on the brake and bent down to check on Rose.

"I'm nae sleeping," said Rose, opening one eye a fraction. "But as I canna see, I may as well rest my eyes."

"We're in the priory," said Annie.

"Aye, I kna. I can tell from the smell."

"The smell?"

"Cut grass, stone, seaweed on the air, but not too close. I canna hear the waves on the shore, so we're nae at the harbour, and there's a peace here that ye dinna feel elsewhere."

"Yes," said Annie, "I suppose there is."

Rose tilted her head to the sky and took a series of shallow breaths. She let out a shiver, and sweat began collecting in pearls on her brow.

"Grandma, I think we'd better get you back."

"Aye," said Rose, wiping her forehead with her sleeve. "But before we go, tell me something."

"What?"

"Is all that business with Blaine McCloud over? Have ye come to yer senses yet?"

Annie swallowed hard. "Yes, Grandma, I have. You were right all along."

"I usually am," said Rose, letting out a cackle that turned to a cough. "That was all I needed to kna. We can gan home now." She patted Annie's hand. Annie clicked off the brake and turned back towards the hotel.

Chapter 81

September, 1953

The knock on the door was so soft, Annie wondered if she had dreamed it. She pulled herself up in bed and listened. The knock sounded again. "Hello?" she called, her voice thick with sleep.

Clara walked into the room, her face grey with tiredness, her eyes red-rimmed from tears.

"What time is it?" asked Annie.

"Not yet six," said Clara. "I'm sorry to wake you so early, but your grandmother had a turn in the night. The doctor came over from the mainland, but there's little he can do besides make her as comfortable as possible."

Annie climbed out of bed, any trace of sleep banished. "Shouldn't she be in hospital if she's not well?"

"The doctor didn't think she'd survive the journey. He said the kindest thing was to let her slip away peacefully in her own bed."

"This is my fault," said Annie, her voice shaking. "I should never have taken her outside yesterday."

"Oh, Annie," said Clara, sitting down on the bed. "This isn't your fault. Rose wanted to go out onto her island for one last time. I think she knew the end was coming. What you did was a blessing. She was so much more peaceful when you returned from your walk."

"Can I see her?"

"That's why I woke you. Rose is slipping in and out of consciousness, but during her few moments of alertness, she has been asking for you."

Annie pulled on her dressing gown and a pair of thick woollen socks. With no further conversation, she followed Clara down through the hotel towards Rose's bedroom. When they reached the door, Clara turned to her. "I'll wait out here, let you have some time alone with her. But if you need me, call and I'll come straight in."

"Thank you."

Annie opened the door and stepped into Rose's room. Rather than death and decay, the air held a floral scent, and as Annie's eyes adjusted to the gloom, she saw a vase filled with white roses on her grandmother's bedside table. A chair was already pulled up beside the bed and she sank into it, taking Rose's hand. The old lady's breaths were shallow, her eyelids closed, but flickering, as if in the middle of a dream.

The door clicked open and Jimmy walked in. "Do you mind if I sit here with you?" he asked. "If you'd rather be alone, I understand."

Annie smiled. "Don't be silly, Uncle Jimmy, Rose is your mother. You've more right to be here than me."

Jimmy stood beside Annie and squeezed her shoulder. "You know," he said, "I was expecting Mam to go months back. It's you she's kept going for. You've brought so much happiness into her life, Annie."

"I've not really done anything."

"That's not true. You've spent much of your free time with Mam, and I can see how much she's grown to love you. I may be wrong, but I think her closeness to you has healed some past hurts."

"Like what?"

"Mam never had an easy relationship with her children, at least not when my da was alive."

"But you and she seem very close."

"We are now, but there were plenty of lost years."

Rose stirred in her bed and her eyes flickered open. Jimmy walked to the other side of the bed and took her free hand in his. Rose's eyes darted between Jimmy and Annie, and with great effort, her lips curled up in a smile.

"We're here, Mam," said Jimmy, his words catching in his throat. "We're here, and so if you're ready, you can go."

An almost silent whisper slipped from Rose's lips. Annie leaned forward. "Say that again, Grandma."

"Tell... Marnie... I... love her." The effort of speaking seemed too great and Rose's eyes closed once more. Annie was about to sit back up when Rose spoke again. "I... I love ye all."

"And we love you too," said Annie, leaning forward and kissing Rose's cheek.

Jimmy stroked his mother's hand with his thumb. Rose took one last, faltering breath, then her eyes closed for the final time. Annie's eyes filled with tears, and she walked to Jimmy and wrapped her arms around him. "I'll leave the two of you," she said. "I know she's gone, but if there's anything you need to say to her, now would be the time."

"You're very wise for someone so young," said Jimmy, tears swimming in his own eyes.

"How I wish that were true, Uncle Jimmy."

Annie let herself out of the room, and Clara looked at her. "She's gone?"

"Yes," said Annie. "She's gone." Tears broke free and Clara wrapped her arms around Annie, letting her sob against her shoulder, stroking her back, and soaking up her tears.

When Annie's sobs eased, Clara reached into her pocket. "Rose wanted you to have this," she said, handing her a letter. "I know what's in it as I transcribed it for her. Why don't you take it up to your room? I'll bring a cup of tea up to you in a little while."

Annie nodded, took the letter and made her way back upstairs.

At the small writing desk which looked out on views of the harbour, Annie opened the envelope and pulled out the paper inside.

Dear Annie,

If you are holding this letter in your hands, it means my time on this earth has come to its end. Please don't cry for me, for I have lived a long life, one which has at times been hard, but has ended with great happiness. I never deserved the kindness shown to me these past few years, but I am more grateful for it than any of you will ever know.

Your arrival on this island has brought much joy to me. I'm not sure you'll take it as a compliment, but I see a lot of myself in you. I may be gone, but part of me lives on in you and the thought brings me a lot of comfort.

I've no wise words as I leave this life other than to say embrace your future. Don't let others drag you down. Go after the life you dream of, and be happy, my bonny lass.

All my love, your grandmother, Rose.

Annie reached down and placed her palm against her stomach. Her future was uncertain, she was at risk of disappointing everyone she cared about, and yet she was free. Free from Blaine's lies and cheating, free from the madness of love which had held her hostage these past months. If Rose could be strong after all she'd lived through, so could she. With Rose dead and Blaine's lies exposed, it was time to grow up and look to the future, even if that meant being alone.

Chapter 82

October, 1953

"Your mam and Frank are coming up for the funeral," said Jimmy as Annie sat down to breakfast. "As we're closing up the hotel, the logical course of action would be for you to travel back to Lowestoft with them."

"Yes," said Annie, barely able to force sound out through a throat constricted by fear. She stared down at her hands, wondering how to get herself out of the mess she'd created. In the days since Rose's death, her earlier feelings of resilience and capability had drained away. Instead, reality was looming large in her mind. She couldn't return to Lowestoft, not carrying Blaine McCloud's child.

As for Blaine himself, even if Annie had wanted to speak to him it wouldn't have been possible, for whenever their paths crossed, he pretended she wasn't there. It was as if she was dead to him. For her part, now the scales had dropped from her eyes, love had quickly turned to hate. His lush long hair now appeared lank and greasy, his handsome weathered face now looked old and sagging, his confidence seemed more like arrogance. Annie had even had dreams about killing him and burying him at sea. A step removed from his charms, Annie now saw his romancing as coercion, and she hated herself almost as much as him for falling for it.

But the fact remained that she might be carrying Blaine's child, and he deserved to know. Besides, he had responsibilities, not least to offer some financial support. The child would tie them together, whether they liked it or not. A conversation would need to be held, however much Annie was dreading it.

Clara joined them at the table, and Annie snapped out of her day-dream. "Annie, there's something we need to talk to you about."

Annie saw a look of uncertainty pass between her aunt and uncle. "What is it?"

Clara sighed. "The last thing we wanted was to burden you with this so close to losing your grandmother, but you'll find out eventually, and as the two of you were friends of sorts..."

"Please," said Annie, her voice quiet, "just tell me what's happened."

Clara fiddled with a teaspoon and Jimmy took charge. "It's about Blaine McCloud. He left the hotel last night."

"Left? What do you mean, left?"

"Ran off into the night," said Jimmy, his mouth pulled into a thin line, "and although we've no way to prove it was him, it seems among his belongings was cash from the hotel safe. I've informed the police and they're coming here later to take fingerprints, but I suspect our Mr McCloud would have been too clever to leave any."

"I don't understand why he'd do such a thing?" said Clara, shaking her head. "I had a soft spot for Blaine. And still find it hard to believe he'd steal from us."

"He was a skilled manipulator," said Jimmy. "I can see why you both fell for his charms, but I've met his sort before. Charming when they need to be, ruthless when they don't. I expect he came up with some sad life story to make folk feel sorry and place their trust in him. There was plenty about the man that didn't add up, but nothing I could ever prove."

"Excuse me," said Annie, standing and running from the room. She made it to the toilet just in time, leaning over the toilet bowl, throwing up amid tears of despair. She hadn't wanted to see Blaine McCloud again, and certainly didn't want to marry him, but there was no getting away from the fact he was father to the child she was likely carrying. Now he was gone, she was completely alone.

Annie flushed the toilet, splashed water across her face and rinsed out her mouth. She studied her reflection, eyes puffy and bloodshot, skin grey. She dried her face and hands on a towel, then climbed the stairs to her bedroom.

Unable to settle to anything, Annie pulled on a coat and ran downstairs. On her way through the village, she was greeted by islanders who accepted her as one of them. They doffed caps, wished her a good day, and Annie felt a pang of regret that she'd devoted so much time and energy to Blaine McCloud when she could have been throwing herself into island life. She added it to her list of wasted opportunities.

The bell rang as Annie opened the post office door. Genie looked up from a book she'd been reading. "Hello, Annie."

"Hello, Genie. Do you have a few minutes spare for us to talk?"

Genie turned away from her and yelled through to the room behind, "Mam, I'm off out for a few minutes. I won't be long." She marked her page with a bookmark, slipped on a coat, and followed Annie out onto the island streets. "Here alright?" Genie asked, pointing to a bench outside an old cottage.

"Yes, here is fine."

"So," said Genie, when they had both sat down. "What did you need to talk to me about?"

"I owe you an apology."

"Another one?" asked Genie, eyebrow raised, a grin spreading across her face.

Annie's cheeks turned pink. "Yes, another one. I've been a terrible friend to you, Genie. I should have listened to you all along."

"Does this change of heart have anything to do with Blaine McCloud doing a midnight flit?"

"You heard about that?"

"Of course I did," said Genie with a chuckle. Her lips dropped, and she frowned at Annie. "So what is this? Now Blaine's gone, you need a new friend?"

"No. I've known Blaine McCloud's true colours for some time now."

"I hoped so, but having not seen you this past couple of weeks, I was worried he'd hooked you again with his lies."

Annie blushed an even deeper read. "I would've come to see you sooner, but with my gran dying..."

"Aye," said Genie, taking her hand. "I heard about that. I'm so sorry, Annie, I know the pair of you were close. Any news of when the funeral will be?"

"The end of next week, to give my parents and Rose's other children time to get here."

"I'll be by your side that day, don't ye worry about that."

"Genie, I can't go to the funeral."

"What? Why on earth not?"

"Because straight after, my parents will want to take me back to Lowestoft, and I can't go back there."

"Sorry, Annie, I don't understand."

Annie let out a long breath. "I think I'm expecting a child."

"What?" Genie jumped to her feet, staring down at Annie. "Whose child? Oh, surely not..."

"If you were going to say Blaine McCloud, then you'd be right."

"Are you sure about this?" asked Genie, sitting back down.

"No, but my monthly is late by several weeks, and we... well, we did the thing needed to make a baby. Oh, Genie, I've been such a fool."

"Did you tell Blaine about the baby?"

Annie shook her head. "I found out the truth about him before I had a chance."

"And what truth is that?"

"That Blaine McCloud is a liar and a thief. You were right about him stealing from the Knights Templar, and I suspect Amy was right about him pinching that wallet, too."

"Good God."

"I haven't got to the best bit yet," said Annie, raising a small smile.

"I heard about him stealing from Clara and Jimmy."

"Oh yes, I'd forgotten about that. Also, he stole from his father. That's the reason he was here. He was running away from trouble. It's why he had to leave his wife and children."

"Wife and... no," said Genie, her eyes wide. "Surely not?"

"I found a letter from his wife."

Genie took Annie's hand again, and they sat in silence for a few minutes.

"Now you see why I can't face my parents," said Annie. "It would break their hearts to know what I've done."

"I'm sure they'd understand."

"No," said Annie, shaking her head, "I have to leave the island before they get here."

"Running away won't solve anything."

"I can't stay, I can't. Oh, Genie, I know this is an awful thing to ask, but will you help me?"

Chapter 83

October, 1953

For the next few days, Annie pretended everything was normal. She helped Clara close up bedrooms for the season, ate breakfast with Jimmy each morning, and took long walks around the island, drinking it all in.

Annie hated her own cowardice, but remained set on her decided course of action. She had made plans to run away two days before the funeral and would leave a note, so no one was worried. By the day of her escape, she had packed a suitcase with her small amount of belongings and collected all the money she had saved into a leather purse. The tide was due to open at eight in the evening, and Annie would depart in tandem with it.

At four o'clock, she sat at her writing desk to pen the hardest letter of her life.

Dear Clara and Jimmy,

Thank you for the hospitality you have shown me since I arrived on the island. I can't thank you enough for the welcome I've received, and I have thoroughly enjoyed my time with you both.

Please forgive me for leaving without saying goodbye, but it is time I struck out on my own. I feel terrible for missing Grandma's funeral, but we said our goodbyes whilst she was alive, and I know she'd understand my reasons.

When Mum and Frank arrive, please tell them I am taking a few weeks away from everything to think about my future, but that I will get in touch with them in due course.

Your loving niece, Annie

Annie folded the letter, slipped it in an envelope, and addressed the front. She propped it up against the lamp on her writing desk and glanced around the room. She had stripped the bed and folded the bedding in a neat pile. Every surface had had a thorough dust, and she'd even polished the windowpanes and mirror. If it weren't for her suitcase sitting in the middle of the floor, it would look as if she had never been there.

During their last meal together, Annie joined in conversation as best she could, pretending to be excited about her parents' arrival, and agreeing with Clara over her choice of hymns for the funeral. When Jimmy asked if Annie would read a bible verse during the service, she politely declined, suggesting she'd be far too emotional to speak in front of a large congregation.

"Would you like to spend the evening with us?" Clara asked, as they finished washing dishes from their meal.

"No, I've a nasty headache," lied Annie. "If you don't mind, I'll spend a quiet evening in my room and have an early night."

"Alright," said Clara, looking doubtful. "But are you sure you are alright? We've not spoken about whatever happened the day you helped me with Rose. From your face, I'd say you'd been crying."

"Oh, it was nothing," said Annie, waving a hand and forcing a smile. "I was sad at the thought of leaving, that's all."

"Oh, you lovely girl," said Clara, pulling Annie into her arms. "It's been an absolute joy having you here with us and we will miss you terribly when you're back in Lowestoft. But you know you're welcome here anytime?"

"Yes," said Annie, swallowing tears, lies, and shame at what she was about to do.

"I won't keep you," said Clara, releasing Annie. "You go and get your rest. Shall I bring you a cup of tea up later?"

"No, thank you," said Annie, fighting a rush of panic that her escape might be discovered so soon. "I'll probably fall asleep as soon as my head hits the pillow."

"Alright, we'll see you in the morning, and if you need anything, you know where we are."

Annie retreated to her bedroom, pulled on her coat and picked up her suitcase. She took one last look around the room, spent a moment soaking up the view from the harbour, then slipped out into the corridor. Her heart hammered as she walked down the long corridor, descended the stairs, and crept towards the back door. No one saw her, no one heard her, and as she stepped out onto the island streets, Annie breathed a sigh of relief.

Dusk was settling in, but she didn't want to take any chances. Instead of going through the village, she turned right, crossing a field that led down to the beach. She picked her way along the pebble-strewn shoreline, struggling in the fading light. With relief, Annie turned a corner and saw the orange glow of a lamp reflecting on the pools of water left behind by the tide. She increased her pace, hurrying towards her prearranged rendezvous.

"You made it," said Genie when Annie reached her. "I wondered if you might change your mind."

"No," said Annie. "Even if I wanted to, I couldn't turn back now. Are you sure you'll be alright coming back to the island alone?"

Genie laughed. "I've crossed these sands thousands of times."

"I know, but it's almost dark."

"Put me in a blindfold and I'd still find my way back," said Genie. She took Annie's hand, and the two stepped beyond the stony beach and onto damp sand.

Tall wooden poles stood proud against the darkening sky and Genie expertly navigated from one to the other, pulling Annie away from areas where the sand was too soft, encouraging her to follow the imprint of footsteps Genie left in her wake. Only once did Annie turn back, feeling a pang of regret for her own cowardice. Her namesake had crossed these same sands in the opposite direction decades before, an act of bravery fuelled by love, and yet here she was, slinking away into the night to avoid the consequences of her fall from grace.

After an hour of walking and with the mainland in touching distance, Genie stopped and turned to Annie. "You'll be alright by yourself from here on out." She took Annie's hands and gave her a small smile. "Part of me wishes I was coming with you. Do you remember when you arrived, you promised to broaden my horizons? I thought it would be me leaving and you staying, but looks like I'm stuck on the island for a while yet."

"Couldn't you come with me?"

"And leave my parents to fend for themselves?" Genie shook her head. "No, I couldn't do that to them."

"They're lucky to have you."

"Right, ye know what to do next?"

"Follow the track to Beal station and catch the nine o'clock train to Berwick."

"Aye, and be sure not to miss it or ye'll be spending the night on the station platform for the nine o'clock is the last train of the day. I must say though, as running away goes, Berwick isn't much of a distance."

"It's far enough," said Annie. "I need to take some time to plan what I'll do next. Berwick is as good a place as any to do that."

"You've got the address of the boarding house I told ye about?"

Annie nodded.

"Good. Once you get there, ask for Mrs O'Brian. She'll be expecting ye and knows which train you're coming in on."

"Thank you so much for helping me," said Annie. "I couldn't have done this without you."

"Dinna be daft, of course ye could."

Annie wrapped her arms around Genie and gave her a tight hug. "Thank you," she said, before turning and walking towards the mainland.

Annie didn't stop walking until she had reached the brow of a hill. She turned back to see the island, but it was shrouded in darkness. All she could see was a pinprick of orange as Genie crossed back to the island by lamplight. With a loud sigh and a squaring of her shoulders, Annie headed for the station.

Chapter 84

October, 1953

Annie jumped down onto the platform and looked around her. The station was even quieter than the train, few people travelling along the north-east coast after dark. Throughout the brief journey, she had mulled over Genie's comment about Berwick not being far from the island. Should she have continued on to Edinburgh and put more distance between herself and those who would look for her? No, Annie had made it clear in her letter she needed time to herself, and hoped Clara and Jimmy would respect those wishes.

The town was almost as quiet as the station, a handful of people hurrying along the main street, their collars raised against the evening chill. Berwick-upon-Tweed was more charming than Annie had imagined. She walked down the cobbled main street, an array of bay-windowed shops displaying everything from fresh fruit and veg to fabric and tins of paint. From the variety of shops, Annie decided the street must be the bustling heart of the town during daylight hours.

A large town hall dominated the far end of the street, the clock in its tower showing it was already ten p.m. Annie stopped a woman as she passed and showed her the address on the paper Genie had given her.

"Down the street, at the end, turn right, then you'll find Cora O'Brian's place five houses along. It's easy to spot. She has a bright red door and pots of plants beside it. Takes pride in her place, does old Cora."

Annie thanked the lady, picking up her suitcase and following the directions she had been given. The woman's description sounded promising. If Mrs O'Brian took such care of the outside of her boarding house, Annie hoped the inside would be just as nice.

When she reached the boarding house, Annie gave a tentative knock, aware of the late hour and not wanting to disturb fellow residents. Seconds later, the door swung open and a tiny woman of about fifty, with permed grey hair and wearing horn-rimmed spectacles, gazed out.

"Miss Hearn?"

"Yes. Good evening, Mrs O'Brian."

"Ah, a polite one. That's a good start. Come in, lass."

Annie followed Mrs O'Brian over the threshold of the three-storey Victorian stone-built property. In the tiled entrance stood a hat stand and a bucket for umbrellas. A dark wooden staircase rose against one wall and the smell of cooked meat filled the air.

"Will you be half board or full board? Miss Guthrie didn't say."

"Um, do you mind me asking the difference in price?"

"Not at all, lass. It's ten shillings half board, fifteen for full, per night, of course."

Annie mentally counted up the money in her purse. She needed to be careful with her earnings, but given she didn't know what facilities were provided and wouldn't be staying long, she decided the extra five shillings would be well spent. "I'll take the option of full board, please."

"Very well. Breakfast is served between seven and eight, lunch is at midday and dinner is from six until seven. We eat in the dining room through there." Mrs O'Brian pushed open a door to their left. "If you know you will be late for a meal and give me plenty of warning, I will save a plate of food for you, but if you're late with no notice, you'll have to go hungry."

"I understand."

"How many nights will you be staying?"

"I'm not entirely sure. A few days at least."

"Right, well, you can pay me for three nights now, then we'll see how you get on."

"Of course." Annie opened her purse and counted out a handful of coins.

Mrs O'Brian's fist clenched around the coins before slipping them into the pocket of the apron she was wearing. "Your room is on the first floor. Follow me."

Annie followed the landlady up the stairs, trying to make her out. She was friendly enough, but her matter-of-fact way of speaking suggested the relationship between host and guest was a professional one and she was running the boarding house as a business, not to make friends.

At the top of the stairs, they walked down a long landing. "This is you," said Mrs O'Brian, turning the key in a door marked with a brass number 6. "Bathroom is two doors along. If you need me, my flat is downstairs at the back of the house, but unless it's an emergency, I'd rather not be disturbed. There is a telephone in the under-stairs cupboard with a list of prices beside it. I operate an honesty box system, but I check the bills carefully and will know if anyone has been cheating me and using the telephone without the appropriate recompense."

Annie nodded, too tired to reassure Mrs O'Brian that she would pay her way.

"It's late, and I need my sleep. I'll see you in the morning at breakfast."

"Goodnight."

As Mrs O'Brian walked back along the landing, Annie stepped into her room and closed the door. The room was clean, but more like a cupboard in size than a bedroom. A narrow bed covered in a faded floral quilt was pushed against one wall, a small nightstand beside it. There was no space for a wardrobe or chest of drawers. Instead, a hook had been nailed into the door, and four wooden hangers attached.

Annie kicked her suitcase under the bed and walked to the window. Her previous harbour view had spoiled her, but here there was no danger of staring out of the window in a daydream. The window looked out onto the stone wall of a neighbouring building, and was so close, if she reached out of the window, Annie could feel the cool roughness of the stone.

Whether because of the uninspiring view, tiny room, or tiredness from the journey, Annie was suddenly enveloped by the realisation of all she had left behind. If this room was any sign of what her future held, it didn't look bright. As she climbed into bed, Annie couldn't shake the feeling she had made a terrible error of judgement. Her recent experiences had told her to trust no one, but from where she lay, the alternative looked bleak. She was on her own, and didn't enjoy the feeling one little bit.

Chapter 85

October, 1953

If it weren't for fear of Mrs O'Brian's disapproval, Annie would have missed breakfast and stayed in bed. She'd tossed and turned all night, trying to see her predicament from every which way, but still finding no solution. By now, Marnie and Frank would be on the island, and everyone would know about her midnight flit.

"How did you sleep?" asked Mrs O'Brian when Annie arrived at the breakfast table.

"Very well, thank you," said Annie, wincing at how easily lies tripped off her tongue these days. She sat down at the table and introduced herself to the other guests. There was a middle-aged man come up from North Shields for something to do with fishing, although from his smart suit and tie, Annie guessed he didn't venture out onto the water himself. Another even older, smarter gentleman turned out to be a travelling salesman with appointments at several local shops. The only other guests were a young honeymooning couple who were too interested in each other to take any notice of their fellow guests.

Annie ate her breakfast as quickly as was polite, her tired brain struggling to make small talk with the strangers opposite. After clearing away her dishes, she paused in the hallway, eying up the telephone. The honeymooners burst out of the dining room, giggling and holding hands. From behind the door, Annie heard the two older gentlemen engaged in a political discussion. Much as she needed to use the telephone, it felt too public an area for the conversation she needed to have. Slipping on her coat and checking she had enough coins, Annie left the boarding house, hoping to find a public telephone somewhere among the deserted early-morning streets of the town.

She didn't have to walk far before finding what she needed. Annie entered the small, brightly painted kiosk and closed the door behind her. She pulled her address book from her pocket, slipped her coins into the slot, and dialled the number she needed. She prayed Helen would be home.

"Hello?" Helen's voice sounded crackly and unsure down the line, as though still getting used to the telephone she had so recently installed.

"Oh, Aunt Helen, it's me, Annie."

"Annie? Is everything alright?"

"Not really, and I need to talk to someone about it or I'll go mad. Oh, Aunt Helen, I've made such a terrible mess of everything."

"I'm sure that's not true. Calm down and tell me what's happened."

"I thought going to the island would solve all my problems. But then there was a man..." Annie's last word came out as a wail.

"Annie, I really need you to calm down. You're scaring me, and I want to help, but I can't hear a word you're saying."

Annie took a series of deep, steadying breaths. "There was a man on the island."

"Has someone done something terrible to you? Have you been attacked?"

"No, nothing like that. I thought I loved him."

"Are you talking about Sam?"

"No, not Sam, someone else."

"I think you'd better go back to the beginning, Annie, and tell me everything. But before you do, can I ask why you rang me and not your mother?"

"Because I can't bear the thought of speaking to her, or Frank, or Aunt Clara or Uncle Jimmy. You were like a second mother to me once, and you were always so kind." Annie sniffed.

"Well, I promise to be kind now. What has happened?"

Annie began her sorry tale from when she had left Padstow, feeling a sense of unease and with a big question mark over where she belonged. "I loved it on the island at first. It really felt like home. Then I met Blaine McCloud and everything went wrong."

"Who is Blaine McCloud?"

"He works at the hotel, worked at the hotel."

"Doing what?"

"A bit of everything. And he's an artist, and very charming."

Helen sighed down the telephone, as though she knew what was coming.

"I thought I was in love. I thought Blaine loved me. He told me he'd take me to Paris. He said I could trust him. But all the while he had a wife over on the mainland, and not only that, he was a thief to boot."

"But you've broken it off now?"

"Yes, but I've been left with the consequences of my actions."

"Your actions?"

"Oh, Aunt Helen," said Annie with a sob, "I think I'm going to have a baby."

The line went quiet and Annie wondered if they'd been cut off. She was about to replace the receiver when Helen spoke. "Not again," she whispered.

"What do you mean?"

"Nothing. So, what are you going to do?"

"I don't know. I've heard of other girls in my situation who have taken matters into their own hands, but aside from the physical dangers, it's illegal and I don't want to end up in prison. Also, I don't think I could do that to the baby, even if I don't want it."

"Have you considered adoption?"

"Like Grace, you mean?"

Helen sighed. "Yes, like Grace."

"I'm not sure."

"Sometimes it's the best way. And there are so many loving couples out there who would do a wonderful job of raising a child but are not able to have one of their own."

"Was that the position you were in?"

"Yes."

"I still don't understand how you came by Grace. In fact, it's been on my mind ever since I came to visit you."

"What has?"

"Her strong resemblance to Jack. And don't try denying it. Not now, when I've just spilled my heart and its wicked secret to you."

"It's not my place to talk about it."

"Then whose is it?" Annie knew her voice was rising, her own problem momentarily forgotten. "I know I've been lied to since I was a child. I think it's part of the reason I ran away to the island. There's no one I can trust anymore." By now, Annie was sobbing, tears running from her cheeks and soaking into the neckline of her jumper.

"You should talk to your mother," said Helen quietly. "As I said, it's not my place."

"Please, Helen, please tell me."

"I can't."

In the end, it was Helen's refusal to speak which enabled Annie to see the truth. *Talk to your mother, I can't say.* There was only one reason Helen would want Annie to speak to her mother. A memory flashed through Annie's mind. She was still a small child, wrapping her arms around Marnie's thick waist. Marnie had always been film-star thin, and Annie could remember being terrified Marnie had some mystery illness which caused her stomach to expand.

"Annie, are you still there?"

"It... it was my mum, wasn't it? My mum and Jack. They... they..." A sob escaped Annie's lips and her stomach flipped, making her want to throw up.

"Annie..."

"No." In an instant, Annie's sadness was replaced by anger. "All these years, you've all been deceiving me. All these years of thinking I was an only child, longing for a proper family, longing for a sibling, and I had one right in front of me."

"It's not as simple as that," said Helen. "Oh, dear, I wish you hadn't found out over the telephone like this."

"Does Grace know?"

"She knows she was adopted."

"Why not tell her the truth?"

"Because..."

Annie heard the crack in Helen's voice, could tell the emotional toll the conversation was taking on her. "Just tell me why."

"I'm not sure how much you remember of those war years," said Helen. "I think on the whole they were a happy time for you, but only because the adults around you shielded you from the fear and danger."

"I wouldn't call losing my father a happy time."

"I'm not talking about that," said Helen. "Losing Tom was a horrific tragedy. That's never been in doubt."

"But Jack... I thought my mum loved my dad..."

"She did, Annie. Tom's death broke your mother. What happened with Jack had nothing to do with love. Believe me, I was as angry as you are now when I first heard what had happened, but as the years have gone on, I can understand it. But this is really something you should speak to your mother about. It's her place to explain things to you."

"I never want to talk to her again."

"Really, Annie? You'd judge her so harshly, even though you've now got yourself in a very similar situation to the one she found herself in?"

"It's not the same."

"No? What about Sam? I thought the pair of you were stepping out."

At the mention of Sam, Annie flinched. "Does Grace know about Jack and my mother?"

"You're changing the subject."

"Does she know?"

"No, she doesn't, and for her sake, I want it to stay that way. I offered your mother the chance to remain part of Grace's life all those years ago, but she didn't feel it would be fair to Grace, or to you. That decision was made a long time ago, and to tell Grace the truth now would upend everything she thinks she knows about herself and where she came from. It wouldn't be fair. In fact, it would be cruel. Promise me you won't say anything to her. Please, Annie."

"I need to go," said Annie. "I'll ring you again soon."

"Annie, please..." Helen was still pleading when Annie put down the phone.

Chapter 86

October, 1953

"Jimmy? Jimmy?"

"What is it?" asked Jimmy as Clara ran into the room waving a piece of paper.

"It's Annie, she's gone."

"Gone? Gone where?"

"Heaven knows," said Clara, throwing herself down in a chair. "Marnie and Frank are arriving at lunchtime. What on earth are we going to tell them?"

"Let me read that," said Jimmy, taking the letter. "Oh, the silly girl. Whatever was she thinking? Do you have any idea what all this is about?"

"No," said Clara, "but I can think of someone who might. I'll be back soon, I'm going to speak to Genie."

"Good idea. Do you want me to come with you?"

"No. If she's been keeping Annie's secrets, we don't want to scare her into keeping quiet by turning up mob-handed."

"Alright, but don't be long. We need to decide the best way to proceed with all this before my sister turns up, expecting a reunion with her daughter."

"I won't be long, I promise."

Clara kissed Jimmy, then ran out of the hotel and through the village streets. The post office wasn't open, so she knocked on the door until a light went on in the back room. Clara watched through the glass panels as Genie walked towards her. Her face went from white to red, and she kept her eyes to the ground.

"Good morning, Clara. Is everything alright? I'm afraid we're not open for another half an hour."

"I think you know why I'm here," said Clara, pushing past Genie and walking into the shop.

"I'm not sure I understand."

Clara turned, hands on her hips, staring at Genie, whose face turned a deeper shade of red. "I'm here about Annie. I found the note she left."

"Annie? What's the matter with Annie?"

"Genie, don't even bother trying to lie. You've practically got steam coming out of your ears. Tell me what you know about Annie's departure."

Genie kept her eyes to the floor, fiddling with her fingers. "I told her not to run away."

"I suppose that's something. But I'm assuming you helped her? Annie wouldn't be able to cross the sands alone after dark."

"I'm really sorry," said Genie, looking up at Clara, her eyes filled with tears. "She didn't have anyone else to turn to."

"What about me? What about Jimmy?"

"I think she was too ashamed to come to you with her problems. But also, Annie doesn't trust anyone," muttered Genie.

Clara frowned and folded her arms. "What reason could Annie have not to trust us?"

"She heard you talking right before Amy and Ben's wedding. She knew her mam was keeping secrets from her, but that day she found out you were in on it too."

"Secrets? What secrets?" Clara ran a hand through her hair, trying to make sense of the situation. Suddenly, it dawned on her. There was only one secret Annie could mean. But how much did she know? Clara silently cursed Marnie and her insistence on keeping something so huge from her daughter. Hadn't Clara warned her it would all end in tears? "Do you know where Annie is now?"

Genie's cheeks flushed again.

"Genie, if you know where my niece is, you must tell me."

"She wants to be left alone."

"Enough of this nonsense," snapped Clara. "Tell me where Annie is this instant."

Genie scowled, then muttered, "at a very reputable boarding house in Berwick."

"Thank you for your honesty. I'd like the name and address of this boarding house, please."

"I promised I wouldn't tell. She wants to be left alone."

"Fine," said Clara with a long sigh. "I'll give my niece her time alone, but when I come back here in a few days' time, I'll expect you to hand over the name and address with no quibbling."

"That sounds fair enough," muttered Genie.

"Tell me one thing, Genie. Why did Annie run away? I know you mentioned secrets, but Ben and Amy's wedding was months ago, so that doesn't explain why she'd choose to run away now. I've come to know my niece well these past few months. She wouldn't miss her grandmother's funeral because she felt left out of a secret. What's happened?"

Genie kept her lips pressed firmly together.

"Please, Genie, at least tell me if Annie's in any physical danger."

Genie shook her head. "She's quite safe where she is."

"Well, at least that's something." Clara sighed again. "I'd better be getting back. My sister-in-law arrives in a few hours and I'll need to explain Annie's departure in a way that won't scare the living daylights out of her. But don't be surprised if Marnie comes around wanting a word. Whatever has happened to Annie, you should have convinced her to come to us with her problems rather than helping her run away. I'm very disappointed in you, Genie."

Before Genie could respond, Clara marched out of the shop and onto the street. She felt a pang of guilt at how harsh she had been with the young girl, but her worry over Annie eclipsed any social niceties.

"I'm home," called Clara as she let herself back into the hotel.

"How did you get on?" asked Jimmy, limping into the foyer and leaning heavily on his stick.

"You're in pain," said Clara, rushing forward and leading him to a chair.

"Not in pain, just stiff."

"It's always worse when you feel under pressure. Goodness me, I could throttle that niece of ours. What on earth does she think she's doing?"

"What did you find out from Genie?"

"I had mixed results," said Clara. "It turns out she's only run away as far as Berwick, so that's a relief. Genie wouldn't tell me where, except that she's staying in a reputable boarding house, whatever that means. I still have no idea why she's gone. I don't believe a word of her letter. Her and Rose were thick as thieves, and Annie wouldn't miss her funeral without good reason."

"So we're not much further forward in either understanding or finding her."

"I'm sorry," said Clara, shaking her head.

"You've nothing to apologise for. Now, why don't we sit down with a cup of tea and work out what we're going to tell my sister when she arrives?"

Chapter 87

October, 1953

Clara and Marnie wrapped their arms around each other, sharing the weight of emotion compounded by grief for Rose and worry over Annie. Both had secretly hoped she would reappear in time for the funeral, but despite spinning around in their pews each time the church door creaked open, there was no sign of Annie at the service. Clara had done her best to reassure Frank and Marnie that Annie was quite safe, and had left the island to deal with her grief alone, but neither seemed entirely convinced by her explanation and Clara was sure there would be more questions once the funeral was over.

"The vicar did a good job," said Marnie, dabbing her eyes with a handkerchief.

"Aye, he did. Rose was well respected on the island. We're all going to miss her."

"I should have visited more," said Marnie with a sniff. "Here I am, expecting my daughter to share her life with me, and I rarely saw my mother. I'm a damned hypocrite."

"Mother and daughter relationships can be complicated. But Rose knew you loved her, and so does Annie."

Marnie gave a weak smile. "Do you need any help to prepare the wake?"

"No, Olive and Steffie came in to help and everything is ready. All we need to do is to be there to greet those wanting to pay their respects and express condolence. I'm hoping folk won't stay long, but it's rare for the bar to be open at this time of year so I suspect they'll want to make the most of it."

"We'd best get back then," said Marnie.

The two women left Rose's graveside and walked back to the hotel. It wasn't long before the entire island was filling the bar, the windows steamed up, the noise of chatter deafening. If Clara hadn't needed to fetch more plates from the kitchen, she would never have heard the telephone ringing. She ignored it, but after she returned from the kitchen, it was still ringing five minutes later as she made her way back to the bar. With a groan of frustration, Clara balanced the plates on the reception desk and picked up the receiver.

"Mrs Watson speaking."

"Oh, hello. I'm sorry to trouble you. This is Mrs Trevorn, Helen Trevorn."

Clara paused, the name familiar but unable to place it.

"Helen Trevorn from Padstow. You came to visit once."

"Ah yes, of course, Helen. How lovely to hear from you. Is everything alright, only, we're in the middle of a wake and..."

"Oh my goodness, I'm so terribly sorry. What a dreadful time for me to ring."

"Please don't worry, you weren't to know. Would it be alright to ring back tomorrow?"

"Oh dear, well, I suppose I could, only I'm ringing about Annie."

"Annie? Hold on." Clara placed the receiver on the desk, closed the bar door so she could hear herself think, and resumed her position at the telephone. "That's better," she said. "I can hear you properly now."

"Good, and I really am sorry for interrupting, but I wasn't sure who to contact. Marnie doesn't seem to be at home and the news I have is rather urgent."

"Marnie is here on the island with us. Has something happened to Annie?"

"Yes and no, she telephoned me yesterday. Goodness, she'll be so cross that I've rung you, but the girl needs help, and there's little I can do from hundreds of miles away."

"You'd better tell me what she said."

*

For the rest of the wake, Clara forced herself to play the graceful hostess. She accepted condolences, joined in reminiscing, and refilled glasses, all whilst wishing everyone would leave the family in peace. She needed to speak to Marnie, but her reaction was too difficult to predict, so the news was best delivered without half the island looking on.

"You look exhausted," said Jimmy, pulling Clara into his arms. "Is everything alright?"

"I had a telephone call from Helen Trevorn."

Jimmy took Clara's elbow and pulled her into the corner of the room. "Why was Helen ringing here?"

"She's spoken to Annie."

"What? Why did Annie contact Helen and not us?"

"Apparently, she doesn't trust any of us, although she can add Helen to her list after their conversation."

Jimmy's eyes widened as realisation dawned. "Helen told her about Grace?"

"No, but Annie guessed, and Helen didn't deny it."

"Oh, no."

"That's not the worst part," said Clara with a grimace. She leaned over and whispered in Jimmy's ear. His skin lost all colour, and his eyes darted to where Marnie and Frank were chatting with locals.

"I suspected an infatuation, but never thought Blaine had reciprocated. The man's old enough to be her father! It was plain from the day she arrived Annie was a little lost. How dare that man take advantage of a vulnerable young girl! How did we not see it?" he whispered.

"I've no idea. But given what we've recently learned about Blaine McCloud, I can't say I'm surprised that he seduced our niece right under our noses. If there's one thing that man's good at, it's deception."

"We need to get people to leave so we can discuss this with Marnie and Frank."

"I know, but isn't it rude to end the wake abruptly?"

"Most of the family members from the mainland have left with the tide. The only folk still here are locals taking advantage of a free pint. I think we've shown them enough hospitality for one day."

Without further discussion, Jimmy strode behind the bar and rang the bell. "I'm afraid it's time to draw this gathering to a close," he announced over the hum of voices. "If you'd like to join me in one last toast to my mam. To Rose Watson," said Jimmy, raising his glass.

"To Rose Watson," chorused the assembled islanders.

It took another half an hour to remove the stragglers from the bar, and Marnie and Frank seemed surprised the wake had ended so abruptly.

"If you were both too tired to continue, Frank and I could have held the fort," said Marnie.

"It's not that," said Jimmy. "We need to talk to the pair of you in private."

Marnie frowned. "What is it?"

"Not here. Let's go through to our rooms."

Before leaving the bar, Jimmy grabbed a bottle of whisky and four glasses, deciding that the news Clara was about to impart was best accompanied by a stiff drink.

"What's going on?" asked Frank as they settled themselves on sofas and armchairs.

"During the wake, I received a telephone call from Helen Trevorn."

"Oh," said Marnie, surprise spreading across her face. "Was she ringing to offer her condolences?"

"No, she wasn't aware the funeral was happening today."

"Then what did she want?"

"She wanted to talk about Annie."

"Annie?" Marnie leaned forward in her chair, frowning.

"Aye," said Clara. "It seems we have two problems."

"Here," said Jimmy, handing out glasses of whisky. "You might need this."

Frank took hold of Marnie's hand. "What's going on, Clara?"

Clara took a deep breath and relayed part of her earlier conversation with Helen.

"Good Lord," said Frank when she had finished. "But I don't understand how something like that could have been going on right under your noses?"

Jimmy leaped to Clara's defence. "It was our busiest time of year at the hotel. By nine p.m. we're usually wiped out and ready for bed. Annie must have been sneaking out to meet Blaine after dark. I understand your frustration, Frank, but we invited Annie here to work, and besides, she's eighteen, hardly in need of babysitting."

"Has a doctor confirmed the pregnancy?" asked Marnie.

"Not from what Helen gathered, and if Annie is indeed expecting a baby, it will be very early days."

"So this could all be a storm in a teacup? We might all be worrying over nothing?"

"It's possible," said Clara. "But whether Annie is expecting is not the only thing we need to worry about."

"Oh, Lord, what now?" asked Frank, taking a glug of his whisky and holding out his glass for a refill.

This time, Jimmy took the lead. "It seems Annie knows Grace is her sister."

Colour drained from Marnie's face and she clutched a trembling hand to her heart. "Knows about Grace? But how?"

"Helen got the impression Annie had been suspicious for some time. Genie, Annie's friend here on the island, said she had overheard you and me talking about it when we were preparing the flowers for Amy's wedding. When Annie spoke to Helen, the puzzle pieces finally slotted into place."

"Secrets always have a way of coming out," said Jimmy.

"That's unhelpful," said Frank. "Annie must be so confused and scared. We should go to her immediately."

"For starters, the tide is in, so no one is going anywhere tonight," said Clara. "But from what Helen said, Annie is furious with us all. I think it may be best if I visit her first."

"Clara's right," said Jimmy. "She can try to calm her down. If you two go straight there, there's every chance Annie may run away again, and I doubt it would be to anywhere as close as Berwick."

"It doesn't sound like we have much choice," said Marnie. "But please, Clara, when you see Annie, do everything you can to bring her home."

Chapter 88

October, 1953

"Annie, it's me, Clara."

"Go away. I don't want to talk to you."

The door opened, and Clara strode into the room. Annie was vaguely aware of the clothes strewn across the floor and empty cups littering the worktop, but couldn't bring herself to care. Clara stood with her hands on her hips, staring down at Annie, who lay curled up on her bed.

"Helen telephoned us at the hotel. We know why you ran away."

Annie didn't answer.

Clara let out a dramatic sigh. "Honestly, Annie, I really don't understand how you feel able to take the moral high ground in this situation. Not after the way you've behaved!"

"I've done no worse than my mother, and I don't see you being angry with her."

"Annie, you've run away, like a coward, like a little girl, missing your own grandmother's funeral because you couldn't face your own family. You want to be treated as the woman you are, but allowed the indulgences of a child when it suits. Do you have any idea how worried we were when we found you gone? You were under our care! We went out of our minds worrying about what could have happened to you."

Annie tucked a strand of hair behind her ear and looked up at Clara for the first time. "I really am sorry about that. I didn't mean to worry you, I was just so ashamed of what I'd done."

Clara sighed again and sat down on the bed beside her. "I feel partly to blame. I was as much taken in by Blaine's charm as anyone. Jimmy and Rose tried to warn me about him, but I couldn't understand why they didn't trust him. I've always considered myself an excellent judge of character, but it seems I was wrong."

"None of this is your fault, and I am truly sorry for what I've done. But nothing changes the fact you've all been lying to me for years about Grace."

Clara stood up, walked across the room, and pulled Annie's coat from a hook on the door. She threw the coat to her. "Come on, we're going for a walk."

"I'm too tired."

"You need some fresh air, and we can air out this room while we're at it." Clara flung open the windows and Annie shivered. Before she could argue further, Clara had opened the door and was striding back down the corridor. Annie pulled on her coat, slipped her feet into her shoes and ran after her aunt.

"Where are we going?"

"I thought we could walk around the town walls. Have you done that yet? They're really rather wonderful."

For a few minutes they walked in silence, the wide expanse of the Tweed rushing towards its final destination. "What did Mum say about all this?"

"That she's very worried about you."

"Does she know I might be pregnant?"

"Helen told me, and I told Marnie, so, yes. I must say, it came as rather a shock when I heard."

"I'm so sorry."

"No, Annie, I'm sorry. I should have seen what was happening right under my nose. I should have protected you from Blaine and his manipulation."

"I'm an adult."

"Only just."

"When did you find out about Grace?" asked Annie.

Clara continued walking and said nothing.

"Clara?"

She sighed. "I suspected before I knew for certain."

"How?"

"I knew something had happened between your mother and Jack. She told me that much. Then months later she was suddenly heading back to Lowestoft, in the middle of a war, when the town was coming under attack."

"She told me she had to care for my grandparents."

"Yes, and that was true, she did. But I wondered at the timing of it all..."

"When did you find out for certain?"

"After she'd told Jimmy what happened. He told me, but I wasn't surprised."

"Weren't you angry with her?"

"Why would I have been? I was in no position to judge. I'd made plenty of mistakes of my own. Besides, I felt she'd made the right decision, giving Grace to Helen and Richard."

"But what about Grace? Didn't she have a right to know her parents?"

"Perhaps, but I wonder what that would have achieved. From what you've told me of Grace, she's had a very happy life."

"But the lies," said Annie, becoming exasperated. "So many lies."

"Sometimes we hide the truth to protect the people we love."

"But the truth always comes out in the end."

"We should talk about your own situation, Annie."

Annie turned on Clara. "Should we? And why is that? Honestly, I feel as though I don't know any of you anymore. What else have you been keeping from me? You all say you care about me, then spend years lying to my face. No, I'll find my own way through this mess I've made. I don't need any of you."

Annie turned and ran back the way she had come. When she reached her boarding house, she locked her bedroom door and buried herself beneath her covers. She waited for Clara to return and try to reason with her, but no knock came, and although Annie hated to admit it, part of her was disappointed. For although the prospect of arguing with the aunt she adored wasn't a pleasant one, neither was spending another night in a coffin sized room alone with her worries.

Chapter 89

October, 1953

For the past few days, Annie had only left her bedroom at mealtimes, where she sat quiet and sullen around a table of guests who all wished she wasn't there. If she could, she would have stayed in her bedroom all day, but she knew she needed a good wash, and needed more soap.

After using her fingers to detangle her hair, Annie pulled on her warmest coat and left her bedroom, locking the door behind her. She was almost at the front door when Mrs O'Brian appeared.

"I hope you're not thinking of doing a runner."

"Pardon?" said Annie, turning to face her landlady. "And how would I do that without any of my belongings?"

Mrs O'Brian gave a grudging tut. "So where are you off to, then? You've barely left your room since you arrived."

"If you must know, I'm off to the chemist to buy a bar of soap."

"What an exciting life you lead. I need to know if you're staying longer. If so, you owe me more rent."

"I'd like to stay for a few more days, please," said Annie, pulling out her purse and counting out more coins. She handed them to Mrs O'Brian, who nodded her approval, then walked back into the dining room. Annie caught her reflection in the hallway mirror and sighed. If her appearance was anything to go by, staying at the boarding house wasn't doing her much good, and she had found no solution to the immediate problem of her possible pregnancy.

As Annie let herself out onto the street, someone called her name. She spun around, saw Jimmy, and began walking hastily away in the opposite direction.

"Annie!" he called. "Please slow down. My leg isn't too good today."

Annie paused. Much as she wished her family would leave her be, she loved Jimmy, and hated the thought of making him limp along in her wake. "Why have you come?" she said when he caught her up. "I told Clara I didn't want to see anyone. You've all lied to me. There's no one I can trust."

"For goodness' sake, Annie. All this talk of trust is stuff and nonsense. As it happens, I agree that Marnie should have told you about Grace. In fact, I've suggested it several times over the years, but I can also see things from her point of view. She was trying to protect everyone. She was trying to protect you. Surely, now you've got yourself in a similar position, you're able to show a little empathy?"

"I'd never give away a child."

"No? Then tell me how you expect to clothe and feed yourself and your child with no family support."

"I'll get a job."

"And what will you do with the child while you're at work?"

Annie continued walking and Jimmy limped on beside her.

"I'm not trying to be unkind, Annie, but you need to face the reality of your situation."

"And what do you think I've been doing these past few days? All I've done is play different scenarios over and over in my mind."

"Then let us help you find a way through this."

"I'm better off on my own."

Annie pulled open the door of the chemist, and Jimmy followed her inside. He waited by the door as she chose a bar of soap and paid for it at the counter.

"You may as well go home," said Annie, as they stepped back onto the street. "There's nothing either you or Clara can say to change my mind."

"What about your mother? Will you speak to her?"

"Did she come with you?"

"She's waiting in the car."

"Then she'll be waiting a long time."

"Please, Annie, show a little kindness. All Marnie wants to do is help you."

The heel of Annie's boot caught on a cobble, and she swore. Part of her longed to see her mother, to be held in her arms and told everything would be alright, but she couldn't do it. It wasn't just anger at Marnie's lies, but shame at her own actions.

"I'm sorry, Uncle Jimmy, but I can't bear to see Mum at the moment, not when I've got worries of my own to deal with. Besides, I'm too angry to speak to her rationally."

"Annie, please, listen to me. You're going to need our help, and the sooner you realise it, the better."

"What I need is to be left alone, just for a few more days."

Jimmy sighed and ran a hand through his grey curls. "If I agree to that, I'm going to need some reassurance that you won't go running off again."

"I've just paid Mrs O'Brian for another three days and I'm not in a position to be wasting money."

"So you promise to still be here by the end of the week?"

"I promise."

Jimmy nodded, and Annie walked away, her thoughts so confused that three days felt a very short time to untangle them.

Chapter 90

October, 1953

Sam stood outside the thick oak door and knocked.

"Come in."

With a deep breath, Sam opened the door, marched in and stood to attention in front of a polished walnut desk covered in neat piles of paper. "Good afternoon, Chief Petty Officer Brown. You asked to see me?"

"At ease, Leading Seaman Thorn. Yes, I asked to see you. It seems you've *another* family emergency requiring your attention."

The way Brown emphasized the word *another* irritated Sam. The only other time he'd taken additional leave was during the great flood, and he'd still been employed in service during that time. "Can I ask the nature of this emergency, chief?"

"Your mother was vague on the telephone, but very insistent."

"Insistent about what, chief?"

"That you are the man required during your family's hour of need. I must say, I'm not given to allowing my men to go off base willy-nilly, but given your exemplary record, and the fact this is a bereavement, I have decided to comply with your mother's wishes and release you from duties for a period of one week."

"A bereavement?" asked Sam, his heart hammering.

"As I said, Leading Seaman Thorn, your mother was vague on details. You have permission to use the telephone in the officers' mess to gain further information from your family. Your mother suggested you ring one Mr James Watson, who will appraise you of the details you need."

"Thank you, chief."

"I shall expect you to report back to base at zero seven hundred hours on the twenty-sixth of October. Do I make myself clear?"

"Perfectly, and thank you, Chief Petty Officer Brown."

Once dismissed, Sam left the room on shaking legs. As he walked to the officers' mess, his palms were sweating, his heart hammering. Someone had died, but who? Sam prayed it wasn't his father, or one of his siblings. But why had he been asked to telephone Jimmy? With a rush of horror, Sam prepared himself for the worst possible news. Annie. It had to be Annie. Oh, God, no.

At the officers' mess, Sam gave a garbled explanation of why he was there and was shown to a telephone booth in a quiet corner of the room. He dialled the number he had been given and waited to be connected. The telephone rang and rang, but no one answered. Sam racked his brain for anyone else in possession of a telephone in their home, but could think of no one.

"I can't get hold of my family member," he told an officer at the door, "so I will pack a bag and ring them en route to Lowestoft."

"Very well," said the officer.

Sam packed with less care than usual, flinging items of clothes into his kit bag and slinging it over his shoulder. He walked as fast as he could through the barracks, then once beyond its boundary, broke into a run. He only stopped running when he reached a public telephone box, pushing coins into the slot and praying this time he would be connected.

"Hello, Mr Jimmy Watson speaking."

"Oh, thank God, Jimmy, it's Sam."

He heard a long sigh down the line. "Sam." Jimmy sounded weary, and if Sam wasn't mistaken, cross.

"Please, Jimmy, just tell me. Is it Annie? Is it my dad? Please."

"Oh, Sam, you should never have been dragged into this mess."

"Just tell me!"

"No one has died."

"What? But my superior told me there had been a family bereavement."

Jimmy sighed again. "A foolish notion cooked up between my sister and your mother, one I wholeheartedly disapproved of, I would like to add."

"You mean, no one's dead?"

"Well, my mother died last week, but that's no reason for you to be called away from National Service."

"Then why would Mum ring my base demanding I be given leave?"

"Oh, good God, what a mess this is," said Jimmy. "There's been a situation with Annie."

"Annie? Is she hurt?"

"Only her pride."

"What do you mean?"

"I'm sorry to be the one to relay this information, but it seems Annie got herself involved with that no-good cad Blaine McCloud. She is possibly carrying his child and, as a result, has run away."

Sam held the telephone to his ear, unable to find any words.

"I expect you're wondering why your services have been called upon?"

"Y... yes."

"Annie is in a bad way, but won't listen to any of us or accept our help. Your mother and my sister felt you were the only person she would listen to."

"They lied to the navy?" asked Sam, horrified as the implications sank in. "I can't go swanning off and leave my duties for a woman who has made it clear she wants nothing to do with me. I need to speak to Chief Petty Officer Brown and tell him this has all been a terrible mistake."

"Have you already left your base?"

"Yes."

"Oh dear. In normal circumstances, I would agree that telling the truth is the best course of action," said Jimmy, "and please believe I did everything in my power to put a stop to this subterfuge. But, the deed is done. You've left your base under false pretences. Goodness knows what trouble you, not to mention your mother, could get into if you tell your superiors she lied to them."

"Then what should I do?"

"Catch a train to Northumberland?"

"But if I'm caught?"

"We'll cross that bridge when we come to it, which hopefully we won't."

"I don't want to see Annie."

"I understand," said Jimmy, "and in your position, I'd probably feel the same. But she is one of your oldest friends, and she could really do with a good friend at the moment." Jimmy's voice cracked as he added, "I'm worried about her, Sam. Really worried."

"Very well. I'll come up there for you, Jimmy, not for Annie. But I'll need to have words with my mother. She's put me in an awful position."

"I know."

"I'll let you know which train I'm getting. Will you be able to meet me at the railway station in Berwick and give me all the information I need?"

"Of course."

Sam hung up the phone and let out a long breath. It was Annie's fault he'd been put in this terrible position. And all because she had chosen some no good bounder over him. But much as he hated her, he hated himself. For the thought of seeing her made his heart flutter. He shook his head and swore. He would help her because he was her friend, nothing more. But even as he told himself these words, he knew they were as much a lie as the one his mother had told. For he could go back to base and tell them it was all one big misunderstanding, but he wouldn't, because his oldest friend needed him, and whatever she had done, he couldn't stop loving her.

Chapter 91

October, 1953

Annie jumped at the knock on her door. Assuming the knock would be Mrs O'Brian demanding more rent, she buried herself back beneath her blankets. The knocking continued, and Annie lifted her head free and waited. Whoever was there wasn't about to give up, so she climbed out of bed, walked to the window, and opened the curtains. Bright daylight streamed into the room. She turned to the clock on the wall, shocked to see it was eleven a.m. No wonder the boarding house was quiet. Everyone else would be at work by now.

Annie pulled on her dressing gown. "Coming," she called, crossing the room.

"Hello, Annie."

Annie's mouth hung open as she saw Sam standing on the landing. "What? How?..."

"It's best not to ask. I shouldn't be here, in fact, if I'm caught... Never mind. Everyone's so worried about you."

"But why are you here?"

"Like I said, everyone is worried about you, and as you've turned everyone else away and are refusing to speak to your parents, I was asked to come as a last resort."

"Who asked you to come?"

"It was your mother's idea, but I think Jimmy, Clara and Frank agreed."

"So everyone's been talking about me behind my back?"

"What did you expect?" asked Sam, letting out a frustrated sigh. "You've caused so much worry by running off like you did. Do you have any idea what I've risked to be here with you?"

"Do you want to come in?" asked Annie, ashamed her behaviour had resulted in Sam travelling so far.

"Your landlady let me in, but only on the condition I didn't step inside your room. I had to tell her it was an emergency just to be allowed across the threshold. She gave me five minutes, so we had better find somewhere else to talk. I'll wait for you outside."

"Alright," said Annie, closing the door and leaning against it. She dressed quickly, her heart pounding. Sam was the last person she expected to see and she was mortified that he'd been dragged into her mess, especially after the way she had treated him.

Annie found Sam sitting on the front step. When he saw her, he jumped up and straightened his jacket.

"Would you like to go to a café for a cup of tea?" asked Annie, suddenly shy around the man she'd known her entire life.

"No, I drank a year's worth of tea on the train. Let's walk."

She let Sam take the lead, despite him not knowing the town or where he was going. They walked in silence to a long narrow stone bridge which spanned the width of the Tweed. The day was cool but bright, a gentle breeze caressing their faces as they walked. Annie glanced at Sam, who kept his eyes straight ahead. His features were so familiar, and although not that much time had passed since his last visit, Annie felt so changed herself, it was like seeing him for the first time.

"You don't need to keep staring at me like I'm an apparition or have two heads," said Sam, catching her eye and smiling.

"Sorry," said Annie, blushing. "I can't believe you're here. I owe you one heck of an apology."

"No, you don't," he said. "I was dreadfully hurt at the time, but just because we've been friends our entire lives doesn't mean I can expect you to fall in love with me. That's not how these things work, and I was naïve to think it was."

"You weren't naïve," said Annie. "I gave you every reason to expect romance, and I wanted it myself."

"But you found someone you liked better. It happens. I've moved past it. Besides, I've had a lot of time to think things through and calm down on that long train journey."

Annie stopped walking and leaned against the wall, watching the water rushing below.

"Careful," said Sam, placing a hand on her waist.

"Don't worry, I'm not about to jump." Annie smiled at him, the movement feeling strange after a week of frowns and tears. "I've been a complete fool, Sam."

"I may have heard a rumour…" he grinned and Annie laughed. "I'm sorry, I shouldn't be making light of your situation."

"Come on," she said, linking her arm through Sam's and continuing to walk. They left the beach and walked along a street lined with industry. Several small factories occupied the area parallel to the river, along with fishermen's sheds and a large area where boats lay stranded, ready for repair.

"I'm assuming we'll reach a beach eventually," said Sam.

"We're walking along an estuary, so there's a high chance," said Annie, with no small amount of sarcasm. Sam nudged her in the ribs and the easy familiarity of their lifelong friendship brought tears to her eyes.

They continued on, the street giving way to sand dunes, then climbed down onto a stretch of sand which wrapped around the mouth of the estuary.

"Do you want to talk about what happened?" asked Sam after several minutes of silence.

"I'm not sure I'd know where to start. Ever since I turned eighteen, I've made a mess of everything."

"Alright, why don't I ask you some more specific questions?"

"Only if I can ask you one first."

"Go on."

"Did you know I had a sister in Padstow?"

Sam's mouth fell open. "A sister? This isn't Grace you're talking about, is it?"

"Oh," said Annie, "so they only told you part of why I ran away and won't speak to anyone."

"Sorry," said Sam, placing a hand on Annie's arm to stop her walking. "Are you telling me your mum had a baby while you were in Padstow?"

"Turns out she did, yes. And for the past thirteen years, everyone has lied to me about it."

"But didn't you realise at the time?"

"I remember being told mum was ill, but I suppose I was too young to put two and two together. I've had my suspicions about Grace being Jack's daughter for a while, but not once did I think we shared a mother."

"Good God, my list of questions has suddenly grown," said Sam. "That's a bombshell and a half."

"I'm surprised Kitty never said anything."

"My mum knew?"

Annie nodded. "At least from your reaction, I can assume I'm not the only one who was in the dark."

"Goodness," said Sam, running a hand through his hair. "Your mum's always seemed so... so... proper."

"Do you remember me telling you about that letter I found?"

"Yes. Do you think it was about Grace?"

"I'm certain it was."

They turned a corner, and a large stretch of yellow sand came into view. "I think I can spot a tea stand over there," said Sam. "Come on, I have a feeling we're going to need something to wet our whistles, the amount we've got to talk about."

Chapter 92

October, 1953

"Before we talk about your mum and Grace, I'd like to talk about your time on the island, if that's alright?"

"It's the least I owe you."

"What happened, Annie? What did that chap Blaine have that I didn't? I don't mean to sound rude, but he was rather haggard."

Annie laughed, marvelling at how one visit from Sam had brought into use facial muscles she'd lost hope of using again. "What he had was a pack of lies. And I was stupid enough to believe every one of them."

"Was he really an artist?"

"Yes, that part was true. I thought he was so exotic, so different from any man I'd met before. He made me feel grown up, womanly. I was flattered by the way he looked at me. Yes, I know I'm being ridiculous."

"Maybe, but you're not the first woman to be charmed by a no-good cad. But I still don't understand why you let things go so far. I mean, to be expecting his baby..." Sam flushed and Annie looked at the ground.

"I'd like to say he tricked me into it, but I could have stopped it if I'd really wanted to. You don't want to hear about all this."

"Does he know? About the baby?"

"I didn't get a chance to tell him. We had a big falling-out after I found out the truth, then one night he just ran away."

"Well, I suppose that's something you have in common."

Annie groaned. "I know, I've behaved terribly. I was so confused by everything, but it's no excuse. To miss my grandmother's funeral was unforgivable."

"Forgive me if I'm wrong," said Sam, his voice gentle, "but do you think your refusal to see or speak to your family could have as much to do with your own actions as Marnie's?"

"What do you mean?"

"You seem to regret what happened with Mr McCloud?"

"Yes, of course I do."

"And you seem racked with guilt over missing Rose's funeral."

"Yes."

"Might you have run away from shame as much as anger?"

Annie kicked sand into a pile, the toe of her boot jabbing into the sand. "Suppose what you say is true," she said eventually. "It still doesn't excuse what my mum did to me and Grace."

"Perhaps not, but equally, you've not given her a chance to explain why she did what she did, have you?"

"You mean like you've just done for me?"

"Precisely."

Annie flopped down onto the sand, not caring that the dampness would soak into her skirt. She pulled her knees up to her chin and let out a sob. "I'm such a horrible person. What on earth am I going to do?"

"We can think about that once we've got a hot cup of tea in our hands. Wait here."

By the time Sam returned with their tea, Annie had dried her eyes and was staring out to sea. "Sam," she said, as he handed her a mug. "Why are you here?"

"I told you why I'm here."

"I know, but after the way I've treated you, for you to have come all this way."

Sam sat down, picked up a handful of sand, and let it run through his fingers like a timer. "When I heard what had happened, I hated you. Part of me wanted to return straight to base and never see you again. I almost did. But stronger than hate was a desire to help you, and it seems as if I'm the only one who may offer a solution."

"A solution?"

"Yes." Sam took a sip of his tea, but didn't speak.

"Sam, what are you talking about?"

"What if... what if you and I were to marry?"

"Marry? But, Sam..."

"I know, I know," he said, kicking at the sand in frustration. "You don't love me. I'm not a fool, Annie. If you don't love me now, you're unlikely to change your mind. But if you don't marry me, what else are you going to do?"

"I've been making plans to raise the child alone."

"Without money? With no support?"

"The past few days I've realised the flaws in my plan," said Annie quietly. "But I can't marry you, Sam. It wouldn't be fair to burden you with another man's child. And what if one day you meet another woman far better than me and fall in love? You'd be trapped."

"That's unlikely to happen."

"But it could."

"The way I see it, and I've thought about it a lot during the journey to get here, is that it would be you making all the sacrifices."

"Me?"

"Yes. Annie, I've loved you all my life. Whilst those feelings are not reciprocated, I would still get the chance to spend my life with my best friend. It would be you giving up on the chance of a fairy-tale romance."

"I'm not sure such a thing exists."

"And besides, I'm a simple fellow. As you made plain when I visited, my ambitions don't amount to much. I'd like a quiet life working on the boat, with a family to come home to when I'm back from sea. You want more for yourself and I want you to know if we married, I wouldn't stop you heading off on adventures, as long as you came back to me once you'd had them."

Annie shook her head. Sam's offer was too great to take in. "I'd need some time to think things over."

"I agree. But you also need to stop running away. This afternoon I'm taking you back to the island."

"Oh, no, I can't face everyone."

"It won't be everyone. Your mum and Frank are back in Lowestoft, so it would only be Jimmy and Clara. The least you owe them is an explanation."

"Alright."

"Really? You'll let me take you back to the island?"

"If you can travel all this way to talk sense into me, the least I can do is travel eleven miles to apologise to people I love."

"Goodness, I really didn't expect you to say yes."

"I'm not always irrational and stubborn."

"Just most of the time."

Annie gave Sam a light punch on the arm, and they both laughed. "Come on," she said , standing up and holding out her hand, "we'd better get back so I can pack, or we'll miss the last train."

Chapter 93

October, 1953

"It's alright," said Sam, squeezing Annie's hand.

She nodded, but could feel the beginnings of a headache thanks to the tension in her face and neck. She had been so rude to Jimmy and Clara, and wouldn't blame them if they took one look at her and sent her packing.

The taxi wound its way through the village streets and Annie kept her eyes lowered. Rumours of her midnight flit were bound to have circulated in her absence, and goodness knows what locals were saying about her. The taxi drew up outside the hotel, but Annie made no move to leave the car.

"Come on," said Sam. "This taxi's cost me an arm and a leg and I can't afford for us to sit here with the engine running, racking up a higher fare."

Annie noticed the wink pass between Sam and Mick, their driver, but pretended she hadn't seen. She pushed back her shoulders, took a deep breath, and climbed out of the car. With her luggage in one hand, and Sam gripping tight to the other, she walked towards the entrance. They stood at the front door, Annie suddenly paralysed with nerves. Should she ring the bell? After the way she'd behaved, surely she'd lost the right to call the hotel home?

Before Annie could dither further, the door opened and Jimmy and Clara stepped out, their faces inscrutable. As tears rushed to Annie's eyes, Clara smiled, nudged Jimmy, and they both wrapped their arms around their niece.

"You gave us such a fright," said Clara, kissing Annie's head.

"Thank you for bringing Annie home," said Jimmy, releasing his niece and shaking Sam's hand. "I know the risk you've taken in coming here, and I hope she does, too."

"I'm so sorry for..."

"There'll be plenty of time for that," said Clara, holding up a hand to stop Annie speaking. "But we have important matters to discuss, and these things are best tackled with a cup of tea in hand."

"A woman after my own heart," said Sam as they followed Jimmy and Clara inside.

"I hope you don't mind, but I've made a list of discussion points," said Jimmy as they sat down around the dining table and Clara poured the tea.

"A hangover from his headmaster days," said Clara, shaking her head.

"Perhaps, but we're dealing with some big topics, and a bit of structure to the conversation could be useful."

"Whatever you feel is best," said Annie, mentally preparing herself for an interrogation.

"Right," said Clara, "let's get to the most important point first, your pregnancy."

"Actually," said Annie, "I'd like to begin with an apology. Sam's helped me see how dreadful my recent behaviour has been and I'm so sorry for all the worry I've put you through."

"We've all had moments in our life when we've gone off the rails or made poor decisions," said Clara. "It's what you do from now on that matters. But whatever path you choose, you won't be walking it alone."

"That's more than I deserve."

"Nonsense," said Jimmy. "You weren't the only one fooled by Blaine McCloud. Clara thought the sun shone out of his..."

"That's enough, thank you," said Clara. "What Jimmy is trying to say is we understand how you could have got yourself into this muddle. Blaine could be very charming and manipulative when he wanted to be. I presume he knows about your situation?"

"No," said Annie. "We argued when I found out he was a thief with a wife and children. After that, he avoided me at all costs and before I could tell him he'd run away."

"We've been in contact with the police," said Jimmy, "but it seems Blaine McCloud has vanished off the face of the earth, if Blaine McCloud is even his real name."

"We were going to run away to Paris," said Annie, her voice quiet, a single tear running down her cheek.

"Paris?" said Sam.

Annie nodded. "I know how ridiculous it sounds. But Blaine convinced me I couldn't trust any of my family, and we were better off going somewhere new and starting again."

"Oh, you poor thing," said Clara.

"Please," said Annie, "don't pity me. I don't deserve it."

"I didn't know you wanted to go to Paris," said Sam, his eyes on the ground.

Annie reached over and took his hand. "I didn't know what I wanted, Sam. All I knew was I didn't feel at home anywhere and all the people I loved were keeping secrets from me. I understand now that running away isn't the answer, but when Blaine suggested it, it was tempting. I suppose I thought that if I felt so ill at ease in my life, I may as well create a new one somewhere else."

"What will you do now?" asked Jimmy. "You can stay here as long as you need, but we will need to make some decisions about the baby."

"Thank you," said Annie, "but I've been running and hiding for long enough. I've loved being on the island and part of me would like to stay here forever, but it's time for me to go back to Lowestoft."

Jimmy pulled out his piece of paper and tucked a pencil behind his ear. "I think we should tackle some practical topics, such as how you're going to manage with Blaine's child on your own."

Annie glanced at Sam, her cheeks turning pink. "Uncle Jimmy, do you think we can talk about this in the morning? I'm exhausted."

"Of course," said Jimmy, laying the paper down on the coffee table. "You go off and get some rest."

"I'll bring you up some cocoa," said Clara.

"Thank you. Thank you all for being so kind."

"Sam, how about we go for a swift at The Ship?"

"What a good idea," said Sam, a look of relief crossing his face at the prospect of escaping the intensity of the afternoon.

*

"It's probably best to leave the women to it," said Jimmy, as they stepped out into the cool early evening air. "Thank you so much for bringing her home to us. I know what it might have cost you."

Sam winced. "I hate having to lie to my superiors, but Annie is my oldest friend and when I found out she was in trouble, I knew I'd have to help. I suppose I should thank Mum and Marnie for giving me the nudge I needed, although I'll be having words to make sure they don't pull a similar stunt in the future. But it all seems to have worked out for the best, and if I can help Annie, I will. That's what best friends do, isn't it?"

"You love her," said Jimmy, his walking stick clicking against the ground as they moved through the quiet village streets.

"Yes," said Sam, "I do. But I could never compete with the excitement of a man such as Blaine, and who's to say she won't find another Blaine one day?"

"Oh," said Jimmy with a smile, "I think our Annie has learned her lesson. She's been like a feather caught on the breeze ever since she returned from her evacuation to Padstow. All this nonsense with Blaine was a symptom of what she's been grappling with. I know my niece, and I think this recent experience has grounded her. Who knows, it may all turn out for the best?"

"Even with a baby in tow?"

"Ah, yes. Well, that will be quite a challenge, no doubt."

They walked into the quiet pub. A handful of locals gathered around the bar, but there were none of the tourists Sam had encountered on his last visit.

"You find a table and I'll get us a couple of pints," said Jimmy.

Sam nodded and found a table in the room's corner where they wouldn't be overheard. "Thank you," he said, when Jimmy returned with their drinks.

"So," said Jimmy, "Annie might not be up to talking about practical matters, but there's no reason you and I shouldn't try to hash out a solution."

Sam took a sip of his pint and glanced at Jimmy. "Actually, I have come up with one solution and put it to Annie, but you might think it's madness."

"I'm all ears."

Chapter 94

October, 1953

Annie woke after a deep sleep and winced at the low ache in her stomach. She pulled herself up against the end of the bed and rubbed a hand against her nightdress.

She inched her way out of bed, feeling a familiar stickiness between her legs. With all she needed collected in a towel, Annie let herself out of her bedroom and rushed along the corridor to the bathroom. She felt sick, scared about what she would find, but she had no choice but to face whatever was happening to her body.

When Annie emerged from the bathroom half an hour later, her legs felt unsteady. What had shocked her was not any distressing discovery, but how ordinary everything had been. The realisation that there was no baby, and most likely never had been, hit her with full force and she leaned against the wall for a moment to gather her thoughts. Whether fantasy or nightmare, all her recent actions had been dictated by a belief she was carrying Blaine McCloud's child. All those people she had upset for nothing. Annie bit down on her fist to stifle a sob.

"Good morning," said Sam, coming out of his bedroom. "Oh, is everything alright?"

Annie raised her eyes to Sam and slowly shook her head. She had planned to accept his proposal, had even become excited at the prospect, but now he had no reason to stand by her. "I'm not feeling too good, but we should have a talk. Do you want to come to my room for a moment?"

"Of course."

Sam followed Annie along the corridor and into her bedroom. He stood for a moment admiring the view, before perching himself on the end of her narrow bed.

"I may as well come right out with it," said Annie, taking a deep breath. "There is no baby, Sam. I was wrong."

"Oh my goodness," he said, reaching for her hand. "I'm so sorry, Annie. When did this happen?"

"This morning, but I'm not sure anything out of the ordinary has happened. I was late, but that's not so unusual. I jumped to conclusions and have made such a terrible mess of everything."

"I don't know what to say. How are you feeling about this sudden change?"

"I'm not sure... there's certainly relief among my emotions, but also disappointment."

"That's a very natural reaction. You would have made a wonderful mother."

Annie shook her head. "No, you don't understand. I'm not disappointed about the baby. The thought of raising Blaine McCloud's child alone was terrifying. I'm disappointed about you."

"Me?"

"Yes. I was up half the night thinking not just about your proposal but about the fact you'd made it. It spoke of the man you are. I've been so blind and foolish, Sam."

"Blind to what?"

"To the fact I've loved you for years. I've been too focussed on myself to see it until now. But given there's no baby, you no longer have any reason to be lumbered with me."

Sam stayed quiet, his eyes lifted to the ceiling. "It certainly changes things."

"I know, and I'm not expecting you to forgive me for what I've done to you. The way I discarded you as soon as Blaine caught my eye was unforgivable, but believe me when I say I've learned my lesson. I wonder though, do you think we could remain friends?"

"Of course we can," said Sam. He cleared his throat. "I'm sorry, but I need to return to base today, and it's probably for the best. A little time apart will give us both a chance to think about how we'd like our futures to turn out."

"I understand," said Annie, disappointment hanging over her like a cloud. "Thank you for all you've done for me. You've been a loyal friend."

Sam leaned over, gave Annie a chaste kiss on the shoulder, then stood and left the room.

"Sam, wait!" Annie ran from her room and caught up with him in the corridor. He turned, and she flung her arms around him, squeezing him with all her might. "Thank you. Thank you so much. Whatever happens next, I know I'm the luckiest woman alive to have a friend like you." Annie clung on to Sam, her tears dampening his shirt. She breathed him in, not knowing if she'd hold him again, but knowing for certain that if she did, it would be because of his grace, and not because she deserved it.

Annie released Sam, and he took a deep breath. "I think you might have broken a rib," he said, rubbing his chest. He laughed, took her face between his hands and kissed her on the forehead. "You know, Annie,

I can give and take orders in the navy, can lead a group of men from all walks of life, in fact, I'd say I'm growing into quite a capable chap with a good understanding of the folks around me. But you?" Sam shook his head. "I'm not sure I'll ever get the measure of you. You're one of a kind, Annie Rose Hearn." He kissed her once more, brushed a lock of hair from her eyes, then turned and walked away.

Annie returned to her bedroom and watched from the window as Sam said his goodbyes to Clara and Jimmy, then climbed into Mick's old Ford Anglia, ready to cross the sands to the mainland. She held a hand to the window and waved, but he didn't see her. Sam was right that time apart was the best thing for them. Too much had happened to be able to think clearly. But as the ache in her stomach reminded her, she was now free. She could make her life whatever she wanted it to be, wherever she wanted it to be. But in order to move forward, she must first confront the past and all it held. It was time to return to Lowestoft. It was time to speak to her mother.

Chapter 95

November, 1953

As the train pulled in to Lowestoft station, Annie felt a rush of gratitude that Clara had convinced her to stay on the island an extra month. Not only had she gained perspective on her future, she'd been able to do all the things she'd missed out on while wrapped up in Blaine McCloud; a trip to Edinburgh with Genie, attending a village dance, helping Amy sew clothes for the baby she'd be welcoming in the spring, and exploring not just the island's physical beauty, but its history as Jimmy and Clara told stories each night beside the fire. Through their stories, they'd shown Annie she wasn't alone in stumbling through life, in making mistakes, in forging regrets. But their stories also gave her hope. Life might not follow a straight line, or move in the ways one might expect, but happiness could be found in the unexpected, and love found in the mess and muddles of humanity.

The train creaked to a noisy halt, and Annie took hold of her suitcase. It felt like a lifetime since she'd last been at the railway station, about to head off on an adventure. Now she was back, changed, happier, and with a sense that she was finally coming home.

Her optimism didn't salve the nerves which caused her stomach to churn though, and as she walked along the platform, her eyes darted around, simultaneously dreading and longing for the moment they would alight on her mother.

"Annie?"

Annie spun around, her eyes filling with tears as she saw the worry in Marnie's. "Hello, Mum."

"Welcome home." Marnie held out her arms, then dropped them to her sides, giving Annie a shy smile. "I thought we might take a walk before going to the house? I'd like to explain things to you, clear the air. We could leave your suitcase here and come back for it once we've had a talk?"

"I'd like that," said Annie. "Lead the way."

*

Annie kicked her heels against the sea wall, the cool concrete beneath her hands and legs keeping her firmly in the present as Marnie spoke of the past.

"Do you still hate me?" Marnie asked, as her story drew to a close.

Annie shook her head. "Who am I to judge you after all I've done?"

"My actions maybe, but you have every right to be upset at the unintended consequences of what I did. I've deprived both you and Grace of a sibling."

"But had you kept Grace, goodness knows where we'd be now, or the life we would have led."

"True. If only we could look into the future," said Marnie with a sad smile.

"Of all the upsetting things about what happened, I can see what a gift you gave to Helen and Richard. And don't forget, I've seen them far more recently than you. Grace is so happy there. Even after Richard's death, or perhaps because of it, the bond between Helen and Grace couldn't be stronger if they shared a bloodline."

"You've grown up a lot lately."

"I've grown up a lot in the last ten minutes. I should have done it far sooner. I'm sorry, Mum."

"No, I'm sorry for everything. I should have been honest with you from the start. What are you going to do about Grace? Are you going to tell her the truth? I know poor Helen has been beside herself worrying about what will happen next."

"I've thought about it a lot, and talked it through with Clara and Jimmy. On the one hand, I feel she has the right to know. The anger I felt on finding out the truth is nothing compared to what Grace would feel if she found out. Not to mention the fact that keeping it from her would add me to the list of people who've lied.

"On the other hand, she's just lost Richard, and I'm not sure I want to be responsible for her losing Helen too, even if she gained a sister and birth mother in the process."

"She wouldn't lose Helen."

"No? Goodness knows how Grace would react to the news. It could drive an irreparable wedge between the two of them, and I don't want to be responsible for that."

"So you won't tell Grace?"

"No, but I'm going to take a far keener interest in her life. We used to be such good pen-pals and I've let my letter writing slip lately. I can't be a sister to Grace, but I can be her friend." Annie looked round as Marnie let out a sob. "I'm sorry, I didn't mean to upset you."

Marnie shook her head. "No," she said, "you haven't upset me, you've overwhelmed me with your love and understanding. I wish things could have been different for you. You've had so much to contend with in your young life."

"And I've had you by my side through it all. I'm just sorry I didn't realise it sooner."

Marnie turned to her, undid the clasp of the locket she always wore, and dropped it into Annie's palm. "The letter you found all those years ago from Helen also came with this."

"What is it?"

"A lock of Grace's hair. It seems right that you should have it."

Annie opened the locket and stroked a finger across the soft ribbon-secured lock of hair. "No, Mum, you keep it. We'll add a lock of my hair to it and you can keep both your girls close to your heart."

Marnie took back the locket. "Thank you," she said, her voice husky as she fought back tears. She squeezed Annie's hand, then stood up from the sea wall. "Come on," she said, "it's freezing out here and we need to be getting home. We've a guest coming for tea."

"A guest? What guest?"

Instead of answering, Marnie tapped the side of her nose, gave an enigmatic smile, and began walking back toward the town.

*

When Marnie and Annie arrived home, they were chilled to the bone and longing to warm up by the fire with a cup of cocoa.

"We're home," called Marnie as they walked through the door and slipped off their boots.

"In here," came Frank's voice from the sitting room.

Annie walked in and her mouth dropped open. Sitting in an armchair, a cup of tea in his hands, was Sam.

"Hello, Annie."

"What are you doing here?"

Sam laughed. "I've made a habit of turning up when least expected lately, haven't I? I'm here to see you."

"Marnie, why don't we make a fresh pot of tea?" asked Frank. "Welcome home, Annie." After a brief hug and a promise to catch up on all her news shortly, Frank and Marnie left the room.

"Sit down," said Sam. "I'd like to talk to you."

Annie did as she was told, throwing Sam a nervous smile. They'd written to each other a few times in the past month, but their letters were brief and Annie had no idea about Sam's feelings towards her.

"Is everything alright?"

"Yes. I've had a lot of time to think about our situation. As you know, I'm a simple chap, and one thing that has no place in my life is holding a grudge. Life's too short."

"What do you mean?"

"I mean that whilst what happened between you and Blaine McCloud hurt me, all that sadness and anger isn't something I want to carry. And if you look at our history, the Blaine episode is a mere blip. You're my best friend, Annie. I know we've grown apart since I began my National Service, but the closeness we once shared can be found again, I'm sure of it." Sam stood up, crossed the room, and knelt beside Annie's chair. "What I'm trying to say is my offer still stands."

"Your offer?"

"My proposal. I've loved you all my life and if this past year has taught me anything, it's that I can't stop loving you even if I wanted to. But I don't want to clip your wings. If you feel you'd be bored being married to me, I completely understand, but you'd be free to travel, have your adventures. I'd never stand in your way."

Annie looked at Sam with tears in her eyes. She reached down and cupped his chin in her hand. "Sam Thorn, what did I ever do to deserve you?"

"Is that a yes?"

"No, I don't fully agree with all your terms."

"Oh..."

Annie smiled. "The restlessness I feel may always be with me, but if I never settle, I'll never allow myself the chance to feel at home. To travel would be interesting, to have adventures would be exciting, but I don't want to do all that alone. I want to do those things together."

"But I'll be running the boat."

Annie laughed. "Sam, I'm not talking about gallivanting off on some world tour. I'm talking about the occasional holiday somewhere that might broaden our horizons."

"I'm not sure I could afford anything too exotic."

"I'm also not asking for any five star treatment. But aside from occasional jaunts, what I realised lately is that I want much the same from life as you do. So much of my recent destructive behaviour has had a feeling of rootlessness at its heart. I want to put down roots, have a family of my own. And I want to do that with you."

A single tear trickled down Sam's cheek. "Are you sure?"

"Yes, my darling, I'm sure."

"Crikey," said Sam, wiping his eyes. "This is all rather marvellous, but I have one more request."

"Name it."

"We wait, just until I've finished my National Service. That way, we will both be certain it's what we both want."

"Alright."

"Thank goodness, as I haven't got around to buying a ring."

Annie laughed, leaned forward and kissed the handsome, kind man kneeling before her.

"Annie Hearn," said Sam, when they finally pulled apart, "would you do me the honour of being my girl?"

"Why yes, Sam Thorn, I think I shall."

From behind the door came an excited squeal.

"How much of that did you hear?" called Annie.

A sheepish-looking Frank walked in carrying a tray, followed by a red-faced Marnie. "We weren't eavesdropping," said Marnie, "but we gather there might have been a proposal?"

"Yes," said Sam, "but before you go off hat shopping, we're not engaged. We're stepping out, with a view to making a bigger commitment once I've finished my National Service."

Marnie clapped her hands. "I never thought something so sensible could sound so romantic." She beamed at the pair of them and they laughed.

"Let's forget about this tea," said Frank, dumping the tray on the coffee table and opening the drinks cabinet. He poured out four glasses of sherry and handed them round. "I think we can all agree it's been a rough old year in so many ways, but as 1953 draws to a close, I'd like to make a toast to brighter days ahead."

"To brighter days," they chorused.

"To young love," toasted Marnie.

"To young love."

Frank put a record on the turntable and the sweet sound of 'I Believe' filled the room. He took Marnie in his arms, waltzing her around the room. As they danced, Annie knelt down beside Sam, took his hands, and kissed him again. "To young love," she whispered in his ear, before pulling him up for a dance.

***

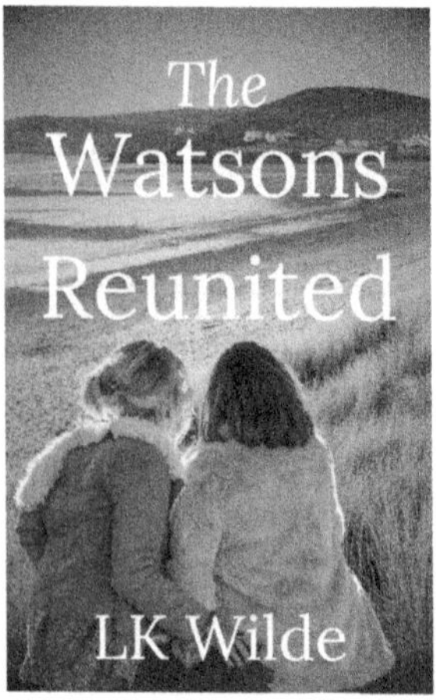

Coming soon...

Padstow, 2018

In Padstow, **Elle's** life is unravelling, much like the seaside cottage she shares with her mother, **Grace**. As Elle struggles to hold everything together, a discovery in the attic changes everything—letters stretching back decades, and photographs that reveal a wartime secret intricately tied to Grace's past.

In Lowestoft, **Sophie** struggles to reconcile the guilt of sending her mother, Annie into a nursing home. **Annie** is haunted by the past, and Sophie knows the only way to bring her mother peace is to uncover her closely guarded secrets.

As their lives begin to intertwine, the four women are about to discover family ties which have remained hidden for generations. But with Annie's health failing and time running out, they must find a way to reconcile the past before it's too late...

Acknowledgements

Before writing this book, I was considering making *The Hope She Found* the final book in this series, but there were several loose ends I wanted to tie up. Firstly, the issue of Grace's adoption. It was a comment in an email from my proofreader Julia Gibbs along the lines of 'storing up problems for the future' that made me wonder what effect it would have on Annie if she discovered her friend was actually her sister. Alongside this, the long-term effects of being a child evacuee were something I was keen to explore.

While researching earlier books in this series I'd come across the 1953 flood, and was shocked to learn of the damage caused, and loss of life in the Netherlands among other places. The flood had a lasting impact on Lowestoft and The Grit, and contributed to the decline of a place and way of life not yet recovered from the war years. It was this important episode in the town's history that dictated when this novel would be set. The fact it coincided with Annie turning eighteen was an unexpected bonus for me as a writer (although I should probably pretend I planned it that way)!

I hope in this and previous books I have managed to bring to life some lesser known areas of history and that these have been interesting to readers. For anyone interested in knowing more about the fascinating history of Lowestoft, in particular The Grit, I can't recommend

The Grit, by Dean Parkin and Jack Rose highly enough. The personal accounts and stories from a lost way of life have been invaluable during my research. It also happens to be a beautifully illustrated book that is a joy to have on my bookshelf!

I'd like to extend a big thank-you to Lowestoft resident Heather, for sharing her memories of living in Lowestoft in the early 1950s. Her recollections of dances at the Palais really brought the period alive in my mind.

Thank you also to Jo for your editing advice, Jarmila Takač for the wonderful cover, and Julia Gibbs for your expert proofreading.

Thank you to all the readers who have been following the Watson Family Saga up to this point. I hope you enjoyed Annie's story, and didn't become too frustrated when she lost her way! There is one final instalment of the Watsons to come, and I can't wait to share it with you.

About the author

Author and musician LK (Laura) Wilde was born in Norwich, but spent her teenage years living on a Northumbrian island. She left the island to study Music, and after a few years of wandering settled in Cornwall, where she raises her two crazy, delightful boys.

To keep in touch with Laura and receive a 'bonus bundle' of material including the Watson Family Saga prequel *The Island Girls*, join her monthly Readers' Club newsletter at-

www.lkwilde.com

Or find her on social media- @lkwildeauthor

Also by LK Wilde

People say you get one life, but I've lived three.

I was born Ellen Hardy in 1900, dragged up in Queen Caroline's Yard, Norwich. There was nothing royal about our yard, and Mum was no queen.

At six years old Mum sold me. I became Nellie Westrop, roaming the country in a showman's wagon, learning the art of the fair.

And I've been the infamous Queenie of Norwich, moving up in the world by any means, legal or not.

I've been heart broken, abandoned, bought and sold, but I've never, ever given up. After all, it's not where you start that's important, but where you end up.

Based on a true story, *Queenie of Norwich* is the compelling tale of one remarkable girl's journey to womanhood. Spanning the first half of the 20th century, Queenie's story is one of heartbreak and triumph, love and loss and the power of family. It is a story of redemption, and how, with grit and determination, anything is possible.

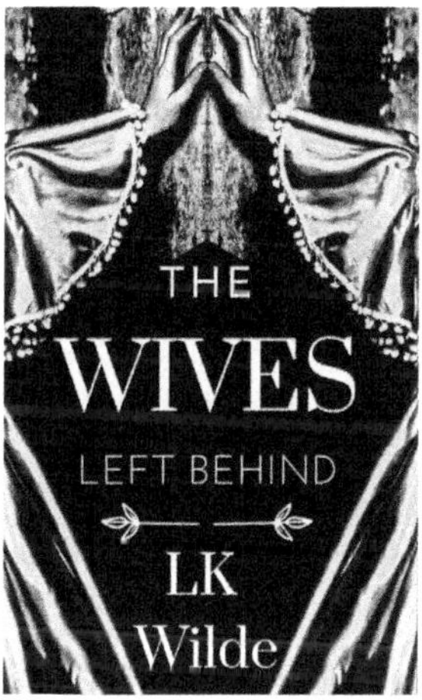

1840, Cornwall. The victim, the accused, and the wives left behind. Welcome to the trial of the century...

Based on a true story.

When merchant Nevell Norway is murdered, suspicion soon falls on the Lightfoot brothers. The trial of the century begins, and two women's lives change forever.

Sarah Norway must fight for the future of her children. Battling against her inner demons, can Sarah unlock the strength she needs to move on without Nevell?

Maria Lightfoot's future looks bleak, but she's a fighter. Determined to rebuild her life, an unexpected friendship offers a glimmer of hope...

With their lives in turmoil, can Maria and Sarah overcome the fate of their husbands? Or will they forever remain the wives left behind?

Book 1 in the Cornish feel-good *The House of Many Lives* series

Kate is stuck in a rut, She works a dead end job, lives in a grotty bedsit and still pines for the man who broke her heart.

When Kate inherits a house in a small Cornish town, she jumps at the chance of a fresh start. A surprise letter from her grandmother persuades Kate to open her home and her heart to strangers.

But with friends harbouring secrets, demanding house guests, and her past catching up with her- can Kate really move on? And will her broken heart finally find a home?

Printed in Great Britain
by Amazon

61175576R00272